Confessions *of a* Homing Pigeon

Books *by* Nicholas Meyer:

The Love Story Story
Target Practice
The Seven-Per-Cent Solution
The West End Horror
Black Orchid (with Barry Jay Kaplan)
Confessions of a Homing Pigeon

Confessions

of a

Homing Pigeon

a novel by

Nicholas Meyer

The Dial Press
New York

Published by
The Dial Press
1 Dag Hammarskjold Plaza
New York, New York 10017

Manufactured in the
United States of America
Third Printing—1982
Design by Francesca Belanger

Library of Congress Cataloging in Publication Data

Meyer, Nicholas.
    Confessions of a homing pigeon.

    I. Title.
PS3563.E88C6   813'.54   81-3154
ISBN 0-385-27198-0

for Antonie, *for* Ronnie *and for* Kitty

Confessions *of a* Homing Pigeon

꙰ ꙰ ꙰ ꙰

One

In Which I Take Notice

I find my earliest recollection is of two huge, gleaming eyes
staring at me from utter darkness. These orbs, though they
filled my infant imagination (as I can recall) with dread
malevolence, turned out to be nothing more than the eyes
of our family cat, an affectionate Siamese by name Hieronymous, who, for unexplained reasons, lived to the ripe old
age of twenty-five, the oldest feline that anyone had ever
heard of. This cat, then, whose glistening eyes began or
begat my sense of consciousness of the world (he liked the
electric coil heater in my room, which was why he was always
to be found there), was more or less companion and witness
to my growing up. Or I to his, if you care to take it that
way. And though as the years passed and I grew first to take
him for granted and later still to ignore him altogether, I
find, as I try to piece together the mystery of my life, that I
recall the eyes of Hieronymous as the first pieces of the
mystery. Would that other mysteries were as easily and
pleasantly resolved, for Hieronymous was, as I have noted,
an affectionate animal, tolerant of babies who yanked on his

tail, and (aside from a propensity to shed at certain times of year) otherwise without fault or flaw. He was actually rather like a dog in some ways, would come when you called him and was fond of licking your face with his tiny, rough, sandpaper tongue.

After Hieronymous' eyes, a host of other memories and images crowd in upon me, and yet I cannot remember anything else of my room— Wait! I remember now it had a closet, and in this closet I attempted once to conceal myself in order to avoid the application of painful unguent to a cut on my chin. Mercurochrome, I think the name was, or was it something called Medafin? Anyway, it stung, and with a child's instinct in such matters (much like a dog going to the vet) I knew it *would* sting, and hid in the closet accordingly, hoping to avoid my fate. Crying, no doubt. Later, in the darkness of my room, lying in my bed (crib?), I remember picking at the scab that had formed on my chin. Enjoying the picking, not knowing how the scab got there or what it was.

The apartment occupied the sixth of seven floors in a small building on West Fifty-seventh Street near the Automat. It had a small balcony with a window box, where Hieronymous liked to bask in the sun on warm spring and summer days. He was capable of remaining motionless and ecstatic there for hours.

The neighborhood has changed considerably over the years (what hasn't?), though I remember its layout from my time there quite vividly. Its principal attraction, in my view, was the Automat itself, shiny and mysterious, where sandwiches swooped round at you from behind little windows for twenty-five cents and for a nickel hot chocolate poured into thick china cups from magnificent silver spouts imbedded in the wall. What mysteries lurked behind that wall I scarcely dared imagine. How did the sandwiches get there? Who made the hot chocolate that erupted from the wonderful silver spouts? Matters were not simplified when Madelaine, my black nurse, addressed the window when she pulled out my sandwich and said, "Charlie sent me." She always thought this very funny, and as her laughter was infectious, I thought it funny, too, though I was oddly disturbed by it at the same time. Who was Charlie and why did they keep him immured behind the wall? How did he get out and what if he had to go to the bathroom? (Was there a bathroom behind the wall as well as endless supplies of hot chocolate?)

On one of the corners of the intersection of Fifty-seventh and Sixth (the northeast or -west I can't say now) there was a Liggett's drugstore, the word *Liggett's* inscribed in heavy, dark-blue cursive against a orange background. It was in this drugstore that Madelaine introduced me to a heavenly brew that surpassed even the hot chocolate at the Automat, and this was a wonder called the chocolate malted. It was made before your eyes by a light-green machine and came in a huge silver vase, whence it was poured into a thick glass, velvety brown and very cold. The alternative to the chocolate malted was the strawberry malted, an equally delicious concoction. I can remember to this day deliberating between them, as perplexed as the sages contemplating the meaning of life were said to be.

There was a Chinese restaurant on the west side of Sixth Avenue. I have an early and fond memory of egg rolls. Across the avenue, in the ornate Steinway Piano Building, was my dentist, and a good thing, too, considering. Beyond the Steinway Building, appropriately enough, Carnegie Hall, where Madelaine took me to concerts on Saturday mornings. She took me to Central Park, too, which wasn't very far away. There I delighted in the animals, especially the frisky seals and the majestic if somnolent tiger. The agitated pacing of the cheetah I did not quite trust, and the monkeys startled me with their sudden leaps and swings, but it was a nice startle, one that provoked a giggle. Best of all I liked to be given a bag of salted peanuts with which to feed the pigeons. They dropped onto my head and shoulders from the sky and ate themselves silly on my largesse.

When I was four I had a best friend, a lawyer's son about my own age named Jake, who lived in our building. Jake and I were inseparable and enjoyed that special sympathy that characterizes best friends. We were agreed on almost every important point concerning the universe, right down to our passion for Junket, a pudding variant made by Madelaine to which we were hopelessly addicted. Jake and I could have gone through life happily eating Junket and concerning ourselves with little else.

Actually we were rather different in our personalities. Jake was a bit standoffish and diffident, while I—so long as he was there—was prepared to dare anything. One day Madelaine took us to the park and Jake and I ran away. I do not know why we ran away; possibly it was an accident —we may have turned around and simply not found her— but we were not distressed to find ourselves abandoned, not panicked, not even put out, though other four-year-olds might well have been. We might have been upset had either of us been alone, but together we assumed the confidence of any of history's dynamic duos: Batman and Robin, Quixote and Sancho, Phileas Fogg and Passepartout. I can't even recall our searching very diligently for Madelaine. Perhaps we didn't even think of her. Instead, with what I distinctly recall was a sense of elation, we set about navigating our way home without her. It was no mean feat for two small babes on chubby legs, but we brought it off. We couldn't read, we could barely speak and we had certainly never negotiated a car-filled street by ourselves before, but that didn't stop us. We rose to obstacles as they occurred, got handy policemen to help us breast the automotive surge and, steering by familiar landmarks, made it back to Petey, the black elevator man, who was astonished by our unassisted and inexplicable arrival. He held on to us until the return of a frantic Madelaine, who wept to find us safe and well. She had, as it turned out, done a deal of weeping all afternoon, presenting herself to the police department's Lost and Found in an almost hysterical condition and asking after two lost male children and giving—between sobs—our ages. Alas, the only children fitting her description were two misplaced black boys, and it was with difficulty that the police dissuaded her from claiming them. She did try to take them home with her on the theory that perhaps our parents wouldn't notice anything amiss. With my parents, who were never home, she might have had a point, but Jake's were not so likely to be fooled. As it was, the crisis ended upon her hapless return. When I saw how hard she cried to find me safe, I cried, too, and bitterly repented of having frightened her so.

Thus I spent almost the first five years of my life in a pleasant neighborhood, and it must be said that my life was as pleasant as my surroundings. It was a world filled with familiar faces—Petey the elevator man's, the man who made the chocolate malteds and also the strawberry ones, the fat man who sold us the peanuts and the balloons at the zoo and wore the same shirt, even the unseen face of Charlie at the Automat. These comprised the human geography of my little life.

Of my parents it is more difficult to speak, and I must own at the outset to only the faintest recollection. They died together before my fifth birthday, and most of my memories derive from the faded scrapbooks I possess and the anecdotal reminiscences of Madelaine and my Uncle Fritz.

My parents were circus trapeze artists and very successful, too, though today not many remember the Two Flying Berninis. They worked years for Mr. John Ringling North, playing without a safety net, as was their custom (and, one may infer, to an extent the basis of their appeal), and died as the result of a curious mischance that has never been satisfactorily explained. For some reason both of them left their bars and sprang for each other in midair.

Circus experts, learning the manner of my unfortunate parents' deaths, have assured me that such a catastrophe is impossible. (Why, then they must be alive, I am tempted to reply.) In trapeze acts, I am continually informed, one partner, known as "the catcher," never leaves the bar. I am then obliged to explain that in the case of my parents, part of the novelty of their act revolved around my mother's ability to act as the "catcher" for my father. As I understand it, they switched roles with blinding speed and dexterity. Working without a net, my parents, more than others in this world, could not afford the single mistake they evidently made. Clearly one of them ought to have caught the other while maintaining his (or her) hold on the bar, but for whatever reason or missed signal, they plunged to an instantaneous death, locked in each other's arms. When I was old enough to understand exactly what had happened, it struck me as perhaps a happy way for them to have gone, for certainly they were devoted to each other and had been for fifteen years.

"Your mother came from one of those white-collar Irish families," my Uncle Fritz confided, "and she was always jumping up and down from the time she was a little girl, so they say. She was a champion gymnast all the way through that convent school she was in, and she went with a group of girls from the school to visit the circus when it came to town. She wandered off somehow"—I listened to this with a start of recognition!—"and caught sight of Bruno [my father] doing his warm-ups. It was love at first sight and she ran away and married him. All of fifteen and he a year older. I don't believe she ever saw her family again. She'd found what she wanted and had the brains to recognize it, which not everybody does," he added in a meaningful parenthesis. "Bruno taught her the ropes—literally—and with her background in gymnastics added to her natural inclinations in that direction, she took to the trapeze business like a duck to water.

"When her father died she got hold of some money, but circus people are never much good at holding on to money. They blew it on that apartment you grew up in and on paying for Madelaine to look after you. Can you imagine anything more silly? Circus people maintaining an apartment in midtown Manhattan?" He shook his head, wondering at it. "They sure liked the trapeze business, though," he reflected with wry amusement. "Sometimes I think they liked flying round up there better than—" Here my uncle, probably because he was speaking of my parents, lapsed into uncharacteristic reticence. "Better than you know what," he ended up mumbling.

She had a conservative or proper streak, though, my mother—probably the only remnant of her upbringing. Why else had she insisted on the absurd apartment and Madelaine to care for me when I came along? How far did she expect her little inheritance to go, or hadn't she troubled herself over that issue? Probably not. Circus people are just about as silly as you'd expect them to be, which may explain why I have never had much to do with them.

I don't know how or where my mother chanced on Madelaine, but it was a great arrangement for all concerned and I had no complaints, having no other arrangement with which to compare it. Madelaine, who was single and a frustrated mother if ever there was one, had ipso facto a child and a proper apartment in a fashionable section of Manhattan. It was just the two of us and Petey in the elevator, plus Jake. I realize now that with Petey Madelaine was having some sort of intermittent affair. He was sometimes to be found asleep on the living-room sofa and at breakfast, groggy, unshaven and smiling in the morning. I saw nothing irregular in this, as I liked Petey, who let me have some of his coffee in my milk and would sometimes allow me to operate the controls of the elevator.

At odd intervals during the year, whenever the circus was near the city or when they had some time off, Petey would retire to the elevator and my parents would return and stay with us. I recall these descents indistinctly—there were always gifts, but I remember the elaborate packages more than I do their contents—and associate the memory of my parents chiefly with the introduction of alien smells into the apartment and our lives. My father, I seem to remember, always wore a heavy after-shave with an orangey scent, and my mother favored some sort of lavender cologne. This was in the days before the enormous sophistication and variety of deodorants that now flood the consumer market, and I think my parents—who were, after all, athletes—were self-conscious about working up anything resembling a sweat outside the ring and away from the big top, for they went to some extremes to avoid the accidental giving of offense. Madelaine, by contrast, used no perfumes except a faint touch of something she called "musk," which, mingling with her own sweet scent, made her smell better than either of them. Smell is a powerful memory-provoker, as we all know, and to this day the merest whiff of any of these smells takes me sharply back to West Fifty-seventh Street, with musk (whatever musk is) providing the most jarringly poignant reminiscence of them all.

Another odor I associate with my parents' infrequent stops at the New York apartment is that of Italian food prepared by Bruno, who, like many Italians, was fond of a spicy cuisine. Madelaine's cooking was varied and nourishing but (except for Junket) lacked the color and daring of my father's, and it was supplemented by a good many trips to the Automat. Bruno, on the other hand, loved home-cooking, especially his own. He enjoyed puttering about the kitchen, brandishing saucepans and ladles with careless enthusiasm as he chatted with me, or rather at me, perched on a sideboard and watching his easy movements with absorption. I do not recall these conversations in particular, but I remember that a large portion of them was musical rather than verbal. Like all Italians, my father was devoted to the opera. (He listened on Saturdays between performances to the Texaco broadcasts from the Met and had at home a large collection of 78's.) Bustling about the kitchen, Bruno was fond of humming snatches of this and that and the other, sometimes bursting forth for a few bars in a full-throated tenor voice that startled me with its abrupt commencements and equally abrupt subsidences. The meals were invariably successful, but as I look back on them I summon up most vividly their odor of garlic and the rituals surrounding their preparation.

My mother I don't think had any interest in kitchens of any kind. Her lavender cologne preceded me on trips to the barber's and the Best clothing store on Fifth Avenue for additions to my wardrobe ("You keep right on growing, sweetheart!"). I recall her brisk and lengthy stride down the avenue, but little else. She was efficient with tradesmen and store clerks—not a person, as I gather, to try and fool with. I seem always to have been hanging on to the hem of her coat, burying my face in its mysterious folds when she wished to present me to anyone—the barber, for example. I harp on this business of the barber because I hated having my hair cut and loathed and feared the barber with his sinisterly snipping scissors and smile of false bonhomie. Not even the promise of a beige balloon afterwards, with red lettering on it, was sufficient to undeceive me. "George—" my mother would say in a voice torn between teasing and exasperation addressed to my hiding place, "George, come out of there."

I was shy. Who wouldn't have been in the company of parents at once so flamboyant, so glamorous and so indifferent? I would not abandon my sanctuary in her skirts without considerable coaxing, and when I did present myself, spoke rarely and usually in monosyllables. My mother worried about my silence. She thought it unnatural in a four-year-old and wondered if there was something wrong with me. Maybe I ought to have speech lessons, she soliloquized out loud when I was near, obliquely threatening me with the prospect. In later years, hearing her worries repeated, this raised a good laugh, considering how voluble I became.

I did not need lessons, as it turned out. I needed my Uncle Fritz and I needed France, and these two requisites her untimely death provided.

Two

Of Steamship Whistles & Nocturnal Revels

There is no telling what sort of life might have been mine had it not been for the unexpected death of my parents. Certainly it would have been a very different affair, but what sort of affair I cannot begin to imagine. At any rate I tell myself my life would have been different had they lived, but as I grow older and less certain of my opinions and perceptions (the older I get, the more there is I don't know), it now occurs to me that perhaps it mightn't be so very different after all. Who knows what part genetics and heredity play in one's fate? If Aristotle is correct and character is destiny, then the death of my parents and the upheaval caused in my circumstances thereby may have had less to do with my subsequent life than I think.

As it was, my parents' deaths caught all parties unawares and threw everyone connected with them—and me—into confusion. I was ignorant of most of the details at the time— Who am I kidding? I was ignorant of all the details at the time. It was only years later that I was able to piece together the chaotic arrangements my parents had made—or rather, had failed to make—in the event of their deaths. So little had they planned for this eventuality that it seems, in retrospect, to have been a kind of denial of the very possibility—a curious failing in a couple whose hazardous profession (or art, whichever you care to term it) would seem to have prepared them for the contemplation of it at the very least. When I first discovered how scanty had been their provisions where my future was concerned, I went through a period of hurt and resentful reflection: The memory of their selfish lack of foresight galled me.

Later, brooding on their lives and discussing the matter with a circus ringmaster whom I chanced to meet when I was in college, I was made to see the thing in a different light.

"Of course you'd expect people in their line to prepare for it better," the ringmaster had solemnly agreed over his schooner of beer. "But that ain't the way it works. Do you think people like your folks could have done their jobs every day if they thought about the likelihood of dying? Something going wrong up there? Damn right they couldn't. You ask why they didn't make provision and that's why. It would have been anticipating in a way, and some 'artistes' are so superstitious they put those things off, never get around to them; some can't even bear to think about them. Plus the fact that it's mighty hard to get insurance if your act don't have a net. And even if there *is* a net, sometimes you can't get any decent coverage." The ringmaster was old and bloated with beer; without his Pan-Cake makeup, his pale face and pocked skin looked like the craters of the moon. And he didn't work for an A1 big top. (A1 big tops didn't play Iowa City.) Nevertheless, his observations were cogent enough and I found myself turning them over in my mind for days afterwards. I realized, finally, that between his two points lay the truth: Between my parents' reluctance to consider the possibility of death in the ring and the insurance companies' refusal to consider it either, we had been left penniless victims, Madelaine and I. Of course Madelaine wanted to keep me, but she had no money of her own and now found herself without a salary. I don't believe that would have stopped her, but insuperable objections did present themselves. Madelaine lived in Black Harlem when she was not in the West Fifty-seventh Street apartment. She came from Rochester (where I had never been), had been to college and was cultivated, musically inclined and sophisticated—but that didn't alter the fact that as a white child I was unlikely to survive handily on her present home turf, the more especially as she had no money. Nevertheless, she offered to continue caring for me. In the midst of funeral arrangements, lawyers' phone calls and the opening of empty safety deposit boxes (and heaven knows what else—consultations with city social workers, an attempt to locate my mother's family in Michigan!)—in the midst of all this my Uncle Fritz wired from Paris and agreed to have me. "Send young George to me," ran his cable, still in my possession. "I am named guardian in Bruno's will."

As no one could even locate Bruno's will, there are grounds for supposing that Fritz made up the bit about being named guardian in that elusive document, though why he should have been so eager to assume responsibility for a child not yet five whom he had never seen was and remains beyond me. Possibly he was sober at the time and didn't know what he was doing. I asked him once about it, but he was drunk and in a surly humor and didn't seem to understand my question as his answer was incoherent. "Whas I spoose do? Big broth's oney son—no one else—whaya spec?" he snarled unevenly. I let it go at that.

The arrival of the telegram, however, gave immediate shape and structure to everyone's plans for me. I was to get a passport first—I had to have my picture taken in a studio, a process as similar and disagreeable as having my hair cut, likewise involving my sitting immobile in a chair—have my bags packed (not that there was much; I continually outgrew my clothes, hence there was little point in taking most of them) and sail on the *Ile de France* for Cherbourg, there to take the train for Paris, where Fritz would collect me at the Gare Saint-Lazare. Lest it be supposed that an infant was undertaking this lengthy voyage alone and that the grown-ups responsible for these arrangements were lunatics, let it be said at once that I was to be escorted by two companions. The first of these was my friend Jake Jablow's father—the lawyer—who was bound for Europe on business and kindly offered to share his tourist-class stateroom with me and generally to see me safely delivered into my uncle's hands. This convenient notion was hailed by all connected with it except Mr. Jablow's son, my best and only friend. Jake instantly perceived a double defection on our part, and no amount of reasonable explanation offered by various grown-ups could deflect his feelings of hurt and betrayal. It was symptomatic of a great deal of his character that was to reveal itself that Jake did not manifest his reaction with tears or hysteria. He simply went into his room, closed the door and refused to speak to me or his father. He played quietly with his toys, a large collection of automobiles and trucks that he (sometimes with my help before our rift) manipulated with great concentration along a labyrinth of streets formed by a huge assortment of building blocks. The only sounds he uttered when I tried to establish communication with him in the wake of the unfortunate decision were a series of murmured *Vroom, vroom, vroom*'s as he shoved the little cars around. He wouldn't even look at me. When I protested that none of this was my idea, that I didn't want to go to wherever it was they were sending me, Jake gave no sign that I had ever spoken. The cars absorbed all his attention.

I later learned that the marriage of Jake's parents was unraveling at about the same time, so the poor little fellow had a good deal with which to contend. Jake's silent withdrawal from our friendship increased my alarm about the impending Voyage—*Voyage* was the word everyone kept using. I had no idea what it really signified. It assumed several dreadful meanings to me, this Voyage, all threatening, in which the Voyage came and ate me up or carried me off in its claws or put me in jail or something.

My anxieties multiplied to the point where, in order to soothe them, I was granted a second companion for the trip: Cuddly, comforting, furry Hieronymous I was allowed to take with me. I was lucky, though I didn't know it. Had Fritz insisted on pursuing his postwar musical studies in England, a six-month quarantine would have made Hieronymous' visit to that country so impractical as to be unfeasible. The French, however, are less frightened of alien cats and dogs, and some extra paperwork cleared the way for "Hairy

Mouse" (which was all my inexperienced tongue could make of Hieronymous' long and difficult name) to go with me to France.

If I have not alluded to my feelings about the death of my parents, it is because they (the feelings) were so slight. I did not know them well, was a bit frightened by the pair of them and had only a hazy idea of what was meant by "the accident" (variously known as "the tragedy") and generally what had become of them. I did not attend the funeral, as I was deemed too small and had no real sense of exactly where they were.

On the other hand I had a very lively terror of being separated from Madelaine, the very fulcrum and center of my world, and my terror was not diminished by my perception of her own anguish. She did what she could, poor creature, to put the best face she could on our plight, assuring me that all was for the best, but try as she might, her valiant efforts to reassure me by painting a glowing picture for me of the fine adventure I was off to in "Gay Paree" always ended with both of us in tears, hanging on to each other for dear life. Of all the separations I have experienced, the hardest and saddest I ever endured was being wrenched from her musk-smelling arms in the midst of the crowded and steaming Forty-sixth Street Pier. Mr. Jablow held me gently but firmly in one arm as I screamed and shrieked Madelaine's name above the general din. In the other hand he held Hieronymous, equally terrified in his new wire-mesh traveling case.

"Good-bye, George! Good-bye, good-bye," sobbed Madelaine from the pier. We stood on the bridge beneath the forward funnel and waved to her now tiny form sandwiched amidst the throng; those around her shouted sweaty and gay farewells to friends and family next to us, who responded by hurling blue and white crepe-paper streamers back at them over the side of the ship. "Good-bye! Good-bye!" Mr. Jablow held me up to see her, but she could no longer be heard. I could only see poor Madelaine, choked by the press, her honest, kindly face twisted with passion and shiny with tears, mouthing the words over and over.

To comfort me, Mr. Jablow took Hieronymous from his box and let me hold him. This almost proved disastrous, as the ship's monstrous whistle, located in the forward funnel directly above our heads, suddenly let forth an enormous sustained bellow. I shrieked with yet another attack of abject terror, and Hieronymous, likewise provoked, bolted from my arms. In later years I have seen many times *The Wizard of Oz,* and the scene at the end, when Toto flies out of Dorothy's embrace in the balloon, brings back, uncannily for me, the moment when Hieronymous almost got away for good. Fortunately a passenger standing beside us scooped him up in an automatic gesture and Mr. Jablow wisely returned him to his box. Poor man, he had gotten a good deal more than he had bargained for, as he must have supposed; the tugboats pushed and pulled and pummeled the *Ile de France* out of her berth and into the Hudson ass-backwards, bearing on her bridge a squealing little boy who had not the least notion in the world of where he was or what was happening to him or why, and who was in sight of losing the only person in that world whom he loved. His parents, Charlie the unseen sandwich man behind the wall of the Automat, Jake and even Petey the elevator operator would soon fade like the skyline of Manhattan from his conscious-

ness. But Madelaine, dear and loving and as heartbroken
as he—Madelaine I would never forget.

> *A capital ship for an ocean trip*
> *was "The Walloping Window Blind!"*
> *No wind that blew could scare her crew*
> *Or trouble the Captain's mind.*
> *And the man at the wheel was made to feel*
> *Content in the wildest blow-ow-ow—*
> *Though it often appeared when the gale had cleared*
> *That he'd been in his bunk below!*

The age of the great transatlantic liners has passed; it has
been superseded by the age of jet planes, and to my way of
thinking it's a pity, though heaven knows I'm not old
enough to pose as a true authority. All that's left now of that
once glorious era is the inglorious *QE II,* a wretched craft
built of stainless steel and plastic that rolls more in light
swells than she should, sports miserable food and geriatric
passengers. The *QE II* is to a real ocean liner what Amtrak
(Amtrak, the son of Gad?) is to the old *20th Century Limited* as I've heard it described by Lucius Beebe and others
who took her. (As a matter of fact, as you will hear, I had
occasion to take the *20th Century Limited,* but that's later
in the story, and as I was traveling coach at the time, my
observations aren't as informed as Mr. Beebe's anyway as
regards the luxury of the appointments.)

In 1946, when I set forth to join my uncle in Paris—
wherever that was—the ocean liners were still in their hey-
day, though heading proud and unsuspecting into a rapid
twilight. The ships glistened with polished wood, polished

brass and polished service. Romance flourished at sea, as every ship was crammed with young innocents on their way abroad, and truly Cunard's boast was on the money: Getting there was half the fun. There was just something instinctively liberating about a voyage at sea; in later years I concocted a somewhat self-conscious theory that ocean travel represented the nearest approach to a return to the womb— everything done for you, no responsibilities, and you are surrounded by water. Now wouldn't you call that fun?

It was certainly fun for a five-year-old boy, no mistake. And while I whimpered myself to sleep for many nights to come, longing for Madelaine and missing her most cruelly before I lost consciousness, by daylight I forgot her a little, my curiosity and imagination fueled by the dreamlike wonders of this new world, the world of a great ship and its gleaming accoutrements, friendly crew and delicious food.

Hieronymous spent the voyage in our little cabin, where all had orders to see that he never left it. These orders were scrupulously observed. He complained a good deal at first, but regular meals and fresh strips of newspaper in his box daily, along with my own presence in bed each night, helped to calm him. His was basically an easygoing disposition, open and affectionate with all, and since all responded in kind, he soon grew accustomed to his confinement, though I don't know how he would have behaved if it had lasted longer than five days.

Our cabin was a marvel of ingenuity and architectural economy, filled with strange gadgets and paraphernalia whose purposes I could not guess. Its chief attraction from my standpoint was the double-decked beds, the first of their kind I had ever beheld. On our first night out I had timidly requested the lower berth, and for all I know, I slept the second night there as well. But Hieronymous preferred the upper (I think he liked to be near the air vent in the ceiling —there was no air conditioning) and I took my cue from him. The agreeable Mr. Jablow changed places with me— with some relief, I now feel—and allowed me the use of the glamorous upper, where you could touch the ceiling with your fingers and you had to climb down a ladder every time you wished to leave! At night, with the ship rolling gently in the darkness, I recall with a thrill my discovery that I had to urinate. The prospect of quietly descending that ladder in the dark to reach the bathroom was an adventure I had contemplated with relish, and my successful negotiation of all the obstacles between me, the john and bed again gave me a welcome feeling of accomplishment.

The cabin, however, paled before the other curiosities of this endlessly fascinating place. First there was the infinite ocean itself, with bracing sea air that dizzied you as you ran up and down the decks past row on row of passengers in deck chairs and sunglasses. They sat motionlessly soaking up the sun's rays beneath thick red or blue blankets, like bands of esoteric idol-worshippers. I had never beheld anything as hypnotically beautiful as the sea and could sit next to the stern railing for what must have been hours, admiring our wake. The ocean's blue-green colors, churned to a boil by our propellers, looked good enough, in a funny way, to eat.

The ship was an endless labyrinth of stairs and corridors and rooms of various sizes and designs, all of which I was free to explore. Technically, as a matter of fact, this was not so. We were tourist-class passengers and theoretically not entitled to wander into those areas labeled Cabin or First, but as I did not read or understand in the least what distinctions were being made and why, I examined what and where I pleased. It must be said that the ship's personnel were largely indifferent to my trespassings. Everyone smiled at me wherever I went, and though I got lost frequently (despite Mr. Jablow's best efforts to keep me in view), I was always returned without incident sooner or later, thanks to his happy thought of pinning our stateroom number to whatever shirt or sweater I was wearing, rather the way Madelaine fastened my mittens to the ends of my coat sleeves to prevent my losing them. In this way he was able to remain with his briefcase full of important papers and leave me with a clear conscience to my own devices.

There were big rooms and little rooms, rooms with pictures on the walls and smooth white statues of people without any eyes or any clothes. There were strange games people played on the decks, using long poles, colored disks and white painted designs on the floor. There were so many children, they had a playroom for us that included a hobbyhorse, whose ownership was hotly contested by all for the duration of the voyage, being clearly the prize item in the assorted collection of toys assembled for our amusement. There was a puppet show every afternoon. I had never seen puppets before and sat fascinated and a little uneasy as I viewed their grotesqueries. They were frequently violent, and my neighbors in the audience screamed with laughter at their brutal antics. There was a beauty parlor into which I strayed one morning, amazed at all the ladies sitting under steel helmets and pale blue sheets, their faces like masks under white cream. There was Ping-Pong, but I was too small to play. Nevertheless, I enjoyed holding on to a spare racket as I watched older children and adults slam the little white ball hither and yon.

Meals were considerable events held in a huge room (I fancy it wouldn't look so big today), with more silverware at each place than I had ever seen. It was of no use to me, as I couldn't even cut my own food without the assistance provided by the children's matron or the parents, but I marveled at the prodigality of all of it.

I sat at the children's table (its riotous revels reminiscent of a birthday party I once attended at Jake's house) and made friends with a little girl named Roxy. She was perhaps a year older than I, with freckles and slightly pudgy, but she didn't shout with joy when the puppets beat each other, which gave us something in common. We commenced roaming places together, tireless in our joint pursuit of the unknown—of which there was heaps. We even succeeded in joining up with a tour of the engine room, the guide evidently under the impression that we belonged to one of the grown-ups he was showing around.

The engine room gave me much to think about. Later I associated it with Hell, though I didn't know then about Hell, religious indoctrination being something I have managed successfully all my life to escape. But when Hell was described to me by a young Greek Orthodox friend (about whom more later), I instantly conjured up our visit to the ship's engine room. We started off crammed into a small elevator, each having been given a paper towel to hold and our shoe soles checked to make sure they were not made of rubber. As the elevator slowly and endlessly descended, the temperature inexorably rose. When we stepped out the heat was terrific, the hottest I'd ever experienced, and the purpose of the paper towels became evident: They were to be used in holding on to the steel handrails to which we were obliged to cling as we followed the guide throughout the steamy maze. Without them our hands would have been burned, and with rubber soles we should have melted into the metal floor plates.

The world of the engine room was a shocking contrast to the blue sky and fresh air on deck. The air was thick as well as hot, and it was very dark, with glistening steel and silver-colored objects shining at us with sweat, and huge machinery that thundered so that it was impossible to speak without cupping your hand over your mouth and screaming into the ear of the person next to you. Roxy became frightened and started to cry, but as no one could hear her above the roar, she allowed me to pull her along behind me as I followed the group. What an odd place it was, like a jungle gym gone mad and twisting on forever in and out of shadows. All around stood men staring at dials and watching gauges and meters, but otherwise there was no human activity but our own.

That night I went to bed exhausted but not sleepy. I lay in the dark for a long time—Hieronymous curled in my arms—and listened to his contented purring merge eerily with the dark distant throb of the ship's machinery as though another cat, a giant one, were sleeping somewhere far away. But now I knew better. I thought about the motionless men I had seen down there staring at those dials and wondered if they were asleep now and if they ever saw the sky. I thought of Charlie buried somewhere deep in the Automat's recesses.

On our last night I assisted at a curious incident, the meaning of which was not clear to me, though it made a deep impression and caused much puzzlement. There was a party all over the ship. The children were given fancy hats to wear and noisemakers to blow. Someone said there were to be horse races after supper, and this seemed too wonderful to be true. I had seen with my own eyes that the ship possessed a real swimming pool, but I could not imagine that it boasted horses as well, nor could I think where they might run, unless it would be around the deck beneath the lifeboats. As things turned out, I was destined to be disappointed. The horses, it devolved, were not real but wood, and they did not run under the lifeboats or anywhere else. They never moved at all except when picked up or shoved forward by a sailor a space or two on a green rug with white markings.

Everyone appeared to be having a good time. Grown-ups cheered lustily for the mounts by different numbers. They were all dressed up, though the men wore identical black clothes and funny little sideways black ties like waiters. The ladies were far more interesting to me and captured my attention with their bright jewels and piled-high hair, their lips brilliant with red paint. The long dresses they wore I had never seen before on any women except in pictures in a book of fairy tales Madelaine used to read to me at bedtime. Roxy and I had wandered into the opulence of first class— the wooden horses were bigger and painted brighter colors —and some fool in a black suit gave us some of his champagne to taste. I told Roxy about Hieronymous in my cabin and we went to see him. He was asleep in the upper berth and we climbed up to disturb his slumber and play. Roxy was intrigued by the fact I was allowed to travel with so furry and friendly a companion, but the wine must have made us sleepy, and in the close air of the cabin we lapsed into unconsciousness. I don't know how much time passed before I was awakened by a widening shaft of light from the hall as the cabin door opened, followed by a throaty giggle and another voice admonishing "Sssh!" in a sharp whisper. The light disappeared and the room was again plunged into darkness. Roxy slept on, but I was now awake, aware that we were no longer alone and probably not meant to be there, though how I knew this I cannot say.

"You sure he's asleep?"

"Yeah, yeah. Sleeps like a log, poor little tyke."

"Hey."

"Hey."

"Do that again. Again."

"You like that?"

"Umm. *Ummm.*"

There was the sound of kissing and the rustle of silken clothes such as I had heard the long dresses make earlier in the evening when the ladies crossed their legs or trailed their dresses on the dance floor.

"Oh, God!"

Irresistibly curious now, I peered cautiously over the protective side ledge of my berth. The cabin lights were out (the steward must have flipped them off earlier, not knowing anyone was there), but the moon had risen and streamed faintly through our porthole, providing sufficient illumination for the peculiar sight that greeted me. A woman stood in the middle of our small room; in her gloved hands she held up the front of her dress, her legs spread slightly apart. At her feet, kneeling between them, his face buried between her thighs, was Jake's father. I knew it was he, although I could not make him out except for his voice and the fact that the moonlight struck the back of his prematurely silver-grey head. For a few moments they remained motionless; then the woman sighed again and opened her eyes, at which point they looked directly into mine.

"Oh, Jesus!" She sprang backwards awkwardly but kept her balance, at the same time letting go of her dress in the process, which fell automatically back in place. Mr. Jablow seemed confused and purposeless there on his knees on the middle of the floor without her. He might have been praying, but he realized quickly enough what was wrong and rose to his feet, instinctively dusting off the knees of his black trousers. The woman in the meantime had recovered her composure and giggled again, covering her mouth with a gloved hand to muffle the sound.

"Holy cow. Holy *cow*." She took her hand away and approached me with frank curiosity where I had frozen in the bed, rooted to the spot. She climbed a step or two up the ladder.

"Leave the child alone," Mr. Jablow said quietly behind her.

"Hang on to your horses," she responded without impatience. Her face rose large before mine, blocking out the light from the porthole behind her, her breath heavy and smelling of something that later in life I would handily identify as booze. Her gown was extremely low-cut, and my last vision before the light was completely obliterated by her form was of two shimmering orbs of flesh jiggling or heaving with her exertions an inch or so below my nose. A distinctive odor emanated from them as well.

"Well, for heaven's sake," she cried in astonishment, "he's been doing just like us."

"What are you talking about?" Jablow demanded from below across the room. "Leave him alone." A match flared briefly in the darkness as he lit a cigarette.

"Mark, he's got a girl up here."

"What?"

"See for yourself." She fell or rather slid down from my upper berth like a tenacious wave reluctantly backing out to sea, taking her scents with her and allowing me, a drowning man, to breathe again. Jablow appeared in her place, his hand giving the top of my head a gentle, reassuring tousle. Little pudgy Roxy was still asleep with Hieronymous purring across her chest, his tail flicking every now and then beneath her freckled nose.

"All right," he said mildly after a moment's reflection. He handed the woman his cigarette to hold and proceeded deftly to extricate Roxy from under Hieronymous. He got an arm under her back and carried her, still sleeping soundly, down the ladder. "Open the door," he instructed the woman, then called over his shoulder to me quietly, "Go to sleep, George. It's late."

"Well, that's that," I heard her sigh as she followed his instructions and they left me there in the dark.

For the second time in as many nights I couldn't fall asleep. I stared at the dark ceiling inches above me, listened to the distant throb of the engines and woozily pondered the scene I had just witnessed, trying to decide how I felt about it. I had no very clear notion of just what had been happening, but one phrase kept repeating itself over and over: "He's been doing just like us." It is not sidestepping the issue to say that I cannot now remember what I made of this repetition then. I find it impossible to reconstruct my thoughts on the matter without the self-conscious knowledge I possess today of what was going on that night in our cabin. All I can honestly say is that the entire incident robbed me of most of a night's sleep and that somewhere, in a portion of my mind that I was imperfectly able to acknowledge, I wished I *had* been doing just like them, whatever it was. I thought of Madelaine, wondered where she was and if she had stopped crying and what she might be doing. I missed her most when it was time to fall asleep, and I knew that had she been there, she could have explained things to me.

꙳ ꙳ ꙳ ꙳

Three
My Uncle Fritz

"Now then, let's have a look at you."

These were the first words I ever heard from my Uncle Fritz, and I remember them distinctly because they coincided with the disorienting moment when I opened my eyes and found myself looking directly into his. I shifted my gaze and looked about in perplexity. I was in a house, a strange house, with a strange person looking at me, and had not the least idea how I came to be there.

"You slept all the way from Cherbourg," Fritz explained lightly, reading my mind. "You were sleeping when I took possession of you like a sack of groceries at the Gare Saint-Lazare. You kept right on sleeping on the train out to Marly. Had a big blowout your last night at sea, did you, chum?" he inquired with a friendly twinkle and a suggestive twitch of a neatly clipped mustache. I believe he was the first person I ever knew who grew hair on his face. I had never seen a mustache close up, but I perceived that it suited him while fascinating me. All I could do for the moment was blink wordlessly and stare at his mustache. "Welcome to Marly-le-Roi," Fritz resumed, seeing that I made no move to speak. *"Bienvenue à Marly-le-Roi.* I would like you to meet my housekeeper, Mme. Berthe," he added, and for the first time I became aware of a white-haired woman in black staring down at me behind Fritz with a glum expression. *"Giorgio, je te présente à Mme. Berthe; Madame, je vous présente le petit fils de mon frère, Giorgio Bernini."*

"My name is George," I corrected, sitting up and looking about me. At the moment I was going to cling very hard to the things of which I was certain.

"Well, so you talk!" Fritz laughed with simulated hearti-ness and clapped me on the back. "You had me worried there for a minute. Good for you, okay, George it is, if you say so. Hell, I don't care. It's my opinion that everyone should name themselves anyway. Names are too important to leave in the hands of strangers, like parents, wouldn't you say? Christ, they already saddled you with life—didn't they?— never asking if you wanted any. Isn't that bad enough with-out adding to it by giving you the wrong moniker? You don't suppose Fritz is my given name, do you? Hell, no. It's Ernesto. Ernesto Bernini. Now I ask you straight out, George: Do I strike you as an Ernesto? Do I *look* like an Ernesto? Damn right, I don't. God, you're quick—" Here he paused to raise a small glass to his lips and knock off its contents with a swift backwards jerk of his head. He smacked his lips appreciatively and went on, "Anyways, that's how I became Fritz. I am a Fritz, wouldn't you say?"

There was little doubt of that. I understood very little of what he said, for he spoke quite rapidly, used many words I had never heard before and interspersed his conversation with rapid gulps from his small glass, the contents of which he continually and dexterously replenished from a green bottle of amber liquid on a little table to his right. (Uncle Fritz was what we call an alcoholic.) I didn't understand much, but I did grasp the salient point that he was not and never could be an Ernesto, whereas he was indisputably a Fritz, down to his Viennese comic-operetta mustache.

"Only one thing," he was saying, filling up the glass and sloshing the contents over the rim as he waved it in Mme. Berthe's general direction. "You can be George instead of Giorgio all right, if you say so, only you'll have to say it in French 'cause no one around here speaks any English."

I didn't understand anything this time. What was French?

"*Je m'appelle George,*" Fritz intoned very carefully, and repeated it several times. "That means 'My name is George.' *Je m'appelle George.* You try it."

"No." It came out ornery, but that wasn't my intention. I was simply too frightened at the moment to ingest any more strangeness. Fritz looked at me without expression, trying, I suppose, to understand what he'd gotten himself into. Finally he sighed.

"Suit yourself, chum, but you'll find it pays to learn the lingo. When in Rome, chum."

As with so many things, Fritz managed to be both absurd and right at the same time. It was his particular curse, like Cassandra's. As the days went by and things assumed their bizarre shape, which was no shape, I discovered for myself that it paid to learn the lingo. And so, with a child's adaptability, I did. I wasn't troubled by grammar, irregular verbs or syntax; I learned the way babies learn, by imitating what I heard. I rolled my *r*'s with increasing relish and mimicked the expressive hand-gestures that seemed so much a part of the French tongue. I used idiomatic phrases (like *ma vieille* when talking to Mme. Berthe) without knowing or particularly caring exactly what they meant. Within a year I spoke nothing but flawless French and pronounced it like a born Parisian.

We weren't exactly in Paris, in point of fact, though not so far from it as to impinge upon the purity of my accent. Marly-le-Roi was located in a small wooded suburb not far from Versailles (where I was occasionally taken to play), about twenty minutes by train from the heart of the city.

Fritz was also five years younger than Bruno and was a musical fanatic in the manner of his father (that would be my grandfather), a trumpeter who emigrated to the United States from his native Bari at the beginning of the century. Niccolo Bernini performed with a good many orchestras and bands but wound up playing with the Ringling Circus band, which, as I understand it, was where he met my grandmother, Edna, who worked for Mr. John Ringling North in some sort of secretarial capacity. The nomadic life of the itinerant troupe appealed to my grandfather, who enjoyed discovering the country of his adoption from the unique and ever-changing perspective offered by the peripatetics of a traveling circus.

In due time my father was born, grew up amidst the spotlights and the sawdust and rose to become a part of them both, as we have seen. Some years later Fritz came into the world as Ernesto. With his arrival coincided the departure of my grandmother, to the despair of her husband, who, try as he might, could not help blaming the child for his wife's death. Fritz grew up wild and guilty, trying on the one hand to atone for his crime (I think he first became interested in music out of a desire to placate his father) and, on the other, given to fits of violent rebellion, drink and eventually his change of given name, which could be viewed as yet another attempt to throw off the culpability of the miserable Ernesto. Both children managed to avoid much in the way of formal schooling, my father through his dedication to the trapeze and Fritz through a natural cussedness that manifested itself in disinclination and truancy. This form of protest ended when it was succeeded by another: He lied his way into the army in 1934 at the age of sixteen. He had a varied and colorful career in the military, played in the army band, saw action with Patton's inexhaustible Third, was invalided out (because he *was* exhausted), signed up again and returned to the army band, where he played the trombone, learned conducting and could sight-read anything.

When the war ended, there seemed no reason to return to America. My grandfather had died in the interim (he is buried in the circus cemetery in St. Petersburg) and the GI Bill would let Fritz—the name was even on his dog tags— stay on in the City of Light and study piano and composition. He got a scholarship with Emile Laurent at the Conservatoire and supplemented his stipend with a series of odd jobs (ah, those jobs!) that enabled him to lead a sort of Walter Mittyesque existence while studying music and drinking himself to death. He was not yet thirty when I came to live with him.

It might have been more practical for us to have lived in the city instead of commuting to it every day, but a twist of fate had ingratiated him with Mme. Berthe, who, it devolved, was not his housekeeper, as he had so grandly advertised to me in English under her nose, but his live-in landlady, the owner of the house. He had performed some obscure act of kindness or generosity for her when he had arrived in Paris with Patton's liberating forces, and in addition, she found in him, she felt, a replacement for her own son, killed at twenty-three at Dunkirk.

Their arrangement was a curious one: Fritz had the ground floor to himself with the exception of the kitchen, and Mme. Berthe retained the upstairs. How she managed any rest I shall never know, for Fritz was a chronic insomniac as well as drinker who played the piano (the trombone he never touched after the war) at odd hours of the day or night, and when he wasn't thundering at the keyboard, he was making love to a succession of young girls who paraded through our lives at spasmodic intervals, some lasting only a night, others for a few days and occasionally one who'd survive us for a week or three.

When he was in his cups, which was often, Fritz's character underwent no radical alteration, unless you count his rapid ascents and descents. His mercurial temperament swung back and forth like a pendulum, only without any perceptible rhythm. He swung from wild energy and good humor, alert, penetrating conversation at the one extreme, to an almost Russian depression on the other in which tears, occasional abuse (and once, I recall, an ineffectual, half-hearted round of Russian roulette with a British service revolver won in a crap game) were all possible. His pendulum swung back and forth when he was sober; when drunk, it was simply likely to swing faster. And harder.

Overall, however, Fritz was nothing if not filled with an appetite for life, and he filled me with it, too. As he never patronized me, I never felt self-conscious. He treated me in a funny sort of way as an equal, perhaps a younger brother, rather than assuming the avuncular role for which he was so clearly unsuited. I recall wandering into his room, shortly after my arrival, to find his pale rear end waving up and down in the air like a steeplechase jockey's as he plunged arhythmically in and out of someone whose thin legs were all I could see. I retreated in confusion, noting that the sounds coming from his bed were reminiscent of those I had heard on my last night at sea. I went to the kitchen and sat morosely by myself, frightened and bewildered by the recurrence of this phenomenon. Whatever did she mean, crying again and again, "Do it to me"? Do what? As I pondered this enigmatic request—really more an urgent command—Fritz walked in wearing his ratty bathrobe and a sheepish expression.

"That probably didn't make much sense in there," he began, with a jerk of his head in the direction of his room, "but it's not really terribly important; nothing to get upset about. You want some beer?" He opened a warm bottle and sat with me as we passed it back and forth. I was too rattled to know even how to frame my questions.

"Is she all right?" was all I could manage, eyeing him intently.

"God, I hope so. Come on, I'll introduce you. Come on." He took me by a reluctant hand and did it, too, pulling me into the bedroom and letting me sit with both of them, warm and fussed over until, happily reassured, I fell sleep.

As my French improved, I was allowed to accompany him into the city, where we attended concerts, rehearsals, performed some of his odd but lucrative jobs, sat in on jazz sessions in Montmartre and once or twice slept overnight in a brothel in Pigalle called Mlle. Isabel's, where a lively party seemed always to be in progress and where, as he played the piano so well, Fritz was always welome. To me, all these wonderful places were more or less interchangeable, and I viewed them without any prejudices or reservations. (If I had any bias, it was a positive one in favor of Isabel's, where there were always so many pretty girls and so much laughter. The jazz clubs, on the other hand, reeked of cigarette smoke, which gave me headaches.) If I fell asleep at one or other of these events, my uncle carried me with never a complaint or reproach. He held endless philosophic discussions with me, usually on the train into and out of Paris. These conversations would begin with Fritz staring out the window at the passing scenery, then, turning to me to pose the question of the day: "What's the difference, do you suppose," he might begin, "between thought, fantasy, dreams, and imagination?" Such a question might seem pucrile to an adult, but demanded of a six-year-old, it kept me on my toes. Although he had eschewed his opportunities for a formal education, Fritz was one of those self-informed types who know so much more than anyone else because their thirst for knowledge has been prompted by some genuine curiosity rather than a compulsory regimen. Our rooms at Mme. Berthe's were cluttered with books, volumes upon volumes of every description. There was a good deal of music lying about and music paper was everywhere; in addition there were biographies of composers and other historic figures of interest; texts on orchestration, harmony, counterpoint, musical theory; books on art and European history. They filled the chairs and choked the corridors; they held open doors and propped up the legs of tables; periodicals rose like growing trees from atop the piano and even shared the small cot that was mine.

Is it any wonder that I learned to read? I learned, I think, both French and English through a kind of osmosis, absorbing words in both languages through my pores. With all the volumes cascading down and round about me, it seemed impossible that I should fail to ingest some of their contents. Later I was an irregular student at the nearby École du Saint-Esprit in Sèvres, and there they put the finishing touches on my literacy, though they confused me with a great many arbitrary rules on the subject, which seemed almost specifically calculated to rob the process of the natural pleasure I had found in it.

Fritz and Mme. Berthe disagreed on the matter of my education. Fritz distrusted and disapproved of schools and didn't care whether I attended class at the École du Saint-Esprit or not. Mme. Berthe, on the contrary, was of the opinion that formal schooling was essential. The result of their dispute was my on again–off again attendance, with consequences that—as will be shown—affected more than my education.

Hieronymous soon got used to the home and environs of Mme. Berthe, although the poor woman never especially got used to him. She didn't enjoy finding him constantly underfoot and sooner tolerated the succession of pretty musicians who boarded with us (Fritz displayed a marked preference for young violinists) than a Siamese who liked to jump into her lap the moment she found time to take a load off her weary feet. Hieronymous didn't mind; he wandered about indoors and out until he had found his favorite haunts—the warm ones—and soon felt quite at home. He developed a knack for catching birds and field mice, which the apartment in New York had not provided, and his *meow*'s in French were perfectly understood by all who heard them.

I had a somewhat harder time adapting to these new surroundings. Aspects of my life to which I had never devoted any conscious attention or acknowledgment, suddenly altered or removed, caused me anxiety and confusion. There was, for example, no central heating in the house, and though I wouldn't have known the term, I certainly knew what it felt like. There was no plug-in electric coil heater such as I had known in West Fifty-seventh Street either. The house was frequently chilly, especially in the morning before Mme. Berthe had lit the fires and late at night if I had not been fortunate enough to fall asleep before they went out.

Instead of cold homogenized, pasteurized milk from the refrigerator, I was awakened each morning by the clanking of the hand-pulled milk wagon of M. Jacopo. The milk was warm, yellow and tasted odd. It had a scummy surface that I was obliged to pick off and throw away. I never got used to the milk, though I did learn to enjoy M. Jacopo, who played with me and let me ride on his milk cart as he pulled it about the grounds.

There was no plumbing. Not only was water pumped from a well that rose next to the kitchen sink, but Hieronymous was not the only creature among us who had a litter box. Ours were called chamber pots and were kept under our beds. Mme. Berthe emptied and cleaned these pots daily and seemed to feel no resentment or embarrassment in connection with this task, but I was terrifically self-conscious using them. Even at five I had been accustomed to the idea of privacy for bowel movements (peeing I wasn't so particular about—Jake and I used to have sidewalk contests to see who could go farther and longer) and took entirely for granted the existence of the flush toilet. But the chamber pot, an attractive if slightly chipped white china affair with blue piping around it, disgusted me.

You can get used to anything, however, given sufficient time and the discovery that no one else is looking. I became so familiar with that chamber pot that I would slide up and down the corridors, performing my business on it as though it were a sort of combination toilet-sled, using my legs on the tiled floor to propel me past piles of books or in pursuit of the cat. So much for plumbing.

In 1946 the house of Mme. Berthe on rue Saint-Denis in Marly-le-Roi was very much in the country. Today it has become a Paris commuting suburb on what now constitutes the outskirts of the city, with many apartment houses, condominiums and immobile rush-hour traffic. When I lived there it was a tranquil countryside with few houses, little villages and a great many woods, formerly used by the kings of France when they sallied forth from Versailles to hunt boar and other animals that did them no harm. In my day the only distinct evidences of modernity were the railroad tracks and nearby station platform and the telephone poles and electricity wires. Television antennae had not yet sprouted everywhere like cracks at the base of the sky.

The house of Mme. Berthe was situated directly off the rue Saint-Denis, but behind her house was considerable land. On the back portion of this land I soon discovered that there was another house—almost a shack, really—and this house was inhabited by tenantry. They were an interesting group and I was soon involved with them, for they had a little boy two years older than I and a daughter of fourteen with whom I fell instantly and hopelessly in love. The father, a widower, was a Russian Greek Orthodox priest, a refugee named Ogareff. His little boy was called Sasha and his beautiful daughter Olga. It was never clear to me just how Ogareff made his living. He had a long reddish beard and his house was a dark place with so many trees and bushes growing unchecked over the windows that yellow oil lamps were continually employed to illumine the interior. There were many animal skins lying about, a bear rug on the floor and more furs on the beds, which were all in the one central room that dominated the architecture of the place, so that the whole thing reminded me of a caveman's abode as I imagined one would look, except for the candlelit ikons on the walls.

Ogareff himself was an amiable if distant man. He seemed always to be reading a book when I showed up to play with Sasha and would glance briefly at me over the top of some massive tome so that I could only see his eyes beneath bushy orange brows and guess at what expression was occupying the rest of his face. But when he lowered the book he was always smiling.

I discovered the existence of the Ogareff family when I realized that M. Jacopo had other deliveries to make at Mme. Berthe's besides our own. Riding on the milk cart to his next stop, I chanced upon the little house near the woods and quickly made friends with the lively Sasha.

With Ogareff busily ingesting theology (I presume it was theology) and with Olga at school, Mme. Berthe occupied with cleaning house (and chamber pots) and Fritz in Paris, studying, drinking or performing one of his peculiar labors, Sasha and I were left much to ourselves. I can't imagine what he did with himself before my arrival. We devised all manner of games and wandered unsupervised from dawn till dusk around the property, sometimes straying down by the railroad tracks, a pleasant place of wild flowers, buzzing insects and a tarry smell from the railroad ties. Hieronymous sometimes went with us on these perambulations, whose tranquility was only occasionally interrupted when a train thundered by.

"Are you a Catholic? Do you accept the concept of the Holy Trinity? You must be a Catholic," Sasha insisted when I made no reply. "My father says all Italians are Catholics."

"Which shows how much his father knows," Fritz scoffed when I repeated this conversation to him and demanded to know the answer. "You're not Catholic—or only half-Catholic, anyway, on your mother's side. You're a Jew, chum. The Berninis are all Jews."

"What's that?"

"Oh, Christ, I knew I shouldn't have started this," Fritz moaned, clapping a hand to his forehead and reaching for his bottle. He tried explaining to me what it meant to be a Jew, but there was a naked violinist on his lap at the time (they'd just finished playing some duets), and as he became increasingly absorbed in the stiffness of her coral nipples as he kneaded them with a free hand while talking to me about Moses and the Israelites, he soon lost interest in his topic and so did I.

"We're Jewish and we believe in wolves," I announced solemnly to Sasha the next day.

"What the hell does that mean?"

I didn't know; I had simply said the first thing that came into my mind.

"You're damned," Sasha assured me with satisfaction.

"I know *that*," I shot back in a tone of lofty superiority that baffled him.

CHAPTER

Four

Vocations & Avocations

"Sit down, chum, and have a look at this."

"What is it, chum?" At first I did not like being called "chum." I did not know what it meant except that it was not my name. To give Fritz a dose of his own medicine, I began calling him "chum," and to my surprise he was amused. Thereafter we addressed one another by this absurd appellation.

"It's a paragraph of handy facts and figures about the Eiffel Tower. One copy's in English and this one's in French. Think you can learn them both by heart?"

Fritz's latest job was at the Eiffel Tower, where he worked the topmost elevator from ten until four each day except Thursday. He had a great deal of time to think up there, and what he came up with was not a rondo for the piano sonata he was supposed to be writing but a scheme involving my participation, by which he hoped to add a hefty per diem to his weekly salary.

Briefly, the idea was this: After he reported for work every morning, I would surreptitiously join him in his elevator.

Once there, Fritz would offer my services to the ascending passengers, charging them by the head to listen to me spout a few facts and vital statistics concerning Gustave Eiffel and his mighty skyscraper. This information I would rattle off in French, and for an additional sum—a little less (Fritz was nothing if not a psychologist)—I would repeat the thing in English for the benefit of all the postwar American tourists. Fritz calculated that the idea of a child dispensing this data would prove to be both endearing and provocative. Maybe I could be milked for tips as well—who knew? So taken was he with his plan that he actually invested money in a small dark suit for me, the nearest possible approximation to the uniform worn by the Tower employees.

We were a success, though not without some period of shakedown. I duly learned the paragraphs in both languages, my excellent memory helping me leap this first hurdle with ease. My suit was perfectly tailored to my small frame and I arrived at work with Fritz at nine-thirty, when he was due to report. I kept his watch and understood that at ten-fifteen ("when the big hand is on the three and the little hand is just past the ten") I was to buy a half-price ticket for the *troisième étage* and join him at the last elevator.

So far, so good. Our problems began with our arrival at the base of the huge tower, which I had never been close to before. From a distance it was not especially awesome: a curious needle poking into the sky and nothing more. Close up, it loomed over me, terrifying. When I gazed up at the top, the clouds moving past it made me dizzy and frightened. Nevertheless the thing appeared structurally sound from the point of view of its shape, squatting on four huge legs and not looking as though it were likely to tip over.

At ten-fifteen I screwed my courage to the sticking place and purchased my ticket on line at the Pilier du Nord.

Each part of my ascent was more frightful than the last. I was obliged to rest several minutes on the first platform, gathering my nerve before proceeding to the second. The first elevator began by going up a sickening curve in the leg (it's actually on a cog wheel at this point), and the fact that this first ascent is at an angle came as a disagreeable shock. I got out at the first level, bathed in sweat and needing desperately to go to the bathroom. Fifteen minutes later, anxious not to disappoint Fritz, I got back on and made it to the second level, where he was waiting impatiently for me.

"What took you so long?" he demanded testily when I found him.

"It's scary," I explained, and went to the bathroom again.

"There's nothing to it, chum," he reassured me in an urgent undertone when I returned. (He had been to the top and back again in the meantime.) "The thing's perfectly safe: They've never had an accident or even replaced a single strut since it was built. Come on, let's give it a try."

So, wondering when the first strut would need replacing and which one it would be, I tried. I stood next to Fritz as a new load of passengers got on, listened earnestly to his announcement of the destination of the lift and the safety precautions all were enjoined to observe—"Hands inside the windows at all times, please. . . ."

We started off.

"And now, ladies and gentlemen, for five francs my young associate here"—pushing me forward—"will deliver a brief history of the Tower as we move to the top."

Francs were duly proffered and I tried to speak. Alas, all I could do was stand rigid, with my eyes bulging at the windows as the steel struts outside grew thinner and fewer the higher we went. Fritz kicked me as though I were a piece of machinery that had stuck or a pump needing to be primed.

"La Tour Eiffel," I gasped in a squeaky voice, but could go no further. Ominous grumbling from the passengers resulted in a refund hastily distributed among them. Fritz muttered something good-naturedly about my being new to the job, which understatement was typical. Surprisingly he wasn't angry. When the tourists left, he kneeled beside me, his hands affectionately holding on to my shoulders.

"It's all right, chum. You've just got to get used to it, that's all. Come to think of it, I was frightened, too, when I started here."

We dispensed with the routine for almost an hour while I rode up and down with him; sure enough my terror turned to familiarity, and by and by familiarity gave way to a kind of boredom. (I was fine from then on, except for those infrequent occasions when I would look out the window and see a workman sitting on one of those thin, isolated beams, a hundred miles above nothing, chipping away at loose paint. That would always throw me, but I learned to look the other way quickly.) As I grew calm in the elevator I began mumbling my speeches under my breath in rehearsal and finally was introduced to an unsuspecting crowd and successfully performed in both languages. I even managed to get out the two paragraphs before we reached the top. There was an elevator change midway up the last portion and it was there that I switched languages

as well. There was nothing to it. I was the center of attention and admiration, and we took in a tidy sum—Fritz's
phrase—from which I was given what he called "a little
off the top." I left before closing time and waited for
him at the bottom of the Tower.

"Didn't I tell you?" Fritz crowed for the twentieth time
on the train home, counting the coins spread out on a
handkerchief on his lap. I could do no more than smile
tepidly, as I was exhausted. We had celebrated that night
with dinner at a sidewalk café on the boulevard Saint-
Germain and then gone to an American movie—the first
film I had ever seen—and it was so realistic (or rather, so
dreamlike, which is to say more than real) that, coming as
it did after my tiring labors, I was now completely spent.
The film was *Casablanca,* and though I have seen it many
times since, I will never forget this euphoric and traumatic
first exposure to it and to movies. Fritz was obliged to
whisper explanations in my ear so that I could follow the
story, but I understood all that was important. Ilsa was
loved by Rick and also by Victor; then Rick, for reasons I
could not grasp, sacrificed his happiness and sent Ilsa off at
the airport with Victor. It was an exhilarating experience
to see images so huge, and the black and white of the film
added to its dreamlike effect. I could not get over the beauty
of Ilsa Lund, and at the end, when she left without Rick, I
dissolved in tears.

"What's wrong?" Fritz asked gently, putting an arm
around me to comfort me.

"I want to go on to the next page," I declared, sniffing
into his shoulder. He laughed, caught me up in his arms
and carried me to the train.

Thereafter, for a number of weeks we plied our trade. If the ticket-taker at the Tower saw anything irregular in the same little boy showing up in the same dark suit every day (except Thursday) and staying until almost closing time, she did not appear to find it worth investigation, let alone comment. Possibly she was as bored with her job as I soon commenced becoming with mine. Blasé with my status as a wunderkind, I spoke my piece so quickly and so devoid of inflection that it became almost impossible to understand me, whichever tongue I happened to be speaking. Fritz had to rewrite the speeches to give me something to stay alert. They soon became outlandish, for his researches began turning up quaint and rococo variations that I suspect may have been discovered in the eccentric recesses of his own mind. I remember tearing through a passage about how the syphilitic Maupassant despised Eiffel and his wretched construction and urged fellow Parisians to "tear the iron monster from the skies." Passengers grew restless hearing a seven-year-old (I think I was seven by this time) speak glibly of venereal disease, though of course I had no idea what I was talking about. As usual.

Sometime after the information about Maupassant's illness, the whole thing ended. I'm not sure who blew the whistle on our lucrative enterprise (my suit had almost been paid for!), but Fritz no longer worked at the Eiffel Tower and neither did I. He refused to discuss the matter but simply looked for another preposterous line of work. I was left with some change, a slightly shiny dark suit, a good deal of incidental (and uncertain) knowledge about the construction and history of the Eiffel Tower and an odd, persistent affection for the place, considering how bored I eventually had got with it. Possibly my affection originated in the memories it evoked of Fritz and myself cheating the world and enjoying ourselves at the same time.

I mention this interlude because it was in so many ways typical of the kind of jobs Fritz held, while at the same time being rather more pleasant than most. He drove a taxi for a time, which was awkward because he had no license and couldn't steer very well. He lost what he earned repairing a succession of dented fenders. Another time he worked at Les Halles (this time at a profit) and again dreamed up a scheme that involved my collaboration, this time at four in the morning, but this one is a little too disgusting to mention. Suffice to say that it was years before I again touched steak or any other kind of meat.

He poured a great deal of energy into his jobs and money-raising adjuncts to them, far more than he allotted to his composing. I think concocting his Byzantine financial plots was a way of avoiding a long-overdue confrontation with his dreams and ambitions as a composer.

As a pianist Fritz was first rate. He worked hard at the piano and managed to practice at least three hours a day, drunk or sober. Hieronymous and I loved to listen to him from our favorite vantage point, on the floor underneath the instrument, where we could watch his legs animatedly pumping up and down on the pedals. Alternatively Hieronymous would perch on one side of the music stand and sit contentedly for an hour or so. Then, seized by a sudden whim to stretch his legs, he would jump down to the keyboard and meander along the blacks and whites, producing a few haphazard musical effects before leaping up to his perch on the other side of the piano. Fritz and I were always amused by this action and waited for him to do it.

Fritz was a good accompanist as well. Never intrusive, he played with a deft, supportive touch, not competing with the soloists, taking his tempos from them and following adroitly, always tasteful. At least once a week there was some form of chamber music at Mme. Berthe's. Sometimes there were as many as eight, other times just a violinist or flautist. Invariably one of the musicians was an attractive girl who stayed behind to empty the ashtrays "and help clean up." This cleaning was usually done in Fritz's bedroom to the accompaniment of distinctly unmusical sounds. I have associated sex and chamber music ever since, and certain particular pieces—the Dvořák Piano Quintet and the Mendelssohn Octet especially—continue to hold an ecstatic significance for me.

It was not as a performer that Fritz experienced difficulty, but he had violent theoretical objections to the role. He felt that a performer, even a great performer, like a great actor, was merely an intermediary between the artist or creator and his public. Interpretive art, he sniffed at me when I told him how much I loved his playing, was a secondary form of expression. Unfortunately the primary form eluded him. As an interpreter he was exquisite, introducing me to the delicate joys of Mozart, Chopin, Bach and his personal favorites, Fauré and what he called a newcomer, Francis Poulenc. (Beethoven he never played.) As a composer he was totally out of sympathy with his idols and utterly unable to manufacture music of the deft and subtle kind he so admired. He didn't write atonal music, but what he did produce had a heavy, almost atonal sound, devoid of melodic content or appeal. As a composer his entire musical character underwent a disagreeable metamorphosis and a pounding djin emerged in place of the quicksilver whiz of the Chopin études and Schumann's *Carnival.*

He worked very hard for some months on a symphonic tone poem inspired, he admitted, by existentialism, of all things. It was to be some sort of counterpart to *Thus Spake Zarathustra,* a piece that I didn't know and couldn't pronounce. He conducted the piece, titled *Equations,* in my presence at the Conservatoire before a good-sized audience of teachers, pupils and other interested parties. He conducted well—an interpretive art that he had polished as assistant leader of the army band—with authority, his precision all the more remarkable because he was quite intoxicated at the time. The piece was tepidly received and only politely acknowledged with a scattering of perfunctory applause followed by a hasty scraping back of chairs. "A little of this, a little of that," I heard someone say as people filed out of the auditorium. "Adds up to a lot of nothing," someone else supplied, reaching for a scarf.

Later we repaired to the Café de la Paix with the platinum-blonde first violinist.

"I liked it," I told Fritz, uneasy at his distracted air. He looked at me and smiled kindly, taking off the wire-rimmed glasses he wore when conducting and pinching the bridge of his nose before putting the glasses away in the breast pocket of his frayed, ill-fitting oatmeal jacket.

"You're a good boy and a real friend, George." He so seldom called me by my rightful name that I was startled and further alarmed.

"Perhaps they didn't play it right—the way you wanted," I ventured, groping for consolation.

"No, chum, it's only a poor workman who blames his tools. They played what I wrote as I directed them to play it. It just doesn't happen to have much merit, I'm afraid." He stared for a long time at his empty glass of cognac as if searching for something or someone there.

"Time is the final arbiter in these matters," the blonde violinist offered gently. "You may discover more merit in your work than seems apparent today. Who knows . . . ?" she trailed off before a withering glance shot in her direction that plainly instructed her not to patronize him. There was an uncomfortable silence as we tried not to watch one another and waited to take our cue from Fritz. At length, with a brief but eloquent shrug of his shoulders, he threw off maudlin introspection and transformed himself by an act of will into the loudest and funniest I had ever seen him be. Patrons at nearby tables stopped their own conversations to enjoy his antics. We laughed until we had tears streaming down our faces; our bellies hurt to be so convulsed. Fritz's anecdotes were culled from his early life with the circus and later with General Patton ("the *big* circus," as he called it) and included much grotesque mimicry and miming faintly resembling the puppet shows I had seen on the *Ile de France*. Now I could not help joining in the gales of laughter. Only later, thinking about them, did I come to realize that all his stories had the same point: They were tales told at his own expense, histories of his failures and shortcomings.

Later he fell asleep on the train back to Marly, and I had to wake him up for our stop and help him up the station stairs and down the rue Saint-Denis. The blonde violinist had not come home with us, which at the time surprised me, but I realized that if she had, it would have been in vain. Fritz was in no condition to help her "clean up." He fell backwards into his bed when I led him to it, and lay there, staring up at the ceiling, motionless, unable to get undressed. I set about helping him, untying his shoes and pulling them off, then pulling off his moth-eaten socks and trying to heft his legs onto the bed. Absorbed in this task, I was startled to hear a muffled sob from the indention on the mattress where his head was. I stood up and peered over at him, horrified to find tears spilling out of his eyes and glistening on his cheeks.

"What's wrong? What's the matter?"

"Oh, God" was all he replied, and now his entire frame shook with convulsive heaves. I thought his heart would break, judging from the sounds he made. I put down the socks and climbed onto the bed next to him and lifted his head onto my lap. I didn't know what else to do. He didn't resist, but threw an arm across his eyes and continued to weep behind it.

"It'll be all right," I told him, touching his hair hesitantly. If he heard me he gave no sign, even when I repeated this foolishness.

"We can't always have what we want," he mumbled once or twice as he drifted towards sleep. Another time he referred to the shambles that was his life and how he had destroyed himself and disappointed his father. Finally his eyes closed and stayed closed. I sat perfectly still for as long as I could, not daring to move for fear of waking him when I judged that rest was what he needed more than anything.

Finally, my back aching from rigidity and one leg falling asleep, I slid by degrees out from under his head and fell asleep by his side. "Sorry," he mumbled without waking.

The next day he was unaccountably distant, his humor cold and teasing. There was nothing in his words or manner, not even a gleam in his eye, that acknowledged the events of the night before or my part in them. Whatever it was I felt for him, he didn't want any of it.

Occasionally I would get letters from Madelaine. They arrived regularly at first, and as I was learning the rudiments of spelling, I endeavored to answer them. But it is hard to write often to a child, and after a time her letters commenced reading like mine: How are you? I am fine. Do you miss me? I miss you. I hope you are well. I hope to see you soon. How is France? It is hot in New York today. Tomorrow I will see Petey and tell him you said hello. I have to go now. Much love. Stay well.

I had no trouble remembering Madelaine, but it was hard, as time went by, to associate the generalized sentiments of her correspondence with the living, breathing person I had known. I understand now that she wrote simply so as to enable me to understand what she had to say, but that choice compelled her to become repetitious and had the net effect of making her less vivid to me. It was almost like viewing snapshots of someone and trying to remember how they looked when they moved and spoke. The letters, at first eagerly, desperately awaited, grew to occupy less space in my consciousness.

Our routine was no routine. The days became weeks without anyone's seeming to notice, and the weeks accumulated as months, with no sense of any specific progression except my own expanding horizons of knowledge. And even that, from my subjective vantage point, was invisible, at least to me. No one else seemed to be paying any attention to my progress, let alone calling the fact of it to mine. I learned things—books and vast amounts of music—without being aware that I had learned them. My worlds were multiplying effortlessly, like rabbits, without discipline or order. I continued my irregular appearances at the École du Saint-Esprit in Sèvres, too infrequent to make friends or to come away with any codification for the miscellaneous scraps of information I was accumulating. There were odd and unexpected gaps in my knowledge of facts, things and how they worked. These gaps appeared abruptly out of nowhere, like potholes in a swiftly traveled road. All you got was a sudden yawning glimpse of the chasm just before everything went *bump!*

Sasha and I ran away—one of my lifelong specialties. That is, we went for a long walk, and each daring the other to go further, found ourselves inside and soon lost in the forest of Marly. This time there were no policemen or handy landmarks to help guide us home. I remember the experience of being lost in the woods, not with the elation that surrounded my escape from Central Park, but not with apprehension or panic, either. The woods were alive with beauty and not at all treacherous or menacing. It was like walking through one's own dream, and to this day the real events of the walk are obscured in my memory by the dreamlike sense my memory makes of them. What I really did and really saw remain unclear. My most pronounced recollection of the day is of the soft yellow sun-light penetrating the leafy canopy above us and darting through in bright rays to the moss beneath our feet and ahead of us. Somehow, as an aural accompaniment, I hear in my mind's ear not the actual sounds of the forest but the "Forest Murmurs" from *Siegfried,* which I probably learned at about the same period on Fritz's Victrola. Certainly my rational self insists that Wagner was not playing in my ears during our actual hike—unless I was mentally replay-ing it at the time. I suppose it is a question not much worth pondering, for the indisputable fact is that we *were* lost, and lost for hours.

Sasha began as the leader and suggested various routes he thought were sure to extricate us from the maze of woods that entrapped us, but he was no better than Hansel at this sort of thing and hadn't even thought to leave a trail of bread crumbs in our wake. When I pointed out that we had passed the same lightning-felled tree three times (and showed him the snapped end of one of his own shoelaces left there to prove it), he was humbled, and the torch of leadership passed to me, despite my being his junior.

Only once did either of us taste real fear, and that was when we realized it was getting darker and we were faced with the prospect of spending the night in this unending forest. And if we survived the chilly night and whatever wild animals chose to venture out into it, what guarantee was there that we would reach civilization the next day when we had failed so completely to rediscover it on this one? We were beginning to feel hungry, too, and weak as a consequence. How far could we traipse through the roots and brambles and thickets on the morrow with nothing to fuel our energies?

The entire series of questions became moot when we suddenly perceived the end of the trees and popped out into the open field not far from the familiar railroad tracks where our odyssey had begun. It was twilight, and the field had a number of dark-clothed figures roaming through it who turned out to be the police summoned by Mme. Berthe, Fritz and Sasha's father to search for us.

"Where in God's name were you?" Fritz demanded when the fuss was over and the police had gone. He was drunk and enraged but held himself together with a sort of wild calm that I failed to recognize as the one that precedes the storm.

"Playing tennis," I hazarded, not knowing in the least what tennis was or how it was played. It was probably a phrase I had come across in one of the damn books lying about.

It was not a wise choice. Fritz hauled off and slapped me across the face. The blow was so powerful it twisted my head and threw me backwards off my feet, stumbling over more books behind me as I fell across the room in a heap. It was so powerful and (more to the point) so unexpected that I don't even think it hurt until later. For the moment I was numb with astonishment. I had never been struck before in my life, certainly not by a grown-up using his full force. Roughhousing with Sasha didn't count.

"Are you crazy?" he roared at me, gasping for breath with the unaccustomed exertion. "Don't you know there are unexploded mines in Marly? You want to go to Kingdom Come? You might have blown yourself to bits, you little goddamned shit."

Here was another pothole in my knowledge. I had heard of Germans—Mme. Berthe called them *"les Boches"* and spat whenever she mentioned them—I had heard tales of the war and Sasha had given me his version of who Hitler was and what he had done, but his stories of mass annihilation were so ludicrous that I knew he had gotten it wrong or was possibly making it up with the object of frightening me. None of it had any reality; or rather, it had the same unreal reality as the fairy tales I read. I certainly had never heard of unexploded mines in the forest—in any forest. The only mines I had ever heard of were those in which dwarfs labored.

"Well, say something," Fritz barked, suddenly avoiding my eyes. "Don't just sit there with your ass on the floor like a baby."

"I didn't mean to. I didn't know about the unexplored mines."

"Unexplored?" He looked at me for a moment in exasperation, ran a nervous hand through his hair and gave a choked laugh. Something I had said evidently amused him. He came over, knelt beside me and gave me a ferocious hug, burying his head for a long time in my shoulder and breathing heavily there. Then he lifted me up. "Come on, let's put some cold water on your face, chum. It's going to burn otherwise."

It did anyway.

After the episode in the forest I was not allowed to leave the property, even as far as the railroad tracks, without the supervision of Olga. School was out for the summer holidays and to her was assigned the disagreeable chore of looking after me. I don't think she minded baby-sitting for me, but Sasha was her responsibility as well, and they despised each other with a mutual contempt that only brothers and sisters seem capable of generating. She called her brother a little monster, a disgusting cretin and other suchlike terms of endearment. He responded in kind, telling her how ugly she was, making fun of her newly sprouting breasts and putting frogs into her bed to show the esteem in which he held her.

"Why can't you be nice, a little gentleman like George?" she would coax him in a condescending tone, smiling over at me while she said it.

"He's not a gentleman, he's a little fairy who picks his nose," Sasha would wittily retort, shoving me in the chest for good measure. Olga would gasp, continually amazed at his effrontery, and hit him ineffectually on the rear. Sasha would then shift his attack to her, pulling without mercy on her long orange braids, and I would rush to the rescue, grabbing his ears from behind, and the fight was on. In later times as we grow up we forget what a purgative a good fight can be, and we take its healthy effects for granted when we are children. The natural release that results from being knocked about, rolling around on the floor or ground and squeezing some part of someone as hard as you can is bred out of you by grown-ups, who make no distinction between aggression and letting off steam. Learning to "settle our differences peacefully" is the series of misnomers that parents and psychologists give to this process, and it is too bad, because I know of no substitute for a good fight unless it is a violent bout of lovemaking, and even though that releases something, it is not quite the same.

I was, as I have said, in love with Olga. There are people who make certain useless distinctions between different kinds of love. Some friends are fond of saying, "You're not in love; you just *think* you're in love. Let me tell you what love is. Love is when—" and they then proceed to their own empirical definitions of this phenomenon. As far as I am concerned, if you think you are in love, then you *are* in love, and there's no one qualified to qualify your feeling.

If an eight-year-old boy is in love, it is called puppy love. If he is in love with a fourteen-year-old girl, I am sure there is yet another quasiclinical term for it. All I know is that it felt like love to me. I doted on Olga and watched with eagle-eyed attention every move she made. Her banal observations and commonplaces I received as Holy Writ. She was an utterly conventional girl really, proper, religious, conformist (though not without natural high spirits) and with a streak of greeting-card poetry about her that she—and I—took to be romantic refinement. She could not believe ill of anyone except her brother, whose aberrant behavior shocked her each time as though she had never been exposed to such antics before in her life.

She thought me, as she often said, a little angel and a perfect gentleman. I tried not to disoblige her in these views and carefully censored my conversation and actions in her presence, for I was neither a gentleman nor an angel, especially where she was concerned.

My thoughts about Olga were dark, unspecific and carnivorous. Unfamiliar with sexual intercourse personally and too young to contemplate it for myself as a consequence (what I understood of it from Fritz's goings-on disgusted me), my appetite for Olga expressed itself in vivid dreams and daytime fantasies. I imagined being in the Ogareff shack alone, going through Olga's bureau and looking at her pairs of white cotton underwear. The merest inadvertent glimpse beneath her dress of these innocent yet somehow wickedly intimate garments was enough to distract me for the rest of the day. I longed to kiss Olga, to hug her and to smell her. I concocted little scenarios compounded of my eccentric reading on the one hand and the unexplored corners of my imagination on the other. We were alone on a picnic somewhere. We were alone in her house, her father off taking Sasha to the doctor. (Why he needed to go to the doctor was not covered by the fantasy.) She was with me at Mme. Berthe's, only Mme. Berthe was dead and Fritz was in his room with a violinist.

All that came of these varied and passionate daydreams, however, was that I became tongue-tied in her presence, incapable of expressing myself except in small gestures, the significance of which entirely eluded her.

"How pretty!" she would innocently exclaim when I presented her with a hand-picked bouquet of violets. Then she would plant an affectionate kiss of thanks on my cheek and it would burn there worse than the blow from Fritz.

To make matters worse, she had a boyfriend of sorts. He lived a half-mile or so away, was a year or so older than she was, tall and gangly, with a faint mustache and dark aviator sunglasses. His name was François and his aviator glasses were appropriate because he intended to become a pilot, he said. (He was right: Now he flies 747's for Air

France.) He would show up and collect her for walks or trips to the cinema at Sèvres, and though Olga was a good girl with a strict curfew to obey, it nevertheless galled me to see her with fresh ribbons in her hair, listening to me with only half an ear and looking always over my shoulder in eager expectation of his arrival. Then he would spirit her away and out of my child's grasp, beyond my circumscribed confines of house and garden, to a wider world where children could not go.

The summer dragged on. I would go to sleep thinking of Olga, and one night something peculiar happened. I was lying on my stomach, thinking about lifting up the hem of her checked gingham dress and examining what was underneath it. I was not aware of my body at the time, so absorbed was I for the moment in the fantasy, but I realized later that I must have been unconsciously rocking myself back and forth to the accompaniment of these sweetly pleasant thoughts.

All at once something exquisite and odd erupted in my loins. For an instant I panicked at the unfamiliarity of it. It seemed as though I had sneezed from the wrong place (with my elbow, say), and then it was gone. I had used some part of my body in a way it had never been used before. I rose off my belly and felt the sheet beneath me. There was a small, warm and sticky damp patch, and I could feel the stickiness on the tip of my penis as well. Was I bleeding? I turned on the light by the bed and discovered no blood, just a peculiar milky-white foam that was getting colder by the minute. It had an unfamiliar scent that reminded me of ammonia. I sat up in bed for a while, examining it and myself. Apparently whatever had happened had not injured me; I got my towel and absorbed what remained of the mess, feeling none the worse for it, whatever it was. Looking back on it as I lay my head on the pillow in the darkness and considered the matter, it had really been rather pleasant.

I was Columbus, Admiral Byrd and Galileo rolled into one. I had just discovered yet another new world and set a tentative foot on the edge of a vast and unknown continent.

Five

Scandals & Traumas

Fritz had begun giving lessons at the Conservatoire lately, the closest thing to a normal job he'd held since his days with the army band. He practiced at home on me, as you might say, and then incorporated the methodology he found comfortable with his students in Paris. They were, of course, far more advanced than I, but he warmed up for them on me.

Teaching was something he did really well. He was endlessly patient and so clearly enjoying himself that it was contagious. I learned rapidly under such circumstances, since I was already a music addict (carrying on at least one of the Bernini traditions) and actually enjoyed practicing, though Mme. Berthe had to remind me more than once to do my scales, always the most tedious part of learning to play an instrument. Our lessons always began with the exchange of a few jokes and that ridiculous game you play with thumbs and closed fists, whose object—in this case— was to warm up the hands.

"Did you hear about the couple who were one hundred years old and wanted a divorce?"

"No."

"Well, they went to the lawyer and asked him to help, and he said, 'Look, how come you waited all these years before you decided to get divorced?' Know what they said?"

"What?"

"They wanted to wait until the children had died."

I always laughed at Fritz's jokes; they went a long way towards defining my idea of humor, as did his outlook on life generally. The fact that many of his jokes were just plain silly or perverse or weirdly bleak (what was later referred to by the cognoscenti as "black humor") made no difference to me. Children are usually more open to everything than adults, if only they are exposed to things soon enough. It is as adolescents that we start closing ourselves off to ideas we haven't heard or assimilated before. I had no trouble with *Le Sacre du Printemps* at five: At fifteen it baffled me, and I had to wait until I was twenty-five before I was free enough to recapture my childhood acceptance of it. (Later, at school in America, Fritz's jokes would elicit blank stares from the other kids. "That's dumb" was the most frequent rejoinder I got for my pains. Unless they were about sex, I discovered, no one even told jokes. My store of silly stories soon helped turn me into the ostracized figure I remained at school.)

In the meantime I continued my fantasies about Olga during the long, hot summer days and nights. Masturbating while thinking of her became a happy addiction, but orgasms did little to satisfy my insatiable if unspecific desire. At most they defused it briefly, but the merest sight of her crossing the garden or returning the milk pails to M. Jacopo was enough to inflame it all over again. I worried about doing myself an injury.

One day, quite without my planning it (not that I could have done any such thing), one of my fantasies actually occurred. Fritz was teaching at the Conservatoire, Mme. Berthe was in Ville d'Avray, visiting with her younger (maiden) sister and Sasha was with his father at the Greek Orthodox church in Châtelet, attending some sort of special service. Olga was looking after me, wandering about the house as I did my piano exercises. When lunch time approached, she suggested we picnic by the railroad tracks, as it was such a lovely day. Her suggestion fell in so uncannily with my secret dreams that it savored of the miraculous. All I could do was stare at her.

"Well, yes or no?"

"Yes."

She made up a picnic basket, humming an approximation of some of my little piano pieces as I watched, breathless with anticipation. There was bread, cheese, pâté and cold vinegar potato salad, along with a bottle of wine not quite full. I carried the basket and Olga managed the food.

Lunch with her felt like an hour in heaven. I ate silently as she prattled on, unable to believe I had this ravishing creature all to myself, safe from any distractions or interruptions. No window would open with a summons for either of us to do this or that. Sasha wouldn't spoil everything by inciting her to exasperation with his loutish behavior. She was all mine.

Our conversation, to be sure, verged on the desultory. Olga had little to say to an eight-year-old, and as I have

intimated before, her remarks were not likely to be provocative or original in any case. On the other hand I, who
was bursting with important things to tell her, found myself
tongue-tied as usual. Dialogue was tapering off, and in an
attempt to keep it going, seeking some gambit that would
reanimate her, I asked:

"Are you going to marry François?"

Bull's-eye. She blushed and began putting away the lunch
things, but it was certain she was all attention now.

"He hasn't asked me. Besides, I'm only fifteen."

It took me a while to come up with anything else.

"I think you should, if he asks you."

Better and better. Her features became suffused with
pleasure and she looked over at me with shining eyes. True,
they were not shining for me, but it is not the best of all
possible worlds, as I knew even at eight, and I was thankful
for what I could get.

"You do? Why?"

This was a poser, the more so as I was frantically jealous
of François and now had maneuvered myself into the
ridiculous position where I must sing his praises. I attempted
to dodge the issue.

"Because he likes you."

Worse and worse.

"He does?" She gasped at this intelligence as though
learning it for the first time. I might have been bringing
her news of life on Mars. "How can you tell?"

"He always comes to see you, doesn't he?"

So it went, she sitting on the edge of her blanket, so to
speak, and I mumbling in reluctant monosyllables, she
pursuing the tiniest scraps I had to toss out and I trying

not to throw her anything she could chew on. I cursed myself for having mentioned the scarecrow's name.

Eventually she grew tired. The heat of the day, the food, the wine and my unenthusiastic replies to her boring questions combined to make her sleepy.

"I think I'll stretch out for a little bit," she said finally, suiting action to the word. "Don't wander off, now."

Small likelihood of that. I hadn't the slightest intention of leaving her side. She lay on her back on the blanket, bare legs outstretched and a napkin spread over her face to protect it from the sun. For a while we were both motionless, like two statues, with only the buzzing insects of the field making any noise.

"Aren't you going to lie down?" she asked after a while from beneath the napkin.

"Pretty soon."

"It's hot," she remarked contentedly and drifted off.

For a while I did nothing. I looked at her, drinking in her dormant form with my eyes, my pores. Her legs were splayed across the blanket, and as she moved in her sleep, the hem of her pink dress rose slightly, exposing a pair of dimpled knees. I didn't dare move for fear of waking her, but by inches adjusted my position so as to be looking up her dress. There wasn't much to see, as her legs were close together, but the backs of her thighs, angled slightly off the ground, were sufficient to enrapture me for a quarter of an hour.

Looking at her knees, an idea occurred to me. It took some minutes to work up the courage to try it, but finally I eased myself to the edge of the blanket and plucked a blade of grass. My entire body was now bathed in perspiration; it wasn't due to the sun's heat but emanated from a nether reigon between my legs and spread outwards so that the grass was slippery in my hands. I crawled cautiously towards her beautiful hairless legs as though I were a soldier trapped in no-man's-land, aware that the least detection of my movements could prove fatal. She stirred once and I froze in place for another interminable five minutes.

At length, trying to control the shaking in my hand, I scraped the blade of grass along her right calf. No response. I touched her leg with the grass again, a little harder, and moved it back and forth. Wonder of wonders, her legs spread apart, the door to her haunting white underwear ajar as if by magic. I was Ali Baba and had spoken *Open Sesame,* only it wasn't a grain that had forced her portals but a lowly bit of green weed.

The white of them was dazzling in the sunlight, blinding me with possibilities as if it had been burnished porcelain. I realized that I had not swallowed in over half an hour but had refrained, frightened that the gulping sound might awaken one of us and put an end to this dream. From either side of the underpants, little tendrils of red hair peeked shyly out like infant creeping vines that haven't yet latched on to a wall.

I inched forward between her legs, scrunching my shoulders until they ached to avoid making contact with the inside of her creamy thighs. The underwear grew more distinct, and I could make out the weave of the fabric. At the very center where her legs joined each other, her pubic hair underneath the cotton subtly darkened the shade of white in that one area. I moved closer still and hoped that no trains would come roaring by and rouse her. My nostrils drank in a pleasant if unfamiliar scent. Without knowing any more what I was doing, I stuck out my tongue and touched the darker white spot of the underpants with the tip. She didn't move. I grew bolder. Or more desperate. Or both. I moved my tongue up and down, barely making contact. Nothing. I stretched my neck out still further and created a greater friction between my tongue and Olga herself through the thin material, involving more of my tongue's surface. Up and down I bathed the small area like a mother cat cleaning her kittens.

Olga moaned in her sleep and her body undulated slightly. Either I knew that she was not waking up, instinctively understood that this was an unconscious response to the stimulus that I was offering her, or else I simply was past caring. I continued lapping and lathering, lost in a haze of ecstasy. Her thighs now clamped tightly over my ears, but I paid no heed. My tongue now met her undulations in an insistent rhythm, a private dance to which we both miraculously understood the steps without ever having practiced. By degrees we found ourselves pushing harder and harder. I was aware of my penis rubbing madly up and down in my trousers against the blanket and dimly sensed it was only moments before it would explode.

Suddenly she woke up. I could sense the shift in her position as her torso raised itself on her elbows; her thighs loosened their grip on my head. I jerked away in time to see her pluck the napkin off her face. When she saw me she screamed. It was just a horrified squeal at first, but then it resolved itself into words, phrases like "What are you doing?" and "You filthy, disgusting boy!" and others like that. Her invention was not lively, though it must be ac-

knowledged that she was severely rattled. Shortly thereafter she burst into tears and, converting the napkin to yet
another use, dabbed at her eyes and her reddened face with
it. I crawled over to her to say something—to this day I
have no idea what it might have been, for I never got it out
—and she began to slap me viciously about the head and ears.
This time I was not as resilient as I had been when Fritz
struck me. I, too, burst into tears and sat next to her, sobbing
in accompaniment on the blanket. I suppose I was hurt, I
suppose I was ashamed, but in truth I cannot remember
thinking anything in the way of coherent thoughts. I *felt,*
that was all, but such a confused tangle of different and
conflicting feelings that they made war with each other
inside my head.

She stopped crying but I continued, lying on my stomach
now and pounding the blanket with my fists, furious,
heartbroken, wanting to die, wanting to live, wanting not
to be a child. Wanting. It was a long time before I became
aware that she was staring at me; when I realized it, I
stopped crying and looked over in her direction on the
ground. Not *at* her, for I could not bear to lock eyes with
hers, but from the corner of mine I could see them, red
and puffy, staring at me as though I were some new form
of life. Her lip trembled.

At last, compelled by her will, I raised my face and, with
some settling, looked her in the eye.

"Why?" was all she said. She infused the word with
tragic eloquence as though demanding of a murderer his
motivations. Her *Why?* penetrated my inmost depths and
buried itself like an arrow in my bowels, searching there
for an answer. I could only think of one.

"Because I love you."

She continued to stare at me with no change of expression upon hearing this, but after a moment her eyes blinked. She looked away, surveyed the sky and then, standing, seized the picnic basket and strode off without another word.

I spent a tortured week wondering if Olga would reveal my scandalous behavior to anyone. I felt intuitively that she would not, that our encounter had been too intimate for that, but I couldn't be sure. I have read since on the subject of rape and discovered that many women never report having been violated out of a misplaced sense of shame, as though they and not their rapists were guilty of some outrage. Instinctively I felt that Olga would see the matter in this light and I hid behind that fact of human nature.

Unless she confessed. The thought popped unbidden in my mind. I knew what confession was—Mme. Berthe was always confessing, and Fritz in his inimitable fashion had explained it to me—but did Greek Orthodox people confess? And if they did, would Olga include this item in her report? And if she did, would the priest take it upon himself to take some sort of action? Would he contact Olga's father and warn him to keep his daughter away from the eight-year-old maniac? Or would he, when (and if) he learned of my transgression, simply send for the police? I was so terrified by these thoughts that I could not even bring myself to ask Fritz if Greek Orthodox people went to confession. (They do.)

At the end of a week, however, nothing stirred. Neither Father Ogareff nor the police pounded on our door, demanding my blood. Nor did François make an appearance.

I think I had dreaded this possibility most of all, feeling with the same series of intuitions that if Olga confided to anyone anything of what happened, it might soonest be to François. But no doors were pounded upon and by degrees I felt myself safe and likely to remain so.

I need scarcely add that Olga's behavior towards me underwent a pronounced alteration. She no longer planted spontaneous kisses on my cheek, nor did she ever again refer to me as an angel or a perfect gentleman. Indeed, she avoided talking to me altogether when she could, and when she could not, confined her remarks to the barest minimum. And she never looked me full in the face.

"Olga doesn't like you anymore," Sasha sneered, and gave me a heart-stopping moment. But as he failed to pursue the matter, I judged he had merely seen fit to give me the benefit of his observations.

I languished in shame and misery. God knows, I had not meant to do what I did. I had neither premeditated nor arranged it; it had simply occurred, one thing leading inexorably to another. Looking back in my mind and attempting to replay the incident, I found I could hardly believe it really happened. How could I have conceived, let alone carried out, such a revolting act?

The question gnawed at me as I waited to fall asleep at night, and I was the more confused as, guilty as I felt, I could not help remembering with pleasure the ecstatic sensations that had enveloped me right up until the whole thing ended. Truly I had been lost in a maze of pure rapture to the point where I had been beyond the claims of reason. It may have been disgusting, what I had done, but it was also wonderful.

And I had not been alone in my enjoyment. In her sleep, untrammeled by any inhibitions or sense of propriety, Olga had responded to the pressure of my tongue, arched her body and pushed enthusiastically back at me, crying out with pleasure. When awake, however, she hated me for what we had done, for what I had tricked her into doing. Why?

These were knotty paradoxes for an eight-year-old to wrestle with and reconcile, and I could not reconcile them. All I could do was feel miserable with guilt and remorse, while at the same time longing to do it again.

Six

A Bang & a Whimper

In addition to his other quirks and eccentricities, Fritz was a gambler of sorts. He was eclectic about his choice of medium and by no means compulsive, but he liked a game of cards or an occasional few hours with a pair of dice. His luck was undistinguished either way as a rule, but since he played for infinitesimal stakes, it didn't much matter whether he won or lost. His enthusiasm during the play, however, was enormous and more than made up for the ante. You would have thought millions were riding on the next hand or roll of the dice from the way he carried on. He yelled, he chortled, he prayed; he hummed when he was winning and groaned when he was losing. He clapped his hand to his forehead, his heart or any other handy surface and drank the whole time.

Gambling was not permitted at Mlle. Isabel's—though whether this was the law or simply because Isabel felt it interfered with the flow of commerce I never knew for sure —so it was that my experience of Fritz the cardshark and crapshooter, Fritz the comic-opera version of Dostoevski's gambler, was obtained on the rue Saint-Denis on a sort of biweekly basis. Sometimes, but not always, chamber music preceded the game. Afterwards the cards and chips were produced, but the players were not exclusively culled from the ranks of musicians. Some were people Fritz knew from his various jobs—and a colorful assortment *they* were around a poker table!—while still others came to us from I don't know where, possibly referred by friends of friends. I can't remember more than eight of them at a time, but in our crowded quarters, making a lot of noise as they played, they might as well have been eighteen.

Once things got underway, there was no telling how long they might go on. It usually took two days to air the place out after a particularly grueling contest, and all the books lying nearby were impregnated with stale cigarette smoke and branded by glass-ring watermarks. On more than one occasion I fell asleep to the sounds of Fritz crowing with fervor over the turn matters had taken and slapping his hand down on the rickety card table in a way that made the poker chips clatter and bounce, to the annoyance of the other players. He played with a comical ferocity as though nothing but blood would satisfy his lust for victory, but scarcely remembered ten minutes later what he had been so wrought up about when he lost.

One time, shortly after the Olga debacle, I walked early one morning through the piles of books to our "music room" —which is to say, the room where the Bechstein was kept and in which music and all other social activities, including card games, took place—and discovered Fritz, rather pale, still seated at the card table, staring blearily at a pile of crushed currency spread over the play area before him. He looked up at me, slightly dazed.

"Things got out of hand last night," he commented, running his fingers through his thick, curly hair in an effort to collect himself. Then he stared at the money some more.

"How much is it?" I asked, approaching the table, waving away stagnant clouds of tobacco smoke. The money, scattered in profligate disarray, looked impressive.

"Lots." He pushed the bills around a little with his finger. "No one wanted to call it a night and there were two fellows from Lyons who dropped a bundle between them. The question is," he went on, still poking at the stuff, "what to do with it."

It didn't take him long to figure that out. He decided to blow it all on something. It was, after all, "found money," whatever that meant, and ought to be squandered on a suitable extravagance. After some deliberation (he realized with chagrin that he had not made enough to commission a ballet from himself!) he settled on a trip to Rome. He had never been there, and as an added bonus, he said he would take me with him. Once the idea took hold, he got quite worked up over it. When he told Mme. Berthe of his plans she was appalled.

"Rome at the end of August?" she cried in horror. "You are out of your mind. You will roast!"

"Nonsense. We'll tan."

"But you don't speak a word of Italian. How will you manage? And with the child—?"

"Don't speak Italian? Of course I speak Italian. I *am* Italian! Besides, I'm a musician, aren't I? *Allegro vivace*— don't tell me I don't speak Italian." He was hurling clothes pell-mell into a battered suitcase now and addressing both of us carelessly over his shoulder. "Besides," he assured us, "all you need to know is one word: *Dov'è*."

"What does that mean?" I asked, not liking the idea of this trip.

"It means 'Where?'."

No one could dissuade him, and he certainly was not about to heed the uneasy reservations of an eight-year-old on the subject. I didn't want to go to Rome for reasons that were unclear to me. My objections were a compound of those raised by Mme. Berthe and other less specific qualms—the whole thing sounded crazy. For one thing, I had never been to Rome, and doing things I had never done before, especially in Fritz's company, by this time held an ominous significance and always made me nervous. I knew with a child's intuition that it was one thing to go tearing around Paris with him—his home turf, so to speak—but that it would be quite another to go with him to a strange place where we wouldn't be able to communicate with anyone.

Fritz was stunned by my lack of enthusiasm.

"I can't believe my ears," he declared, sitting on his suitcase to close it (I had seen him throw in three sweaters) and favoring me with an expression of amazement. "The chance of a lifetime, to see sunny Italy, the land of your ancestors! And Rome, mother Rome! The Eternal City! Romulus and Remus! The capital of the empire that bore its name for a thousand years! Julius Caesar, Nero, Michelangelo! Vivaldi! Rome, with its seven fabled hills and thousand churches—the land of your fathers, and you don't want to see it? What about the Colosseum?" he dared me. "Where gladiators shouted"—and he stood up for this and stretched forth his arm—"*'Ave Imperator!* Those who are about to die salute you!' We'll see it by moonlight—the only way. No? Honestly, George, I blush to think you're a nephew of mine.

Haven't I had any influence at all? Haven't you the least curiosity to eat real pasta? Is that blood in your veins, or Junket? I can't imagine you letting a chance like this slip through your fingers.

"Of course, if you insist," he continued, sighing, altering his tone and swinging his feet back and forth over the side of the bed and staring listlessly at the ceiling, "we'll forget the whole thing. I don't know, maybe you're right—"

"All right, I'll go," I mumbled, cowed by his unquenchable flow of oratory. Bringing up Junket, which I had told him about and missed, was a low blow. You couldn't trust Fritz that way: He remembered things you told him when you thought he wouldn't; then he used them on you.

"You mean it?" He sprang back to life as though I had thrown a switch. "That's sensational. I knew I could count on you. I knew you were a real Bernini!" Abruptly he snapped his fingers. "Bernini! I wonder if he ever spent time in Rome." And he went on with pie-in-the-sky predictions and preparations. I comforted myself with the thought that at the very least, if we went to Rome, the Eternal City (I remember thinking it must go on forever), I wouldn't have to see Olga for a few days, and that prospect was enticing enough to override my fatalism about sightseeing with Fritz.

From my point of view at the time, the trip was an unmitigated disaster from start to finish, a roller coaster out of control. But in retrospect, having got out of it safe and sound, it plays back in my mind as a sort of grand adventure, typical in many ways of Fritz at his maddest and most wonderful. And also, though I had no way of knowing it, it was to be our last adventure together.

But one.

Things began with a bang. We took the overnight Paris–Rome express, and Fritz, sparing no expense, booked us berths in something called a *couchette,* a compartment that contained six stacked sleeping pallets, three on each side. Ours was shared with a stolid German couple traveling with their sixteen-year-old daughter, a hefty, sullen, sultry blonde with smoky blue eyes and a thick-lipped perpetual pout. She took a smoldering interest in Fritz and his dashing mustache, an interest that was not shared by her parents, who viewed both of us—but especially my uncle—with undisguised suspicion. There was no sixth passenger.

And I suppose they were right to be suspicious. All I remember of the trip is a ruckus that took place in the middle of the night, plunging under the Alps, when we all woke up and Fritz was discovered more or less in an upper berth with the pouty-mouthed daughter. He explained reasonably enough that he had been searching for the bathroom and had lost his way in the dark, but changed his story and insisted that he was a chronic sleepwalker when the girl's father pointed out how unlikely it was for the bathroom to be located on the ceiling of the compartment, at the top of a ladder. The language difficulty was invoked to account for the discrepancy between alibis, but I could tell from the murderous look in the father's eye and the harsh quality of his German expostulations that he was not entirely satisfied with either fiction. He sat up the rest of the night, guarding his treasure, as I was able to see because the unfamiliarity of my surroundings and my own forebodings about this trip made my own sleeping intermittent.

The next morning, with the dazzling blue Mediterranean

coastline on our right, the smoldering look was gone from the face of the daughter. It had been replaced by a kind of dreamy, faraway expression. Whenever she looked at Fritz, she wore an abstracted smile.

We reached Rome about midday and it was very hot. I did not mind. Eight-year-olds—even if they are almost nine —do not notice such things as heat, and Fritz was likewise impervious to the temperature. Rome filled him with instant ecstasy.

"Everything's in pastels!" he exclaimed, awestruck by the fact as we left the station. "Everything's yellow and pink!" His only concession to economy was to book us into a tiny hotel (called an *albergo*), where we paid by the day for our room. "No sense spending money on a place we'll never be in except to sleep," he theorized with the last bit of cogency he was to display for several days. He was right. We were never there, though more than once I wished we were.

The moment the bags were dropped off, he started in. He dragged me all over the place, pointing out this and that with the authority of a native. He prompted his disquisitions with the aid of a Michelin guidebook (which I grew to hate) and used *"Dov'è"* on the local folk to get wherever he wanted us to go. We climbed the Palatine Hills and viewed the Circus Maximus, which seemed little more than a de-serted racetrack to me. "A racetrack indeed!" Fritz said scornfully and cupped a hand dramatically to his ear. "Lis-ten! Can't you hear the mob howling for their favorite charioteers?" We scrambled among the ancient walls of the city—"Think, *think* what these walls have kept out!" he cried, prancing among the ruined red brick. "Hannibal never breached them and neither did Freud!" We played with stray cats in the Forum, though none were as affectionate as Hieronymous and several looked quite hungry.

And all the while Fritz kept up an incessant running commentary from that book. This was where they had murdered Caesar—*"Et tu, Brute!"* he declaimed solemnly, gasping, clutching his tummy and searching for something he called Pompey's Basis, where, he assured me, Great Caesar fell. "Oh, what a fall was there, my countrymen," he shouted, alarming other tourists in the area—"then you and I and all of us fell down, whilst bloody treason flourished over us—" and on and on in the same manner, while I chased after the kitties. He was impressive, all right, completely out of his mind but, as it happened, perfectly sober. I had to admit he was fun to watch gamboling about. I didn't know the term *disturbing the peace,* but instinctively hoped no one would show up and take him away.

We went to the Castel Sant' Angelo, where I was informed that from these battlements the singer Floria Tosca jumped to her death after the murder of the wicked police chief Scarpia. There seemed to be a lot of death and destruction connected with all Fritz's Roman anecdotes, but he told me that when Tosca dies in the opera, she only lands on a mattress.

"I saw a production once," he cheered me by saying, "in which the bounce of the mattress was so strong that Tosca bounced right back onto the battlements again. Very droll; wish you'd been there, chum."

In another place he showed me where Il Duce had harangued the crowd from his balcony. I did not begin to understand all his references: There were so many kings and tyrants and murders and she-wolves that they all got jumbled in my mind. Fritz was not the best explainer because he refused to trouble himself over details and jumped around so much while he was talking that he kept losing his place in the guidebook. I think I assumed Caesar and Tosca were contemporaries and that Romulus was the father of Il Duce (which, in a way, you might argue he was). And I never did understand why the Spanish Steps were not located in Spain.

What an amusing little boy I must have been.

We saw many gigantic fountains spewing water in all directions. Fritz insisted these were the creations of a man named Bernini, undoubtedly an ancestor of ours. When I asked him how he came to conclude this, he responded, "Intuition, chum. Fountains and music have one thing in common—they are absolutely useless. They exist only to give pleasure, to delight the eye or ear. This fellow was working the same line of country as all Berninis. Even your late father—my brother, the trapeze artist—was following the family tradition of silly activity. Now me, I'm the only boy in history who ever ran *away* from the circus, but I'm still in the fountain-making business, as you might say."

"Music isn't useless," I protested, staring at the soaring water, hypnotic as fire.

"It isn't," he agreed quietly, "but neither is this thing. They only appear to be useless." I did not understand him and would have pursued the subject, but we were off and running again.

We spent money on a prodigious scale—I don't believe Fritz ever once bothered to count how much we had—ate lots of pasta, and when communication was essential, Fritz made himself understood with phrases from Italian opera libretti. He got a cabdriver to take us to Ostia, the defunct harbor city of ancient Rome, and I had to admit that the sight of this ruined ghost town was impressive. There were lots of cats there, too, poking their noses in and out of a thousand roofless, wall-less houses.

"*La commèdia è finita*," Fritz intoned sagely to the cabdriver, who shook his head in delighted agreement.

We went to the Vatican and I marveled at the Swiss Guards sweltering in their heavy woolen uniforms and armor.

"If they are Swiss Guards," I asked, "where is Switzerland?"

"Far away."

"Then why aren't they guarding it there?"

"Maybe they don't even want people getting near the place. Come on, chum, we'll miss the ceiling."

We saw the Sistine Chapel. Fritz explained to me how Michelangelo, reluctantly undertaking to paint the ceiling, had lived atop scaffolding for years to achieve the spectacular results. I took this information quite literally, I recall, and having only the haziest idea of what scaffolding looked like, I tried picturing the artist perched precariously on top of a very tall and shaky ladder. Every morning he lowered his chamber pot to the ground on a long rope.

Over my objections we rented a car. I gently reminded Fritz that he didn't really know how to drive.

"Not to worry, chum," he countered, blithely filling out forms. "As you may have noticed, no one else around here does, either."

As it turned out, he was right again. We scratched up the car a little bit when we went through places where everybody went around together, and narrow streets gave us some trouble, and we had a noisy altercation at one point with another driver, who shook his fists at us and questioned Fritz's sanity in two unfamiliar languages. Fritz responded gamely in French—which the other man gave no signs of understanding—to the effect that the man's mother wore shoes that had been purchased in the military, or words to that effect, and we went our several ways.

It never stopped and never let up. I know I slept and was carried through some of it. Parts were beautiful and parts were fascinating, but overall I was oppressed by the headlong, nightmarelike rush of it, the sheer manic intensity that infused the entire enterprise. Sooner or later something was bound to go wrong. I eyed with alarm our dwindling supply of poker winnings.

Someone told us that a good dinner could be had at a place called Otello's, and nothing would do but we must go there. The name alone cemented it as Fritz's choice. It was, he told me as we made our way there, the very best of Verdi's operas (possibly excepting *Falstaff,* his last) and was written when the composer was in his seventies.

"So you see," he commented with gusto, "there's hope for me yet. Of course, having Böito for a librettist didn't hurt."

The place, when we found it, was packed, but Fritz slid some bills into the palm of someone with authority and we were given a small table in the corner of a room dominated by a huge and raucous party. Some years later, viewing the paintings of Brueghel's peasant feasts, I was reminded of this scene. The diners sat at long tables stretching end to end around the room, laughing and shouting across at each other. The place was hot with the heat of bodies. The waiter explained that these were cinema people, but that didn't mean anything to us. If they were cinema people, I couldn't understand why they were not on a screen. All I gathered, watching their antics as we ate, was that they were all trying very hard to amuse a little man at the head of the first table who was slightly chubby, had dark curly hair and wide sad eyes. They strove hard to make him smile, which he did from time to time, but he said little and appeared shy, speaking only occasionally to a small, waiflike lady seated on his right.

Later we walked off our dinner along the Via Veneto and Fritz decided on a nightcap at the sidewalk café outside the Hotel Excelsior, which he told me was the fanciest hotel in Rome. He hadn't been drinking since our arrival, interestingly enough (not counting red wine with the pasta). He didn't need to: He was drunk on Rome.

"What about our money?" I demanded, tugging ineffectually at his sleeve.

"You're being a wet blanket, chum," he replied airily, mussing up my hair with an affectionate gesture that served to push me forward at the same time. "Learn to live a little. Who knows? You might never get to have a drink at the Hotel Excelsior again. There'll always be more money, but how often do you get to spend a night like this?"

As it turned out, he was destined to be right again— though in more ways than he had anticipated.

At the café the tables were all occupied, but two middle-aged American couples, overhearing Fritz's American speech (English was more readily understood, we found, than French) and with a few drinks under their belts already, invited us to join them. They looked nice enough, though overweight and flushed. They were amused by me and wanted to know what a child was doing out so late. They were from Maryland and the wives laughed a lot in high, grating giggles. I think even Fritz began to realize we had made an error in accepting their hospitality. Fritz had envisioned himself sipping his cognac in the cool of the evening and watching the world go by. These noisy, nosy people were spoiling it. They were eating fattening desserts and squealing over how good they were. Fritz ordered his cognac ("*Rémy Martin* is the same in every language," he'd assured Mme. Berthe) and a Coca-Cola for me. The service was a bit delayed, owing to the waiter's stopping to take the order of a young Negro couple a few tables from us.

"Don't worry, boys," one of the men assured us, "after the niggers we come first." And they all laughed.

Except Fritz and me. I didn't laugh because I didn't understand what he had said and didn't know what it meant. Fritz didn't laugh because he went crazy.

"What did you say?" he demanded, letting his chair fall forward off its hind legs. I knew him well enough to detect the subtle change in his manner: The quaver in his voice, the sudden pallor of his complexion—even under the night lights—and the telltale tic over one eye all assured me he was no longer disinterested: He was angry.

The others didn't notice.

"I said, after the niggers we come first," the man guffawed, and his friends found it just as funny the second time.

"That's what I thought you said," Fritz replied, and seizing the nearest of the creamy desserts, he leaned across the table and mushed it into the man's face, turning it slowly while all the rest of us looked on in shock. I could not imagine why he had done this.

In any event all hell broke loose. The other man reached for Fritz, swinging, but missed and socked the first man's wife in the eye. She stood up screaming, knocked over the chair she was in and flung back her purse for what I suppose was instinctive retaliation, but during her wind-up the purse slammed the back of a waiter's head, causing his tray and its contents of drinks and ice creams to go flying into the faces and laps of several other patrons, one of whom took an irate poke at the waiter, who poked him right back. The next thing you know, both the ladies at our table were screaming and so was everyone else, and the fight was on, with everyone doing things to each other and not seeming to care whom they struck. Or bit. Or throttled. In films I have seen since, such melees are are always played for laughs, and the audience understands that windowpanes are made of sugar, furniture of balsa wood and liquor bottles of something equally harmless. It looks like fun.

But if you have ever actually been in a real bar fight— and this has been my only one to date—I can tell you that it isn't all that humorous. The furniture in that café was wrought iron chairs, and people were bringing them down on one another's heads with predictable results. The bottles were made of glass, and splinters exploded all over the place whenever one of them was broken. People yelled with rage and pain as they fought. I took refuge under one of the tables. All I could see were Fritz's legs as he danced nimbly back and forth next to where I was sheltered and did battle with all comers. But then someone picked up the table that was hiding me and threw it at someone else, so I was obliged

to seek safety elsewhere. Some people from the café next to
ours came over to put a stop to the fight, but they only
succeeded in getting caught up in it. I noticed a party of other
patrons trying to escape into the lobby of the Excelsior, but
the hotel closed its doors and wouldn't let them in. Somebody
fell over me. More things were thrown about, more screams
were heard as people got beaned or fell on glass shards.
Mingled with the yells were the grunts of effort that soon
accompanied all punches.

I looked around for Fritz and couldn't find him. Panic,
which had been hovering dormant on the edge of my consciousness—right behind shock—now awakened and in an
instant stole over me completely. The whole trip, I now perceived in a crystalline flash, had been irrevocably building up
to this. I knew I was only a child, I knew I had no money,
I knew I couldn't speak the language and now I had now
lost my only friend and protector in this strange place. As I
looked frantically around, bobbing my head back and forth
to catch glimpses of people between people, I heard in the
distance the rhythmic *bo-bee-bo-bee-bo* of the police sirens
approaching, the same as the ones in Paris. They grew
louder, forming the perfect accompaniment to my increasing terror.

"Come on, chum," said a familiar voice at my elbow, "it's
time we ran along." Before I could respond, a muscular arm
—an arm that played Liszt's *Hungarian Rhapsodies* and
won—grabbed me around the waist and carried me off.

We hotfooted it away from there for several blocks of
twisty streets until Fritz was satisfied we were in no danger
of further involvement. Another huge Bernini fountain in
the middle of a deserted square stood invitingly before us,

cool water spritzing from the mouths of green naked men, women and fish. We walked over to it, sat on the edge and splashed the delicious if not quite clean water on our faces. Fritz started to laugh and let out a whoop.

"That feels good," he sighed, throwing water by the handful at his face and chest, letting it dribble all over him. "Nothing like a little fisticuffs to test the reflexes, I always say." He touched himself gingerly on the face in a couple of places. "Am I all right?" he asked, not seeming especially anxious. I inspected him by what light there was and made out a purplish bruise on one cheek with a tiny bit of torn skin at the center. His shirt was ripped by the collar, but otherwise he appeared unharmed. By this time I was shaking.

"Well, maybe that's enough for one night," he conceded, and we headed for the hotel.

Our troubles were not over, however. When we reached the little *albergo,* Fritz discovered that the last of the money had been spent or left—he couldn't remember—at the café. This fact, coupled with his disreputable-looking face, torn shirt and generally disheveled appearance, caused us to be turned out, bag and baggage. He called the manager all the Italian he knew, including *"Traditore!"* which means "traitor," if you know anything about opera. No use. *"Perfido!"* and *"Misericordia!"* didn't get us anywhere either. We were out on the street.

"Now what do we do?" I whined. He sat on his old suitcase in the middle of the night, with no money, in the middle of the street, looking at the ground before him, his brows knit with concentration. For a moment or two I believed circumstances had finally beaten him. But I was wrong. He stood abruptly and smiled at me.

"*Vittoria!* Come on, chum," he cried, "it's almost bed-time," and gathering up our belongings, we started off on foot into the warm night.

"The one thing our trip lacked until now," he proclaimed, after he had helped me climb over the high iron fence and tossed our bags over after me. "Didn't I promise you the Colosseum by moonlight?"

So that's where we spent the night. He insisted on climbing around a bit first to see the thing, and unfortunately for me there was enough moonlight for his purpose. The place was eerier than anything that had preceded it, and I was exhausted with fear. The high jagged walls defined by the light of the full moon cast monstrous shadows, and we tripped over stones and misplaced bricks.

Finally he calmed down and selected a spot for us to sleep. The air was warm and he made little cushions for us out of the contents of our suitcases. ("Lucky I thought to bring these sweaters," I heard him remark to himself.) I heard a noise.

"What's that?"

"Probably rats or something." His tone was offhand. "They won't bother us."

I started to cry. "How will we get home? I want to go home," I sobbed. He put his arm around me.

"We'll go home tomorrow," he promised softly.

"But how?" I wailed. "We don't have any more money."

He held me tighter.

"Don't you worry so much, chum," he said in my ear, quite serene now, so that I relaxed in his embrace despite myself. "You worry too much. You just trust your old uncle. If I say we'll be on our way home tomorrow, we will, and that's all there is to it. Okay? Okay?"

"Okay," I whispered.

"Good. Now, do you have to pee?" I nodded against his chest. "Well, you've got the whole Colosseum to do it in. The world's biggest chamber pot. Go on. Come to think of it, I'll join you."

We found a spot a little ways off and let fly. He started to laugh. "Want to know something interesting that it says in the book? It says they paid for this whole thing by taxing the toilets. How do you like that? Every time you wanted to pee you had to pay money, and they used the money to build this place."

This seemed too strange to be true, but I found it provocative. "What if you peed somewhere and they didn't know?"

He shrugged. "I don't know. Maybe they had people follow you around or something." The thought was so funny I laughed out loud. "That's better." We settled down again and laughed some more about it, and then we were quiet for a time.

"Fritz?"

"Right here, chum."

"Why did you put the dessert in that man's face?"

He was silent for a long time while he fished out a cigarette and lit it, the match revealing his taut jawline for an instant in its flare.

"That probably was not a good idea," he admitted finally. He sighed then and told me what the word *nigger* meant. "The thing is," he explained quietly, "that the one thing civilized ladies and gentlemen do not do is judge one another by the color of their skin. It simply isn't done, chum. You don't make fun of a person's skin, you don't make jokes about it and you don't call people names because of what color they are or which way their eyes slant or how their hair grows. It is considered very bad form. You understand?"

"Yes," I said sleepily, hypnotized by the undulating glow of his cigarette in the dark. There was another silence; then he chuckled.

"On the other hand, you remember all the pie-throwing in those silent movies we went to last time? Charlot? I guess it was something I always wanted to do." He took me in his arms again and held me close, and we noticed the stars shining brilliantly overhead, framed by the shadows of the ruined stadium. "You know anything about astronomy?" he demanded. I didn't even know what the word meant, I don't think. He roused himself with mischievous enthusiasm at that point and told me that the stars had names and that clusters of them had names. "You see that bright one over there on the right? Over there? That's Vivaldi. Down there is Mozart and that group by the bottom is the Great Harpsichord; if you imagine connecting the dots you get a harpsichord, sort of. Then over there is the Budapest String Quartet, and to the left, the Arm of the Waiter bringing them tea in tall glasses. Of course I'm serious. You think I'm making this up as I go along?"

And that's the way I fell asleep, quite happy, despite everything, just to be together.

And he kept his promise. The whole thing was so simple and comparatively uneventful, I had to wonder at the fuss I had kicked up when, the night before, it had seemed so impossible.

If you haven't seen dawn break over the Colosseum from *inside* the Colosseum, you have missed a lot. Fritz nudged me awake to watch it with him, and the effect was staggering.

The place is composed of ten million nooks and crannies—some of them too large to be described as nooks, I suppose, but that's the way they look from the other side of the stadium—and the light, slowly washing into each and every one of these fissures, was a spectacular display of pyrotechnics. It was mesmerizing to sit there, pick out a spot towards which the light was inching and wait for the illumination to creep into it, changing its character completely. Lots of times our projections of where the light was going would be off by a little bit, and that was interesting, too.

The sight was beautiful enough to remind me of Olga, who, with her romantic sensibility, would have enjoyed it. This brought back the memory of what had happened between us and gave me a dull pang, but truth to tell, at the moment Olga and all of my normal life seemed miles and light-years away.

We must have watched the sun bathing over the Colosseum like the tide coming in for about three hours, and then Fritz decided we should probably get out of the place before the tour people arrived. As we were leaving, I asked what all the stuff in the center was, and he explained that those ruined buildings were not part of the original structure but had been added years later; he wasn't certain by whom.

"It was just a sandy area," he told me. "Somehow, somewhere, the word *sand* and the word *arena* are related; isn't that interesting? Down there is where the early martyrs were thrown to the lions—*chomp chomp chomp*—Lions 500, Christians nothing." Sometimes I didn't understand a thing he said. "The other thing they did here was to flood the whole place with water and have men on big boats fight each other to death—naval battles where those buildings are now." I squinted at the center of the Colosseum and tried to picture the place filled with water. Just when I wanted to tear that guidebook out of his hands and stamp on it he'd tell you something like that to keep you interested.

We left the Colosseum without incident, and although Fritz didn't like hitchhiking, we thumbed a ride to the beach in a Jeep driven by an Englishman with an enormous red beard (it reminded me of Father Ogareff's) who wore a funny hat Fritz told me was called a pith helmet and that helped to ward off the heat from the sun. We had a few giggles together about the name of this kind of hat, but the Englishman appeared not to have heard us, or didn't mind, or had heard those jokes before.

The beach—don't ask me which beach it was—was certainly a pleasant place to pass the morning if one had to go without breakfast, which was our case. We lazed in the sun for a bit and took off our shoes and went wading in the water, which was quite warm. I tried not to think about our problem; in broad daylight, aside from being hungry, things didn't seem so bad.

Around noon we found ourselves in conversation with three American sailors on shore leave who, tiring of monuments in the heat, had come to the lido to cool off, hoping to meet girls and generally to take it easy during the siesta time of early afternoon. I suppose they were little more than boys really, though they seemed from my perspective to be quite grown-up. Nevertheless, there was something eager and naive about them. They didn't speak anything but English, and that in a way that I could scarcely understand what they said. I didn't speak much English anymore—Fritz and I always conversed in French—and the English of the books

I read was all period stuff about knights in armor and had little of the twentieth century in it.

The sailors liked Fritz right away. He was clearly a man of the world and gave them the impression he knew Rome like the back of his hand. He recommended restaurants and even threw in the name of a sporting house we hadn't bothered to visit as evidence of his familiarity with the terrain.

One of the sailors said he wouldn't mind a little action.

"Action?" Fritz inquired mildly. "Do you mean you fellows are interested in games of chance?"

That they were, but the blond Nordic type among them said it could be anything but cards. They had sworn off cards. Fritz casually asked if they were up for a little crap-shooting. They withdrew to a huddle for a few moments to discuss the matter while Fritz sweated it out, pretending indifference as he helped me to build a sand castle.

"We don't have any dice," I pointed out, scooping out a moat.

"Don't remind me. Just keep your fingers crossed."

The huddle broke up and the sailors decided that they hadn't anything better to do for the siesta time, so a game of crap was all right with them. They asked if Fritz knew of a game and he said he did, but it would take too long to go back to town: Why not play right here?

"With what?" the beefy, jolly one asked. "We ain't got dice. You?"

"No problem," Fritz soothed. "I'll be right back. Watch the kid." And so saying, he gave me a reassuring squeeze and took off in the first direction that was handy, not knowing, as he told me later, what he was going to do, only that he had to find a pair of dice.

He returned within a half-hour, during which time I had convinced the sailors to help me with my castle. He had come across a restaurant by the sea and filched two fistfuls of cubed sugar from the sugar bowls on the tables. With the aid of his music-writing pen, he put dots on the cubes as the sailors watched, whistling with amazement at his ingenuity. Under a tree at the edge of the sand, the game got underway. They found the lid of an old garbage can and used that to toss the dice in.

It was a daffy game all right, as the sugar dice kept fragmenting and had to be replaced. It wasn't the impact of them hitting the garbage can lid that caused the attrition rate so much as the sailors forgetting what they were made of and rubbing them rapidly back and forth between their sweaty palms before shooting.

"Come on, baby!" the beefy fellow would coo before each roll, and everyone had to caution him not to rub the damn dice.

I didn't exactly understand how the game worked. Fritz had been on the point of teaching me once when he had no one else to play with, but Mme. Berthe had caught him at it and said it was a shame to bring up a child so. She went on at such length that Fritz came to see the thing her way and refused to instruct me, though he did teach me to play gin rummy and some kinds of poker. But even without a formal education, I grasped the rudiments of crap, though certain idiomatic French expressions, now heard in English for the first time, made no sense to me.

Fritz began playing with no money at all, which was chancy to say the least, because if he had lost, we should have been out of the game before we got started. I don't think

I understood this until he explained it to me on the train home, where he was in high good humor.

At any rate he didn't lose: With those ridiculous dice he had the most astonishing run of luck, and those sailors could scarcely believe it. On the other hand they could hardly accuse him of cheating, since whenever anyone felt like it, they were entitled to draw a new set of dice from the supply of sugar cubes. Anyone could mark them with dots, provided all witnessed the tattooing. As the game wore on, you saw a lot of people licking their hands and getting black ink around their mouths. Fritz kept the dice for a very long time before he threw snake-eyes and the Nordic sailor took a turn.

Two Italian youths at the beach joined the game for a while. They lost more money than they'd planned to and decamped, soon to be replaced by a fat priest who had noticed the commotion from his folding canvas beach chair, and so it went. Fritz, uncharacteristically lucky for the second time in as many weeks, couldn't seem to lose. I got bored watching after a time and returned to work on my sand castle. I could hear them whooping and groaning from where I sculpted, and every so often when I looked up I could see another stranger sitting in to take on Fritz.

When they finally decided to call it quits, sometime around four, Fritz had pocketed another wad. The sailors didn't seem particularly to mind—one of them had done rather well against the priest, as it turned out—and they had passed the time in a congenial if unorthodox fashion. It was very hot and everyone stripped down to their underwear to go swimming, while I was left to guard all the clothes and money. Then Fritz took me in for a cooling dunking and we made our way to the train station. The Rome–Paris express was due to leave in another forty-five minutes. We couldn't have timed the whole thing better had we planned it.

"You sure you want to get back?" Fritz asked with a hopeful glint in his eye. "We have a new bankroll. Wouldn't you like to hear some music while we're here besides Mass at St. Peter's?"

But I threatened to cry again and he relented. We didn't have a *couchette* this time: There weren't any available on such short notice and he hadn't made enough money to purchase space in one anyway, so we had to sit up all the way home. I didn't much mind. I wasn't very big and could stretch out with my head in his lap, which was where I remained for most of the journey.

We arrived grubby and tired the next day around noon and had just enough cash left to change to the commuter train for Marley after crossing Paris by bus.

"I know you think you've had a rough time," Fritz said a trifle defensively, feeling the unshaved stubble on his chin. "But in the years to come, mark my words, you'll look back on this whole thing with fond memories and thank your old uncle for having shown you Rome as few tourists have ever seen it."

Damned if he wasn't right again.

About a month after we got back from the Roman roller coaster, Fritz began to receive a strange visitor. When I say a visitor, I mean to distinguish him (as he instantly distinguished himself) from the usual ruck of musicians, card-players and cronies who frequented our rooms of an evening, playing chamber music, arguing politics or tossing cards at one another.

This man was quite a different sort. He arrived alone every few weeks. He actually drove up to our house in a late-model Peugeot. He always wore a dark suit—though not the same dark suit—and a grave expression to match. In addition he was never without an ominously fine tan attaché case.

One afternoon in early autumn, as Mme. Berthe and I returned from the market, I pulling her shopping cart for her up the incline of rue Saint-Denis, I saw the familiar automobile parked before the house. Even outside the gate I could make out the sound of raised voices, Fritz's uncharacteristically high and strident, the stranger's tones reasonable but audible nonetheless. "—only prolonging the inevitable—" the stranger was saying.

"Nothing is inevitable," Fritz's voice shot back angrily.

"—think you're being most unreasonable" drifted through the air from the stranger.

I left Mme. Berthe with the cart and ran into the house. Both of them appeared to stop in mid-sentence and looked at me.

"I must be on my way," the dark-suited man said, stuffing some papers into his attaché case and closing it with two sharp clicks.

"Good idea," Fritz called unceremoniously to his back as he started out. At the door where I stood, the man stopped and looked down at me.

"This is the child?"

"What does it look like, a midget? Go on, get out of here."

The dark-suited man sighed and went out without another word, closing the door softly behind him.

"Who was that?" I demanded. I wondered if his unpleasant appearances were in any way connected with my

attempted rape of Olga. His reference to me, so particular—
the child—renewed my terrors of exposure and punishment.

"It's none of your business who that was," my uncle responded with asperity. "It's time for your lesson, chum; come
and get it. Have you worked on the Clementi?"

He grabbed the familiar-shaped bottle, started to pour
some of its contents into a glass, then impatiently changed
his mind and tilted the entire thing into his mouth for a
couple of sustained glugs.

I had reached the stage of sophistication where I understood his various moods and, understanding their differing
origins, found it relatively easy to accommodate them. But
the origin of this mood escaped me, save that it was occasioned by the visits of the man in the dark suit.

"Did I do something wrong?" If it was about Olga and
I was going to jail, I wanted to know the worst.

"If you don't start playing your Clementi you're going to
be sent into next week," Fritz snarled. "Clementi," he snorted
with disdain. "What an awful composer."

Summer drifted into fall. The dark-suited man visited a
few more times, each visit clearly an upsetting experience
for my uncle—increasingly upsetting. There seemed no way
to keep him from returning again and again. Each time he
went away I hoped we had seen the last of him, but it was
always a false hope.

One morning I came into the house lugging our morning
milk from M. Jacopo and was astonished to find Fritz up
and shaving. Normally he did not rise much before nine and
usually he brushed his teeth with brandy. Today he was
using soap and staring into the mirror at his image as if he
beheld a total stranger there. He shaved with great care, but

managed to nick himself in a couple of places anyhow. Shaving was a chore he didn't much relish and avoided for days when he could, but when he cut himself, all of Marly knew of it. Today, however, he made only a little hiss and used toilet paper to staunch the wounds as he continued with his determined labor. He was stone cold sober and didn't much care for the feeling, I could tell.

"How come you're up?"

He didn't answer, but pushed past me to his bedroom, where I followed and watched as he stepped into his best trousers, shirt and the "good" oatmeal jacket he used when conducting. He even put on a tie *and* buttoned his collar underneath it, which I had never known him to do. His shoes he had polished until they gleamed like mirrors, something the army had taught him but which he rarely practiced anymore. His hair, I noticed now, had been freshly washed and was carefully slicked down and parted—another rarity.

"Where are you going?" I pressed him as he made to walk by me again. He stopped, looked down at me and patted the top of my head.

"Nothing to worry about, chum." He smiled, but the smile was artificial and unlike his own toothy grin. "I'll be home for supper."

But he did not come home for supper, or indeed for some hours later. He reeled in very drunk long after the house had gone to bed. I was in my bed and I could hear him, boiled, tripping over books and hurling his shoes at different targets on the walls. He had what sounded like a fit of coughing and then collapsed onto his own mattress with a crash.

The next morning I was engaged in a heated game of mumblety-peg with Sasha when the back door opened and Fritz stood there in his undershirt, calling my name. I didn't hesitate, for I knew something had been brewing lately and was eager to know just what it was, which I sensed I was about to learn. I think I still assumed that in some way it concerned my picnic with Olga and its unfortunate aftermath.

He held the screen door open for me as I climbed the steps, and I noticed for the first time a muscle twitching by his right eye. He was sober again, which made two mornings in a row. It was so unlike him it increased my anxiety.

"Sit down, chum," he instructed when we reached his cluttered bedroom. He couldn't wait for me to obey, but pushed me gently into a seated posture on the edge of his bed. He stood up and paced in the cramped area before me, running a nervous hand through his hair as he went about collecting his thoughts.

"Chum, I've got some news for you. Maybe it's good news and you'll like it and maybe you won't, but either way it's news and it's going to happen. If I had any money we might try and make a run for it— Ah, that's no good," he interrupted himself angrily. "Anyway, the long and the short of it is that you're going back to the States to live with your mother's sister and her husband in Chicago."

He had to explain it to me several times before I could grasp what he was saying, as the tale was long and rather convoluted, involving as it did a lengthy ongoing search by the sister of Kathleen Bernini for her nephew, a search that had entailed tracking down first Madelaine Brown and then my uncle in Paris. At the same time French authorities had become interested in my case because of reports concerning my irregular attendance at the École du Saint-Esprit. They had, it now appeared, contacted Fritz on several occasions, questioning his propriety as a guardian for me, and he had contrived for over two years to put them off the scent with paper chases, evasions, outright lies and even a bribe or two.

"I did everything I could think of to keep you." Fritz's remarks were nominally addressed to me, but as he walked back and forth, he appeared in fact to be addressing himself, reminding himself, assuring himself. He rambled on, "They got lawyers; *I* got a lawyer. It seems I couldn't afford the best." His face flushed as he added this, but the specifics, like the details of the plot of *Casablanca,* were lost on me.

"I don't want to go."

"You don't have anything to say about it. Besides"—he interrupted his brusque rejoinder to smile his new false smile at me—"you didn't want to leave Nursie and come to live with me in Paris, did you? No, you damn well didn't. And it can't have worked out so badly because now you don't want to leave. But who knows? Maybe you'll like it even better than here. That's always possible. They're supposed to be nice; they've got money—more than I do, anyway. They even say you can bring the cat," he put in as a happy afterthought, snapping his fingers with feigned enthusiasm. Looking at him with that desperate expression fixed on his face as though it had frozen there, I felt my eyes fill with water until, even while I was blinking, Fritz existed before me only in a milky haze.

"Please don't send me away. I want to stay here with you and Mme. Berthe and Sasha."

"Listen to me!" he shouted, purpling, then passed a hand

over his face as though to mop the passion off it. "George," he continued in a milder tone, breathing in the wrong places and speaking very slowly so that I might understand, "George, I am not sending you away. They will not let me keep you. It's not the same thing."

It was to me, however, and I hated him for it.

Seven

Chicago

My life was like a train that I could not get off; the train might make very long stops here and there—in New York, in Paris—and I might make friends and learn things at each stop. But in the end the train would move on, trundling me and Hieronymous away from every place, leaving behind, obscured in the choking dust of memory that soon obliterated their features, the eyes, the ears, the hands, the hearts of all the bits and pieces that had constituted the mosaic of my life.

I flew towards the United States with a deal of excess baggage in the form of grief, bitterness and betrayal—betrayal not only by the Harris family, whom I had never thought of, let alone met, but betrayal by those in whom I had placed a blind, implicit, thoughtless trust. Not only Fritz but even Madelaine in retrospect was now viewed with grave disfavor as a contributor—if not the initiator— of a sinister pattern that was apparently inherent in human nature and to which I vowed never again to succumb. My heart was effectively broken and I hated with an even-handed loathing all those who had broken it. I trusted no one today and I would trust no one tomorrow. Looking back, I wish I had not made such choices. Unbeknownst to me, their ramifications would be long and far-reaching, and the day would come when I would find myself caught in their coils and tentacles, strangled by the defenses I had so deliberately forged.

There was, however, no way that anyone could have explained to me, convinced me or predicted for me the consequences of what were, after all, instinctive responses. That sad irony—that we cannot foresee the consequences of all our decisions—is a great and mysterious part of life. Sometimes our fates seem tragic as a result and sometimes comic, but like death itself, they are the price we pay for having been born.

The America towards which I flew late in the year 1951 was the America of Joseph McCarthy, Dwight David Eisenhower and the Man in the Gray Flannel Suit. *Brown* v. *Board of Education* had not yet altered irrevocably the landscape of American society; Elvis Presley had not been photographed from the waist up on *The Ed Sullivan Show;* the cold war was at its coldest as America competed desperately with its former allies for dominion and sway over what was left of the world in the wake of the war. Richard J. Daley was not yet the lifelong mayor of Chicago; television was still a novelty, not yet a necessity; everyone had more gasoline than they knew what to do with, and no one much had ever heard of Korea.

I neither knew nor anticipated any of these things as I landed at Chicago's snow-covered Midway Airport in the TWA Constellation (there was no commercial jet travel yet, either). And though I was destined to grow up amidst many of these problems, trends and developments, I would interact

with few of them and understand still less. I had bigger
problems to concern me, or so it then seemed—namely, my
own.

All I knew was that I was the half-Italian, half-Irish, half-
Jewish, half-Catholic child of dead circus acrobats who had
been raised so early and so long in France that I couldn't—
and never would—speak English without a foreign accent.
Eventually I scraped away most of it, but I still sound
vaguely like the French actor Louis Jourdan, who speaks
perfect English, but you are always aware that he is not
American. In later years people who learned how young I
was when I returned to America professed surprise over the
fact that I had not been able to lose the accent entirely. By
age nine (I was told by those who seemed to think they
were in a position to know) it is still possible to change
languages and accents completely. I had no way of explaining my failure to conform to accepted linguistic theory save
one interpretation, advanced by a shrewd English teacher
in the fifth grade, that I hated so intensely that I never repeated it to anyone: "It's your unconscious mind's way of
being loyal to a time and place where you were happy," she
speculated. "You won't let yourself learn unaccented English
because in some way that means you would be abandoning
a time in your life to which you find it necessary to cling."

In my strongly accented English I assured her she was nuts.

In addition the English that I did speak (and write) was
—and remains—slightly stilted in its employment of syntax
and vocabulary. English had never been spoken by me except
for three weeks on the Eiffel Tower and except for the word
chum, continually inserted by Fritz into all of our conversations. Chum, I discovered soon enough, was an absolutely

ludicrous appendage to a mid–twentieth-century American adolescent's vocabulary. The English that I knew I had learned from reading Robert Louis Stevenson and Arthur Conan Doyle and other authors who were calculated to appeal to a precocious eight-year-old. It was as though I had learned my native tongue in a time warp.

The Harrises, who met me at the airport with slightly anxious expressions and a winter coat and gloves in case I didn't have any (I didn't), saw at once how exhausted I was from the flight—I had never been on a plane in my life, and Hieronymous was still under the influence of the powerful tranquilizer he had been given twelve hours earlier in France and was no better off—and greeted us with a minimum of fuss. Our bags—meager possessions, again—were collected and we were driven into the city, sleeping in the backseat of the Harrises' Hudson Hornet.

My mother's younger sister (Who knew how many siblings she may have had, coming from a family of serious Catholics?) had attended her funeral and there learned of my existence. Her name was Susan, but everyone who knew her called her Suki. She had a dark pageboy haircut that was beginning to show traces of grey here and there, now and then. When she discovered a grey hair, she always plucked it out with a little yelp, though whether the yelp was occasioned by the discovery itself or her method of dealing with it I could never tell. She had the slender figure of a young schoolgirl and the giddy disposition to match. It was only with some difficulty that she could be persuaded of the necessity of addressing a serious topic seriously. If the topic was related to sex she got the giggles, but her laughter concealed a deal of prudery beneath it. Like my mother she had been reared in a convent school, but unlike my mother (Mother wore tights!) she had not the wit nor the will to make a dash for freedom and leave it. Though she no longer practiced her religion, it had nevertheless left several indelible impressions and repressions on her, which made their claim forcefully at predictable times.

The man to whom she was married was quite another sort. David Harris, some six or seven years her senior, came from a prominent Chicago family, but he was not a man to rest on genealogical laurels. He went to Harvard, stayed there for his Ph.D. and was now a tenured professor of nuclear physics at the University of Chicago, delicately treading his way on tiptoe through a mine field of loyalty oaths. In his own way, however, David Harris was as much a prisoner of his background as my aunt was of hers. Although a scientist and liberal intellectual by natural aptitude and inclination, he was nevertheless caught up in a great many social and cultural snares that he could not rationally defend; neither could he completely escape their pull. He did not, for example, make his home on the South Side, anywhere near the university campus. He could afford better, and with some foresight had purchased a slightly rundown brownstone on Dearborn near Schiller, not far from the prestigious Racquet Club, to which he belonged. He rarely went there, but he belonged. Perhaps that best expresses his ambivalence towards the familial traditions in which he was enmeshed. Instead of lunching at the Racquet Club, he toiled in his office on campus weekdays, ate hero sandwiches and spent weekends working on the house until it became quite a showplace. (To the left and right of us down the block, other savvy folk were engaged in similar renovations. The value of the real estate in the area as well as its look and appeal improved enormously during the years I grew up there.)

In appearance Professor Harris reminded me of a wise old owl. He had a pinkish complexion, the beginnings of jowls and thinning brown hair that retreated yearly from an already high-domed forehead. He wore transparent-colored horn-rimmed glasses and rarely removed them. When he did, his eyes peered myopically at the world and he looked like quite a different person, not himself. He spoke slowly and with an agreeable nasal twang and was seldom without a curved pipe in his mouth that he was forever lighting. Sometimes he spoke so slowly you wanted to finish his sentences for him.

Looking back on it—and everything makes more sense when we look back, it seems—I would guess that David and Suki had been drawn together by a mutual desire to flee the clutches of their parochial pasts. Suki, less dramatic than my mother, saw in David a respectable refuge from Irish Catholicism, and David found in her a cheerful companion who would lighten his intellectual burden and help him break the constricting bonds of straitlaced, conservative Chicago society. They were both partially right in these assumptions. They had no children, which seemed strange to me, for my arrival was clearly an intrusion into the lives that they had long relished. Later on I discovered the reason for their childless state, and that proved to be even stranger.

I was now, in any event, to be their child. A room had been set aside for my occupancy. It had a bed and assorted necessities, but was otherwise unfurnished so that I might choose my own surroundings and decorations.

"We want you to be happy here," Suki said, looking earn-

estly into my tired eyes after showing me the room. "We all
have a big adjustment to make, but we want you to know
how glad we are that you are here. We've waited a long
time for you and we're going to try our best."

I closed the door against her without replying.

"Give him some time," I heard David say from outside the
door, overriding her muffled expressions of anxiety.

They gave me years, but my "addled-essence" was not a
success. I should resist the temptation to write sarcastically
about it: The only amusing thing I can honestly say of it is
that it ended. And I am now aware that while I was having
my adolescent problems, everyone else was having theirs.
Some people's problems, I was to learn, were worse than my
own. But I venture to suggest that in some ways my difficulties during those years were not principally caused by the
age or stage through which I was going, but were rather
the unfortunate result of where I had already been. To plump
down amidst an emotionally constrained middle-class,
middle-aged couple living in the American Middle West, a
nine-year-old who had been weaned on brandy, cigarettes,
sleepover dates at Mlle. Isabel's, as well as violinists who
stayed the night—all this in a foreign country, to boot—was
like planting flowers from Jupiter in a cornfield and hoping
they would take root and flourish there. In retrospect the
fact that I survived at all smacks of the miraculous.

I was tested and admitted by the skin of my teeth to the
fourth grade of the Marcus Leader Workingman's Progressive School, an institution of learning in which I was destined
to toil for four years and about which some words are now
in order.

I very much doubt that many people have heard of Marcus

Leader; in case you are among the benighted billions writhing in ignorance, allow me to enlighten you. Marcus Leader was a nineteenth-century American educator and philosopher (who owned a great many textile mills in Indiana as a hobby) greatly influenced by the ideas and works of Emerson, Thoreau, Owen and that group of self-reliant questers who hailed from New England. Leader was determined to see their ideas, theories and practices made available, accessible, and comprehensible (he seems never to have used one word where three would do) to the masses. Masses was a word that had not yet taken on the suspicious connotations others would soon attach to it. To implement his own ideas, Leader founded and became the chief architect of a religious philosophy that he called Moralistic Pragmatism. Moralistic Pragmatism was not intended to be the contradiction in terms that its name implies (though for my money that irony was ominously symptomatic of many to follow). Moralistic Pragmatists were good people trying to reconcile ethics and the Industrial Revolution. They sought a meaningful code to live by that did not necessarily include God in a world where His existence or relevance was increasingly called into question, but which did not exclude His possible contribution if some practitioners insisted He had one to make. Easy does it. Rather, it was Leader's contention that morality was a function of each individual interacting with his conscience, a process of contemplation and reflection based not on the hope of reward or fear of eternal damnation, but on the Rousseauian conception of the basic nobility of all men if left alone to discover it.

If one didn't know better, one might suspect Leader of cutting and pasting together the best moments of Rousseau,

Marx, Emerson, Thoreau, Jean-Paul Sartre and Scientology, then cutting them up again and throwing them in the air before a large circulating fan. Whatever scraps of paper he was able to retrieve after they had settled all over the room he pasted together again in the order in which he found them and called the result Moralistic Pragmatism. I feel certain, however, that he did not do this. It is just my fancy.

For one thing Scientology came along too late to be of use to him. About the only religious conceits that failed to reveal themselves to me when (in a perverse humor some years later) I endeavored to catalogue as many as possible were those to be found in the Book of Mormon. Possibly Leader was acquainted with this ideology, though in Illinois, where he lived, this seems unlikely. For whatever reason, there is no Mormonism to be found in the basic tenets of Moralistic Pragmatism. The Mormons, for some unaccountable cause, got off lucky.

Leader's new religion (he called it a society) took off almost at once. Several times, down on my luck and looking enviously about me at the riches being reaped by people like Werner Erhard and Arthur Janov, I have seriously considered starting a movement of my own—something based on horse racing and hat sizes ought to set me up for life, I think —but I always shrink from the work load involved. Anyway, followers flocked to follow Leader, drawn by the magnetic force of his personality and his ideas. Money was collected and in almost no time a meeting hall was built. As in several other religions (Leader was a great exploiter of precedents: They were so reassuring) the word *church* was eschewed. Leader called his building the Gathering Place, and this day the Gathering Place and the Marcus Leader

Workingman's Progressive School stand shoulder to shoulder in a section of prime Near Northside real estate that Leader and his band with great foresight bought up after the Great Chicago Fire. Songs were written, including one that runs:

> *O Moralistic Pragmatism,*
> *We Come to Learn Thy Wisdom;*
> *O Font of Goodness Great and Dear*
> *We Listen to Our Lea—der.*

The tune to which this and assorted other verses were sung was "O Tannenbaum, O Tannenbaum." It was a tricky business getting *wisdom* to rhyme with *pragmatism,* but with practice you could if you really tried and were serious. It was also a bit knotty to get the words to fit the tune exactly, but I think all derived a measure of pride and satisfaction from the way in which the name of the founder had been wittily used to describe his function as well. Even hearing the rumor in later years that Leader's real name had been Avram Moscowitz did not dampen my enthusiasm for this part of the song.

Moralistic Pragmatism attracted enlightened liberals or liberals seeking to be enlightened, people who were wary of organized religion but felt guilty about sleeping late and reading the papers in bed on Sunday mornings; they felt they ought to go someplace and renew themselves. It was a group of agnostics holding hands, as you might say, a perfect haven for self-conscious Jews, lapsed Catholics and rebellious Protestants. As such it was the perfect compromise for my aunt and uncle (though as the years passed they didn't much gather at the Gathering Place either) and the logical choice, where school was concerned, for me.

In the last years of the preceding century, Leader founded the Workingman's Progressive School, designed for the children of those parents who were both obliged to work during the day. It was a good school, where surprisingly there was no proselytizing for the organization's adjacent religious arm—with the single exception of a required class called Morality, about which more later.

The school was progressive at first, with an ambitious curriculum and no grades. As the twentieth century gathered steam, however, a richer class of parents discovered the merits of the school and began sending their children to it along with large endowments, upon which the school soon grew to depend. Soon the workingman's children were excluded from it altogether (they couldn't afford the tuition), except for a few token scholarship kids who were easily distinguished from the ruck of spoiled, bright, competitive, nouveau-riche children who, having taken it over, now constituted the majority of the enrollment. Grades were introduced and eagerly sought after. The MLWPS's reputation soared on SAT scores and in Merit Scholarship finals. Having gone there was a sure bet on getting into a good college.

"And what with the postwar baby boom," Uncle David explained to me, "you're going to need all the help you can get. Graduation from Marcus Leader will go a long way towards getting many a young man into Harvard."

Well, I showed them. Poor Uncle! That statement may have been true, but I was not destined to be one of those young men.

The Marcus Leader Society for Moralistic Pragmatism had long been without the benefit of its founder, whose death in the year 1918 (of influenza) was a deprivation still mourned by some of the senile members of the movement.

A number of replacements attempted to fill his shoes, with indifferent success. Their portraits, alongside Leader's, line the hallway that leads to the present directors' offices. Despite having been painted by different artists, the portraits all look essentially the same: They all appear to have been sat for by individuals whose countenances would be improved by a closer acquaintance with lemon meringue.

Some fifteen years before, the Society fixed on the real difficulty of adequately replacing Leader: No one man had sufficient knowledge, energy, and multifaceted charisma to head both the scholastic and religious arm of the Society. It was therefore decided to divide the responsibility into two equal halves. And here fate played into the hands of the board of governors in a fashion that can only be termed unique: Herman Blue, a long-standing member of the Society and a disciple of Marcus Leader, was named Headmaster of the Workingman's Progressive School, *and his twin brother, Waldo,* became the Guide (as the title was called) of the Society for Moralistic Pragmatism. It was a most satisfactory arrangement, though complicated in ways that, candidly, might have been foreseen but were not. With both institutions housed under the same roof and both Blue brothers looking exactly alike (they resembled Woodrow Wilson and like him wore identical pince-nez, compounding the problem), it was almost impossible, meeting one of them in the hallways, to know if you were addressing Herman, who had Ph.D.s in education and biology from Harvard and Columbia respectively, or Waldo, who had a degree in divinity from Yale (or possibly Woodrow Wilson, who had been president of Princeton, but who was now generally agreed to be dead). The brothers didn't help matters much by dressing similarly, as twins apparently are wont to do. One of these twins—and to this day I don't know which it was—formed part of the panel before which I was examined to determine if I was eligible for admission for the school. That would seem to indicate it was Herman, but I can't be sure, for the twins were fond of attending meetings in one another's place, to make sure they both kept abreast of what was going on in each business.

As for the test itself, it is my impression that I was accepted at the school more on the basis of my perceived potential than on any actual competency I displayed during the questioning. The panel felt, talking to me, hearing me speak perfect French and telling them all about *Treasure Island,* that I *ought* to make a good student. Clearly I was intelligent—there's the paradox that was destined to confound so many teachers, tutors, testers and educators, who would dash their theories to pieces when given the opportunity and the money to take a whack at me. I really think I ought to have been exhibited at Ripley's Believe It or Not Museum. Who, ladies and gentlemen, can explain why this boy with an IQ of 145 has a C average—barely? Step right up, folks, and let's have your views.

But all this was in the future. For the moment the tests proved that I could read French and English fluently, speak the latter without difficulty, but couldn't spell a sentence in either tongue to save my life. I could not add; neither could I subtract, multiply or divide. I had no idea where Chicago was located or who Thomas Jefferson might be. My appalling ignorance was greeted with pursed lips and impatiently tapping pencils on desk blotters, though the four examiners (who were teachers in the school) made every effort to let me see them being nice to me. My knowledge or interest in music cut no ice with them either way.

"He's got a lot of catching up to do," one of them explained to Suki at the end of the interview, "but he's bright and we're going to take the chance."

Suki could hardly refrain from squealing with joy. She left the school with me, trying to contain herself, but once outside on the sidewalk, emitted a whoop that was probably audible on the other side of Lake Michigan and followed it with a crushing hug.

"You made it, George! You're in! Now everything's going to be just fine."

Eight
In Which I Fail

It was never just fine. When I entered school my problems began right away. Within three weeks it was quickly determined that a mistake had been made in putting me in the fourth grade. While my age and brainpower may have corresponded with those of the other children, my previous experience of school and academic discipline (a word that was to haunt me) clearly was inadequate to aid me in conquering the curriculum. A series of conferences were hastily convened and the decision was made to start me again in third grade. David and Suki tried to put the best face on this humiliating solution to my problems, but they could not disguise from me the galling step backwards I was being obliged to take.

And so, with the burden of my first defeat already upon me, I became a late entrant in the midst of the third grade and found myself among an insular group of boys and girls who had known each other since nursery school, which is to say, since birth. They had already stratified themselves into a rigid series of concentric cliques in which your status

depended on your wealth, your address, how you arrived at
school, what clothes you wore and what grades you earned.
In addition to my presumptuous lateness and newness,
there was the matter of my being conspicuously a year
older than the rest of them. They knew whence I had
come and why, and they were not shy about letting me
know it.

And if all the foregoing did not represent two and a half
strikes against me, there was the matter of speaking. I
didn't dare speak French, which no one understood, nor
did I like to frame a sentence in English where my odd
accent was sure to contribute to securing my position as a
figure of ridicule. In my new class was the son of the
Italian consul. He spoke with a slight accent, but he was
known to be the scion of a ranking diplomat and his speech
was deemed a part of his birthright. Besides which, the
Italian consul was quite wealthy and Guido arrived each
morning in a chauffeured limousine, complete with consular
markings on its doors and Italian flags on its fenders. I, on
the other hand, was as American as apple pie. Why then did
I not speak like an American? Why did I not speak at all?

Because when I finally did, I quickly acquired the name
"Frenchy."

But the real problem went deeper than my age, the snotty
children, the philosophy of the school and its smug, self-
satisfied faculty or my ludicrous accent. It had to do with
the concept of school itself, to which I had never before
been truly exposed. I had never in all my nine short years
experienced anything that approximated the regimen of
school. The idea of showing up at the same place every
morning, at the same time, and going through some inter-

minable disagreeable ritual every day, then returning home to more of the same after supper, was an adjustment (to use Suki's word) I could not make.

At first my terror of the new experience, its very unfamiliarity, lent it a certain piquant novelty. It was not unlike traveling to a new place for the first time on an unknown road. Each bend in the road, each virgin vista, is so interesting that you are distracted from the fact that the trip takes one hour and fifteen minutes. But if you are obliged to make that same hour-and-fifteen-minute trip to and from your dreary job each day, the scenery quickly loses its attractions and you soon become aware only of how long it takes. You would be quite happy to go to another place, using the same length of time to get there, if only you were not compelled to look at the very same billboards along the way.

So it became with the dull pattern of my days at school. Whatever spontaneous curiosity had once been mine about the this and that and how and why of things—when I had been allowed to follow the erratic educational footsteps of Uncle Fritz and teach myself the things that interested me —now vanished utterly before the stultifying and (to me) incomprehensible demands of Discipline. I was like a savage, whose two feet served him well in every wind and weather until the white missionary insisted on cramming them into constricting shoes.

I do not mean to blame the school for my inability to become a scholar. It could be argued that my chances of becoming one were actually better at Marcus Leader than they might have been at many another school, however less "progressive" or pretentious. Nor do I fail to acknowledge the great gaping potholes in my education that wanted filling. I needed to learn arithmetic, biology, spelling and civics. It is no one's fault but my own that I never learned them.

I was soon labeled an odd duck (see "Frenchy," above) by the other children, and though I was not the only odd duck, I was the only odd duck I wished to know. I was too observant not to realize that this business of being an odd duck did not perforce give me anything in common with the other odd ducks swimming in the same pond, who might have been my friends, if I had let them. The one thing we had in common I pegged at once: I saw that they were losers like myself and wanted no part of the compromise of their company. They were ugly, stupid or poor, or they were even more neurotic than I. And I had trapped myself, in a way, by my childish oath to trust no one. That vow bound me, despite my efforts now to break it.

I wanted, more than anything, to belong. All the things about me that set me apart from the norm—however disgusting I might know that norm to be—I devalued to the point of hatred. I despised my absurd parentage, my absurd parents, my absurd accent; I despised the Harrises for having no limousine with which to drop me off at school (let alone one with flags on the fenders), and I tried to despise classical music, which had been such a mainstay of my sanity for upwards of four years in France. I despised the very frivolous, cruel and capricious cliques to which I longed to belong and disdained their vulgar members while secretly envying them. As I frowned on their cruelty to the outsiders, I would gladly have joined their cruelty, so long as it was not directed at me. I even envied them their lack of humor and cursed my own, for every time I opened my mouth to make what I thought was a joke, they stared at me in dumb disbelief, wondering that anyone could utter something so stupid.

Instead I coveted their brains, the brains that allowed them to survive with honor in the competitive world of Marcus Leader. Somehow—whatever social barbarities they practiced to one side—the fact that they got A's gave them in my sight the right, the moral justification, to be contemptuous of me. Up until the Marcus Leader School, I had always thought of myself as extremely intelligent. The school (with my collaboration) did its best to disabuse me of this delusion, and the shock of being ground down to intellectual rubble reduced me in the process to a kind of numbness that compounded itself over the years. "George stays aloof," read one of my Teachers' Assessments (they were not called report cards). "He seems not to know or care how to make friends."

It was certainly not easy to know how to make friends. I once got into a conversation with Larry Hayes, one of the most popular boys from school, when we both found ourselves waiting on the same street corner for our rides home. Alone, Larry seemed friendly, reasonable and nice. He listened in a half-attentive way to what I had to say and made intelligent and not unsympathetic responses. I thought that perhaps some companionable headway had been made. The next day, walking down a corridor, I came upon this same Larry Hayes laughing and talking with a knot of ten or so charter members of his inner circle. He ignored me even though he saw me, and when I spoke to him it was almost as if we had never met. Realizing my mistake, I continued down the hall and listened to the laughter half-heartedly suppressed in my wake and could distinguish Larry's laugh easily enough at its center.

To top off all my miseries, I fell in love my first day of third grade. Students of the human mind and heart will find nothing astonishing in my attempt to anchor both of these possessions to someone or something stable in my new surroundings. Be that as it may, I could hardly have made a worse choice. She was the Princess of the third grade, the undisputed feminine pinnacle of the class, whose every move and mode of dress had instantly three dozen imitators. They copied her every idea, sartorial or otherwise. I saw her at once as I entered Miss Rosenberg's class. She sat at a desk in the front and wore a pleated navy-blue skirt, white socks and saddle shoes; her blouse was a lighter blue and there was a little circular gold pin attached to the collar. Her hair was an ordinary middle brown, drawn back in a ponytail and gathered in a dark velvet ribbon that matched the color of the skirt. Her eyes matched the blouse. Her name was Delilah Kirstein and she was to dominate my fantasies and ambitions for the next five years, to become the invisible yardstick by which I measured every girl I met.

She soon enough became aware of my attraction to her and made it equally plain that she found my attentions grotesque. Once, I seized the opportunity to squeeze into the place next to hers on the school bus we shared. She never said a word to me; in fact, she never turned her face away from looking out the window so that I might see it. It was hard to misinterpret this message. In fact, she had already made her choice, as I quickly learned. (Things being what they were, she had probably made this choice

in kindergarten.) Richard Revere was her male counterpart, the Prince of the school, and he was everything that I
was not. He was handsome, clever and seemingly indifferent
to status, his own as well as everyone else's, the school's, the
world's. He got straight A's without appearing to study for
them, and he won Dottie Kirstein's affections by not appearing to care whether he won them or not, a disinterest I
could not even pretend to emulate. (My desperate desire
for Dottie Kirstein was the poorest-kept secret since the
defeat of Adlai Stevenson.) The two of them—Dick and
Dottie, as they were known throughout the years—always
succeeded in making me feel clumsy and foolish. To do
them strict justice, they didn't have to work at this. I almost
compelled them to with my insistent and absurd hanging
about. Dottie was understandably vexed by my improbable
persistence, while Dick always was friendly in his diffident
fashion. It was the crowd that revolved around them like
satellites who decided my fate and kept watch to see that
it never varied. Whatever choices I made in those early
days were invariably the wrong choices, and they marked
me for life in the eyes of this tiny world. For example, when
school was let out during the frigid winter months and we
waited for our various bus and car rides home, the boys
would gang up on the girls and throw snowballs at them.
This struck me as ungallant behavior on their part and I
instantly took up with the girls, hurling snowballs with
devastating effect at my own sex and assuming the role of
knight-errant defender, such as I had read about in books
like *The White Company*. If I thought this action would
ingratiate me with the ladies, I was quickly disabused of
that idea. Evidently I had missed some subtle form of court-

ship or communication between the warring parties and failed to realize that the girls *liked* being attacked by the boys and had no wish to be championed. They would defend themselves and love every minute of it. My defection to their ranks was viewed by both groups as dumb at best. At worst, only the fact that (then and for years after) I happened to be the strongest child in my class prevented my being tarred with an even more hideous brush.

I had various methods of dealing with this cluster of miseries and phobias called school. My first line of defense was employed in the morning, to see if I could avoid going there in the first place. Malingering. I complained of headaches, stomachaches, sore throats, diarrhea and whatever other likely ailments I could lay my tongue to. Suki was surprisingly naive about these ruses at first. For a time she honored my complaints and I was allowed the bliss of remaining in my room, where time passed agreeably enough reading the books and comic books that suited me, listening to my phonograph, building model boats and masturbating. In the last two areas of endeavor I became a proficient addict. Masturbation involved no great skills or technique (as someone remarked, you don't even have to look your best), but model-boat–building was another matter. It required hours of back-breaking patience and very steady, nimble fingers. As boat-building was an occupation that took up much more time than masturbating, it suited my purpose better, which was to get through as much of my life as I could. (Masturbating functioned as a kind of coffee break, a brief physical interruption to get out the kinks in my body and soul.) I began with relatively simple model boats, but graduated quickly and with astonishing ease to complex five-hundred piece, yard-long square-rigged sailing vessels like the clipper ship *Cutty Sark* and the USS *Constitution*. These projects involved not only a lot of delicate trimming, fitting, gluing and painting of tiny parts and tiny crewmen, but also an interminable amount of rigging, which was accomplished with a tweezers and different-colored threads. For hours I was capable of shutting out school, Chicago and all other forms of reality as I drew these little strings into place and created, as time mercifully went by, objects of great beauty and interest.

It was my hope that David and Suki would put one of my ships in a glass case. Without protection the ships became dust-traps the moment they were finished. Of course, with some of my allowance I might have purchased a case for one of the smaller vessels myself, but I never did. Looking back on it, I see now that I waited for David and Suki to buy one as a sign of interest or approval on their part for what I had done. Unfortunately what I had done was not what they wished me to do, and though they casually admired my models as I finished them, it seems never to have occurred to them to pay my efforts the formal tribute of acknowledgment that a glass case would have signified.

At school my attendance record for this period was bleak and would have gone on to even bleaker depths, but Suki and David put their heads together. David explained to her the high improbability of anyone who seemed so healthy (and who was growing so fast) being so often under the weather. She grew less willing to take my symptoms at face value. Nevertheless, staying home was my first choice if I could arrange it. I slept much during this time and would gladly have slept away the next four years if I could have managed it, but a new rule was instituted, and if I had no fever or other perceptible ills, I was packed off to face life at Marcus Leader.

At school my next line of defense came into play. At each opportunity I visited the nurse's office, there renewed my litany of ailments and played possum. I complained of blinding headaches, terrible stomach cramps, and as time went on, I was amazed to discover that these complaints became genuine. I so believed in my pains that by degrees they took me over, and soon I was indeed unpredictably subject to both. My stomach has remained my emotional barometer ever since.

Another attempt to delay, deny, evade and generally avoid reality at school made me become the class clown. I spoke out of turn, was not to the point and was silly. In the face of our lessons I could not conceal what I took to be my wit. It welled up inside my brain feverishly, like pressure on a boiler that needed the steam governor of my mouth to release it or all would burst. Neither teachers nor students appeared to enjoy these compulsive sallies, but I was unable to stop myself from dreaming them up or giving them voice when I felt them too good to suppress.

I mentioned a while back that there was a sole exception to the rule that forbade the inculcation of Moralistic Pragmatism theology in the school branch of the Society. This sole exception was an oblique one, designed, as it were, far off, to implant in us the seeds of that profound dogma. Thrice weekly a grey-haired lady named Miss Peterson would sit in our homeroom and tell us little stories and question us about them, trying to coax us into investigating their implications. This was Morality class. (Privately I dubbed it Mortality, as I could feel myself growing older by the minute as Miss Peterson spoke.) The kids without exception found her ridiculous. They paid not the slightest heed to her parables, but snuck notes back and forth amongst themselves in which they found amusement bordering on hilarity in attempting to keep an accurate count of Miss Peterson's "Um"s and "Ah"s and "Uh"s, for she was an indifferent orator, prone to the use of these verbal punctuations to help her through her narratives. I rather liked Miss Peterson, personally, and recognized the unmistakable signs of suffering in her face. I felt sorry for the way the other children mocked her behind her back, but I was cheerfully prepared to mock her myself if I thought trouncing her before witnesses would make me popular. I had not understood by then that nothing I could do would have that effect.

"Once upon a time," she might sadly begin, "there was a shepherd who had a flock of sheep and an old sheepdog. The dog knew it was too old to guard the sheep and protect them from the wolf who lived nearby that wanted to eat them. Its sight and hearing weren't so good anymore. Its legs too weak to run fast and many of its teeth were gone. The dog was frightened of what would happen to him when the shepherd discovered these things.

"Then one day the wolf made the dog a generous offer. 'Look,' he said, 'I know you are in failing health and worried about your future. I think I can help you. Let's arrange it so you can see me skulking about the herd of sheep and chase me away in full view of your master. In this way he will perceive you in action and believe you are alert and capable of handling your duties, and so you will keep your job.'

"The old sheepdog thought over the wolf's offer and decided to accept; what did he have to lose? The plan worked perfectly and the shepherd was very impressed on the day when he saw the dog chase away the wolf from his herd. He had been wrong, he decided, worrying about whether the dog could still do his job. Now he knew that he could and the dog's future was assured.

"A week later, however, the wolf came back to see the dog. 'Now that I've saved your job,' he said, 'I want you to do *me* a favor. I think it's only fair that in return for what I've done, you turn a blind eye and let me make off with a sheep now and then.' "

Here Miss Peterson paused and looked about the room. She now had our attention, almost in spite of her indifferent storytelling skills.

"What do you think the sheepdog ought to do?" she demanded quietly.

At this point those children who had not already come to the conclusion that the shepherd and his cursed dog lived too far away to be of any concern to them personally commenced addressing themselves to this tricky question.

I did not help matters when I suggested the dog ought to commit suicide.

On another occasion when we were generally dealing with the issue of morality—what is it? how does it affect us? etc.—I repeated a definition I found useful that I had first learned from my Uncle Fritz, sitting next to him in a pew at Notre Dame, taking in an early morning Mass after spending the night at a friendly neighborhood whorehouse called Le Pussycat.

"Morality," Fritz had said, leaning on his elbows against the back of the pew and staring up at the stained glass, just coming to life with the dawn's early light, "works like this: A man comes into a store and buys a pair of pants for five dollars. By mistake he gives the clerk a ten-dollar bill and walks out of the store. Now the major question the clerk has to face is this: Does he tell his partner about the extra five bucks he just cleared?"

Miss Peterson's face darkened as she listened to my idea of morality. I was ten years old at the time and the rest of the class didn't get it. Miss Peterson got it all right, and I was dispatched—not for the first time—to see Herman Blue.

"Ah, George the Alien," he would dub me, smiling, as I was ushered in for my latest perpetration. What George the Alien signified I don't know, but it was undoubtedly a reference to my curious speech and it was clear that Blue thought it a benign bit of humor—at my expense, to be sure, but harmless. He was so dumb, he couldn't recognize his own sadism and allow himself to frankly wallow in it.

Once, one of the Blue brothers—I never knew which it was—came in to substitute for an ailing English teacher. A composition of mine was read aloud in class and Herman or Waldo found fault with some of my archaic phraseology.

"You write that it was a (quote) 'deal of trouble' (unquote) to find the store, George," he began, holding my paper before him in one hand and pointing to the offending passage with the pinky finger of his other. "Surely you mean a 'great deal of trouble.'"

I replied that I had not meant a great deal of trouble,

because the amount of trouble caused by the problem in the story had not been great.

"Well, why not say 'a lot of trouble,' then?" pursued Herman or Waldo in a still reasonable tone. "'A deal of trouble' is an English construction."

"But it wasn't a *lot* of trouble, Mr. Blue. And besides, I thought English was what we were supposed to be writing. Isn't that why they call it English class?"

There was a faint titter around me. Behind his glasses, Herman or Waldo blanched.

"Stand up."

Hesitantly I obeyed. The class settled attentively in to enjoy the promised fun.

"Why do you write English as though you were living in the last century?"

"I like the way it sounds."

"It is very affected."

"It is my style."

"Why must you be different?"

"It is not ungrammatical to be different. There is no correct style, is there? Would you be happier if I had been the one to say 'Winston tastes good like a cigarette should'?"

There was dead silence. Herman or Waldo stared at me for what seemed an eternity, pursing and unpursing his lips. I wanted to cough or look away, but I was so frightened, I stood transfixed before him.

"You really are a disgusting little boy," he observed at last.

"I know," I mumbled, almost inaudible. He continued to purse and unpurse his lips. I cowered, easing my eyes to the floor at my feet, my face burning, my ears pounding so that

I could not at first hear the bell that signaled the end of the period and my torture.

Another trick I had up my sleeve was to run away. This was no mean feat in a city like Chicago, where to step out of certain circumscribed environs was more than your life was worth. Poles didn't cross the street into Russian sections, Italians didn't inadvertently stray into Irish compounds, and nobody messed with the Czechs. Running away was also difficult if you had no money and it was the dead of winter. Nevertheless, sufficiently desperate every other month, I would dare all and leave home. I had no specific destination in view, as I had no idea where the geography of anything really was outside the city. I took buses, subways and sometimes hitched rides. Mostly I walked. How I survived is a question for the angels to ponder. Usually my defections lasted little more than a day. I would wander along Lakeshore Drive, stroll about Rush Street or make my way to the Museum of Science and Industry, there to distract myself with the real coal mine or the simulated submarine. In warmer weather I used to head for the Riverview Amusement Park. It was a seedy place even then, on its last legs, but it had wonderfully scary rides; as I held my life cheap at the time, it cost me only my allowance to surrender myself to fate.

Once, when I was twelve, I got all the way to Joliet before the police located me and dragged me back to David and Suki.

"Why do you keep running away?" David demanded more than once. Usually I didn't dignify his question with an answer, but on this occasion I had got so far and was so tired, I blurted something back.

"Why did you take me away from my Uncle Fritz?" He blinked at me from behind his owlish glasses and knocked out the ashes from his pipe before answering.

"I'll tell you," he said, and I could see the muscles twitching in his cheeks as he spoke. "You are evidently under the impression that our taking you was a high-handed action performed for our own amusement, for some kind of *whim*. Let me tell you, our lives were just fine without you, George. We didn't need you. In fact, until Kathleen's funeral, we didn't even know you existed. And we weren't exactly overcome with joy when we learned you did. But we did feel duty-bound after learning about you to try and find out if you were all right. We made a lot of inquiries, and what we learned about your life and your Uncle Fritz's qualifications and methods of looking after you convinced us that something had to be done. I'm sure you know better than I what I am talking about. I'm going to be quite candid and say that when we learned how you were growing up, there seemed no question but that it could not be permitted to continue. You would not stand much of a chance in a world where spelling, arithmetic and learning generally are considered prerequisites for almost any decent job. The question was: What to do with you? I don't mind telling you I was all for finding you a decent orphanage. That was how much you meant to me. You have your Aunt Suki to thank for bringing you home, into this house, paying for the clothes on your back, the phonograph and records in your room, the piano you never play and all the other niceties of life you take for granted around here." His voice rose as he spoke and his hands, in jerky, agitated motions, worked inefficiently at refilling his pipe. It was obvious that he was strongly tempted to do other things with them at the moment. "And this is how you repay her kindness," he went on, his eyes glittering behind the glasses. "By worrying her half to death, by fooling around in school, failing your courses so you have to make them up in summer school and God knows what else. As if the world owed you a living. As if you were the only child or even the only person in the world who ever suffered or had a rough time. Frankly I am very disappointed. When I met you, I took you to be smarter than this. I took you to have more grit. I took you to have more style. It seems as though I was wrong."

With this he stood up and went out of the room. I stayed where I was, shaking with terror and humiliation. God knows, I was aware of Suki's endless patience and generosity where I was concerned. And yet I had not wasted a thought on how my behavior had affected her, nor had I ever questioned my divine right to the advantages she and David had bestowed upon me. As for Fritz, I had invoked him in a moment of weakness, since I still regarded his abandonment of me as betrayal, plain and simple. (In response to a letter of his—the only one I read—that he had sent me shortly after I came to Chicago, I had scribbled on the back of a postcard the somewhat melodramatic sentiment

He Travels Fastest Who
Travels Alone

which I had chanced upon in some book or other, like *The Count of Monte Cristo*. "Revenge is the best revenge" was my other working motto at the time—I made it up.)

After thinking the matter over, I went to find Suki to apologize for any unhappiness I'd caused her, but trying to tell her I was sorry was made almost impossible by her giddy refusal to acknowledge anything amiss in the first place. She literally danced about the kitchen, performing inconsequential tasks, and jabbered a mile a minute in order to forestall any discussion of my thoughtless actions or general self-absorption. She was frantic not to admit anything was wrong and not to hear me admit that anything was wrong.

"Suki, I'm sorry I ran—"

"George, do you think you can eat two lamb chops?"

"—but school isn't making me very happy. I ran away because I'm not good at it—"

"I'll bet you can; you're growing so fast you'll wind up eating us both out of house and home! Just look at your shoulders, just *look* at them! Do you know you can get an idea how big a puppy will grow by the size of its paws? It's true—if you don't believe me, take a look at the paws on a Great Dane puppy, they're like horse hooves, practically. Now I wonder if you can tell about boys and girls from their shoulders. Wouldn't it be interesting if that turned out to be true? Hey, I've invented something new—how to predict growth by looking at people's shoulders! I'm a scientist, too, now, just like David!"

Suki existed in the marriage by assuming a kind of childlike relation to David. She even called him Daddy. At first I thought this was a ploy to get me to do the same, but I soon realized that was her favorite name for him. And he allowed her the ungrudging use of it. This parent-child arrangement was apparently agreeable to both and perhaps even necessary. On other than domestic matters Suki had no opinions, or very closely guarded ones, expressed at the dinner table cautiously and with an eye always fixed on David, looking for his approval. On David's part, he frequently expressed opinions for his wife. "Suki doesn't like foreign films," he might say. "She doesn't like to read the subtitles."

On the other hand Suki was perfectly capable of all matters domestic. She ran the house with a Swiss efficiency that formed an almost ludicrous contrast with her little-girl behavior when David was around. She kept an accountant's eagle-eye on the books, was a veritable adding machine and a bargain hunter where all household finances were concerned, leaving David free to work and "think." Suki had a reverence bordering on awe for the times when David was "thinking." "We have to be very quiet," she'd whisper to me. "Daddy's thinking."

Suki was also great at dreaming up things to do. David was something of a stick in the mud, but Suki had a healthy, one might almost say childlike curiosity about most things, and her instincts were uncommonly good. David and I grew to depend on her wild hunches, especially on weekends when we were both inclined (for different reasons) to stay at home and putter. Suki, on the other hand, was always scanning the paper for things of interest. She sent away for tickets and goosed us into going to movies (*Around the World in Eighty Days* was a big favorite; we saw it three times), concerts, shows (*West Side Story*), exhibits at the Art Institute, performances at the Goodman Theatre, you name it. I think it was Suki who actually introduced me to the model-boat–building kits to which I became so devoted.

"What about this Victor Borge?" she would say, showing the newspaper advertisement to each of us at breakfast. "Comedy in music," she read aloud. "Maybe that's good. I hear he's good." She pronounced Borge to rhyme with Norge, our dishwasher.

David and I were incurious. I was the most incurious child I ever heard of. Perhaps I was so abashed by Suki's curiosity that I felt she'd appropriated it all, and decided not to compete.

We would wind up going to see Victor Borge and laugh so hard I thought I was going to be sick. David and I would get more of the jokes than Suki did, but her failure to understand some of the references didn't dampen her enjoyment. David and I wiping the tears from our eyes and our hilarity was ample proof that she'd been right. "I knew my men would like that show," she'd say in the car on the way home. "I just *knew* it." For Suki, every event, even a trip to the planetarium, was "a show," and though she decided what we were going to see and sent away for the tickets and wrote the check, it was always David, in her mind, who took us to see the thing, whatever it was. "I'm so glad you took us to see that show, Daddy," she also would say on the way home.

One day I made a disquieting discovery. Suki and David were at some sort of weekend faculty luncheon and I was at home alone, except for Doris, who cleaned on Saturdays. I don't remember what I was looking for or why I thought I might find whatever it was in David's clothes closet, but I was pawing through it on my knees when I came upon a large cardboard box. In the box was an assortment of neatly folded baby clothes and odd accompanying items: an old rattle; an old, slightly moth-eaten teddy bear with black buttons for eyes and a lot of careful restitching to keep its stuffing in. Baby shoes. Finally there was a folder tied with string that contained documents and photographs. The photos were mainly black and white, but there were some faded color snaps as well.

The pictures featured a sweet-faced, smiling little boy of three or so. He seemed always to be smiling, no matter how often people pointed cameras at him. Suki and David were smiling, too, in some of the pictures as they held him.

"What are you doing?"

I whirled around to find Doris standing over me, her eyes wide with dismay.

"I was just—"

"Put that box away. Put everything back just how you found it." She bent down to help me, carefully refolding the infant's little trousers and sweaters.

"Where is the little boy? Who is he?" I demanded, though I think I knew perfectly well who and where he was. In this instance, however, guessing wasn't good enough.

"He was their little boy. Michael, his name was."

"What happened to him?"

She shoved the box back into its hidden place behind David's row of neatly hanging trousers and heaved herself heavily erect before replying.

"No one knows exactly. Sometimes babies die in their sleep and nobody knows why. That's what happened to him. He was the cutest little thing you ever saw, too." She sighed. "Poor little feller. Now don't you go asking your uncle about poor Michael. He don't like to speak of it, and your aunt can't stand to hear about him neither. She'll bust out crying if you say anything, so keep your lip buttoned up."

I assured Doris that I would, then followed her into the kitchen and watched as she commenced a vigorous mopping of the linoleum floor.

"Doris."

"Uh-huh."

"Why don't they have another baby?"

She stopped swabbing the deck and looked at me, leaning on the mop handle. I could see her trying to make up her mind how to handle this question. Doris was not a gossip, but my discovery of the cardboard box and the questions it raised had placed her in a most delicate position. She understood this quite clearly but was obliged literally to think on her feet.

"They can't."

"Why not?"

"Mrs. Harris—well, she just can't. Having a baby is too much stress for her. They tried it," she added, plunging the mop into the bucket of murky water. "But she lost that baby and now she can't even bear to try."

Much of this explanation escaped me. At ten I didn't fully understand how babies were made or how it was possible to "lose" one. That seemed like a carelessness that even scatterbrained Suki couldn't have managed. Carelessness, in fact, was not her style at all. As usual, however, I had grasped the gist of things. David and Suki had had a little boy who had died. They couldn't have any more little boys.

So they had me. I spent the rest of the afternoon—and many days to come—pondering my place and function in

David and Suki's lives as the result of these disclosures. I dimly perceived now why David hadn't wanted me to begin with and why Suki had; I also saw why she was so protective and even obliquely understood why she would never admit anything was wrong. Later still I was able to infer the presence of an irrational guilt on Suki's part for the baby's death and an equally irrational (and totally un-expressed) conviction on David's part that she was right. These inexpressible ideas were what made the whole subject impossible for them to discuss. I certainly didn't absorb these ideas and inferences at the time, not consciously and not all at once. But when David and Suki came home from the luncheon, I went up to Suki, flung my arms about her neck and hugged her very hard.

"Well, isn't this a nice surprise," she laughed into my ear. She may have said other things, but I didn't pay any attention, just hung on. When I didn't let go, she stopped talking, hugged me back and didn't say any more.

For some time after that I treated Suki with kid gloves. I made allowances for all her giddy insensitivity because of my hot, flushed memories of the boy in the box in David's closet who smiled all the time, which was certainly not the case with me. I knew that little boy—had he lived—would not have been the constant source of worry and trouble that I was. In addition Suki's childish behavior was now perceived by me as a poignantly gallant defense against the tragedy that must—I knew—be daily gnawing at her vitals. I resolved to attempt no more mischief, no matter how bad things got: I would smile; I would make up for Michael.

This noble resolve was, however, of brief duration. As my own difficulties overwhelmed me, my attitude towards Suki

and David slowly relapsed to something like its former con-
figuration. The only difference was that now when I failed
at things, I felt guilty. The dead little boy had receded from
my conscious mind, dominated as it was by the travails and
tribulations I had daily to cope with. But Michael's ghost
festered in my heart.

Nine

In Which Everything Changes

It was in February of 1956, two months after my fourteenth birthday, that I woke up one morning before my alarm clock had gone off. This in itself was uncharacteristic: As I have noted, I would gladly have slept through my entire adolescence if I could have managed it. Finding myself strangely alert, I lay back waiting for the summons to action and stared at the familiar cracks in the ceiling overhead. They reminded me of nothing except perhaps a parched desert such as I had seen in a Walt Disney nature film, an uncanny representation of my life, as I judged. Looking at the cracks provided me with a restful opportunity to think. I was now in my fifteenth year and something somewhere had gone completely wrong. Little of my life seemed to be of my own choosing. It is well for children to understand that they are powerless to control much of their destinies—that privilege being reserved (to a greater degree, anyway) for grown-ups—but in my own case, as I lay there and felt life passing me by (I imagined I could actually hear my cells expiring), it now occurred to me that I controlled none of my destiny.

I had been engaged in a good deal of this reflection lately, owing, I think, to this business of being fourteen amongst a bevy of thirteen-year-olds. Although many in my class were the children of Moral Pragmatists, that did not prevent them from becoming Bar Mitzvah. I was unfamiliar with the ritual and the term—what I knew about Judaism could be squeezed onto the head of a pin alongside what I understood of Christianity (but at least Dumas and Verne wrote about that)—but I understood, without having been asked to any of the lavish receptions that took place in the wake of the ceremonies, what they signified. It was about becoming a man, and though I had no illusions that being Bar Mitzvah would make me a man (I was a ludicrous year late for that, anyhow), I had begun to wonder just what would. David had taken to peppering his criticisms of me with the phrase "You're not a child anymore," or words to that effect, so this subject of manhood had begun to prey upon my mind. I knew, too, that it wasn't the size of the reception following the rite, either, that did the trick, though I had heard that Larry Hayes's at the Palmer House had cost his father some fifteen thousand dollars.

I lay cozy and warm in bed and took stock of my situation. I was no longer fresh fodder for ridicule at school. They were used to me by now; in an odd way I had even earned my own particular niche in their society. Good old crazy Frenchy. In an unselfconsciously patronizing way I had become an endearing figure, the kid who always spoke out of turn and told those incomprehensible jokes that were never funny—which in itself was judged to be funny. There was even evidence of some respectable feminine curiosity on the part of one girl who was not altogether plain. She was by no means a member of the inner circle, the elite, but she had metamorphosed in early adolescence (we were all changing, with interesting results) from an ordinary mousey-looking girl with a deal of baby fat into a surprisingly nice-looking girl with a ripe figure. Her name was Gena. She went her own way, a free spirit, seemingly indifferent to the opinions of the other girls, some of whom noised it about that Gena was "fast." Her father was a well-known Chicago-based novelist of the tough, hard-bitten-typewriter school, which may have explained her successful resistance to peer pressure from a bunch of stockbrokers' children. She was what was then called "beat" and wore her hair long and unadorned, sported pierced ears and clutched translated volumes of French writers like Camus and Jean-Paul Sartre under her arm, neither of which were required reading. No one had ever heard of them. Jack Kerouac (though he didn't know it yet and neither did Gena) was destined to become her hero.

She was interested in me all right, and her approval had engendered grudging interest in some of the other girls. Too frightened themselves to do more than attend dances in white gloves at the Casino Club—or the Standard Club, if they were Jewish—where they trained to be debutantes and engaged in light necking at well-chaperoned "make-out" parties, they nevertheless were intrigued by Gena and her opinions, though protesting the while that she was "gross," had hair under her arms and was guilty of other atrocities too disgusting to do more than snigger about.

I was not particularly attracted by Gena; she *did* have hair under her arms and wore braces on her teeth (she was not alone), but I was aware that some things were changing. I had finally found something I was good at: sports. Despite my years of model-boat–building (and other, only slightly less sedentary occupations), I had a well-developed and well-coordinated body. All those years of wrestling with Sasha and long walks on Rush Street had certainly helped. I found, as I was introduced to exercise via my gym classes, that physical activity helped burn off many of my frustrations. There was nothing like being exhausted. I swam like a fish, could run forever and was generally quick enough so that I could pick up almost any athletic activity and excel at it the way some musical whiz-kids can play any instrument you care to hand them. I sprinted for junior varsity track and swimming (butterfly); I was junior varsity tennis and junior varsity soccer. I was always being threatened with the prospect of not playing on various teams because of my lamentable academic standing, but I was too valuable a player to be without when we played Francis Parker, with whom Marcus Leader had a longstanding rivalry in everything. My school proved to be as utterly corrupt as any university in the country when the chips were down, and I was rarely on the bench. At such times my status soared for the duration of an afternoon, with boys and girls alike (who normally had no use for me whatever) screeching their lungs out on my behalf in Lincoln Park. I was too short for basketball, and a knee injury kept me out of football, but I was cheered lustily when breaking a broad jump record or whacking a grand slam out of the ball park. At one track meet I even won the hundred-yard dash against Richard Revere, much to my satisfaction, though if Dottie Kirstein was impressed I never learned of it. I later discovered she hadn't been there to witness this gratifying event.

Dottie Kirstein. Well-named Delilah. As we reached puberty, strange changes had occurred in the girls. Some of the pretty ones had become plain, some of the ugly ones beautiful. Skin became a problem for many. Not Dottie. She simply grew more improbably beautiful, with graceful long legs, a fetchingly proud bosom and skin with the smoothness of the proverbial peach. She continued to be an A student and was taking Italian. (Someone said she would be going to Italy with a group in the summer to study in Perugia.) I recall getting enormous pleasure out of watching her show up at a school mixer, tottering on her first pair of high heels. By the end of the evening, she had mastered them. Not that any of it made any difference where I was concerned. We spoke to each other now and again, when it couldn't be avoided, but it was as plain as before that she had no use for me. Her childhood vexation had declined into a sort of exasperated amusement at my interest in her. Once, gasping for breath like a beached whale, I had telephoned her and asked her if she wanted to go to a film at the Esquire Theatre.

"No," she had said without embellishment.

Five minutes until the alarm went off. I thought of masturbating to images of Dottie Kirstein and decided against it. I was now perversely summing up my life and reality was taking precedence over fantasy for the moment.

I was in great physical shape—not counting the headaches and stomach cramps—if I wanted to look on the bright side. My shoulders, which Suki had commented upon, I now realized were indeed very large. I had developed an almost muscle-bound physique that made me look somewhat older than I was. I was no longer bussed to Marcus Leader but had a Raleigh bicycle, which I lovingly maintained and rode in all but the most inclement weather.

On the other hand my academic and emotional shape was

deteriorating. There was another prospect of summer school before me, and Chicago in summer was an insupportable muggy hell. And it was terrifying at night to sit next to David as he tried to help me with math. I could practically hear the tension building in his body, the impatience with my slowness, my inability to grasp the simplest equations, welling up inside him until I thought it must explode. I sat next to him, cringing, waiting for him to slap me for my stupidity—wishing he *would* slap me and get it over with. After math Suki joined us for Scrabble—to improve my spelling—and then we sometimes played gin rummy. Suki always won at Scrabble and gin rummy. Her machine-like mind responded to games, like Judy Holliday's in the movie *Born Yesterday*. She squealed a lot while playing, too, while David and I looked at each other, amused. Some Saturday night.

There may have been people more unhappy than I, but I did not know them. At least I did not know that I knew them. All I knew for sure was that I was a poor student and not likely to become a good one; I had no friends and couldn't make the compromises with my own interests or beliefs that would have gained me any. I might try to forget Mozart and listen to Johnny Mathis, but who was I to Mathis or Mathis to me that I should listen so?

And as if all this were not enough, I found myself thinking more and more of the dead Michael Harris and my improbable attempt—which was also none of my choosing —to replace him. That little boy would almost certainly have fit in at Marcus Leader and done it with his ever-present smile. I had come to Marcus Leader and this life that wasn't mine all too late, with too fuzzy and fragmented a past. I could never take Michael's place, and I thought I detected in David's increasingly short temper where I was concerned that he had begun to realize this as well, however much poor Suki protested that everything was just fine.

I noticed, too, that lately I had been thinking a lot about Fritz. We had been engaged in a little comedy of errors via the postal service. When I had first left Paris, he had written me a number of letters, which arrived regularly and which I refused to read, let alone answer (aside from my single nasty postcard), so bitter was I over what I insisted on viewing as his treachery. I didn't like to think about him or my years in France. All these years had done—as I originally saw it—was to twist my tongue out of shape. I also think I blocked out thoughts of France because they sometimes led back to the shame of my encounter with Olga.

Lately, however, I found myself reconsidering. After four years of silence I had sat down five weeks before and written Fritz a letter. It was a hard letter to write and took me some time to say in it what I wished. The letter, to my surprise and chagrin, had been returned to me marked:

ADRESSE INCONNUE
RETOUR A L'EXPEDITEUR

This annoyed me, for now that I had made up my mind to forgive Fritz, it was disquieting to find I couldn't reach him to let him in on the happy fact of his amnesty. After mulling it over for a week, I readdressed the letter very carefully and instructed that it be forwarded if necessary. Again it came back to me. I got a chilled, unsettled feeling in the pit of my stomach at the sight of it on the dinner table. David handed it to me without comment or meeting my eyes. Since then I had been unable to banish thoughts of Fritz, Mme. Berthe, Sasha and Marly. They kept popping unbidden into my mind at odd times.

"What are you laughing about?" my Latin teacher inquired in class, startling me out of a private reverie. How improbable and affected it would have been to tell him. It was a lengthy anecdote that had taken place at three in the morning at a jazz club in Montparnasse where Fritz, very drunk, had taken over the piano and, with the aid of an orange in his right hand, had startled everyone there with his version of several Chopin études. He had used the orange, rolling it back and forth over the black keys, to make the entire treble-clef part. After that, all I wanted out of life was to play "Le Piano Orange." I stayed silent.

"You don't have that much to laugh about, George," the teacher informed me as the class listened in, amused as always by my dressing down.

"Then I think I deserve some credit for doing a lot with very little," I responded recklessly. "After all, there are some people in this world who have a lot to laugh about but who never so much as chuckle. If you ask me, these people are squandering good laughs that the rest of us might enjoy. They're laugh-hoarders, in my opinion. On the other hand I think I have demonstrated a very unselfish willingness to make very little—as you say—go a long way. Anybody who wants to is welcome to join in on my laughs—"

"THAT WILL DO!"

Which rhymed, more or less, with Herman Blue. Ah, George the Alien.

It really wouldn't do. I was headed nowhere unless I got an athletic scholarship to some college, and at the moment I didn't appear likely even to make it through high school. *Where was Fritz?*

I thought of running away again, my lifelong specialty. I hadn't tried it in about six months and I even had some money set aside from my allowance and some after-school jobs, but the idea didn't take hold. For one thing it seemed so hard on Suki, whom I truly had no wish to hurt.

Besides, I always got caught.

At this point my alarm clock, with irresistible objectivity, went off. I abandoned these profitless ruminations for my clothes and gym bag. I biked to school in sleety frigid weather and made it without incident through an algebra and English class. (I did well in English—or comparatively well, Herman or Waldo Blue notwithstanding—as I liked it. I got B's with an occasional B-plus).

I had a free period before lunch and decided to spend it in the gym (which was usually empty at this time), pressing weights, instead of trooping into the nurse's office for a nap. I changed quickly and stepped into the gym, lying down on the pressing bench and lifting a hundred pounds off the stand and onto my chest.

The gym was empty, all right, with one unfortunate exception, which I noticed with the weights in the air above me. Seeing it, I almost dropped them on my chest, which would have been the end of me. As it was, the peculiar sight was even odder viewed from my upside-down perspective and so took me by surprise that the bar almost slid out of my grip. I replaced it carefully on the stand, sat up and turned to look.

Larry Hayes was hanging by a rope from the gymnastics high-bar.

For a moment I didn't think I was seeing correctly. I remember literally blinking my eyes to make sure of what I thought I had seen. This time there could be no doubt. He was swaying gently back and forth by his neck, his body motionless. He was dressed in street clothes and had used a clothesline.

I walked slowly up to where he hung, transfixed by the sight. His face was contorted and his eyes bulged. There was also a strong stench of excrement emanating from a spreading brown stain at the crotch of his trousers.

I looked wildly about suddenly, with the unjustified idea that someone was about to burst in upon us (I thought of it as us), but we were quite alone. Larry Hayes had counted on the gym's being empty at this time, too.

Larry Hayes. Larry Hayes, the boy with the fifteen-thousand-dollar Bar Mitzvah. Larry Hayes, with whom in envious fancies I had traded places a thousand times. Larry Hayes, not fourteen years old and dead by his own hand. If he, whom I presumed to be riding high, wide and handsome in the world, couldn't make it to fourteen, how likely a candidate was I for longevity?

I shinnied up one of the poles and untied him. He weighed more in his inert condition than I anticipated, and his dead weight tore the clothesline from my grip and brought him down on the mat below with a quiet squishy thud.

I spent most of the afternoon with the police and Herman

Blue. In some way I got the feeling that Blue blamed me for Hayes's suicide, simply because I had been the one to discover and report it. Like Persian kings of old, he was prepared to execute messengers who brought bad news.

The police lieutenant told me I oughtn't to have moved the body. I assured him that the next time I came upon a hanged man I would let him swing till hell froze over. He did not appear to find this funny.

"Gallows humor," I explained.

They decided I'd had enough then and sent me home. Suki and David tried to be of some comfort, but I was so lost in my own numbed reflections that I couldn't help them. I ate automatically and retired to my room with only Hieronymous and some dark thoughts to keep me company.

Larry Hayes. With sudden clarity I saw his suicide as the last straw. Everything about this world in which I seemed so helplessly alien (to use Herman's well-chosen word) was a fraud. If Larry Hayes, with everything in this world going for him, couldn't survive it, then I no longer intended trying.

In a continuing epiphany I realized what I would do. I would run away—no, not away. *I would find Fritz.* I would go back to the world I knew, the world that made sense to me and where I seemed to belong. With sudden plainness I saw why all my previous attempts to flee Chicago had failed: I never had any destination. I had simply been escaping, escaping with no plan or aim, running *away,* not *towards.* Now that would change. I had a destination. I knew where I would go. I would return to Paris and learn what had become of Fritz. I would flee this nightmare, flee

Larry Hayes, the Marcus Leader Workingman's Progressive School, flee Chicago, flee Illinois and flee Adlai Stevenson's second doomed attempt at the presidency.

In a frenzy I tore my room upside down in search of my passport, unthought-of for four years. It was still valid for six more months, having been newly obtained for me when I was nine from the American consul in Paris to enable me to return to the United States. I checked my bankbook and cursed myself for spending money on those damn model ships, now collecting dust on my bookshelves. Two hundred and three dollars. I began planning what I would say in a note to David and Suki.

A voice told me to wait a minute. I sat down on the edge of my bed, my temples throbbing, and listened to the voice. The voice said, "Listen to me: You're barely fourteen years old, you don't have but two hundred dollars and you're proposing to go halfway around the world. You better think this one out, chum"—I smiled as my mind reintroduced the word to my consciousness—"because if you're not careful, if you're not downright wily about this, you will get no farther than Gary, Indiana. This time it's got to be for keeps, and it will require a lot of planning."

I crawled under the covers with these sobering thoughts, my heart pounding in my chest.

Ten

I Intrigue

My decision to quit Chicago in earnest and find Fritz, wherever he might be, cleared cobwebs from my head that had been there so long they had begun to petrify. Overnight my perceptions of the world and of myself were profoundly altered. For the first time in my life I had a purpose that was my own and had not been designed or fashioned for me by others, others with their own purposes. I discovered, as I put my mind to the business of my escape, that my intelligence —in which I had begun to fervently disbelieve—was intact and capable of functioning with all the subtlety of a Renaissance poisoner. My ingenuity, as I laid my plans, was a source of continual surprise, enjoyment and satisfaction. I would not need an athletic scholarship after all.

For the moment I went about my life as normally as I could. I was for a time the oblique center of attention at Marcus Leader by virtue of the fact that it was I who had discovered the unfortunate Hayes and notified the authorities. I was frequently buttonholed in corridors or before class by Larry's friends, anxious or curious for details. Death, par-

ticularly to teen-agers, is as a rule so far removed from their
reality or thoughts that its appearance in the midst of a high
school resembles a thunderbolt. Larry's friends were grieved
by his death, but even the grief-stricken were not immune to
curiosity. What was death? What did it look like? How
did it feel to be near it? Death was a phenomenon that not
many knew much about.

I was not about to enlighten them. I had no wish to
exploit the role that fate had cast in my way. Since I was
not staying at Marcus Leader (though the fact was not by
any means known!), it was no longer of interest or importance to me to ingratiate myself—by whatever sordid means
—with any members of the student body. In addition the
topic truly disgusted me. I had perceived the entire world of
Marcus Leader and its environs as fraudulent and was no
longer prepared to envy or cater to any part of it.

In remaining silent on the subject in the face of many
questions, I learned more than I divulged. Perhaps the
saddest intelligence was the rumor that was offered up by
someone for my delectation that Hayes had killed himself
after discovering that he was "queer." (If it had not been
for my chance finding of his corpse, I would not have
become the oracle I now was. People placed their theories
at my feet as though I could explain why he had taken his
own life simply because I had found him.)

I had no way of knowing if Hayes had been "queer," or
if he had recently discovered that he was about to become
"queer." As I considered the matter, I realized that he had
always had slightly effeminate mannerisms. Whether these
mannerisms caused Larry to see himself as a homosexual, I
could not say. And if they made him see himself in that

light—whether this had been sufficient inducement for him to do away with himself—that, too, I could not guess.

But if he *had* killed himself for that reason, I judged him a fool and was angry with him. I gave much thought to suicide during the next weeks. I had considered suicide many times myself, but never seriously. (Just as I had never, I now realized, seriously run away before.) Suicide had been simply a choice, to be numbered among other choices, but was never one that occurred to me in all my years of misery to make. And now, in the midst of my energetic devices to effect a complete departure from the entire Western Hemisphere, it seemed as though it was a choice I could never make, that no sane person could make. As I thought these proud and angry thoughts, a voice whispered, "Never say never."

As I thought about suicide, it seemed to me foolish because death, as the poet has it, will come when it will come, sooner or later, anyway. If there is something interesting after death, well and good, but if there is nothing, the suicide must feel very stupid when he discovers that he has simply deprived himself of any and all possibilities in favor of lying in the ground and rotting. At least alive, things might get better. As Fritz often remarked, "The opera isn't over until the Fat Lady sings."

I could think of only two reasons that might justify suicide: Either you are dying already of a painful and incurable disease, or you are about to be tortured unmercifully for information that you must not divulge as the lives and safety of others depend upon your silence.

With all these clever thoughts and rationalizations, however, I could not help remembering my brief, inconsequential chat with Larry Hayes the day we waited for the school bus together, when I had only been at Marcus Leader six months or so. He had been real with me then, and not unkind.

Nor could I blot out another memory: the spreading brown stench and stain of excrement in his trousers, a humiliation so grotesque that I wondered if Larry had known it would occur.

Against the terror of these fearful thoughts, I plunged with adrenaline-laden precision into my plans. Quickly I sorted my obstacles into two major catagories: The first concerned my travels themselves, and the second dealt with throwing off any form of pursuit.

To get to Europe, I knew that airplanes were useless. It would not be possible to stow away on anything so small as an airplane. I would have to take a ship, and ships left for Cherbourg (as I well knew) from New York. Ergo, I would have to get to New York. I considered hitchhiking briefly, but rejected the idea for a number of reasons. Hitchhiking was uncertain and time-consuming at best; there was no telling what sort of company and in whose power you could find yourself. Even Fritz, who would try anything, always cautioned against hitching if you could avoid it. It did not seem necessary when for twenty-five dollars I could purchase a coach seat on the *20th Century Limited*. The business of getting aboard ship in New York I deferred for the moment.

I decided not to undertake the trip until the weather turned warm: the Midwest in winter would kill you if you stayed out in it too long, and I remembered New York as cold this time of year as well. If I had to do any sleeping out of doors, it would be best to wait until at least early June. With this in mind I went to the La Salle Street Station and bought my coach ticket aboard the *20th Century Limited*. The ticket was good for any trip during the following year, and it was my hope that four months from now, when police were questioning such people, the man who had sold me my ticket back in February would have forgotten all about it. To make additionally sure, however, I wore conspicuous five-and-dime-store glasses and parted my hair differently when I made the purchase. If the man remembered me, he would remember me wrong. Later, when the time came to actually leave, I had another device in mind to throw David and Suki off the scent.

My next question was money. I now had less than two hundred dollars, and while I knew that I could not possibly raise enough money for the entire trip without exciting comment, I would need more than I had. I knew I could not purchase a steamship ticket; I felt fairly certain that my passage across the Atlantic would be an illegal one, but I felt it wise to accumulate as much cash as I could in the meantime for whatever money could buy that a fourteen-year-old would not be begrudged. I withdrew what money I had in easy amounts from my bank account and, using a different bank each time, turned the cash into traveler's checks, which I kept carefully hidden in my room.

Getting my hands on more cash was a problem. I began hoarding my five-dollar allowance, but that sum was designed to cover many of my inescapable incidental expenses and I could only save two dollars of it each week. I continued to work after school at various odd jobs connected with landscaping and maintenance, under the watchful eye of Waldo Blue, who paid fifty cents an hour. I could only work an hour or so before leaving for home and homework, so I netted from school jobs two dollars and fifty cents each week. In other words I was clearing four-fifty a week. Cursing myself for being so poor at math, I counted the weeks until June. There were thirteen. Four dollars and fifty cents over thirteen weeks would net me fifty-eight dollars and fifty cents, or only about twenty-five dollars more than I had originally in the bank before the purchase of the train ticket. And these computations did not allow for illness or accident, and they made it necessary for me to resign from every team to which I belonged that practiced after school. There was considerable protest, annoyance and alarm that followed these resignations, and some effort, particularly by the captain of junior varsity swimming—who had the worst case of acne I had ever seen—to persuade me to stay on. (Butterfly sprinters were not common.) With some difficulty I stuck to my guns. I became aware, as time went by, that my withdrawal from sports was attributed to my discovery of Larry Hayes in the gymnasium. In a way this was true.

That left weekends.

I got a part-time Saturday job at Delisi's, a noisy Sicilian-owned gourmet grocery on State Street. The job involved uncrating fruit, pricing it and putting it on display. I priced canned goods as they arrived and put them on the shelves. I sprayed vegetables and produce with a water atomizer to keep them fresh and fresh-looking. This was seventy-five cents an hour, but Delisi's was a small store, and even after I had mopped the aisles, my work didn't consume more than two hours of a Saturday morning and sometimes less than that. The cash-register position was filled by employees who worked full-time. Add another three dollars a week, more or less, to the escape kitty.

"You're so industrious," Suki complained, though she smiled as she said it. "We hardly get to see you any more."

I smiled and mumbled something about helping to pay my own way.

"Are you saving money for a car?" David wanted to know.

"Not exactly."

But David and Suki were pleased. My grades did not improve particularly (I would still need to spend the month of June in summer school to make up my algebraic deficiencies), but I was clearly being industrious and regular in my habits, which they took to be signs of some sort of improvement. I think they were relieved as well to see me quit all of those teams. Somewhere in the back of Suki's mind there may have lurked the dread that all those sports might somehow lead me to a circus big top, as though it were a kind of hereditary illness. Once, when I lightly mentioned tightrope-walking as an analogy for my life, she had blanched.

"Don't worry," I had assured her, "I don't even go to see the circus when it comes to town. I have absolutely no wish to be a Flying Bernini."

With a shrill laugh she had immediately changed the subject. In fact, I had once identified myself at school as the child of the Two Flying Berninis and the thing had caught on like wildfire for a day or so: "Did you know that Frenchy's a Flying Bernini?"

"I always thought so."

"I always liked flied Berninis for dessert."

"Speak for yourself; I'm sticking with girls."

I bought a grey Norwegian rucksack at Marshall Field. It was a large rucksack fitted on a wood frame. (This was in the days before the widespread use of lightweight aluminum for such things.) It had one main subdivision in its capacious main interior and two side pockets on the outside, with a little zippered compartment under the top flap. It set me back twenty dollars, but it would carry everything I needed.

"Going to climb Mount McKinley?" David asked when he saw the rucksack on my back.

"Take a look." I opened the bag and took out all my notebooks, textbooks, pencils and compass case. I pulled out a sweater. "It's much easier to bike to school with this than putting the books and stuff in the side baskets. They always get wet, and then I have to collect them whenever I get home or to school. Now I just walk away from the bike with all the stuff on my back. Saves time."

"Still looks a little big. You could stash a radio in there and have room for a swimming pool."

"Well, this year maybe it looks big, but I'll have more books to carry next year, and besides, if I go back to any sports, my gym clothes and sneakers and stuff will fit in easily."

"Are you thinking about teams next year?"

I hesitated. Anything to do with after the first of June was only more lies.

"Well, nothing like this year. I was just overextending myself. It wasn't just schoolwork that suffered: I couldn't even make practice for all the teams I was on. Maybe just tennis. Or swimming."

I hated lying to David and Suki. In fact, I didn't much like to think about them during this time because the fact of them and their care for me raised questions I found it difficult to answer. I was taking every precaution against getting caught once I left; I had no illusions about what David's reaction would be if I was returned by the police again. On the other hand, if I did get clean away, I knew that their sorrow—particularly Suki's—might likely be very great. In a way my defection would constitute the third child she had lost, counting the miscarriage. It would probably break her heart.

When I thought these thoughts, my stomach began to throb and tighten. If I was on the bike, I had to get off and walk. I had developed an affection for Suki, despite my youthful resolve not to develop affections, not to trust anyone. I knew that, crazy as she sometimes appeared, you could trust Suki.

Up to a point. Then I would remember the pointless round of drudgery I endured daily at school and how Larry Hayes had found it pointless, too—even with A's and a big Bar Mitzvah. I would remember the cartwheeling freedom with Fritz that had been forcibly snatched from me, and the humiliating loneliness that had been substituted in its place, and my heart hardened, even against the tugs Suki made on it. I was getting out and that was all there was to it. The question of Suki and, to a lesser extent, David, would be shelved for the time being.

Hieronymous was another question mark. I knew I couldn't take him with me this time, and I entertained terrifying fantasies of David vengefully taking out his anger on the cat. This was unworthy speculation on my part, however, for I knew that David's character would never permit him to misplace his emotions so. I also knew for a fact that in spite of a mild allergy to cats, David was quite fond of Hieronymous. I don't think he had ever had a pet of his own, and the honest affection of the cat pleased and surprised him, especially when he was the recipient of it. Hieronymous would jump into his lap, startling him, but he never pushed him off. On the contrary, with hesitant hands, David always stroked him and chucked him under the chin. No, I supposed Hieronymous would be all right if he didn't miss me too badly.

Here was another thought it wouldn't do to dwell on. Hieronymous and I had been together since my birth. I had never been separated from him in my entire life. He was, in a very real sense, the most absolute and constant family I had ever known.

I lay on my bed with a yellow legal pad and pencil, playing with my finances. Hieronymous jumped to his accustomed place on the pillow next to my head and swished his tail back and forth amongst my calculations, nuzzling my cheek for attention and giving my ear a sandpapery lick.

"Don't give me a hard time," I told him in a gruff undertone, but he went on nuzzling, purring now. Hieronymous was another question I couldn't answer.

The weeks passed slowly, but they passed. The weather, imperceptibly, began to warm. Life at school recovered bit by bit from the trauma of Larry Hayes's death. Curious legends began to spring up about him the way such legends seem always to appear in the wake of untimely or accidental demises.

I began talking to David and Suki about a new friend I was making, my first real friend in three years at Marcus Leader. He was new at school and his name was Philip Keller. He lived with his divorced father, who was a prosperous insurance company executive in Hinsdale. They were quite well off. Sometimes I went to Phil's house after my job at school to collaborate with him on homework. His father always had a chauffeured Cadillac pick us up. I first met Phil because we both did after-school maintenance work —despite being rich, he never acted spoiled. I always called David and Suki from Phil's house and let them know where I was and what I was doing. David and Suki were pleased that at last I had made a friend.

Phil had been an easy friend to make because he didn't exist. He and his Cadillac-owning father in Hinsdale were both products of my fertile invention. I called David and Suki from school or various phone booths on Rush Street and told them what a fine time I was having and could I please stay at Phil's for dinner?

One night in late April Phil invited me to sleep over.

"The car will drive us both to school in the morning," I explained reasonably over the phone, "and I left the bike there, anyway. Okay?" I could hear them consulting on the other end of the line.

"Okay, George, but in the future Suki and I would appreciate a little advance notice on something like this. It's putting us in a spot to ask us when you're already in Hinsdale."

"I know—it just came up; I didn't plan it. I'll be sure and ask first next time."

"All right, then."

I hung up and spent a dreary, stiff-necked night in an

all-night movie theatre on Clark Street. The place reeked of hundred-year-old popcorn, cheap stale liquor and the same kind of urine. I wasn't the only person using the balcony as a hotel either, and as if all the preceding were not bad enough, the damned film never stopped playing. To this day I can tell you more than I'd care to about *The Bridges at Toko-Ri*.

But it was worth it. I had established the sleepover precedent, and though I would have to endure three other similarly unpleasant nights in the same revolting place, David and Suki were now mildly accustomed to the idea that I went to Phil's house and spent the night once in a while.

"Why don't you ever invite him over here?" Suki asked. "They're always putting you up, George. I think it's only polite that you reciprocate. We have plenty of room. Besides, I'd like to meet your friend."

"Okay, I'll ask him."

Phil accepted for the following weekend, but unfortunately had to cancel at the last moment. His father, who was away much of the time on business, had telephoned from Omaha to say that he would be home over the weekend and looked forward to spending the time with his son.

"He hardly ever gets to see his dad," I explained. Phil was very sorry, I added, trying not to show my own disappointment as I had been so looking forward to playing host and having him meet David and Suki.

"Another time soon," Suki comforted me.

I turned my attention to ships. I reasoned that a larger ship would suit my purposes better than a smaller vessel for the simple reason that it would provide me with more places of concealment. Gathering information on the subject was surprisingly easy. Not only did the public library offer several up-to-date volumes, but the various travel agencies and Chicago branches of various steamship companies located in and around the Loop all combined to render me something of an expert on the subject. I was surprised and delighted to learn, for example, that each ocean liner had several brochures printed about it, free to the public. These brochures not only contained color photographs of the accommodations, but many informative statistics and detailed architectural plans of the cabin and deck configurations. The prospective passenger could actually locate each and every cabin on a given ship and see in advance (like the floorplans of concert auditoriums at the box office when you purchase theatre tickets) exactly where he would be located.

It soon became apparent to me that my likeliest bet was a choice between the two largest passenger ships afloat, Cunard's RMS *Queen Elizabeth* and RMS *Queen Mary*. While the gross tonnage of the old *Ile de France,* on which I had originally sailed to Europe, was forty-two thousand tons (roughly the size of the famed *Titanic*), the average tonnage of these two leviathans was a whopping eighty-two thousand, with the *Mary* a few pounds less than the *Elizabeth*. While the *Ile de France* offered some seven hundred feet of hull for me to play hide-and-seek with the authorities in, the Mary offered 1,018, which, as I saw it, practically doubled my chances of going undetected. The *Elizabeth* was even longer, at 1,032 feet. As the *Mary*'s brochure proudly proclaimed, her hull (if you stood the ship on end, an admittedly unlikely occurrence or feat) would stand twelve feet taller than the Eiffel Tower. For me, who knew a thing or two about that particular engineering triumph, that seemed plenty big enough to conceal a fourteen-year-old.

The *Mary*, like her sister, had endless public rooms, bars, sports facilities, ad nauseam, which stayed open twenty-four hours a day—also a help, since I was not quite certain where I was to lay my head for the five days I would consume crossing the Atlantic. The *Mary*'s forward funnel alone was seventy feet six inches high and wide enough to accommodate "three locomotives abreast," an unlikely place for them, I supposed, but again an encouraging omen for the prospective contraband traveler. (David and Suki had taken me to see the film of *Guys and Dolls,* and I had visions of my voyage as something not unlike Nathan Detroit's floating crap game—the difference being that this crap game really would be floating.)

The *Mary* had a final feature that clinched it in my mind as my best choice. She sailed at 5:15 P.M. on Monday, the fifth of June. This was crucial to my plans because I was obliged to leave Chicago on the *20th Century* no later than Friday, June second. The reason for this was that Marcus Leader's school term would let out for the summer vacation the following week, and if I was to spend a casual weekend at Phil Keller's house, the weekend of the second was the last chance I would get. The *20th Century* left La Salle Street Station at six in the evening and would arrive at Grand Central sometime in the forenoon of Saturday the third. That would leave me roughly forty-eight hours to solve the most difficult part of this aspect of the journey—namely, figuring out how to board the *Mary*, which would dock at Pier 12 from Southampton on Sunday. If, by chance, I had not resolved the tricky question and missed the sailing, I would get a crack at the *Elizabeth* the following Friday. It was not a prospect I particularly relished, for it would mean surviving in New York for the better part of a week and spending some of my precious funds to do so, but on the other hand the *Elizabeth* was my safety net—and here one may easily discern a difference between me and the Flying Berninis.

I destroyed all the travel material I had accumulated with the exception of all documents relating to the *Mary*. (I could pick up plans of the *Elizabeth*, should I turn out to need them, at the Cunard offices in New York at 1 Broadway and still have five days in which to absorb them.)

I concentrated on the *Mary*'s drawings, staying up late and using a flashlight under the blankets to pore over her myriad intricacies from stem to stern. One hundred and nineteen feet at the beam. Tourist class in the bow, cabin astern (over the props), and first class comfortably amidships. Thirty-five hundred aboard, passengers and crew included: a veritable small town afloat. Twenty-five hundred portholes, if I was interested (I wasn't); twelve elevator banks (I was).

My mind, which could not, apparently, grasp the simplest principles of an algebraic equation or recite a Latin conjugation, had no difficulty whatever remembering where the tourist-class purser's office was located or where the officers' wardroom was. The anchors weighed eighteen tons each (or the equivalent of nine automobiles). Of more importance, there were twelve decks from the sports deck down through H-Deck, which was below the waterline. I knew where the first-class squash court was (sun deck, amidships), the dispensaries, surgery, the nondenominational chapel, the swimming pools, the automobile hold, deck-chair storage area (ditto Ping-Pong paddles), the mailroom and wireless office, as well as the ship's printing press, where the daily editions of the *Mary*'s newspaper, *The Ocean Times,* were run off. I knew where they kept the ice cream and where the butter—all three tons of it—was. I knew which parts of the ship were off limits to passengers and at which points each class was separated from the one above and below it in price range. I even knew that the crow's nest was electrically heated, which—there was no telling—might come in handy.

I ate, drank, worked and slept with the *Queen Mary*'s interminable layout, its Byzantine nooks and crannies. In my sleep I even saw those plans in my dreams.

The only thing I did not know—and I confess it worried me—was how to board her without a ticket. I glossed over this detail again and again, preferring instead to immerse myself in the daily routine of the typical passenger. I tried to decide whether I wanted to take my meals at first or second sitting. I soon perceived that second sitting was much to be preferred, as it allowed the late reveler an extra hour's sleep before breakfast. Since, however, I would not be dining formally at all, the decision was academic.

My only other concern, aside from this inconvenient business of boarding, was the disposition of my belongings, specifically the conspicuous rucksack. I knew quite well that I could not walk around with it on my back the whole time, but it was maddeningly impossible to tell from the ship's plans alone where the thing would be safely concealed from the crew's intermittent rounds of inspection, cleaning and so forth. At times I worked myself into a panic over this issue, but ever and anon another voice would remind me that the thing was bigger than the Eiffel Tower. My rucksack, the voice went on, was small enough to ride on my back. Surely with this discrepancy in size there would be someplace to cache it.

Little did I dream where that place would turn out to be.

It was mid-May suddenly. The preparations I could make at this time were drawing to a close. In my school locker I slowly assembled my traveling gear, including several of the new "wash and wear" items lately preferred by the experienced traveler. I left my bathroom gear at home, but purchased a Gillette safety razor, blades and shaving soap, for I had recently begun to show signs of stubble. (This phenomenon was accompanied by odd uncertain squeaks in my voice as it worked itself into a lower register, but no item for sale that I knew of could do anything to hasten or retard this disagreeable vocal quirk.)

Perhaps as a consequence of these and other inescapable portents, I decided to buy some prophylactics. Strictly speaking, this was a financial expenditure that I could ill afford, and yet I determined on it on the theory that where I was going, anything might happen. The world was wide and some of the women in it might not be as discriminating (or inexperienced) as the females in the ninth grade at Marcus Leader. In fact, the frankly interested glances of Gena were now occasionally to be found in the eyes of some of the other girls, ones who didn't have braces or hair under their arms. I thought it wiser to be safe than sorry and proceeded to a drugstore on Division Street.

The scene in which the virginal young man purchases his first package of prophylactics has been burlesqued to death in story and film. I have no wish to indulge it here, but I did have my own distinctive style, and as I haven't come across it repeated elsewhere, I will say that my idea of appearing casual was to raise my voice in squeaky candor rather than hushing it up. I felt it would appear more routine if I placed my order in a strong, firm, confident tone instead of in a conspiratorial whisper. The result was that several persons at the other end of the counter who might otherwise have had no interest in the transaction became inevitably involved with every detail as I priced and compared several brands. I settled on a twelve-pack of Ramses, unable to decide if I was being optimistic or the reverse. I took them home, burning a hole in my pocket with anxiety, and in the privacy of my closet, illumined by a flashlight held (symbolically?) between my knees, I examined my purchase. So far as I could make out, they resembled nothing so much as the beige-colored balloons I had been given by the barber as a child as a bribe or reward for having successfully endured the agonies of a haircut. The only difference appeared to be in the fact that on his beige rubber balloons, the barber had his name and the name of his shop printed in red lettering.

I felt I was ready.

Eleven

A Hairsbreadth Escape

On May fifteenth, 1956, an event took place that very nearly wrecked all my plans. I was thrown so entirely into confusion by its unexpectedness that all was very nearly lost in the wake of it.

I got an A. It was for an English paper, which was logical, for though I spoke it funnily enough, it was nonetheless the only subject for which I demonstrated any interest or ability, Herman or Waldo notwithstanding. Nevertheless, I had never got an A before, in English or anything else, and its arrival came as a profound shock. I had written an appreciation of the narrative style employed in a novel called *Grasslands* by Arthur Neuburger. If the paper had captured my interest as I worked on it, I had been largely unconscious of the fact, so lost was I between the Scylla of my omnipresent misery and the Charybdis of my machinations to escape that misery. I had worked freely and rapidly on what was just another in a series of interminable homework assignments. The fact that there was no such book as *Grasslands* by Arthur Neuburger—the author's name was a compound of two of my classmates, Artie Herzog and Bob Neuburger—seemed scarcely to figure in the disaster at all. (All I had thought while inventing it was that it would be easier to critique a novel if you could make up its plot and style to suit your evaluation at the same time.)

"A. Good work, George," my teacher had written. "A cogent, well–thought-out, well-developed piece. First class. Watch spelling."

Who needed this? It wasn't, as one might quickly divine, the mere fact of the A itself, nor the friendly accompanying comment, so unforeseen that it hit me between the eyes like a well-aimed bolt from the blue. It was the possibilities raised by the event that so confused me. If I had got this A, might I not get others? In the words of the old song, Could This Be the Start of Something Big? Were there more A's where this one came from? Spectres of future A's loomed enticingly before me, stretching to infinity, and with them a home, friends, acceptance at Harvard, a lovely girl friend to end my Saturday nights of anguished aloneness in my room, where I was surrounded by nothing more friendly than my cat and some plastic model boats. Later, after Harvard, I would go to medical school or law school and get married and have children and live the dream everybody wished me to live but that, up until now, until the advent of the A, I had been so clearly unsuited for and so unlikely to achieve.

Though part of these extrapolations may be humorously exaggerated in these pages, something very like them did take place in my mind at the time, and the dilemma posed by the A was a very real one for me. If nothing else, the A seemed very tangible and had the effect of rendering all my schemes much less so. Suddenly my escape appeared not only improbable but perverse. Why was I, a healthy, not to say athletic (don't forget intelligent, as of my A!) white male child of fourteen who had the good fortune to find myself growing up in the midst of an affluent America—then undisputedly the most powerful and secure nation in the world —why was I preparing—elaborately, desperately preparing —to abandon the secure and comfortable state that I was lucky enough to occupy and exchange the placid world of Dwight D. Eisenhower for an adventure whose outcome I could not guess? Moreover, successful or not, I knew that in the long run it would not add up to the cushy rewards that awaited me if I remained where I was and played by the rules. If I was to be caught, I knew in advance the results would be catastrophic. David had clearly implied as much the last time. And if I got away, where was I going and how could I hope to live? Or find Fritz, if he wasn't where I had left him?

As I said, it wasn't just the A. A girl named Margot Lindstrom passed me in the hall a day or so before I got my paper back with its red printed thunderbolt and casually asked if I was planning to attend the junior high closing-night prom on Thursday, June seventh.

Margot Lindstrom was one of those haughty, mindless, heartless girls who went to the Casino Club on Friday afternoons with little white gloves and studied deportment. She and her crowd of ninnies were at the center of the group from which I was excluded and in which, consequently, I longed to play a part. I knew better than to suppose that Margot's question was an idle one, though I was too stupefied by it to answer. She stopped, looked at me for a moment, smiled deliberately at my confusion and flounced on.

I tried, even then, to tell myself they had merely cooked up some cruel practical joke to play on me if I went to the dance (it was common knowledge that I couldn't dance), but something in my blood told me I knew better. That girl had become interested in me and that was all there was to it.

And now this wretched A. The A and Margot Lindstrom. This was reality. My plans were self-destructive foolishness.

Where was Fritz?

In the midst of the miasma of rationalizations that were clouding my vision and choking off the air of my newly acquired independence, the question jerked me abruptly back to my real reality. Dreams of grandeur that had begun to swirl about me in dizzying patterns squealed to a sudden and reassuring standstill. In the deathly quiet that ensued in my brain, I repeated the question: Where was Fritz? Was it important to find him or not?

The spreading stain in Larry Hayes's pants.

I sat in my algebra class and, setting aside several sheets of clean paper for false starts, I wrote:

Dear David and Suki:

I have gone away where you will not be able to find me. Please do not try. I am fine and I intend to stay that way, but I do not like going to school. I do not think it is for me. I was not happy in Chicago. *This is not your fault.* You are *both great* and I will always remember your kindness to me. Please take care of *Mouse.* Maybe someday I will see him again. You two. I hope so. Stay well and take care.

Love George.

PS: Please pardon spelling.

I wrote and rewrote several versions of this sorry note and was pleased with none of them, but got tired of copying and recopying thoughts that I couldn't seem to express to my own satisfaction. My hand trembled each time I got to the part about Hieronymous and my resolve trembled with it, but I held my tongue between my teeth and pressed the pen more firmly than before to the paper. Finally, as though tired of rereading an exam I was due to hand in, even though I had time left before the clock ran out, I folded the final draft carefully and took it home with me. In the privacy of my room, I sealed the letter in an envelope, which I addressed to David and Suki Harris on Dearborn. There were as yet no ZIP codes. I borrowed a stamp from the roll on Suki's desk.

The letter I took back to school and gave to a boy named Stanley Abrams, who had an egg-shaped head. He was as ostracized as I, though for different reasons: Stanley's idea of a good time was to sit in a large chair, munching an apple, and read the dictionary. In order to break him of this and other antisocial habits, his parents were sending him to a dude ranch in Pinedale, Wyoming. I asked Stanley to mail the letter from Wyoming. He said he would.

"You're sure, now. You're not going to forget about it or lose it, will you? It's important."

He looked at it, then up at me.

"What is it?"

"A joke. A bet," I corrected myself. "I win twenty-five dollars from my aunt and uncle if I can get that letter to arrive with a Wyoming postmark. You mail it when you get there and I'll send you back five bucks for your trouble when I get paid. Here's my IOU for five dollars," I added, thrusting it at him. "Now give me your address out there so I can mail you the money."

My preparations and thoroughness impressed him and he gave me the address, asking no further questions.

"You know I won't get up there until June ninth," he felt bound to point out as I started off.

"That's just fine."

Around the corner I crumpled his address and threw it away.

On Thursday, the first of June, I made stops at American Airlines, TWA, United and Delta. In each office I thickened my French accent and made myself as conspicuous as possible. In each office I investigated the price of a one-way ticket from Chicago to Los Angeles. At each office I feigned dismay on being quoted the price.

"That much? Isn't there half-fare for kids or something?"

I practically cried each time I received a head shake.

Just to be on the safe side, I performed a similar ritual at the Greyhound Bus depot. Their one-way ticket to Los Angeles was so much less than by air that it astonished me. It was harder to do, but even had it been fifty cents I would have reacted with bitter consternation before the ticket window. They would all remember me, I was certain.

Thursday night I asked myself for the thousandth time if I had done everything that wanted doing. I checked my list of equipment and precautions to guide me in case I forgot, but found nothing I had omitted. Still I fretted. Great criminals (and I now felt more like a criminal with each passing hour), it was often said, were tripped up by trifles: For want of a nail the battle was lost, and so forth. There were things I knew I didn't know—in New York, on the *Queen Mary,* in Europe, certainly—but I had reached the point where, so far as I could determine, all conceivable preparations intended by me had been carried out.

I sat on the edge of my bed and looked for the last time at the cozy security of my little room on Dearborn Street. I stroked Hieronymous, who sat beside me, as I let my eyes wander about the place. There were books I had accumulated through school and personal interest, the latter outnumbering the former. There were comic books in stacks tumbling out of bottom bookshelves. There was my portable phonograph and my carefully cared-for collection of records, the long-playing unbreakable kind. There were my many boat models. Assembling these boats had saved my sanity for months at a time as I lost myself happily in the difficulties they presented—difficulties that could be solved. Now, though they sat about my room and gathered dust, I regarded them with gratitude and affection. Sometimes in this life all we need is a form of distraction, however mundane or eccentric, that takes our minds off things. When we put aside what we call our hobbies, we have given our souls a little breathing space and we are ready once more to face life and to do battle with it if need be.

I looked around my comforting room. I knew where I would be tomorrow night if all went as I intended, but what about the night after that? And the one after that? It was almost certain that this would be the last night of simple security and fresh sheets I would know for a long time to come. I had the dreary image of myself huddled somewhere against a drenching downpour.

I climbed into bed with Hieronymous and turned out the light. In the darkness and stillness of the house I could barely catch the sound of David and Suki's voices as they made their preparations for bed. I could not distinguish words, but I recognized their tones and the varying degrees of animation that accompanied them—David's low and sort of humming, Suki's high and jerky.

Soon the voices stopped and all was still except for the regular contented breathing of Hieronymous purring into my ear for the last time. I listened to him and scrunched my eyes closed against the tears I felt forming beneath the lids. Boys are taught to spurn such indulgences. Besides, I had seen people cry occasionally and I always thought they looked ridiculous. I couldn't bear the thought of making myself look that foolish, even if there was no one but the cat to see. Crying, to me, was something shameful and vaguely unhousebroken, like peeing in your pants. I had iron selfcontrol. As I planned never to pee in my pants, so I would never stain my cheeks with anything so grotesque as tears.

And I never wondered where my stomachaches came from.

I felt I would never go to sleep. I wondered why I felt compelled to give all this up, just as it seemed likely to become bearable.

The next thing I knew, my alarm was rousing me for school and Suki was calling up to me from the kitchen, reminding me to pack a toothbrush, for I was spending the weekend at Phil Keller's after school.

I came downstairs with my rucksack after holding Hieronymous in my arms for several minutes, quite smothering him with sniffly kisses. He found the attention pleasant, but otherwise they conveyed nothing to him. Perhaps it was just as well. He responded with a few rough licks.

"You're running late, George."

At breakfast with Suki and David, I sat as I always did, eating the English muffins Suki toasted for me and drinking my coffee.

"What have you and Phil got planned for the weekend?" David asked, getting up and throwing on his coat.

"I don't know. Nothing special, I guess. Just fooling around. We may go down and see what's doing at Stevenson headquarters."

"Well, take it easy. See you Sunday night, and make sure if there's homework to be done, you've got it done. I don't want you up all night again, cramming for Monday morning's assignments."

"I promise."

He patted me on the head lightly, kissed his wife, mumbling something about the evening and left for work.

Shortly thereafter I made to follow suit.

"Hey, don't I get a kiss before you go all the way to Hinsdale for the weekend? I'm gonna miss you, Georgie-Porgie."

I kissed her. It was all I could do to keep it a casual, regular kiss and not fling my arms about her neck and hug her to death. I did neither of these things. I biked to school, concentrating as I seldom needed to on such trivial matters as the flow of traffic.

At school I went to my locker and assembled the rest of my travel gear, which I had stashed there bit by bit, day by day. The rest of the time I functioned as in a dream, watching the hands of various clocks as they inched their way towards three.

As I left school—without a backwards glance—I bumped into Mr. Barlett, one of my erstwhile gym instructors, who remarked that I had forgotten my bicycle. I made some excuse that I cannot now remember. I walked to State Street and caught the bus. My pack was cumbersome and slightly unusual; the day had not arrived when every student around the world (especially in summer) sported such ingenious contrivances. It wasn't much of a journey, those twenty minutes to the La Salle Street Station, but it was the beginning of *my* journey, and my heart pounded with every step I took, with every revolution of the bus's wheels that carried me away from the path from which, in a literal as well as figurative sense, I was not supposed to stray.

La Salle Street Station at three–forty-five was beginning to jam with Friday commuters hurrying for their trains and evening martinis. I opened my rucksack in the midst of the hubbub and withdrew my train ticket. I had confirmed my reservation over the phone a week before, and there was no difficulty finding my assigned seat in the coach section. To get there, you walked down a red carpet, immaculately clean, that said 20TH CENTURY LTD in gold letters. You walked past the brilliant silver Pullman sleepers and dining car, where the stewards were already setting the spanking white tablecloths with dinner cutlery.

My seat faced the window and I looked out at the dark platform, watching people hurrying to find their places, bellowing after redcaps, calling for children. In the window I could observe my own troubled reflection as well. I half-expected to see the searching face of a policeman or, less plausible but more frightening, those of David and Suki, come to drag me off the train and take me home. I wondered if that wasn't somewhere my innermost wish.

Had I left any incriminating evidence behind? I could not

think of any. If only the damned train would start moving, that might lend all of my months-long preparations the touch of reality they still lacked. As it was, I yet had a choice. If I wanted to, I knew I had only to step off onto the platform, leave the station and go home. I could invent easily some plausible excuse for the cancellation of my weekend— a fight with Phil, whom I would never see again—and all would be as it was. I made no move. The train began to fill up. A large, fat man with ruddy cheeks and perspiration coming through his thin white short-sleeve shirt wheezed into the seat next to mine and ignored me. This dashed a hope I had entertained that all the seats might not be taken and that I could lie down part of the way to New York.

" 'BOARD!"

Suddenly I heard shouts, the clang of bells off somewhere, and with a gigantic, reluctant-seeming heave, our engine bestirred itself, and the *20th Century Limited* and I began our lumbering dash for New York. And the wide, wide world.

CHAPTER

Twelve

Of Departures, Arrivals & Computers

I was on the train again. Perhaps (as usual) I had never really got off, only made another of those lengthy stops I kept mistaking for Reality.

I was on the train again, leaving behind a world again (as usual), but this time there was a difference. This time *I* had taken the train, a very real train; the train had not simply (and as usual) taken me. As the miles clicked and clattered away behind us, as we spun a pair of shining rails in our wake like a giant silkworm spewing out twin streams of steel silk, I felt energy and confidence reenter my body like a transfusion. Until the actual moment of our departure, I had been growing psychically weaker by the second. In another five minutes I might have bolted, fled or slipped backwards into my deadly past, which waited to consume me in its gaping, irresistible maw.

But now, with every turn of the wheels that separated me from Chicago, I felt my strength returning.

"School out already?"

I turned, startled, from my hypnotized stare at the twilight Indiana countryside. I had been addressed by the sweating man, who spoke in a high, thin voice.

"Mine is."

He said, "Humph," or something like it, and added something else to the effect that in his day, school had gone through June. I saw little to say by way of reply to this. Presently he altered his gambit.

"Going all the way to the City?" By which he meant New York.

"Yes."

"Ever been to New York before?"

I hesitated. "No."

"And your folks sent you off there by your lonesome?"

"I'm going to see my friend."

"Ah. Best friend, eh."

Why not? "Yes."

He was about to pose another question when the sandwich-and-drink man entered the car with his singsong litany of beverages and food. He spoke his patter the way I had ended speaking mine on the Eiffel Tower: so none could understand a word. I wished I had the money to visit the fancy dining car for many reasons. It would be grand fun; I knew you wrote out your own order with a pencil and gave it to the waiter instead of telling him what you wanted. It would also deliver me from the unwelcome questions of my traveling companion. And the food would undoubtedly be delicious. Part of the train's incomparable reputation rested on its famed cuisine, as I well knew.

There were, however, equally pressing—if not better—reasons for avoiding the dining car. In the first place, I did not have the money to squander on such extravagances. In the second, a fourteen-year-old seen indulging them by himself would attract more notice than might be good for me. I could afford the notice less than I could the meal, if it came to that. Lastly, being of a suspicious turn of mind, I did not see abandoning my rucksack to the inquisitiveness of my fat friend. As I could not see dragging it with me to the dining car either, that settled the matter and obliged me to remain where I was.

Staying put, however, I was unable to prevent my seatmate from buying me a sandwich and Coca-Cola, though I protested I had money with me for the purpose.

"Put it away," he insisted, pushing back my proffered bill with an airy paw. "My treat."

I accepted reluctantly, for though I needed to eat and grudged any nonessential expenditure, an intuition made me resist the idea of being in the stranger's debt. I perceived it as too intimate a gesture on such short acquaintance.

"My name's Ben," he said, unwrapping his sandwich and opening a can of Piels beer with his own church key. "Ben Moran."

"My name is Larry Hayes," I told him, shaking a damp, flabby hand. I gave him the name on pure impulse. I had the idea Larry wouldn't be needing it where he was; he would live again through me; he would escape his fate through me. I would escape for him as well as for myself.

"I'm a salesman," Ben Moran went on, giving his bulging briefcase a nudge with one of his large black shoes. "Did you see *Death of a Salesman*?"

"I don't think so."

"You'd know if you had," he assured me glumly. "Pile

of crap, mainly—well, some of it's true, I guess. Anyway, I'm not exactly that kind of salesman. Ever hear of CCC?"

"No."

"Continental Computer Company?"

"Oh, I think so; maybe." I hadn't.

"Doesn't matter," Ben responded with a shrug and a bite of his sandwich. He went on talking with his mouth full. "Lots of folks never heard of us, but they will. Everybody will, sooner or later. You ever watch *People Are Funny*?"

"We don't have a TV." Which was true, for a change.

His eyes widened at this and he stopped chewing briefly.

"You don't?" He took a swig of his beer. "Well you will. Everybody will, sooner or later. Sooner is my guess. Anyway, on *People Are Funny* Art Linkletter uses a computer—a Univac. Ever heard of that?" He dared me not to have heard of Univac.

"I've heard of it."

"Well, he uses it to help match up people, you know, to date and maybe get married. You follow?"

"Not exactly."

"Simple." He took another bite of his rapidly vanishing sandwich. "Univac is an information storer and matcher-upper of information. You fill out Linkletter's questionnaire: What kind of girl do you want to marry? Blonde or brunette? Tall or short? What religion do you like? What kind of music do you like? How big should her pussy be—everything you can think of, right? And a million other guys fill out the same stuff with their specifications. With me?"

I nodded to show that I was with him, but I was shocked by his casual use of a term I had only heard employed by boys in the locker room at school, none of whom could use it without a giggle. There was something of the locker room about Ben Moran, I was beginning to realize, and it wasn't simply his sweat.

"Meantime, a million broads are doing the same thing with their preferences, just like the guys. Now they feed all this shit into the Univac and the Univac sorts everybody out and matches up all the people who are perfect for each other, who like all the same things. What do you think of that, huh?"

"Neat," I admitted, impressed if disbelieving. There was something not quite believable about anything Ben Moran said, including, it now occurred to me, his name.

Look who's talking.

"But suppose . . ." I trailed off, for I suddenly understood that every time I asked a question, this disagreeable man would answer it. Too late.

"Suppose what? Go on."

I had no choice. "Maybe I'm mixed up by what you said, but if I got it right, the computer goes along on the idea that these people know what they want. But maybe they don't. What if they don't know what they want? What if a person says he wants a blonde lady, but for some reason he doesn't even know about—in his unconscious mind or something—what he really wants is a brunette?" Ben Moran started to reply, but I, enjoying challenging him and reveling in all my lately discovered intelligence, pressed on. "And there's another problem. You said that the Univac matches up people who like the same things, but maybe if people like all the same things, it gets boring after a while. How can you tell if liking the same things makes people happy or unhappy?" I thought of David and Suki as I said this. "Maybe they shouldn't like all the same things because that makes them more interested—in each other. If they don't."

He looked at me, his face darkening as I spoke, perspiration streaming angrily down his brow.

"What are you, a comedian?"

"It's just an idea. I've never been married," I added, hoping to make him laugh. It was a vain hope. He continued to stare at me with an angry expression. When he spoke, it was as if I hadn't said a word.

"Univac's only the tip of the iceberg, Larry." He laid a chubby hand on my knee and looked me in the eye in such a way that I found myself unable to look elsewhere, though I wished to, badly. "You can't imagine what's coming," he rhapsodized. "Univac's already obsolete. In ten years people will laugh at a computer the size of a room. Computers will be the size of this"—and he made a fist of the hand that had lately rested on my knee and held it under my nose—"maybe smaller. Computers will do everything. *Everything.* It's all binary. They teach you about the binary system?" He meant at school.

"Is it to do with arithmetic? I'm not too good at that stuff."

Either that wasn't sufficient to deter him, or else he saw and rejoiced in the possibility of paying me back for my destruction of the Univac's marriage program. He plowed on with an explanation of the binary system (which, as I had feared, had to do with numbers), prefacing his remarks by assuring me the thing was so simple anyone could "get it." I endured his tiresome and seemingly eternal ramblings on the subject, having no alternative. Unfortunately he did not know how to march a straight course in getting from point

A to point B. He was continually taking detours, going off on tangents, sometimes irrelevant examples and unrelated anecdotes about his career in the computer business, whose introduction in the midst of his purported explanation of the binary system—its cause and cure—mystified me totally.

And he kept tapping my knee. These taps were made ostensibly to emphasize a point here and there, but I did not like them any more than I liked his affected voice. (I don't know what he thought of mine because he never alluded to it, for which I was grateful.)

By and by, night fell, and I excused myself to visit the bathroom when he made the mistake of interrupting his monologue long enough to tilt the beer can all the way back in a vain attempt to coax another drop or two from it.

When I returned, I busily unpacked a paperback edition of *The Caine Mutiny,* which I had bought at the station before boarding.

"I think I'll read a bit now."

"Suit yourself."

I tried to concentrate on the volume—I had already seen the film—but was uncomfortably aware that he was watching me.

"You like girls?"

"What?"

"I said, do you have a girl friend?"

The question was none of his business, but I did not know how to say so. I was pretty much used to the idea that when a grown-up demanded information of you, you answered. (Unless you happened to be in Latin class at the time.)

"Not exactly. That is, not yet."

I stared hard at the page before me until the tiny printing swam before my eyes. From the corner of my vision I knew him to be still watching me. Abruptly he shifted his attention and, with a sigh or grunt, bent forward and busied himself with the contents of his briefcase. Again, from the corner of my vision, I was able to discern that it contained clothing as well as papers.

The train barreled through the night. I grew sleepy, and the novel, which had finally succeeded in commanding my attention, was put away. We had made a stop, I thought, but I had been so absorbed in the tale of Captain Queeg that I wasn't sure.

Ben Moran was asleep next to me, his fleshy mouth hanging open and indelicate snores emanating from his twitching, bulbous nostrils. All at once I was exhausted. The tensions connected with my ambivalent departure from Chicago, the preparations, the hesitations, the queasy reaction I had had to Ben Moran while he was awake—these things had all combined to stretch me to my limits. Now, as all the overhead aisle lights were extinguished, I felt myself overcome with stuporous fatigue. Normally unable to sleep in anything but a horizontal posture, I tucked the green sweater I had brought against the window and, using it as a pillow, lay my head against it and drifted off.

I had no idea how long I had been asleep when I became aware of an odd sensation that slowly and at intervals penetrated my unconscious. Something was leaning on me and something was stroking the inside of my thigh. I opened my eyes uncertainly and looked about in the dark without moving my head. Ben Moran had pressed his huge frame against me, apparently in slumber. But the slumber was only apparent, for as I looked down in the darkness, I became aware of Ben's flabby hand making slow investigative progress towards my crotch.

"Hey."

The hand stopped. I tried to sit up but Ben's weight was now pressed actively against mine and his bulk was immovable. I made a brushing motion with my hand, unwilling to make sustained contact with his, but wanting it off my leg as I would wish to free myself from a repellent insect. Ben's voice appeared wetly in my ear in response to this gesture.

"Take it easy. I'm not going to hurt you."

"Cut it out," I said, raising my voice. His hand stayed where it was, daring me. "Cut it out," I repeated, still louder. This frightened him. He withdrew his hand from my leg, his lips from my ear and his crushing weight from off my shoulder. I heard or felt no more of him, but I did not dare go back to sleep. I stayed awake, or strove to, straining my eyes at the darkness beyond the window, my back and neck aching with fear. Every now and again my mind would compulsively replay the incident and I could not suppress a shudder.

When day broke and the other passengers awakened, so did Ben Moran. He avoided looking at me; indeed, he never said another word to me for the rest of the trip.

Only with light and everyone else awake did I allow myself to sleep, and even then it was not easy. Every so often my eyes would pop open to find the train hurtling through the spectacular scenery of the Hudson River Valley.

The sandwich man made a reappearance, offering the poor-man's breakfast. Ben Moran was off performing his ablutions; I didn't think he would be interested in paying yet again for a meal of mine, so I parted with a quarter in return for coffee and a doughnut. When Ben returned, looking no better than when he had lumbered off, I squeezed past him before he resumed his seat and attended to my own needs. I felt grubby and smelly from a night of sitting up and sweating with anxiety. I changed shirts in the bathroom, giving myself a sponge bath from the sink taps between shirts. I brushed my teeth and wished I had another cup of coffee.

When I returned to my seat, I tried returning to *The Caine Mutiny* as well, but my thoughts began irresistibly addressing themselves to my imminent arrival. I was unable to concentrate. Bit by bit, by subtle and hardly perceptible degrees, the countryside was invaded by reaching fingers of the city and the dirty fingernails of civilization. They began to blotch the greenery. Where there had been only fields, a barn and silo here and there and the mighty Hudson itself rolling majestic and undisturbed towards the sea, now cars and signs started to dot the landscape. Then more cars, more signs, more houses, housing projects of red brick, skeins of electric power lines and the smokestacks of factories and utility companies. The very air changed and turned grey as we charged through Tarrytown. Suddenly we were gliding through the slums of The Bronx and northern Manhattan, dismal and hopeless-looking even in the broad morning light. Somewhere, behind one of those million windows, lived Madelaine. My heart skipped a beat as I thought of her, and for the first time it was borne in upon me that I was not merely entering New York as a mere stage in my journey—a stepping-stone to Europe, as it were: I was returning to the place of my birth and to all the memories I had ignored for so many years.

We plunged into a tunnel at Park Avenue and Ninety-eighth Street, leaving the slums and the daylight behind. In the sudden darkness my reflection rematerialized in the window before me like a poltergeist. What was I feeling about this return—to say nothing of the more prosaic problems of food and shelter that confronted me, as well as the nagging question of my getting aboard the *Queen Mary* by sailing time the day after tomorrow? As usual with me, it was hard to know—my thoughts and feelings existed on so many contradictory levels that it was difficult to say which emotion predominated. I was like a man fiddling ineffectually with the tuner of a radio, trying to dial his favorite station, the one that aired the news program he most trusted. My brain received a lot of static being broadcast by my heart. Occasionally this static was interrupted by whispers or blasts from different quarters, stations that went in or out, attempting to make themselves audible. One station was optimistic, full of promise regarding the future, both immediate and far-reaching. They were playing Baroque trumpet music, and sunlight winked and glinted on the brass. I felt good, brave and confident. But just as quickly the station's signal weakened, and suddenly I found myself listening in that tunnel to another wavelength on which they were playing Tchaikovsky's "Pathétique," and it sent melancholy, fatalistic shivers up and down my spine.

I was still monkeying around with the dial on the tuner (figuratively located around my left nipple, I suppose) when the train slowed down, squealing in protest, and crawled dismally through the maze of switches underneath the sky-scrapers of Park Avenue and finally wheezed to a halt beside a platform very like the one we had left in Chicago. With a whoosh of air brakes and more squealing, the first leg of my journey came to its end. I was obliged to turn off the tuner and take action, which was a relief since there is no antidote for doubt like action. I hitched the rucksack onto my back and searched carefully for any belongings (or evidence) left behind. Finding none, I quitted the train without bidding farewell to Ben Moran. He didn't seem too broken up about it, and for my part I hoped I would not meet him or anyone like him again on my trip. (I retain, to this day, an everlasting distrust of computers.)

As I trudged up the inclined platform towards the station proper (that rucksack was heavy!), I had another hot flash: plainclothes detectives, waiting to wave their badges at me by the gate. A little knot of men would attend my coming, flip open their wallets and hustle me out to La Guardia with sirens screaming. From there I would be unceremoniously returned to Chicago by the first plane (handcuffed, the way they transported prisoners?), where David and Suki would be waiting with— I didn't know what, but I knew it wouldn't be open arms. Not from David, anyway, if only because of the hurt I had again caused Suki.

As it happened, there was no one standing at the gate, waiting for me or anyone else. We were all too busy pushing our way into the station, flowing in one fluid mass. I found myself in the huge green-ceilinged main vault of Grand Central. (It was and remains a spectacular room, though they have since wrecked the exterior of the building by plunking

the Pan Am monstrosity behind it. We call this progress.)
I stood for some moments in the middle of the room, gazing
up at the faint astrological murals on the green ceiling with
rapt wonder. I turned my attention then to the walls of the
place and delighted in the huge Kodak blowup of the all-
American family at play. There were lockers for a dime, and
I squeezed the rucksack into one of them and carefully
pocketed the key. There seemed no point in lugging my grey
bundle around town until I knew where and when it would
be needed.

I left the building and emerged a little before eleven A.M.
on Lexington Avenue. I had no specific plan in mind, but I
began to walk, and my feet took me unerringly up to Fifty-
seventh Street. People, like ants, scurried about their business.
Jackhammers thundered. Doors opened and closed; freight
elevators emerged from beneath the sidewalks, bells ringing.
Cabbies sat on their car horns. Why did I seem to remember
the place in winter, with snow on the ground and Santas at
every corner, ringing bells for the Salvation Army?

As though in a trance I turned west on Fifty-seventh
Street and kept walking. I did not know if I was trying to
sort out my new impressions, compare them with my old
memories or what. I noticed WALK–DONT WALK streetlight
signs (minus the apostrophe in the word *Don't*) that hadn't
been there when I left.

In less than thirty minutes, all told, I was standing across
the street from my old building, 49 West Fifty-seventh, and
worrying about crying. I felt like Rip Van Winkle. The
Automat was still there, thank the Lord, but Liggett's had
disappeared. Where were the chocolate malteds of yester-
year?

All at once my eye was caught by an oddly familiar figure. It belonged to someone about my age who emerged from the old apartment building, bouncing a basketball with becoming dexterity and intensity as he turned the corner on Sixth Avenue and headed for the park.

Thirteen

Shooting Baskets

It was Jake Jablow. I am not sure how I knew it was Jake, but there was not a doubt in my mind, even though I had not lain eyes on him since I was five. How strange and yet appropriate that he still lived in the same place. If I had stayed where I was—if my parents hadn't died (a lot of *if*'s here)—I might be going to the park with him. It *was* Jake, all right. He had the same tight curly hair and there was that distinctive loping walk and preoccupied air that were his and his alone.

Almost before I knew it, I was following him. I didn't know what I intended, but I had not made a conscious decision since leaving Grand Central and I saw no reason to start now. I was a prisoner of my spontaneous actions.

He bounced the basketball expertly down sidewalks and through snarled traffic, past the Rumpelmayer's outdoor café —just opening for summer—and on into the park by the bird sanctuary. He was taller than I and probably played junior varsity ball for his school. It was almost noon of a Saturday and he was on the way to practice—what could be more natural?—though whether alone or with teammates, I could not tell. Something in his manner led me to suspect the former.

I trailed him all the way to the basket hoops in the mall, which was not difficult, as he never looked backwards or even up from the ball. Other kids were practicing foul shots, lay-ups and hooks, but Jake was clearly alone, for no one acknowledged his arrival. He found a free basket—the netting had long since rotted away—and began with a few lay-ups. He was not bad, but he appeared slightly distracted, as though the exercise bored him.

It seemed as good a time as any; he was the only best friend I'd ever had.

"Hey."

He waited to retrieve the rebound, then turned to see who called. His eyes were the same startling icy blue, his skin still milky pale. He frowned at me, perplexed.

"Yeah?"

"Take a good look. It's a voice from the past."

He stepped forward, wondering and scratching the back of his head in a characteristic gesture. Expressions succeeded one another across his face like shadows, and his eyes widened.

"George?"

"You just won a box of Rinso Blue."

"George." He broke into a radiant, disbelieving grin and came closer, staring at me with increasing amusement and conviction. "George!"

"Jake!"

"GEORGE!"

"JAKE!"

There was a good deal of terrific back-pounding, which stopped as abruptly as it had begun.

"What the hell are you doing here? Where'd you come from?"

"It's a long, long story."

"And how come you're talking like that?"

"It's the only way I *can* talk, dammit. That's another long story. Let me shoot a few with you." I held out my hands.

Without saying a word, he flipped me the ball. It wasn't my sport, but I enjoyed fooling with it from time to time. And at the moment, shooting baskets gave me time to think, as well as involving both of us in a ritual automatically understood by all boys of our age and place and time.

Between shots I told Jake where I had been for the last nine years. Occasionally he punctuated my tale with whistles, *Gee whiz*'s and later still with *Jesus Christ*'s, and still later with *No shit*'s. Sometimes he was so involved with my story that he forgot to play. I would remind him and he would shoot without concentrating. But when I got to the part about my leaving Chicago, nothing could persuade him to continue.

"Dammit, George. You show up after nine years, talking like Louis Jourdan, and want to shoot baskets. Let's sit down someplace. This is fucking amazing." His use of the word was entirely casual. I told myself this must be New York.

We found a bench by the bike path and I finished the story, or rather brought it up to date to the place where Jake and I sat together on a park bench.

"You really think you're going to find him?" Jake wondered, after remaining silent for some moments when I was done. I shrugged and squinted at the sky. I couldn't answer that one.

"Hell, I may not even get to Europe. I've got to go over to the pier and figure out a way to get on the *Queen Mary*."

"Getting on's nothing," Jake responded, spinning the basketball on an index finger. "I just meant if he's not where you left him and the post office doesn't have any forwarding address for your letters, how will you—"

"*Hold it.*" I grabbed the ball away from him. "What do you mean, getting on is nothing? Getting on has been keeping me up nights for three months."

"You got fifty cents?" I nodded. "Then it's nothing. You're on. Every sailing day loads of people go aboard. You pay fifty cents and get to see your friends off with champagne and stuff. Or you just get to run around the ship and have a good time. I went with my class at school last year. It was a gas. We almost lost one kid—couldn't find him in time to get ashore before they pulled out. He showed up at the last minute, though—fake-out. Too bad," he added as an afterthought.

I could scarcely believe my ears. The pounding in my temples was so intense it was hard to catch what he was saying. All I knew was that I had been obsessing about this until it gave me my famous headaches, and now my friend —my very best and only friend—was telling me it was a snap.

"Are you sure about this? What ship did you visit? Maybe it isn't every company that does it."

"Yeah, they do," he assured me. "They all do. There's always bon voyage parties. Besides, it's good publicity—makes all the visitors wish they were going, too. The money goes to the Seaman's Benevolent Fund or some crap."

I was standing now, shaking, unable to believe it was this simple. A thought crossed my mind before I could shout for joy.

"What if you're carrying something—like a rucksack?"

He didn't even hesitate, but jumped up as well, getting excited and entering enthusiastically into the spirit of the thing.

"No problem! Just stick a bunch of flowers out of it and they'll think it's some kind of going-away present. People bring the dumbest things. Maybe paste a cabin number on it somewhere so it'll look more—I don't know—*authentic*."

I started dancing a spontaneous hornpipe on the bike path.

"Hey, you want them to cart you away?" For some moments I simply couldn't stop leaping about, out of control. When I ran out of breath, I stood there heaving.

"I don't know what to say. You just saved my life here. You're a genius."

"Tell it to the Walden School." But he was pleased, pleased as I was, and pleased as I was to be together. In a strange way that I have experienced with no one before or since, it was as though no time had passed at all. Nine years might have been as many minutes for all the difference it made. We simply took up exactly where we had left off. He filled me in on his life, which in some eerie ways bore an uncanny resemblance to my own, particularly as regarding school. He despised Walden with the same surly antipathy I reserved for the Marcus Leader Institution for the Hypocritically Inane. He insisted Walden was worse. "You want 'progressive'? I'll give you 'progressive,'" he sneered. "Walden is so fucking 'progressive,' they want you to call the teachers by their first names. Can you believe that?" he demanded triumphantly. "Putting themselves on an equal footing with you and me? Some nerve. Christ, I'm tempted to go with you."

"You've done it before," I reminded him. He grinned broadly at the recollection.

"So I have, so I have."

We got hungry about then and strolled to the cafeteria by the zoo. I looked around and told Jake about feeling like Rip Van Winkle.

"You sound like him," he remarked helpfully, but I heard no malice in his observation; only honest, friendly amusement.

"You hear about Madelaine?" he asked as we stood in line with our trays. My heart hit me in the stomach.

"What about her?"

He grinned. "She and Petey got married about three years ago. My pop and me went to Harlem for the wedding—we were the only white people there." He blew air soundlessly out of puffed cheeks. "They're an odd match in a way. Madelaine has a college degree and all, and Petey's—well, you know, just Petey."

"Where are they?"

"Martha's Vineyard. They work for this publishing tycoon from Random House or one of those places. This guy's got a house on the Vineyard; Petey sort of runs the place and Madelaine takes care of the children. I hardly see them anymore."

"Sounds great for them, though." And I meant it.

"I think they're all right." We carried our food to an outdoor table and Jake continued to talk between mouthfuls, rocking back and forth on the hind legs of his chair as he spoke.

"Did you hear about my dad?"

"Jake, how would I hear about him?"

"Figure of speech. Anyway, he's married, too, as a matter of fact. You know what they say—third time lucky."

"And is it?"

He shrugged and knocked himself gently on the forehead. "So far. It's only a little over three years. She's not so bad, speaking from the peanut gallery. They went out for a long time before, so I guess they both knew what they were doing. She paints. She makes babies. She talks on the phone a lot."

"Babies?"

"Well, only one. I have a half-sister named Melissa. She's just learning to talk, so I occupy a lot of time teaching her to cuss, trying to prepare her for life, if you get my drift. Only trouble is, her attention span's so short and her memory's so bad, I have to start from scratch every day. Believe me, it's been hell. But," he added, smiling, "I am comforted by the thought that what I am doing will help to make this world a better place, and I believe that with dedication, with firmness and, above all, with persistence the day will come when Melissa won't be able to open her mouth without being banned in Boston."

"A noble task," I agreed.

"Goddamn hero is what I am."

"No question."

We were silent for a time after this, packing in the food.

"I can't believe you're here," Jake resumed abruptly, letting his chair fall forward with a thud. "I can't believe you actually planned your whole getaway for months in advance. Going to different banks to buy traveler's checks— Gloriosky"—he shook his head in admiration—"it's like *Rififi*."

"Let's just hope it works. If I'm caught my goose is cooked, and it's going to turn into *20,000 Years in Sing Sing*." I looked around again automatically. "I keep expecting someone here to recognize me. In a way I'm glad Madelaine's in Martha's Vineyard. I was really thinking about looking her up, and that probably wouldn't have been a good idea."

"No worse than Smell-O-Vision," he concurred. "I'll give you their address and you can drop them a line when you feel like it. Hey, where are you hiding out until Monday?"

"I hadn't really thought about it, to tell you the truth. I don't want to blow any money if I can help it. I don't want to check into the Y in case they're on the alert for me." I surveyed the park. "If it's warm enough, maybe I'll just stay here on a bench and get cleaned up in a men's room somewhere in the morning."

"Are you kidding? You want to wake up alive?"

"Is it dangerous?"

"Dangerous? No more than Hiroshima. Who writes your stuff, George? Look, you have to stay with me." I started to protest, but he cut me off. "If you think my old man's going to recognize you, you're nuts. You don't even talk like you're from here. Besides, he goes and plays golf Sundays in Westchester, and tonight they're both headed for some fancy-schmancy charity bash. You can help teach Melissa some French cuss words. I want her to broaden her horizons with a cosmopolitan education."

"I don't know. It's an awful chance. If he remembers me, I'm done for. Besides, what are you going to tell him?"

"We'll think of something," he countered cheerfully. "How about vou're trying to find Livingstone?"

"I could be Captain Spaulding," I offered, brightening. I really wanted to stay with Jake, not only because it would be comfortable, but because I was having such a great if unreal time.

"You *are* fucking Captain Spaulding. Just trust me. He'll never figure it out in a million years. Where's your gear? Grand Central? Come on, let's get it."

We trooped back to the station, retrieved the rucksack and returned with it to Jake's apartment. No one else was home except the baby and her inscrutable Oriental babysitter, whom Jake introduced as Lu.

"Lu," he said, bowing, "I'd like you to meet my friend, Captain Spaulding." I bowed. Lu bowed gravely in turn, then shuffled off without a word.

"Chatty," I allowed.

"Her Italian's perfect," Jake informed me. "She'll talk up a storm if you only say *Buenos días*. This way." He led me to his room, which was decorated almost exclusively with huge Rand McNally maps Scotch-taped to the walls. "I like maps," he explained a little apologetically. I said I could see that.

"Where are your folks?" I demanded, trying to stay cool. "The suspense is killing me."

"Keep your shirt on. On Saturday afternoon Sheilah takes him gallery-hopping—walks his feet off, which is probably more exercise than he's ever had on a regular basis. Plus he meets all sorts of people he'd never come across in his work, which is good, 'cause he's a little shy. Here"—he hefted the rucksack—"let's hide the knapsack in the closet; that's the most suspicious thing. I'll tell them you're a friend from Walden—the French consul's son. Thicken up your accent. I'll tell them I invited you for the weekend so we could practice together in the park."

I liked the bit about being the consul's son, but had other reservations.

"Aren't I a little short for a basketball player?"

"I'm telling you, they'll never notice something like that," Jake answered from the recesses of the closet. "Sheilah—that's my stepmother—she's not quite of this world." He reappeared. "You'll understand what I mean when you meet her. I don't think she knows what basketball is. If I remind her that you were spending the weekend, she'll think she forgot all about it. She's that way. Very convenient sometimes."

"I can't wait to meet her. Do you let her roam around without dog tags?"

We spent the rest of the afternoon sitting on the floor, catching up on the details of our lives. I saw in Jake a kind of lone wolf separated from the pack by his mordant humor (which rang a bell), not quite sure of what he wanted but increasingly certain about the things he did not want. He told me to read *The Catcher in the Rye*. I told him to read *King of Paris*. He said he didn't know how to read.

"He wants me to be a lawyer like him," Jake said of his father. "Can you believe that? I'm not even fifteen and he's buried me alive someplace on Wall Street."

"He's a good guy though," I prompted. Not having had

a father, I did not care to be disillusioned about them. Besides, I remembered Mr. Jablow's kindness to me on the *Ile de France*.

"No question about it. He just needs to loosen up a little. As a matter of fact, Sheilah's been a big help in that department. She's so wacky, he doesn't know what to do about it sometimes. Lot of times he just slams the door to his study on her, but she doesn't exactly notice things like that, and by the time he's ready to come out, she's got something else lined up that interests him in spite of himself. Mainly I think he gets a kick out of her."

Sometime later we heard the front door being unlocked and the sound of voices. My stomach started turning back flips in my rib cage and I couldn't seem to catch my breath. Jake shot me a reassuring look and said, "It's open," in response to a knock. Mr. Jablow poked his head in.

"Everything under control?"

" 'We have seen the enemy and they is us,' " Jake replied, quoting Pogo. "Pop, this is Pierre du Bois from school. He's here for the weekend to shoot baskets."

"Hello, Pierre," said Mr. Jablow from the doorway. He didn't bat an eye. He looked pretty much the same, except that his hair was now completely white.

"Hi."

"What are you fellows up to?"

"Talking about law school."

Mr. Jablow's features brightened. "Very constructive."

"Hon," called a voice from the hall, "if you're going to lie down before we have to get dressed, now's the time. Hi, sweetie—" Mrs. Jablow had poked her head in the door beside her husband's as she said this. She was a smiling, attractive redhead with a figure on the voluptuous side, despite her loose-fitting white peasant blouse, calf-length wide-print skirt and sandals. I wondered if Jake had any unstepsonlike fantasies. I felt I would. Also, there was something disturbingly familiar about her. It took me some moments to realize it was her voice, which reminded me of someone, but I couldn't think of whom.

"Hi, Sheilah. Sheilah, this is Pierre from school I told you about? He's sleeping over and we're going to practice tomorrow?" He ended both statements with an upturned interrogatory inflection, but went on without waiting for an answer. "Pierre, I'd like you to meet my stepmother." Mrs. Jablow took me in with a vague but pleasant expression.

"Oh, yes. Nice to meet you, Pierre."

"Nice to meet you," I told her, wondering about her voice.

A few more pleasantries were exchanged and then the Jablows withdrew for a rest before their evening agenda.

"What'd I tell you?" Jake beamed at me when the door had closed. "Didn't I tell you not to worry? Didn't I say it'd be a cinch?"

"Doctor, what can I say?"

"Say you're sorry," Jake said. He did a great impersonation of Groucho Marx. I think he wished he was Groucho Marx. "You play gin, by any chance?"

"I prefer playing it to drinking it."

"Penny a point? Oh, I forgot, you're on an economy kick."

"I've got a better idea. You have any wood matches?" He nodded. "Let's play each match is a thousand bucks."

Jake liked this idea. He went to the kitchen and returned

with a big box of Diamond brand matches. We played until I owed him over four hundred thousand dollars, which Jake was already spending on fast cars, fast women, then slow cars, slow women and a chateau in the South Bronx.

Mr. and Mrs. Jablow looked in on us as they were ready to go out for the evening. Mr. Jablow was in a tuxedo and held a matching black homburg. Around his neck was draped a white silk scarf. Mrs. Jablow was transformed. In a low-cut silver evening gown, she looked like a redheaded version of Jane Russell. Her perfume wafted into Jake's room from the doorway. The scent of it startled me.

"Now, don't stay up watching television till all hours," she admonished. "And don't make so much noise you wake Melissa."

Suddenly it hit me. I thought I was going to cry out in surprise. Jake's stepmother was the woman who had been with Mr. Jablow in the cabin by moonlight on the *Ile de France*.

She started out, then stopped. "Lu will call you when dinner's ready. Be good and help her clean up afterwards." She started out again, then stopped again and, returning, looked at me. Wheels were turning. "Pierre." She tested the name. "Pierre, have we met before?" I thought I was going to faint.

"I don't think so." I tried to keep the adrenaline out of my tone, but I knew I was breathing in all the wrong places.

"Sheilah, get a move on; we're late," Mr. Jablow yelled from the front door. She blew a kiss to Jake, told me it was nice to meet again and with a shrug started out, calling to Mr. Jablow to "hold his horses."

"Are you okay?" Jake asked when she had gone.

I held my breath until I heard the elevator begin its descent and then let out a terrific sigh. "Yeah, I think so. For a moment I was afraid she remembered me."

"Don't be an ass. Remembered you from where?"

I did not choose to enlighten him, but the incident had startled me almost out of my hide. Could I really expect her not to recall our last meeting throughout the weekend? She had, after all, held her face two inches from mine, and her breasts had been . . . On the other hand it had been dark, and what light there was had been on her. I decided to chance it.

We spent a jolly evening eating and watching television— which, as David and Suki refused to purchase one, was very much a novelty for me. We saw Jackie Gleason in funny skits, and the June Taylor Dancers. When we tired of the television, around eleven, Jake woke up Melissa and we gave her some cuss lessons. As Jake had said, she was a poor study, cute little thing, and soon lost interest in our endeavors to corrupt her vocabulary in the cradle.

About midnight Jake decided he was hungry again and we repaired to the kitchen, where Jake went about making pancakes, which he assured me were a specialty of his. "You've never tasted pancakes like these," he prophesied. His culinary efforts were cavalier at best, and a good deal of pancake mix was somewhat recklessly blown about and allowed to settle like a fine mist over everything in the kitchen. Some syrup got spilled as well, but Jake was not disturbed by this.

"We'll let the dog lick it up."

"Where's the dog?"

"We don't have one."

The pancakes, as I was compelled to acknowledge, were indeed different from any I'd tasted. They gave me a kind of gassy feeling that persisted for the next hour or so, but the discomfort notwithstanding, I insisted on cleaning the kitchen.

"They don't give out merit badges around here for this sort of thing," he objected. "You'll only ruin a wonderful evening."

"I don't want your folks so mad with us that they kick me out before tomorrow night."

Jake allowed as how this was a point that ought to be considered and helped me sponge off all the dust-ridden counterwork. At some point during our exertions, Lu, the inscrutable baby-sitter, shuffled into the kitchen, regarded our handiwork with Oriental imperturbability and shuffled out again without comment.

"Think she'll tell?"

"Hardly. She doesn't like to speak—vow of silence, that sort of thing. Besides, she feels it's out of character to speak."

"How do you know?"

"She told me."

We were in bed when Jake's parents returned. It must have been close to three in the morning. We feigned sleep as they looked in on us. The idea of Mrs. Jablow, once again in a low-cut dress and provocative scent, facing me in bed in a darkened room was an eerie recreation of our first meeting.

"He's so familiar," I heard her mutter, closing the door.

We lay for a while in silence after her departure.

"Hey, Cisco?"

"Jes, Pancho."

"Are jou awake?"

"Jes."

"Have jou ever had a wo-mans?"

"Define 'had,'" said I, dropping my Mexican accent.

"You know."

"No. Not yet."

"Ever come close?"

"Yes and no."

"What does that mean?"

"It means no." More silence as we contemplated the fact that I hadn't come close.

"I did it with this girl in my school," Jake said after a time.

"Really?" I was up and on one elbow, staring across the darkened room at him.

"Yeah. Last year. One-shot deal. We were both terrified she'd get pregnant. It was kind of an experiment, only now she won't talk to me."

"What was it like?"

"Well, considering that I didn't know what the hell I was doing, it was the single greatest experience in my life."

"You can't have everything."

"True enough."

"Why were you so worried about getting her pregnant? Why not use a rubber?"

There was a pause in the darkness and a sigh.

"You're going to think this is dumb," Jake said finally, "but I just can't nerve myself to go into a drugstore and buy any. I just can't do it. Isn't that dumb?"

I thought about it, oddly reassured that Jake, who seemed so capable in every way, should acknowledge this simple incapacity.

"These things have a way of working themselves out," I suggested, smiling to myself.

The next thing I knew we were both asleep.

Fourteen

Sailing Day

I woke up and for a moment had no idea where I was. It took me a minute to stare over at Jake and recall the details of our rather surreal encounter. I checked my watch (a thirteenth-birthday present from Suki that gave me a twinge of guilt as I looked at it) and discovered the time to be six-ten in the morning. I couldn't go back to sleep. I was now struck quite forcibly by the precariousness of my position. If Mrs. Jablow suddenly had a lightbulb go off in her head, events would compel themselves like a chain reaction. (I was the first to come up with the Domino Theory.) The longer I lay passively in bed, the more wobbly my head felt on my shoulders. I considered masturbation as a way of calming myself down, but decided the sheets weren't familiar enough to take the liberty. I found myself fantasizing about Mrs. Jablow in bed. These were not romantic fantasies, prompted by my erotic encounter with her as a child aboard the *Ile de France:* In these fantasies Mrs. Jablow suddenly sat up, snapped her fingers with recognition and began throwing on her robe. The idea that she might even now be padding down the hall with a lot of embarrassing questions was more than I could bear. I woke up Jake.

"Whassamarer?"

"I've got to get out of here."

He looked at me, blinking, then sniffed. "Now?"

"Before they wake up."

He thought about this. "Okay."

We dressed quietly, grabbed the basketball and stole out of the apartment. The day that followed was an exhausting kaleidoscope of colors, events and impressions—through shooting baskets at seven in the morning in the deserted mall, eating breakfast at a grungy Nedick's in Times Square, to deciding to visit the Cloisters in Fort Tryon Park and hopping an empty bus to get there. I had never seen the Cloisters and could not imagine the place Jake described.

"Officially it's the uptown branch of the Metropolitan Museum," he explained, as we trundled up Fifth Avenue (which then ran two ways). "In fact, the Cloisters is a collection of European monasteries brought over piece by piece and linked together with period architecture. It's wild. You'd never know in a million years that you were in New York; you can't see any of the city from inside it. How does that grab you?"

It sounded loony enough to fit in with my general mood and in keeping with the dreamlike pattern of events that had unfolded since I had run into Jake.

It took us about forty minutes to get there, and we discovered the place didn't open its doors until noon. It certainly lived up to Jake's description, however—a huge, sprawling castle on the Hudson, completely made of stone blocks, with towers and battlements galore.

"There's a park over there," Jake pointed. "We can fool around till noon."

So we fooled around till noon. Jake couldn't understand the cause of my anxiety, and I, as it happened, could not bring myelf to explain it to him. We threw the basketball back and forth while trotting up and down the paved walkways of Fort Tryon Park and spoke instead of trivial matters —life, death and the Dodgers' move to Los Angeles.

"I lost all hope and faith in humanity when that happened," Jake admitted, staring with melancholy abstraction across at the Jersey Palisades as he spoke. "Life seemed pointless. I felt so bctrayed. Certainly New York seemed pointless, anyway. Shallow, without purpose."

I thought about asking him if he ever allowed himself to be serious. Instead I said gently, "Isn't it about time you went back to your cell now? I think it's almost feeding time."

The Cloisters were truly spectacular. We chased each other through the Unicorn Tapestries, called each other knave and varlet, fought duels on the windy staircases and poured boiling oil on our enemies from the parapets. We saw a pear tree nestled against a wall, trained to grow like a candelabrum. We used a perfectly modern men's room, and Jake allowed as how you'd almost think you were in America, its features wcre so convincing. He led me to his favorite item in the museum, a rosary bead the size of a giant walnut, inside whose two halves (joined by a tiny wood hinge) was carved the Crucifixion.

"I love to think of some old guy carving that out of his selfless devotion to God," Jake said, staring at it through the glass window. Sometimes it was hard to know when he was kidding.

Around three in the afternoon we returned to Central Park, now crowded with Sunday patrons who lined up for the carousel with their children, strolled through the zoo, mobbed the cafeteria and the rowboat lake and milled together at the Bethesda Fountain. Jake looked at me earnestly.

"Is anything beginning to come back? Anything at all?" He spoke with a thick German accent.

"I think so; it's hard to tell. Things come and go in the mists."

"That's the way it is with mists. *You must concentrate!*"

In fact, things *were* coming back—walks with Madelaine, the fat balloon man, pigeons flapping their wings about me as they jockeyed for position next to my supply of peanuts. Somewhere in the zoo was a cheetah with my name on it.

We exhausted ourselves. My trip—indeed, every aspect of my own existence—seemed curiously removed, as though it did not belong to me but rather to someone else—a person I had known intimately, but whose aims and concerns were none of mine. I was a visitor from Mars, to whom every sight and custom appeared strange and new. Life on earth appeared to consist of nothing more than wandering around Manhattan Island, swapping wisecracks with Jake, the first earthling of my acquaintance. It was only when I thought of my rucksack and its contents, stuffed in his closet on Fifty-seventh Street, that my stomach tightened and I came in contact again with my own corporeal self.

"Don't you have any homework on weekends?"

"Walden's very progressive about things like that," Jake explained reasonably. "On my last report card it said, 'Mathematics: cheerful.' "

"That's better than I ever did in math," I confessed wistfully.

Jake called his home to ascertain if Sheilah had gone to play golf with his father, which she sometimes did on Sundays to please him. He found her still home, nursing the remains of a hangover.

"Just called to check in and let you know everything's hunky-dory," he told her when she answered the phone.

It was too much to expect that the Jablows would be out again for dinner, and they weren't. On the contrary, we were taken for Chinese food and I had to endure the tension of sitting across from Sheilah throughout the entire meal, providing her with a perfect portrait and wondering if at any moment she would suddenly flash on the whole thing. Fortunately we were joined almost at once by another couple, Jablow's doctor and his wife. The grown-ups made conversation amongst themselves for most of the meal. Jake and I stayed silent and subdued. It was genially assumed that our tongue-tied silence was symptomatic (and typical) of surly adolescent reticence, and this notion was discussed over egg rolls and spareribs.

"You guys would rather be comparing notes on girls or something, wouldn't you, instead of sitting around with us old farts," the doctor supplied with a knowing twinkle. We smiled shyly, as we were expected to, and the laughter that greeted our response was thought to confirm the doctor's views. Thus reassured, the grown-ups went back to their own conversation, which consisted of speculations regarding Adlai Stevenson's second try, about which all were fatalistic.

"Stevenson's an egghead," Jake's father said with authority. "He was an egghead in '52 and he's still an egghead.

He'll always be an egghead and the country simply never will trust eggheads." No one seemed inclined to dispute this.

"What about tomorrow?" I asked, when Jake and I had returned to his room.

"Simple. We leave for school together. I go to school. You stash your bag again. I'll duck out around lunchtime— one o'clock—and meet you at Columbus Circle. From there we'll grab a farewell hot dog and I'll see you safely aboard."

"You're going to leave school for this? You don't have to; I can figure it out."

"I've left for far less serious reasons," he responded, throwing back the covers and climbing into his bed. "Christ, I'm beat. Anyway, it's not every day that you get a chance to throw a bon voyage party for a stowaway."

"I really appreciate the company," I admitted. "And I appreciate everything you've done for me. I don't really know how I'd have managed without you. I'd certainly have had to spend a lot of money."

"Probably would have had to sell your body to science," he grumbled, embarrassed by my effusion. When in doubt Jake retreated behind flip repartee. I wondered if and when I would ever be permitted to pass through his defenses and what I would find if I was.

Everything went off exactly as we intended. A few minutes after one, Jake joined me under the WINS Radio thermometer in Columbus Circle. He insisted on buying me lunch.

"Any special place you'd like," he offered, "so long as it's cheap. I'm not made of dimes, I'll have you know."

We went to the Automat—not the one on Fifty-seventh

Street, but another one just like it on Seventh Avenue. It was so much like the place of my memories, it even smelled the same as the enchanted domain of my childhood.

"Charlie sent me," I told the sandwich window.

"What does that mean?"

"I was never quite sure."

Over lunch a somber pall descended. Jake toasted me with a Coke.

"Well, good luck. You know I mean that."

"I know." I hesitated. "Can I ask you something?"

"About my sex life, my philosophy—anything—so long as it isn't personal."

"You think I'm doing the right thing?" I blurted. He looked at me but wouldn't take the bait. "We've been together for two days now," I rushed on, "and in all that time you've never said a thing about this."

"You want my blessing?" He made the sign of the cross with his spoon.

"I want your opinion," I lied.

He looked away from me and began playing with his ice cream, mushing it around in its dish.

"George," he said finally, still not looking at me, "I've no idea where you've been for the last nine years. No *real* idea. I don't know your uncle Fritz and I don't know what you feel about him. I'm no one to give advice. Christ, I go to a shrink twice a week, I'm so screwed up. 'Addled-essence,' you called it. Half the time I can't even tie my own shoe-laces. They say it's a phase, but it's hard to understand that when you're in the middle of it. You can't imagine it'll ever end. I can't, anyway, and personally I can't wait for when it does. I'm eager for midlife crisis just as a change of

pace. All I can say is this:"—now he raised his eyes to mine
—"At least you have a purpose. Whether it's a good purpose
or not, whether it's a real purpose or not, at least it drives
you. I'd give anything for a purpose. Except my jockstrap,"
he amended, self-conscious about the seriousness into which
he'd fallen.

At the time I was dissatisfied with his reply. Despite my
disclaimer, I had sought not his opinion but his permission.
Later, however, thinking it over, I realized that it had been
exceptional. When all was said and done, where real issues
were concerned, Jake was a scrupulously careful friend. His
reply may not have been what I wanted, but it was probably
what I needed: His throwing the ball back into my court
meant that my actions might not be validated by his approval, but he had provided a helpful way for me to look at
them.

"I guess it's about time," I said. "If I get on board fairly
early, I get to familiarize myself with the layout. Up to now
it's just a bunch of drawings."

"Let's not be too early," he cautioned. "You want to be
swallowed up and lost in the mob. You know what one
interior decorator said to the other? 'Let's synchronize our
swatches.' "

"What are swatches?"

"I can tell you've been spending time in Chicago."

We stopped at a florist and I bought a bunch of flowers
to stick in at the top of the rucksack.

"This'll never fool anyone," I objected, surveying it. "It
looks just like a rucksack with flowers sticking out."

"Wait till you see what it's like over there," Jake assured

me. "No one's going to notice it in the first place. Have I fucked up yet?"

He was right. It was a madhouse. It is completely different today than it was then. We live in the Age of Terrorism and there are no more bon voyage parties allowed, even on the only ocean liner left, the *QEII*. No visitors are allowed on board the ship, let alone those bringing packages of any description. But 1956 was an easier time for would-be stowaways.

"Look at that!" I exclaimed as we rounded a corner beneath the West Side Highway and the *Queen Mary* came into view, so huge it blotted out the sky. Quite simply, she was the biggest, most beautiful thing I had ever seen, and I fell in love with her at first sight. Her three huge funnels —Cunard red with black tops—swept grandly back from the loveliest, most delicate bridge any ocean liner ever had. (Later, seeing the *Elizabeth,* I was very disappointed: She had only two funnels, which gave her hull—actually longer than the *Mary*'s—a tubby look, and her bridge was nondescript, lacking the two flying wheelhouses that made the *Mary*'s so spectacular and unique.)

We pressed through the throng, paid our money and marched up the visitors' gangway in the midst of sailing-day chaos. As I set foot on board, I caught a brief glimpse of a tiny fissure between the gangway and the ship, below which I saw a bit of the murky Hudson, ten stories down. But it wasn't a mere glimpse of dirty water; it was the Rubicon.

"Didn't I tell you?" Jake whispered as we began our wanderings.

"My hat's off to you," I acknowledged. My heart was pounding wildly in my chest. I needed a men's room before anything else. On the plus side I knew exactly where the nearest one was located.

"This is going to be incredible," Jake commented enthusiastically as we reached the passenger bridge and were there confronted by the New York skyline, where muggy storm clouds had begun to gather. "Do you know how you're going to get off at Cherbourg?"

"According to everything I could learn, it shouldn't be a problem. They don't ask to see your ticket when you debark. The assumption is that you're legally there by that time. They want your passport, immigration and health cards and customs declaration. I've got the passport, my health cards are up-to-date and the customs and immigration cards are given out the night before they dock. I'll nab one of each and put down a cabin number with my name. By the time their tally shows too many people in that cabin I'll be long gone. That's the idea, anyway."

"Sounds good."

We walked over the ship like structural engineers. I was thrilled to find everything as my plans had indicated. I had them with me in the rucksack, just in case I needed them. The ship was so beautiful, it was hard to remember our business. Of her eighty-thousand-odd tons, almost thirty thousand consisted of the world's most beautiful wood. She was getting crowded, too. Every minute more passengers and visitors stepped aboard.

"Can I show you gents to your stateroom?" inquired a friendly steward in a white side-button tunic. He spoke with a strong cockney accent.

"I know where it is, thanks very much," I said automatically. "We're just looking around till my friend has to leave."

"Very good, sir." We walked away down one of the endless alleys on C-Deck that ran past hundreds of cabins. The ship was so long, these alleys actually dipped towards the center and rose slightly at each end.

"I've got to get rid of this damn rucksack. Everyone's going to try and show me to my stateroom."

"At the very least they're likely to remember it," Jake agreed. Wc walked to the next bank of elevators, took a ride up to the promenade deck and stepped outside to where piles of deck chairs were stacked atop one another like cordwood. Jake pointed to a space behind a pile.

"What about here? For the time being, anyway. By the time they pull these things down and set them up, you'll have located a bettcr place. This'll free you of it till you're at sca."

"Good idea. We can stand nearby to keep an eye on it. If the stew comes by I'll collect it fast and we'll move off with it."

Jake did several minutes on "Stew" as Groucho from *A Night at the Opera*. It was a relief to get the cumbersome rucksack off my back, where its wooden frame had been gouging my ribs. We moved a little ways off and watched the hustle and bustle below us reach its zenith. On the outside portion of the pier, well-wishers waved their arms and shouted to friends on board.

"This brings back weird memories," I noted, surveying the crepe-paper ribbons as they were flung over the side.

"I'll bet."

As if on cue, the ship's whistle exploded with a bellow that seemed to shake the very deck. I instinctively cringed. I had forgotten that part of my earlier crossing. It was some sort of omen, but whether for good or ill I could not tell. It rattled me.

"You okay?"

"Fine. It just took me by surprise. What a racket."

Before Jake could reply, the PA system came to life and informed all visitors that it was now time to go ashore, as the ship was making ready to sail.

"Well, this looks like it."

"I'll walk you down to the gangway."

"Better stay here and keep an eye on you know what. I'll find it all right."

"If you don't, history might repeat itself." He grinned.

"I'm tempted, let me tell you."

"Jake." I reached into my pocket. "There's something I want you to have."

"Now don't get mushy on me," he said nervously. "I don't want your old socks."

"I really mean it. They're family heirlooms—not very old, maybe, but precious—and I think you'll value them; for a time, anyway."

"Will you cut it—" He stopped when he saw the package of prophylactics. He was really stunned; it was worth it.

"For me?"

"For you, chum."

"Not your whole supply, I hope."

"Don't worry. Go on, take them." I thrust the package at him and he grabbed it in an impetuous motion.

"Six," he murmured, wondering. "My God, what will I

do with six? You've set me up for life! What I could do with six!" he thundered, turning his question into an emphatic declaration.

"Do it," I urged.

The PA system repeated its message: All visitors ashore. Jake pocketed the rubbers.

"I don't know when we'll be meeting each other again," I said.

"You'll turn up. Or I will. Like bad pennies. When are visiting days? Anyway, write if you get work."

"I will."

"And come back soon—I'll need some more of those things in a year or two, and you're my supplier."

"Get going."

"Yeah, yeah." He started off, came back, gave me a hard and fast self-conscious embrace and sped off, almost colliding with a middle-aged couple in his haste to get out of my sight.

I went to the rail and stood looking over the side. After a few minutes I caught sight of him on the outdoor end of the pier directly opposite me.

"Don't take any wooden nickels," he shouted across at me.

"I'm afraid we haven't been introduced," I shouted back. "What?"

"Never mind. I said NEVER MIND!"

The ship's whistle blew again. I could see the lines being thrown off the cast-iron cleats below. The hawsers were cranked in by windlasses, fore and aft.

It began to rain lightly. Most of the people on the pier took this as a signal to go home, but Jake was one of those who stood his ground. I sheltered myself under a lifeboat (capacity 125 persons) and remained as well.

The last I saw of him as the tugs pushed us out into the river was a sole tiny figure in a wet blue workshirt.

I was alone again.

※　　※　　※　　※

Fifteen

In Which the Fine Italian Hand
at the End of the Long Arm of Coincidence
Raises Its Ugly Head

The older I get, the more I find life resembles a Dickens novel. I refer in this comparison specifically to the issue of coincidence. When we first read Dickens—in our teens— we are struck by the gross implausibility of characters who meet each other, presumably by chance, in out-of-the-way places, at unlikely (but dramatically convenient) times. We scoff with youthful arrogance and confidence at the patent, creaky absurdity of these encounters. Could Mr. Jaggers really have had all those clients? we snort derisively. We jeer because we are not yet old enough to have discovered for ourselves that life is full of such improbable meetings and relations. The older we get, the more people we bump into. Walk down a street in Khartoum and you collide with your third-grade teacher; chat with your insurance broker and you discover he is your college girl friend's brother. It never fails.

The average personal world is filled with only three or four hundred friends and acquaintances. As we travel through our lives, the same four hundred (perhaps that's why someone called them *the* four hundred!) keep cropping up on streetcorners in different combinations. In a way, I suppose, it would be equally true to say that the older I get, the more I find a Dickens novel resembles life, which is no doubt what Mr. Dickens intended in the first place.

Why this literary digression? Why indeed.

The first two days at sea were a nerve-wracking time. I lived the kind of frantic existence a flea must endure, hopping maddeningly about, never allowed to rest in one place for very long. The only difference that I could detect between my modus operandi and a flea's was that, so far as I know, a flea's compulsive hopping does not drive him as crazy as my peripatetics were driving me. And a flea does not have to lug around a forty-pound rucksack wherever it hops.

I slept where and when I could, in deserted lounges in the wee hours. No place was empty for very long: Romance and alcoholism flourish at sea. There was always at least one drunk still drinking and garrulous wherever I wished to grab my forty winks. If it wasn't a drunk, then some inebriated couple would be putting the boozy make on each other, conversing in tones too loud to ignore. I was obliged to feign drunkenness on more than one occasion in order to render myself inconspicuous. It wasn't a foolproof device, for while passengers were not always aware of me, the bartenders kept their eyes open.

I could not go to the dining room—any dining room—as I had no seat assignment. (So much for second sitting!) I subsisted on the tiny cucumber sandwiches that were served gratis at tea time to the accompaniment of a weary string trio playing Strauss waltzes and sorry arrangements from current Broadway hits. These little sandwiches, and the crackers and peanuts that sometimes accompanied drinks, were my sole source of nourishment. When desperate, I would gnaw on some of the salami I had packed in the rucksack (courtesy of Delisi's), but I didn't dare eat too much for it was meant to last all five days. And I didn't dare serve it to myself in public, either, as it was bound to attract attention. I chewed on it at night, furtively, like a rat.

The rucksack was a nightmare. I couldn't move it about in the daytime lest the sight of it become familiar and excite curiosity, which might turn into suspicion. I finally found a place where it seemed relatively safe. In the back of the first-class cinema there was a pile of extra chairs stacked in case the film drew a sellout house. As the cinema was empty most of the time—except for the two daily screenings and an occasional lecture—the rucksack was likely to remain undisturbed and undetected amongst the chairs. However, I could never wander too far away from it and was always obliged to arrive first at every event, retrieve it before the houselights went down and keep it with me in the darkness until the film or whatever it was had ended. It was like being joined at the hip to a dead Siamese twin. And I hope never to see the film *Wee Geordie* again.

I spent a good deal of my time hanging about the tourist-class bar, which in any case was my favorite room on the ship. It remains for all intents and purposes my favorite room anywhere, but its dramatic location in the bow, under the passenger bridge, was responsible for a good deal of its appeal. Opposite the long, curving bar were perhaps thirty high rectangular windows that looked out upon the ship's

majestic prow as we plunged across the restless Atlantic.
The lounge quickly became the favored meeting place for
all the young people on board, not just the tourist-class
youth. (The *Mary,* like the *Ile de France,* seemed not to
care particularly which class you associated with, aside from
your cabin and your assigned restaurant.) All mingled in
that room with the easy familiarity that is engendered by
an ocean voyage. Class distinctions relating to ticket price
were overwhelmed by a wealth of other commonalities
relating to age and interests. Young men and girls my age
or older had guitars and banjos. They stayed up till all
hours, drinking, singing, shouting and romancing. I par-
took of these gatherings but stayed on the edge of them. I
wanted to blend in, to lose myself (and perhaps my problems) in their merry company, but I did not wish to draw
attention to myself or any of my distinguishing character-
istics—my accent, for example. I sang along in chorus but
I volunteered no verses. I laughed at the punchlines but I
contributed no jokes. (This was a great hardship.) The
group was, by and large, attractive, open, friendly and
animated. People sometimes didn't know each other's
names, but that did not prevent them from doing things
together. They played bingo as a team, bet the horses and
entered the fancy headdress competition. Most would probably never see each other after the voyage ended, but some
would stay in touch.

The *Mary* was a happy ship. One amusing reason I discovered for this is that the domestic crew was never sober.
Walking down one of the endless corridors late at night,
you might encounter a portly, red-faced cabin steward with

a big Cheshire-cat grin on his raffish features. The stewards had all been with Cunard, on one ship or another, for at least twenty years.

"Good evening, sir," this one might say, exaggerating the pronunciation of his words and bowing with excessive ceremony.

"Evening," you would respond.

"A lovely night out, in't then?" the steward would comment, though he hadn't been topside in days.

"Yes, indeed. Lovely." You found yourself slipping into his studied, leisurely rhythm.

"Anything I can get you, then?"

And he meant *anything*.

"No, thanks. It's past my bedtime and I think I'll be turning in."

"I'll be saying good night, then."

"Good night."

"Good—night, sir." Again the grave and formal bow. You walk on, and after a few steps, you catch the sound of a gurgle or a hiccup behind you.

The *Mary* knew she was the best. Her officers knew it; her crew knew it; they prided themselves on being the best. The bonhomie that all who sailed aboard her felt was not simulated: It was genuine and pervasive. As I am in a position to testify, even a stowaway could feel it. In fact, if I had to recommend a ship to stow away on, I'd say you couldn't go wrong choosing the *Mary*.

By the third day I had begun to become accustomed to my irregular regimen and had begun to feel some creeping security as well. I was chronically starved, but after some hesitation, decided I had sufficient strength (and daring) to enter the tourist-class Ping-Pong tournament. I played hard all afternoon and had worked my way up to the finals. I was halfway through winning my last game when it suddenly occurred to me that victory might bring me more attention that I could afford. I played a thin and thin-lipped youth of eighteen from Alabama who never smiled. (There were a great many southerners on board.) He was losing grimly fifteen to seven, when I reluctantly threw the match. His features broke into a wolfish grin when he won, twenty-one to seventeen.

There's no telling how pleasantly the rest of the crossing might have been, how uneventful, had it not been for the long and improbable arm of coincidence.

It was after eleven at night, shortly before everyone was due to reset his watches and clocks ahead one hour. The night was the warmest we had had. The rucksack was safe, locked in the darkened movie theatre. I had enjoyed the usual drinking and singing session in the tourist-class bar and left it still in progress, where it would no doubt continue for hours. It was the fine night that called to me and I decided to enjoy some of it. I let the elevator operator (they wore white gloves at all times) drop me off on Prom Deck and strolled beneath the stars. We were halfway across the ocean. Whatever problems I had were both behind me and before me by an equal distance. The stars above, not competing with the bright lights of any city below, shone with an overpowering, almost blinding brilliance. There were millions visible tonight.

I was ambling towards the stern of the ship on the port side, relaxing fully for the first time since boarding, when I became aware of a disturbance in the shadows to my left.

As I approached, I dimly perceived two figures engaged in a familiar amatory struggle. The man was in the act of forcing his attentions on the woman, and she was endeavoring to repulse them. At first I assumed this to be a ritual encounter in which, as Gertrude observed, the lady did protest too much. I supposed her resistance was in some part a formality to be got through, like washing one's hands before dinner—tiresome perhaps, but expected. As I drew nearer, however, I gradually became convinced that this was not the case. The woman was trying to cry out and the sounds of her scuffles and grunts to free herself sounded uncharacteristically urgent.

"Stop making such a fuss. Y'all know you like it," a deep southern voice tried to assure her, though I detected unpleasant exasperation in the tone.

"Please, stop—*please*" was the indistinct and muffled reply. "I'll scream—"

"You do that," the man laughed unsympathetically. I began to recognize him as my Ping-Pong partner of the afternoon. "There's no one to hear," he went on, breathless with his efforts to restrain her. It was my thin-lipped and wiry opponent, all right. I stepped closer and decided to take a hand in the proceedings, nervous as I was. I tried to think how to go about it, but the only words that came to mind, ludicrously enough, were speeches from films in which I had witnessed scenes not unlike this.

"You let her go." My voice sounded a little uncertain to me, a little squeaky, but it had the effect of jerking him around, his body blocking my view of the woman.

"Who's going to make me? Oh, it's you, peewee. Y'all can't even win at Ping-Pong. Beat it, tadpole."

It was a mistake on his part to call me peewee and tadpole, for though I had not yet reached my full height, I
was, as I have said, very strong and a trained athlete into
the bargain. My opponent was a head taller and looked
agile enough; on the other hand I didn't think he was entirely sober, which looked like good odds to me. As he returned his attentions to the woman, I leapt onto his back,
which he had disdainfully presented to me, and I slid a
forearm the size of a small ham under his chin, locking the
bone under his jaw. Using his shoulder as a fulcrum, I pried
his head back, and his body was forced to follow. He released
the woman, swung out of my grip and turned to face me.

"You're going to regret this, kid." He had seen the same
movies evidently. (I had not yet lived long enough to learn
that clichés are the way in which most people express
themselves.)

"I'm ready when you are." I tried to sound blasé, as I
wanted him angry and foolish. I waved him forward like
a traffic cop and he charged like a wounded rhino. If liquor
hadn't slowed his reflexes this mightn't have worked, but
as it was I had no difficulty sidestepping his rush and
bringing a knee into his chin as he went past. I heard his
teeth snap into each other with a pleasing click and he went
down with a sigh like flatulence. He lay on the deck, his
eyes open, considering things. After some moments, while
I stood anxiously over him, not quite sure what to expect
or what to do, he started to get up. I waited until he was
halfway to his feet and then threw all my weight behind a
punch to his gut. This time he did not get up.

My hand hurt like hell. One punch and I was out of

commission. (How different from those movies!) I stood sucking on my knuckles and stared down at my handiwork with no small sense of accomplishment and satisfaction. It pleased me to know that I could have taken him in Ping-Pong as well, if I had wished to. He might have been drunk, but he was taller and older than I—and he had had it coming. Breathing hard, not only from my exertions but from my excitement generally, I turned my attention to the woman. I had been vaguely aware of her making little noises throughout the scuffle. She was staring at me.

It was Delilah Kirstein.

"Dottie."

"George," she overlapped.

"What are you doing here?" we again spoke in unison. "You first," I instructed, my heart sinking into my shoes. For a moment she was unable to answer. Her recent near-rape, coupled with my unexpected rescue and totally unjustified presence, left her at a temporary loss for words. She gulped a few times, like a goldfish.

"I'm on my way to Perugia to study Italian," she said finally. She realized abruptly that part of her wide-skirted blue silk party dress was in disarray and hastily made a few adjustments. "It's part of a tour," she spoke with her head down, examining buttons at her cleavage. "We spend two weeks going to different cities, starting with Amsterdam, and then I get six weeks in Perugia." She looked up, satisfied with her repairs, and took a breath. "Now what about you? What in the world do you think you're doing?" Her tone as much as her words told me she knew I wasn't supposed to be here.

"Are you all right? Did he hurt you?" I was unable to take a step, forward or back, and stood opposite her like a cigar-store Indian.

"I'm fine, thanks to you." More movies. She came forward, walking around the inert form on the deck, not deigning to look at it. "I should have known better than to fall for his line about teaching me a little astronomy. God, I might as well have been in third grade." Now she stood quite close to me, illumined by a floodlight aimed down from the sun deck, as beautiful as ever, her intelligent features wearing a no-nonsense expression. "You haven't answered my question."

I looked at her, sighed and turned to stare out at the water, which was as black as the sky. I needed Dottie Kirstein right now like another hole in my head. How could I have forgotten that she was going to Perugia? Why didn't I check to see *how* she was going? Instead of addressing my present problem (what was I going to do, throw her over the side?), my brain was stuck in a rut of self-recrimination. I had been stupid after all, made the fatal mistake that all clever criminals did that ruined their best-laid plans.

"Well? Come on, George, what's going on here? There's a big hunt on for you back in Chicago. Everyone seems to think you're out west someplace." She moved behind me and addressed the back of my head.

"That's what they were supposed to think."

"Why? What are you doing? You better tell me, because whatever it is, I know too much already." She had her nerve.

"Didn't I just bail you out of a tricky situation?" I

whined, turning to face her. "Doesn't that count for something?" How is it she was always so much more grown-up, so much more self-possessed, that every time I spoke to her I felt like a fool. She placed a hand gently on my shoulder and looked at me with almost maternal condescension.

"George, you're being immature. Of course I'm grateful, but the one has nothing to do with the other. I don't want to—" She removed her hand as she concentrated on finding the right word. "I don't want to hurt you or judge you. And I didn't mean to threaten you just now. Only tell me what's going on."

I looked back at the dormant figure of the Ping-Ponger. He now appeared to be simply asleep. I looked at the ocean again, rushing by invisibly below us, and tried to make myself think. It was no use. My brain had simply stalled like a car engine. I couldn't start it. If it had been almost anyone else, I might have been able to deal with it, dreamt up some story, bluffed it through somehow. But not with Delilah Kirstein, the girl of my dreams, who always intimidated me when she appeared in the flesh.

"Let's go someplace away from *him,*" I suggested at length. "Away from everyone. If you insist, I'll tell you, but it's a long story."

She smiled suddenly. "It's bound to be better than what I've been learning about astronomy. Come on, cheer up. Things can't be that bad."

It was pointless to debate her on this issue. I led her to the first-class cinema and astonished her by letting us in with a cocktail swizzle stick as a picklock. It was totally dark inside.

"Why here?" she wanted to know as I led her, feeling the air before me with a waving arm, to the last row of seats. I pushed her down in one and sat next to her in the dark.

"We won't be disturbed, for one thing. For another, you can't see me; I can't see you. That may make this easier."

"What's so complicated? Were you in the wrong class or something? They're pretty loose about that, I've noticed."

"Dottie, I'm not in the wrong class. I'm not in any class. I'm a stowaway."

I heard a sharp intake of breath, which she tried to exhale quietly.

"A stowaway? George, I always knew you were crazy, but this is—"

"Shut up," I cut her off, louder than I intended to, as I got to my feet. "Please," I added, more gently. "This is really hard. For openers, I am not crazy."

"Sorry."

I tried to collect my thoughts. Outside of the theatre I could hear laughing voices. I wondered if Dottie tuned them in. It didn't matter.

"You don't know a thing about me," I began finally. "And you never have. Now you're about to learn more than you'd ever want to."

I told her the story of my life. I told her about my parents, about their death, my childhood in New York and about Madelaine. I told her about Fritz, about the Eiffel Tower, about the violinists and briefly about Olga. About sugar-cube crap games. I told her about the custody battle and my unwilling arrival in Chicago. I told her about the difficulties I had endured at school, of the horror of being unable to speak fluent English without sounding like a

freak and of my inability to enjoy Johnny Mathis. I told
her about dead baby Michael. And I told her the truth about
Larry Hayes, including the shit in his pants. I told her in
detail how I had planned and executed my escape. As I
spoke, my emotions got the upper hand of me more and
more. I was dangerously close to crying as I ran out of
steam.

"So you see," I blubbed defiantly, "this is what I want,
and I've worked pretty hard to get this far. I am going to
find my Uncle Fritz. I will find him. I am worried about
him. I will find him. I'm not stupid the way everyone at
school almost convinced me I was. I'm smart. I just sound
stupid. They couldn't stop me; you can't stop me," I
finished lamely, exhausted past caring. "But when this is
over and I find my uncle, I'll be a man, not just some spoiled
kid who calls his parents' cook the *schwartze* and learns a
little Hebrew for a dopey ceremony where his father spends
a lot of money on nothing."

There was such a long silence when I had finished that I
asked her if she was awake.

"I'm awake," she replied in a small, thoughtful voice. "I
didn't understand everything you said, but I don't think
you understand it all either. Anyway, I'm awake."

"Well, I'm not." I wiped my eyes with my sleeve. "I
haven't found a safe place to sleep since I got on this tub."

More silence.

"I know a place," she said softly. "Come on, I'll take you
there. Bring your bag," she added, remembering that I'd
said I kept it in the theatre. "You can get cleaned up there,
too."

Drained past thought, I obeyed.

She led me into cabin class, then down to her stateroom, which was on R-Deck.

"Are you sure this is all right?" I asked as she inserted the key in the lock.

"You'll see."

As it turned out, Dottie's cabin had four berths and a small bath unit that included a shower—one of the advantages of a cabin-class ticket. The place was empty. The only neat berth was Dottie's, one of the two lower bunks. The other three were properly made up but strewn about with all sorts of hastily thrown-off clothing.

"You'll be okay here until I figure out what to do with you," Dottie said, locking the door behind her. I looked around.

"Where are your roommates?"

"That's hard to say. They're a bit older than I am and they haven't been back here since we left New York."

"You're kidding." She sat on the edge of her berth and looked around as if seeing the place through my eyes.

"I'm perfectly serious. They come in at odd times of the afternoon to shower and change up for the next round of parties, but they've never slept here once. I've never seen one of them at breakfast either, which leaves me the table all to myself except for one couple in their seventies from Minneapolis. Sometimes one or two make it to lunch, but they're only there to get something for their hangovers and tell each other how loaded they got the night before."

"But doesn't your group have any, you know, chaperones?"

She smiled, in sole possession of the joke. "These *are* the chaperones."

"Jesus."

"The chaperones are a big hit with the junior officers, as near as I can gather. Nobody wants to fool around with me—I may look yummy but I'm under age. Except *him,*" she added, rolling her eyes upwards. She tried not to sound priggish, but finished by shooting me a little sideways glance of nervousness.

What did the boy who grew up in the whorehouses of Pigalle make of all this? I was intrigued by all she said and the fact that it was she who was saying it. I was baffled to find myself alone with her, in the middle of the Atlantic, of all places. But I was also tired and smelly and hungry and aware that she was considering my disposition. Until certain matters were settled, I could not relax, lower my guard or allow myself to be in any way distracted. I decided to tackle things one by one and began by changing the subject.

"Would it be all right if I used the shower?"

"I wish you would."

She stayed on the edge of her bed, absorbed in her own thoughts as I moved past her, dragging my rucksack. She appeared almost to have forgotten my presence or the pickle our discovery of each other had caused. I treated myself to twenty minutes of the hottest water I could stand. It felt so good I almost fell asleep on my feet. When I had done, I wrapped a towel around myself and threw open the door.

"It's all right," I called lightly. "I'm still here." She made no response. I took a step into the cabin. "Are *you* still here?"

She was sitting where I had left her as though she hadn't moved. At the sound of my voice, however, she looked up at me sharply, startled out of some sort of reverie.

"I'm still here. Don't stand in front of me like that," she added snappishly. "Get dressed. I've already seen all your muscles."

"Okay, okay. Take it easy."

I retreated and did as she ordered, trying to keep awake and at the same time figure out what was bothering her. I didn't dare fall asleep until I knew what she intended doing about me.

Come to think of it, what was Delilah Kirstein, Chicago's most desirable Jewish-American Princess and Queen of Marcus Leader Junior High, doing alone in a cabin-class stateroom with three "fast" older girls (who were tomcatting nonstop) on board the *Queen Mary*? I splashed cold water from the sink onto my face and slapped myself awake. My brain was beginning to function again at last, but it churned reluctantly, no longer in shock, but in tired protest. The more I considered Dottie Kirstein's being here in these circumstances, the less sense it made. Dottie Kirstein was always at the center of things, and here she was, alone and vulnerable—literally at sea—actually requiring rescue from some hillbilly lout who in real life would never have found himself alone with her in a million years. Why? What was she doing? Not running away, like me, though the idea flashed across my brain briefly. Anyway, what did she have to run away from? This was the girl who had everything.

But something was irregular here.

She was still sitting in the same spot. When she saw me this time, she made a conscious effort to rouse herself from her thoughts, whatever they were.

"Let's see," she said, with a coolly deliberate resumption

of energy and authority. Clearly she considered herself in command. I suppose she was. "Oh, yes, you look much better. A little thin at the moment, but you were always cute-looking." She said this last in an absent, offhand fashion, but the observation so shocked and pleased me that all I could do was gape. I had never been told by a woman that I was "cute," except by Suki, who was prejudiced and ineligible and therefore didn't count. I certainly never dreamed I would hear it from the lips of Dottie Kirstein. I never thought of her as actively seeing me in all the years she had ever chanced to look in my direction. I assumed she looked through me. Pleased as I was, however, I sensed her persistent melancholy and decided not to tempt fate with some vain and stupid rejoinder on the subject of my looks, her looks, anybody's looks. It was time to take care of my next need.

"You mind if I eat some salami?"

She smiled. "You have a salami?"

"I've been living on it for days. I brought it with me from Delisi's, which is one of the places I worked to make money for the trip. I knew I couldn't go into the dining room because I didn't have a seat assignment. Actually I'm pretty sick of the stuff, but it's done the job. I just hope this is the last salami I ever see." I pulled out the gnawed stub and started to unwrap it.

"Wait a minute." She stood up and pulled open the drawer of one of the night tables. "Here's the room-service menu. Let's order you a decent meal. It's free."

I looked at my watch. "Isn't it too late? Cabin room service closes at—"

"You've done your homework." She looked down, impressed. "It just happens that, like all men, my cabin steward happens to be in love with me, and if I ask him, he'll bring me anything I want."

I could believe that. Just as I could believe the calm, unironic assurance with which she claimed all men loved her. In a strange way it wasn't conceit, it was astonishing self-knowledge. She was perfect and she knew it. We rang for the steward and I ordered enough for three people—an open-faced steak sandwich, a Caesar salad for two and a *croque monsieur*. I got extra *pommes frites* and three Coca-Colas, which was all I ever drank in those days.

"You want any of this stuff?" I asked when the food arrived, hoping she wouldn't as I sat down on the floor with it. She shook her head.

"No, thanks. I'll just watch." She sat down on the floor opposite, modestly arranging the crinoline-supported skirts of her evening dress so that I was not afforded an inadvertent view of anything controversial. By and by she began nibbling on some of the fries.

"Don't eat so fast. You'll give yourself indigestion. *George*."

She was very bossy.

"Sorry."

I made a valiant effort to slow down that was so patently phony it made her laugh.

"All right, all right, go back to your way. Get sick. See if I care." I decided that her mood had improved sufficiently to ask her what she intended doing.

"Dottie."

Instantly, she stopped laughing and set down a French fry she'd been about to eat. "What."

God, but she was tense; too tense to press the question uppermost in my mind. I decided to steer clear of that subject for a while and deal with something else. At the very least, I needed to buy some time.

"I'm just curious: How come you're here like this? Alone. This isn't your—I don't know—it isn't your style."

She looked at me keenly for a moment, then became aware that something was wrong with a thumbnail. She studied it for a moment, then rose with the same decorousness and sat at the desk, continuing her examination of the broken nail under the lamplight there. She became so absorbed by the problem of the nail that I began to wonder if she had forgot my question. Or did she merely choose not to answer it? She was moody and arbitrary that way, as I'd begun to learn.

"I didn't have much choice," she startled me by replying without looking up. "I didn't want to spend the summer with my parents—we haven't been getting along lately— and if I went to camp again, Richard would be there, and I wanted to get away from him, too. I love everything Italian, so it seemed like a good idea to go there and study for a summer. I got accepted by this program and I'm sure everything'll be fine and dandy once the tour part is over. Once I get off this damn boat."

I took this as a reproach and my face fell, but her next words—still directed at the wounded thumbnail—raised my spirits. "If it hadn't been for you—in more ways than one —this part of the trip would have really gotten me down."

"I can see how much I've cheered you up," I said, turning my attention with a little belch to the *croque monsieur*.

"Don't be gross," she said in response to the belch. "The question is, What am I going to do about you?"

I didn't want her answering it at present. I didn't quite trust her moody tone. I needed more time to get a fix on all of this.

"Why didn't you want to be with Dick?" I asked, genuinely curious. Everyone called him Dick except Dottie, who persisted—somewhat affectedly, I thought—in calling him Richard. She looked over at me from her inspection of the damaged nail as if peering over the rims of invisible bifocals. She looked as if she were debating which topic to pursue. I held my breath.

"You know about as much of my life as I used to know about yours," she decided at last.

"Probably less."

"Probably. Stop looking at me like that." She reached for a bottle with a brush in it and started working on the nail. "Look what that creep did to me," she muttered.

"You were going to tell me your life story," I prompted. She didn't look up.

"You don't think I have one to tell, do you? I've seen you staring at me all these years like Rin Tin Tin, staring as if I were—I don't know—Marilyn Monroe or somebody, somebody without a care in the world, somebody who doesn't even have to go to the john. You're the only one with problems. I couldn't possibly have any. Why is that, do you suppose?" She favored me with her over-the-invisible-bifocals look again. "Because I'm so pretty? Is that it? Pretty people

don't have problems? Popular people don't have problems?"
The quiet, even tones, the very smallness of her voice as she
said these things, made me uncomfortable, as though she
had been screaming instead of almost whispering.

"Not the same problems, anyway," I hazarded. Her eyes
flashed and her face clouded over.

"Exactly the same problems! All people have the same
problems, George. How to live, how to eat, where to sleep,
what to do about their parents—or grown-ups, anyway—how
to be happy. You've got some crazy idea of me as this moon
goddess whose feet never touch the ground. And you think
of Richard as Mr. Perfect. Well, I'm not a moon goddess; I
go to the bathroom just like you, more or less, and Richard's
got so many problems it's a wonder he can get out of bed
in the morning and face the world."

She stopped talking to paint something from the bottle
onto her nail, which gave me the moment to reflect that she
was right—I did make these assumptions, and a good many
other like assumptions besides. I couldn't imagine anyone
with her looks, occupying her position at the center of
everything, being unhappy. It did, as she surmised, take an
effort of will to imagine her sitting on a toilet, having a
bowel movement. I don't know how I thought she would
get rid of the French fries she had consumed—immaculate
digestion, I suppose.

"Ever hear of schizophrenia?"

"I think so."

"Know what it is?"

"Uh, no."

"You're in good company, then. No one else does, either.

It's just a fancy word for crazy. When a person's crazy they say he's schizophrenic. It sounds more like they know what they're talking about."

"Oh."

"I have a brother who's—schizophrenic. They used to call it dementia praecox, but as far as I can tell, no matter what they call it, it still means you're crazy. He's sixteen. They keep him in a—place. Sometimes it seems like he's better and he comes home for a while. But it never lasts and he always has to go back."

"Was he always like that?" I heard what she was saying; I couldn't imagine it, though. I couldn't picture what it meant.

"As a matter of fact, he wasn't. When I was little he was my big brother and he took care of me." Her voice changed subtly as she spoke these words; it had been soft before in the sense that she spoke quietly. Now it also became tender and gentle. "I worshipped the ground he walked on; literally followed him everywhere. I didn't know he was walking around on eggshells and that one day they would crack."

I didn't know what to say. I sat there like a lump on the floor. I was tired, yes, but she had jolted me into an alertness of pity and terror.

"As for Richard," she went on, her voice regaining its accustomed timbre, "you seem to think we're made for each other, but the truth is that Richard doesn't know what he wants. He has no passions, including me, which is maybe what drew me to him. That and the fact that he wasn't a nebbish like the rest. But that doesn't mean he doesn't patronize me in private. He's very patronizing. He has nothing to lose. Everything comes too easily to him to be interesting. I have to work for my grades, but Richard just coasts in. It may make life easier in the short run, but it robs it of any meaning for him. He's bored, so bored he doesn't know what to do with himself. He's almost paralyzed with boredom. And in an odd way—" Here she slipped from the desk back to the floor across from me again. "In an odd way," she resumed, "he isn't learning anything. He just grabs hold of enough to pass his courses with flying colors, but he can't remember things and his knowledge has no—what's the word I want? Depth. Width. There's no *thickness* to his knowledge. Do you understand what I mean? Don't just nod. Do you really? I'm attracted to Richard because he's the best at Marcus Leader, the most sophisticated. He keeps me on my toes without half-trying. But at the same time there's very little real excitement, aside from the constant competition between us. He has no energy, no passion. He's never had to develop those things."

"There's plenty of other kids who—"

"Don't talk to me about 'kids,' George," she said earnestly. "I'm not interested in kids. I'm fourteen; most girls my age aren't even going out with boys their own age, so you can see how conservative I've been staying with Richard. If I thought there were any older boys as interesting, I'd let them take me out, but I know that school. I have about as much love for it as you do, with all its hypocrisies. I know that school, and Richard's the only interesting person in it." She looked over at me with a funny expression. "Don't give me 'kids.' Who cares about kids? I'm not even interested in boys. I'm interested in grown-ups. In being grown-up.

I'm interested in men—not just tall boys over eighteen. *Men*." She stopped, embarrassed by her own deadly-serious outpourings. They had been delivered with an intensity I found almost comic. I was afraid to look into her face for fear I might laugh. She tested her thumbnail, sighed and began picking at the cold French fries again, talking almost more to herself now than to me. "Richard comes the closest, but he's slowly wrecking my life. He *will* wreck it if I stick around and let him. I'll drown in his lethargy. His passivity. Know what he said when I told him about going to Italy? He said he thought it was a good idea. Never tried to argue me out of it, stop me or reveal his feelings to me. He doesn't have any. He's locked them away somewhere and now he can't remember where they are."

He certainly sounded strange to me, if what she said was the truth. I couldn't imagine letting Dottie Kirstein—if she were my girl friend—go away to Italy for the summer. I couldn't imagine letting her go anywhere without me. But I did not address myself to the question of Richard Revere. I had only my wounded pride.

"I don't think I'm such a nebbish. I don't think I'm so unmanly. People have funny ideas about what it means to be a man. When I used to fight for the girls, defending them against the boys in snowball fights, that was looked on as unmanly. But where I come from, some would say that was manly."

She smiled sweetly, with real amusement and the first trace of affection I had ever beheld there directed at me.

"Maybe. I remember when you used to do that. I thought you were very strange, but I liked you for it."

"You had a funny way of showing it."

"You're not being fair. In third grade everyone has to do what everyone else does. Everybody conforms to peer pressure, wears the same clothes, thinks the same thoughts."

"I still don't think I'm unmanly. Then or now," I protested bitterly. "And if you didn't think so, you shouldn't have acted as though you did."

"There you go again," she smiled, "putting me on my pedestal. What do you want from me, George? I was scared. You were weird. Everybody said so. Besides, I never really paid much attention. You were so busy throwing up your smoke screen, who cared to look behind it?"

Now I was really interested. We were talking about me.

"What smoke screen? What are you talking about?"

"Showoff. Class clown. All ze funny stories zat were not funnee. You were so busy defending yourself you wouldn't give anyone a chance to even *see* you."

"I don't know what you mean," I protested huffily, though I instantly thought of Jake.

"Then you're not as smart as I was beginning to think you are," she responded with alacrity. In some strange way we were dueling now, and enjoying the duel. "Take your face. You were always so busy saying something—anything, no matter how inane—I never got a chance to see your features in any kind of relaxed expression, like now. How was I supposed to notice how cute you really were? You disguised your features by keeping them in motion. You tried to impress us all with your mouth." She leaned forward. "You should have done it with your lips. Sometimes less is more." I had a brief electric shock as she touched me, then a crazy image that lasted only a second. In this second I tried to imagine myself going through school and never saying a word, just showing my profile.

"Even if I had been quiet, you probably wouldn't have been interested."

"Probably not," she agreed, smiling again. "I didn't like you mooning after me. I didn't want to control you. I didn't want to control any of them. Nebbishes. Richard, at least, I can't control."

Suddenly, and before I could prevent it, I yawned.

"Poor baby. You're all in, aren't you?"

"No, I'm fine. I'm really wide awake."

"No, you're not, and neither am I." She stood up and I instinctively did the same. "All right." She looked about, trying to decide. "I'm too tired to think straight myself. I'm going to sleep on it, as they say. You can do the same. Take any bunk you like—except that one." She pointed to her own and shot me the sidelong come-hither nervous smile again.

"You're sure they won't be back tonight?"

"Positive. If I'm wrong, they'll be so drunk it won't make any difference to either of you." She walked over to the door. "I'm turning out the light. That way we can get undressed without seeing."

She switched out the light. For a few minutes there was no sound but the rustle of our clothes being removed. I heard her bark her shins on the edge of her berth with an angry exclamation. I left my clothes where they lay and found the other bottom bunk. I was unable to suppress a sigh of satisfaction as I crawled into it.

"Feel better than where you've been sleeping lately?"

"I can't tell you."

"All right, then." Her voice assumed the tone of the den mother again. "Get some sleep and we'll talk about this in the morning."

I lay for some moments in silence, letting my body untense from my toes on up.

"Dottie."

"What."

"I would really appreciate it if you wouldn't turn me in."

"I said, in the morning, George."

Sixteen

A Very Pleasant Dream

The next morning she had ordered breakfast by the time I was awake. I longed to press her for a decision, to settle the matter once and for all (and strangle her if necessary?), but she was clearly one of those persons who are not at their best in the morning. She even muttered something to the effect that it was foolish to "mess" with her before a second cup of coffee. I had already detected an incipient grouchiness, as though she were angry with me for being there still, for complicating her day when she was not yet awake, for bothering her with my life. I felt as I did that day on the school bus when I had sat next to her and she refused so much as even to look in my direction.

She had not yet dressed, but wore a man's red tartan bathrobe over her blue silk pajamas. She was the most stylish fourteen-year-old I had ever seen. I, by contrast, sat in blue jeans and a T-shirt and watched her ill-humored movements anxiously.

"I really like that bathrobe," I began, hoping to butter her up with a compliment. "Sometimes a girl can look great in boys' clothes."

"It belonged to my brother."

So much for that. I was about to make a further remark —no doubt digging myself a deeper grave in the process— when there was a knock on the door.

"Who is it?"

"Mr. Jones, miss. I'm the social director."

Dottie and I locked eyes automatically.

"What do you want?" she demanded, never taking her eyes from mine.

"A moment or two of your time, miss, if it's not too much trouble."

I took Dottie at her word and pleaded with my silent face, hoping that she had not underestimated its appeal when speaking to me last night.

"Just a minute. I'm not dressed."

"Please take your time," said the voice. She turned to me, a finger on her lips.

"The john," she whispered into my ear. I started there but thought better of it. I pointed to the closet as a better place. What if he decided—God knows why—to use the bathroom? She nodded impatiently and shoved me towards it. I popped in, dragging my rucksack and crushing its bulk and mine into the shallow recesses behind and beneath her neatly arranged wardrobe. A powerful and familiar scent enveloped me from her clothes: musk.

"I'm coming," I heard her say. Peeking through a crack in the door, I could see a portion of the room, including the tray with my partially eaten breakfast on it and my chair.

Hanging from the seat of the chair was one of my sweat socks.

"Sorry, but I've only just got up," Dottie said, opening the door.

"This will only take a moment of your time. I'm deeply appreciative." His voice was smooth, used to crises of every description, no doubt. What crisis had brought him to see Dottie? The same question had occurred to her.

"What is it? I'm sorry, would you like some coffee?"

"Thank you, no, but I'll sit, if you've no objection."

"Go ahead."

He sat in the chair I had lately occupied, settling himself atop my telltale sweat sock, but he didn't reach under to see what he had sat on. He was very polite. He also was not the social director. All I could see was one white sleeve, but the gold braid on it proclaimed him to be the third officer, according to my researches. He had come to see Dottie and deliberately devalued his importance. It was stifling in the closet, and squatting on my knees, as I was compelled to, made it worse. I began to perspire.

"What is this about?" Dottie asked. I could hear in her voice an attempt to convey the self-possession of a grown-up, but thought I detected as well the lingering accents of a child confronted by adult authority. Fourteen, I decided, was neither here nor there.

"Just a few questions if you don't mind, miss. We understand you were present during a bit of unpleasantness last evening on the promenade deck shortly before midnight."

She hesitated briefly.

"Yes. You could say that. Yes."

"Yes," he echoed. "Well, one of the passengers, a Mr.—" There was a pause and I saw the sleeve move, then heard the sound of a paper being unfolded. "A Mr. Jerry Miller of Mobile, Alabama, claims he was assaulted by a fellow passenger and wishes to press charges. He has, in fact, sustained some damage to his front teeth, which, I am afraid, is permanent."

"Are you asking me if I clipped him in the jaw?"

"If you'll bear with me for a moment, miss, please." There was no hint of levity in Jones's response. "Mr. Miller has identified the man who struck him as someone he defeated during the tourist-class Ping-Pong tournament yesterday afternoon."

"Are you saying he was attacked by a sore loser?"

"I wish this were funny, miss, but I'm afraid it's not."

"Sorry, but I wasn't at the tournament, Mr. Jones. I haven't strayed out of cabin class since we left New York."

"I appreciate that, miss. Our difficulty is that we are unable to locate Mr. Miller's assailant to learn his version of the incident and see if we can't settle the matter. The name we found on the tournament elimination chart doesn't correspond with anyone on the current passenger manifest. There is no one by the name Larry Hayes listed on our present voyage, in tourist class or out."

Even from the closet I could hear her involuntary intake of breath. I cursed myself for having used Larry's name again—I wasn't even sure why I kept doing it—but on the other hand, how could I possibly have foreseen another classmate of his being on board?

"Do you know that name, miss?" His tone was reasonable still, but the question itself told me he hadn't missed her reaction.

"What was it again? I'm sorry."

"Hayes. Larry Hayes."

"Let me think." There was a brief pause. "No, I'm afraid it doesn't ring a bell."

"You're quite certain." Now I heard an edge to his voice.

"Quite." And an edge to hers. There was another pause. Jones sighed and pocketed his paper. "Anything else?" I heard in her voice the impatience to conclude his visit. He heard it, too.

"Just two more questions, if you don't mind. I realize I've taken up quite enough of your valuable time." It must have galled him to say any such thing to a fourteen-year-old, but she was a paying Cunard passenger.

"That's all right."

"Do you know the man who assaulted Mr. Miller last night?"

That, at least, she'd been ready for.

"No, I can't recall ever seeing him aboard before last night."

"Or anywhere else."

"Or anywhere else."

"Are you quite—"

"I am quite sure I don't know him."

"Would you recognize him if you saw him again?"

"What?"

"Could you describe him?"

I could practically hear the gears clicking in that nimble brain. She knew she couldn't falsify my appearance outrageously; it would have to tally in some measure with the one Miller had provided. Sweat was pouring down me in rivulets and my knees ached. I didn't think I could maintain the position much longer.

"Not very well, I'm afraid. It was pretty dark and it happened real fast. I'd say he was—oh, maybe five feet seven or eight inches tall." She was clearly trying to piece me together. He didn't interrupt. "Uh, it's hard to tell about his hair in that light. Medium length and light brown is my guess."

"Not pure black, a little curly?"

"Mr. Jones!" I heard the almost simultaneous scraping back of their two chairs as they both scrambled to their feet. "Mr. Jones," Dottie repeated, in a tone suggestive of rage on a short leash, "you evidently were not told the full details of last night's 'assault,' as you call it. I guess *Mister* Miller"— she had fun mimicking his proper use of the man's name —"didn't see fit to burden you with them. It must not have occurred to him that you would be checking his account with mine, otherwise he probably wouldn't have raised this ruckus in the first place. Let me tell you that if anyone was assaulted up there last night, it was I, *by* Mr. Miller of Mobile, Mississippi, or wherever. I thought I was going to learn something about astronomy—which may have been naive on my part; I'm sure it was—but in any case Mr. Miller had something entirely different in mind. I don't think I need draw your attention to the fact that I am not eighteen years old, even if I look it, but I *will* say that my being under age did not deter Mr. Miller. If anyone is doing any preferring of charges around here it could just as well be me, and my father is one of Chicago's hotshot lawyers, as this company could well find out. As for the man who knocked out Mr. Miller's pearly teeth, I have nothing but gratitude for him, whoever he was. If he was here, I'd fling my arms around him and say so. And so should the Cunard Company, if you want my opinion."

There was a fractional tick of silence, but his next words told me she had blown him out of the water.

"Yes, well, I see," Jones got in when she'd finished this soft-spoken tirade. He hadn't been told the whole story, he confirmed, and with a few other graceful backtrackings, he excused himself and I tumbled out of the closet.

"Are you all right?" she asked, sighing and leaning against the cabin door.

"*I* am. Just frightened out of my mind. What about you?"

"I want my second cup of coffee." I watched her pour it with a trembling hand. She didn't look up and in some way I knew that she was still angry with me. I felt some vague stirrings of annoyance myself.

I knew I ought to guard against it as I was in no position to blow my stack, but I felt dangerously close. I hadn't done anything to her; quite the reverse, as she herself had just been the first to admit. I decided to take it easy.

"Thank you for what you did."

"I'm not through figuring this out yet," she warned, sipping the coffee.

"Why'd you bother, then?" The anger was creeping in; I could feel it but she appeared not to notice.

"I just didn't like the idea of Miller, or whatever his name is, going after you with some sort of kangaroo court. If you'd been a legitimate passenger, I'd have said the same things. But Jesus, George, whatever possessed you to use Larry Hayes's name? That was stupid."

"Yes, I suppose I should have known you'd be on board. Well, thanks very much for all your help. I think I'm going on deck and getting some fresh air."

"Are you crazy? What if you bump into Miller?" I took a breath.

"In the first place, let me remind you that I am not

crazy. Possibly you are confusing me with someone else—
your brother, perhaps. In the second place, if I really knocked
out the man's teeth he's probably in bed somewhere—in the
sick bay, most likely. Lastly, after what you told Mr. Jones,
I don't expect this matter to be actively pursued." She
blinked as I said these things, taken off guard by my words
and the force behind them. I ignored her startled expression
and pulled my green sweater over my T-shirt and tied my
sneakers.

"I think it's too risky, George." Her tone was uncharacteristically mild.

"You don't have anything to say about it," I responded
with undisguised curtness. It gave me great pleasure to
inform her of the fact. She was so damn bossy. She blinked
again at this.

"Why are you talking to me like this?"

"Because you are so bossy. I bailed you out of something
nasty and you've appropriated me and my problem to the
point where it feels like blackmail. Well, if you're going to
turn me in, you go right ahead. I'm going for my breath of
fresh air." I made a move to leave and she leapt in front of
the door, the sudden movement causing her to lose her
breath.

"I'm coming with you."

"Come on, then. Only hurry up." She blanched again.

"I'm hurrying. Just stay here thirty seconds." She grabbed
a fistful of clothes from her closet and dashed into the bathroom. I was left to ponder her curious response to my loss
of temper. I was forced to conclude that she liked it. Hadn't
she said she didn't always want to be the one in control?
That's exactly what she had said. Suddenly I began to feel

there might be a way for me to get out of this mess in one piece.

When she had dressed, I allowed her to trot after me as I climbed staircase after staircase.

"Why don't we take the elevator?" she huffed behind me.

"Go ahead. Take it."

"That's okay."

Once on the promenade deck, however, I ran out of steam, literally and figuratively. I didn't know what to say or what to do. I wandered forward idly, walking towards the passenger bridge, past rows of people blanketed and comfy in their deck chairs. Dottie walked beside me, saying nothing. We both were calming down, a bit embarrassed by how rattled Jones's visit had made us. Sometimes we were grown-ups, or close to it; other times we were just kids, despite all our protestations and aspirations to the contrary.

It was a beautiful, blustery day, with a clear blue sky and whitecaps all over the place on dark-green water. The swells were sufficient to roll the *Mary,* and her bow bucked and plunged among them like a giant hobbyhorse. The wind on the bridge, when we got there, was terrific. You had to hold on to the salty varnished-wood rail with both hands.

"I'm sorry I called you those names," Dottie said loudly. She had to raise her voice against the wind to make herself heard, and her hair blew about her head as though the Furies were playing with it. "It was just—" She searched for an explanation.

"Force of habit?" I supplied.

"All right, just what the hell do you want? I said I was sorry."

"We're not in school now," I screamed back. "Grades don't count here and sorry is just a word. I want to be treated like a regular human being and not—" I couldn't think of the word.

"Patronized," Dottie put in helpfully.

"Right. Not patronized. I don't want to be told I'm crazy or stupid and I don't want to be bossed around either. I'd like to stay this last night in your cabin if you'll let me, but otherwise I'll be just fine. Just—stop acting so put upon. It makes me feel like a creep. I haven't done anything to you, so why are you making such a big deal?" In the midst of my manifesto I noticed her nose. It was delicately upturned at the end, what is called a ski jump. If the curvature had been any more pronounced, it would have resembled a snout; but it wasn't more pronounced: It was perfect.

"Okay," she said simply and at once.

"Okay?"

"Okay to all your conditions. I think they're fair." She was smiling now, an open, friendly smile, while at the same time looking at me in an odd way, as though she were taking inventory of my soul. I felt awkward—again—and didn't like to look back into her face. Had I dropped the ball and had she just recovered it? Or had we stopped playing altogether? "Now what?"

"I don't know. Would you like a tour of this ship? A real tour? I can show you. I know everything about it."

"All right, show me." She had about as much interest in the *Queen Mary* as I had in Frankie Laine, but I didn't know what else to do with her so I took her up on it. I walked her gorgeous legs off. I started with where we were, in the forward section, and worked my way down and back, deck by deck, rattling off every fact and every figure I had memorized. I told her the history of the ship and about her wartime service, when she served as a troop ship and carried sixteen thousand people at a time, leaving New York for England at top-secret sailing times. I told her about Hitler's reward to any U-boat that would sink the *Mary* or her sister. I explaned zigzagging and how the men slept in three eight-hour shifts, three men to a berth, and how one day the *Mary* zigged when her destroyer escort zagged. The result: The *Mary* sliced the destroyer in half as though it had been butter. I changed shoes and we toured the engine room. I showed her all the rare and precious woods that adorned the walls of the public rooms. I showed her the first-class dining room, the largest room afloat. I pointed out the spectacular Art Deco furnishings of the tourist-class bar, the etched glass and steel. Occasionally she would ask a question, interested despite herself, and sometimes she emitted a little exclamation or whistle of wonder. Mainly I talked myself hoarse. After three hours and no lunch, we sat down off in a corner of the cabin-class lounge and she ordered us tea. The dismal string trio was playing. What an image for purgatory: back and forth across the ocean—"Fascination" forever.

"I hope that wasn't too boring," I said a little belatedly, feeling my tired leg muscles uncoil. She squeezed some lemon into a cup of tea and handed it to me.

"It was more interesting than I expected—in more ways than one. George, how could you learn all that stuff so fast and completely and have so much trouble in school?"

I tensed self-consciously at the word. It was as though our former roles had reestablished themselves the moment she uttered it.

"I don't know."

"But there must be a reason," she pursued gently, touching my hand as though to say she meant no harm by inquiring. "It's not just as though you have a good memory. I paid close attention—you also have a very clear idea of how things relate to things. Of what the implications are. That's more than memory: That's intelligence. What about Latin?" she went on briskly. "You speak French without trouble. You're a linguist. What's the trouble with Latin?"

"I'm not a linguist; that's your first mistake. I told you, I learned French the way French children learn it, as a first language. I can't learn a language in a classroom, especially a language no one speaks. I haven't the gift."

"But with your memory the declensions and conjugations should be a snap."

I said nothing.

"What about math?" This was becoming pure torture.

"I never understand it. I get lost."

"But why? Do you study?"

"What is this, twenty questions? I can only learn something if it interests me. In the words of Herman Blue, I don't trouble to 'apply' myself otherwise. Christ, he makes it sound like glue."

"I didn't mean to upset you." She took a sip of tea.

"You didn't," I lied, copying her. I didn't even like tea. "I do well in English," I added, hating myself for telling her but unable to stop, either. "I got an A on my last term paper for Miss Weston."

She positively beamed.

"An A! You certainly kept quiet about it. Well, that certainly ought to prove something to you."

"It proves something to *you,* doesn't it?" I said, getting

angry again. "It's all right to like me; I got an A in something."

"You're reverting, George. Don't give me the satisfaction."

"I don't know what you're talking about."

"I'll tell you what," she said, changing the subject brightly. "Tonight's the last night before Cherbourg. There's a farewell dance. Would you like to take me?"

Now I was completely confused.

"I can't," I fumbled.

"Why not?"

"For one thing I don't have anything to wear that would be appropriate."

"I won't worry about that if you won't. What do you say?"

I fidgeted uncomfortably. Here was my fantasy unfolding, but I wasn't up to it.

"I don't know how to dance, as you may recall. I didn't go to the lessons at the Standard Club."

"Now don't be a snob, George. Take me to the dance. I'll teach you. You're not frightened by a little dance music, are you? After getting halfway around the world by yourself? I'm going down to my room now. You can't go with me because the chaperones will be there, sobering up. Pick me up at eight." She touched my hand again and went off, leaving me with my cold tea and unhappy forebodings. The idea of fumbling around on a dance floor with her filled me with dread. I wanted to do something I was good at, not something that would diminish me in her eyes. I wished we were in Cherbourg. No, that's not what I wished.

I knocked on her door a little after eight. In my mind I was still reluctant, annoyed that this was happening. God knows, I had long dreamed of a date with Dottie Kirstein.

Little had I ever dreamt it would take place in the middle of the Atlantic Ocean, with me a fugitive who had no clothes to wear (my first need was going to be a shower), and the date itself was the last I would have chosen in an effort to ingratiate myself with her. The door opened.

"Hello, you must be my date."

I stared. Where was the long-legged girl in dungarees who had tromped all over the ship with me, her hair blowing all over the place? Where was the impudent, challenging companion of the day, so ready to lock horns with me over anything that struck her as fuzzy or ill-thought-out on my part? In place of that familiar if sometimes irritating creature stood a grown woman gowned in blue silk (as she had been the night before, but I seemed to have forgotten that part until now). Her hair was beautifully arranged off the base of her neck in some sort of chignon—I am guessing at the word for it—and she had put some stuff around her eyes that made their blueness jump out at you. Her cheekbones were more pronounced than they had been during the day, and her lips glistened with red.

"Look, this is ridiculous—"

"Well, thanks very much. I'm sorry it's the same dress, but I—"

"Come on, that's not what I mean and you know it," I amended, following her into the cabin. "I just don't have a suit or a neat pair of shoes, or anything. I can't dance a lick—"

"I never knew you were such a worrier, George," she teased, pirouetting before me to show off how pretty she was. "Don't tell me you're scared by a girl in dancing pumps. We're not in school now," she chortled. "Grades don't mean anything here. There's the shower," she said abruptly, tilting her head towards it.

I grabbed my rucksack from the closet and stomped off, muttering dark imprecations under my breath. If I felt foolish now, in private, how was I going to feel on the dance floor, in public—like a kid with his older sister? I stood in the shower and let the boiling water pelt down on me like punishment until I was almost hypnotized with heat. When I was finished, I cleaned a space of steam off the mirror and shaved before it clouded up again. There wasn't much to shave, but I got rid of what there was.

When I emerged, I had improvised evening attire for myself out of a pair of wash-and-wear khaki chinos and the corduroy sport jacket I had brought in case I had to pass myself off as an adult. It was a little wrinkled from the rucksack and it wasn't exactly clean—like many boys of my age, I was not overly scrupulous about such things. All I had for footwear were my penny loafers (from which I had sponged the dust), and my only tie, a dark-blue knit affair, had a slight stain at the bottom that I think came from an egg yolk landing there, though I couldn't be sure. I was able to conceal the stain by keeping the jacket buttoned.

"What were you making such a fuss about?" Dottie said, turning me this way and that to inspect me and pulling my jacket down a bit in the back. "You look very nice. I like the way your hair looks when it's wet like that. Elvis Presley."

I said nothing, but it is a tribute to my dismal state of mind that what I thought was, Soon it will dry, then where will I be?

"Ready?" She held open the door and took my arm as we went through it, smiling hugely. She was clearly enjoying herself and not about to conceal the fact, the little sadist. (What did I expect from someone named Delilah?) I felt as though I were on my way in the tumbrel to my own execution.

We walked leisurely to the elevator, as befitted our costumes (and her high heels). We stared wordlessly at one another while waiting for the thing to arrive, stepped aboard without comment when it did and let it take us in silence to the promenade deck, where the cabin-class festivities were already in progress. There was a band, colored lights, a good deal of crepe-paper bunting and many people. I had had a nightmare of our entrance being in some way conspicuous, of my incongruity as the escort of this beautiful woman being occasion for sniggering comment among other kids. In fact, no one much noticed, or if they did, appeared to find anything remarkable in our being paired. What were they seeing that I wasn't? Or vice versa?

The band was playing something slow, which was a relief. When Dottie led me unselfconsciously through small tables cluttered with glasses and cigarettes to the dance floor— clearly it did not remind *her* of walking the plank—I at least recalled the box step by the time we arrived. My hands were clammy and my calf muscles tight, as though I had just run a mile. She slipped easily and automatically into my arms and I did the best I could. She was taller in her heels than I was. The fragrance of musk intoxicated me and did not help matters. I felt dizzy.

"What do you mean, you don't dance?" she whispered encouragingly down into my ear. "You're doing just fine."

I stepped on a toe.

"Don't jinx this," I gasped. "Sorry."

"Take it easy. I've got nine more. Loosen up. Enjoy yourself. Everything's okey-dokey. Don't you like holding on to me?"

"Yes."

"What?"

"Yes, I do," I gasped, louder.

"Then do it. Get a grip."

With a clammy right hand—I wondered if I would leave a perspiration stain for her to remember me by on the back of her dress—I drew her closer in an awkward movement.

"You do go to extremes," she laughed.

"Don't make fun of me. You're the one who wanted—"

"Are you having such a bad time?" She looked gaily into my eyes with a challenging stare.

"No." She smiled more broadly still.

"I'm sorry, I didn't quite catch that."

"No," I repeated miserably.

The number ended but, before I could make my escape, was succeeded by another, livelier one: the Lindy. Here I was completely inept and made more so by worrying that we were being watched, which could hardly have been the case on the crowded postage stamp of a dance floor. How I wished the earth (or sea) would open up and swallow me. But Dottie was unfazed. She showed me patiently, politely, not concealing any amusement she felt, but not actually laughing at my discomfiture either—and always persistent. Here was what I was doing wrong, and this was how to make it right. At first my tension made it difficult to listen to what she was saying and act on her instructions, but as dance followed dance, my fears of exposure and humiliation began to abate. They were replaced, finally, as my sense of physical coordination and rhythm began to assert themselves. The sweat evaporated from my hands, and as I got the hang of various steps, I grew more daring, and the tense expression I knew had frozen around my mouth gave way to a sheepish grin.

"Well, look at you. Think you're hot stuff now, don't you?"

"You obviously don't know the difference." I was beaming.

"Hmmm." She rolled her eyes. As the evening wore on, various taller, older and, I thought, more attractive men attempted to cut in. They were always refused with an airy indifference by my partner. She played rough. I was so far gone that when the band took their break between sets I was resentful and impatient for them to begin again. It was not only that I had mastered—to whatever minimal degree —this business of the Lindy; it had gone beyond that. I was now sufficiently comfortable that I began to enjoy, to revel in, the sensation of having Dottie Kirstein, *La Divina Kirsteina,* in my arms. In a curious way the jammed dance floor provided a kind of public privacy. During the Lindy, opportunities for physical contact were not plentiful, but when the slower numbers were played—and they played more slow ones as the night grew longer—I enjoyed pressing her flesh to mine. I did this gradually, not out of shyness, (though I suffered from that, too), but because an instinct told me that beneath all her intelligence, sophistication, self-possession and womanly paraphernalia, Delilah was skittish where things sexual were concerned. I think this idea was implanted in my head by two or three things she had told me, as well as by her overall manner in response to things like the moment the night before when I had stepped out of the bathroom clad in only a towel and wondered where she was. The fact that she didn't like older boys suggested a certain reticence that was not typical of girls at that age. They might mimic her in a thousand ways, but they were eager for contact (and contact was involved) with boys from upper grades, sometimes even college kids. Another statement she'd made that supported this notion and put me on my guard was her description of Richard Revere and his passivity. From what I could gather, sex did not play a great part in their competitive relationship. With some satisfaction as we danced, I recalled his chubby body, the only defect I had ever noticed in him until Dottie's devastating critique.

I went slowly, too, out of my own set of fears. Since my trauma with Olga years before, I had done a lot of frantic fantasizing about girls, but I had not touched a one. Now, to be holding in my arms the girl who was above all others the most desirable to me, was so dreamlike and improbable that I dared not hold her too tightly. I might squeeze her into thin air and wake to find myself in bed on Dearborn Street with another lonely day of school ahead of me. The thought alone was enough to pop the sweat back into my palms.

In the midst of these warring reflections and scruples, I became aware of something: She was pressing back, thrusting her body against my own. I thought quickly, Dottie is not Olga, though she might now be the same age Olga had been; Dottie is far more grown-up, and more to the point, she is not unconscious. True, we were dancing and the music afforded some related license for this sort of behavior (not for nothing have Puritan regimes looked on dancing

with suspicion), but Dottie was neither provincial nor un-
aware.

As we danced, our movements became bolder and more
urgent. We hadn't said a word in hours, but our pelvises
were speaking for us. My penis, confined in my tight chinos,
was hard as rock and ground remorselessly against the top
of her cunt. She held me as tight as I held her now and every
so often emitted a slight groan in my ear.

I began kissing her neck. At first I merely brushed my
lips dryly along her hot scented skin. When she didn't resist,
my mouth became more insistent and wetter. At one point
she drew back sharply and looked at me. Her eyes glittered
and were not her own, or else my vision was similarly dis-
torted. When she returned my close embrace, she sighed as
her hips made renewed contact with mine. Every now and
again she would order me to "stop that" in a harsh whisper,
and I always did—for a time. Then, ineluctably, my body
would take over and her body would take over. We were
like helpless puppets taking orders from some unseen demon
who pulled our strings and compelled us to his bidding. We
might tug furiously on our ropes in an attempt to control
the controller, but always in vain. When the music ceased,
we were unable to separate ourselves, but stood swaying
where we were, like trees that have grown together over the
years, pushed in tandem by an invisible breeze.

"You're embarrassing me. Stop it."

"I can't."

She hesitated. "Then let's get out of here."

We returned to her cabin—the longest and most self-
conscious walk I can ever recall—and there started necking

in earnest in one of the cramped lower berths. At such times, among inexperienced participants, everything happens very slowly. Later, more familiar with the ritual, we make the mistake of rushing it—"cutting to the chase," as someone I know once expressed it.

But not that night. For an hour I didn't do more than kiss her in various ways, wet and lingering, in her mouth, on her neck, around her ears. Her ears were extremely sensitive: She would squirm with pleasure and moan when I darted my tongue inside one and explored there.

For a time I only held her shoulders and the top of her back. Then, tentatively, the base of her spine, coyly, above her rear. Gradually I grew daring and lowered my hand. She didn't notice. Or care. It was exactly like a dream; I had a hand squeezing Dottie Kirstein's perfect ass while Dottie Kirstein's tongue was halfway down my throat.

Ought I to content myself with these riches or go on? I debated the question as another hour of grappling went by. I tired of her ass and began cautiously inching my hand up her heaving torso until it touched the base of her lovely, shimmering breast. I started up from there.

"No."

"Why?"

"Because."

"That's not a reason."

"Please."

And being a nice fellow, I acquiesced. For a time. But my hand was not to be denied. And neither was her breast. I kissed my way down her back, hoping to meet my hand on the way up. There were a number of attempts and a number of rejections—the dialogue much the same—but her sensa-

tions were overpowering her. Soon I was frantically knead-
ing both of them, kissing them through the material of her
dress, and she was flinging her head ecstatically from side to
side, whimpering.

Another hour. I started again innocently enough, holding
on to the outside of her thigh—I had already established a
territorial precedent with her ass—and from there took courage by degrees and started to push up her dress. At first she
didn't notice, but then she did and clamped her hand over
mine like a vise.

"No!"

"Why?"

"Because."

"*Why.*"

"George, no."

It was like laying siege to an impregnable fortress. I attacked when and where I could and she raced from battle-
ment to parapet (undermanned), trying to repulse me at
every breach in the walls. But she couldn't be everywhere
at once. Her defenses were crumbling, her own troops going
over to the enemy, joyously seduced by lust, which ate at
her from within as I kept up the attack from without. Events
now proceeded at an increasingly rapid pace. Soon my hand
was in possession of her most secret charms, and sopping
wet. I did not know anything in the way of technique and
Dottie knew little more. We were inspired amateurs. Desperate amateurs.

"George, wait a minute."

That was easier to say than do. It took several moments
before I could be persuaded to hold still. Finally she got
through to me and we lay panting, bathed in sweat and

staring wild-eyed at one another in the semidark, squeezed together, half out of our clothes in the narrow confines of the bunk.

"We have to stop."

"Why?"

"Because we do."

"Don't tell me you're not enjoying it."

"I am enjoying it. That's the problem.'

"What's the problem? Spell it out for me. I don't understand."

It took a lot more coaxing and stroking but finally she did.

"I don't want to get pregnant." I almost sobbed with relief.

"Is that all?" I tried to sound casual. "I've got prophylactics."

"You do? You really came prepared for this trip, didn't you?" She sat up and I sat up next to her.

"Are you going to bitch because I have them? Or are we going to thank our lucky stars?"

For a long time I couldn't get her to see it my way. Her sense of romance was somehow offended that I had taken this precaution without knowing that I was going to meet her. Nothing I could say would make her accept a more pragmatic view. We were saved by our own lust, which refueled our amorous activities. It took far less time this time to reach the boiling threshold we had reached before. This time I had fumbled her out of her brassiere and sucked her nipples to jutting erections. The bed was wet with her juices and I was afraid that if I did not keep myself distracted, I would ejaculate.

This time we did not speak. I broke free and padded to
the rucksack. I knew exactly where they were. With shaking
hands I tore open the packet and took one out. It wouldn't
roll on and I realized I had it inside out. I turned it around
and pulled it on, then climbed back into the bed. In my
absence she had removed the rest of her clothes. We lay
down trembling next to each other, and for the first time in
my life I experienced the delicious heat of another human
body, unclothed, against mine. We kissed, we stroked. Everything was slippery with passion. I raised myself on top of
her and gently forced open her legs.

At the last moment I hesitated.

"You don't have to do this," I offered. It was gallantry
mixed with cowardice. When she spoke, it was in a voice so
low I could hardly hear.

"I'm not saying no, am I?"

I took this for my answer and set about trying to enter
her. I expected this to be difficult but it was astonishingly
easy. With her hand she guided my rubber-coated cock and
I slid into her without any problem. She grabbed the sopping hair about my ears and held on to me desperately. I
moved slowly at first, my mind refusing to believe that this
was not a dream. Then I moved faster. I was about to explode and I sought to delay this by thinking about something else, anything else. I found myself trying to remember what Jake's father had said about Stevenson in the
Chinese restaurant. He was an egghead; he'd always been
an egghead; the country didn't—

I had never experienced a more exquisite sensation as the
feeling of gliding back and forth inside her. No description
I had read, no fantasy I had conjured up to masturbate with,

could do justice to the searing reality. The country didn't like eggheads—

I could contain myself no longer. As I began to erupt, I said, "I love you."

And meant it.

Seventeen

Waking

For a long time afterwards I simply lay where I had spent myself, passively clutching her. By degrees our breathing slowed and the sweat dried on our bodies, except where they were still pressed together. With my head lying on her breast, I could hear her heart pumping. It was a sound I wanted to listen to forever. She stirred uncomfortably beneath my weight and I rolled out and off her. I wanted to touch my penis and discover how the rubber had reacted to the experience, but I was too self-conscious at the moment. Instead I propped myself up on one elbow and stared down at her in the darkness. All I could make out was the glitter where her eyes were and hear her shallow breath. Some time passed in this way; perhaps it was only minutes, but it seemed longer.

"I can't believe I did this," she said finally, appearing to address no one in particular.

"*You* can't believe it."

She said nothing.

"Aren't we supposed to smoke now?"

She said nothing.

"Are you sorry?" I asked, whispering.

"No."

There was some more silence. Abruptly she sat up and, muttering "Excuse me" under her breath, went to the bathroom. I took the opportunity to examine myself and felt uncertainly for my penis. (It had metamorphosed back into being just a penis again; for a while there it had been a cock.) The covering was still there, though shrunken and loose-fitting with the disappearance of my erection.

The toilet flushed and she came padding back and climbed into bed without comment.

"My turn," I mumbled and heaved myself over her. In the bathroom I removed the funny-looking thing and turned on the light, which made me squint for some moments, to look at it. I could see my captured semen distending the tip. Not knowing what else to do with it, I threw it into the toilet, peed on it and flushed it down. I returned to the bed and she moved silently over to make room. We lay in silence and I stroked her gently. Something odd was in the silence; I knew she was not comfortable.

"What are you thinking?" she asked finally.

"Nothing much. Nice thoughts."

"I guess you can tell I'm not a virgin," she said, by and by. "Did that bother you?"

"No," I told her honestly. "It just made things easier than I thought they would be." I paused. "Does—did it bother you?"

She shrugged. "I didn't like how it happened, mainly. I was at a party at Northwestern. They were all much older kids. I was drinking to keep up." She shrugged again. "Stupid. What are you thinking?" she repeated.

"Is that what's bothering you?"

"Who said anything's bothering me?" she countered listlessly.

"Something is. Please tell me what. This is the most wonderful thing that's ever happened to me. I want it to be wonderful for you, too. If it's something that I did, or something that I didn't do—"

"Oh, come on." Her voice was faint but brusque within the faintness. My stomach muscles tightened.

"Come on what."

"George, I am not stupid. I know why you did this. The funny thing is you didn't have to bother. I wasn't going to tell on you, anyway."

It was the first truly idiotic crack I had ever heard her make, and it was so wide of the mark it took my breath away. My mouth dropped open in the dark where she couldn't see it, then closed.

"Didn't you hear what I said while we were—doing it?" I asked finally.

"Oh, sure. What else were you going to say?"

"Is that why I called and asked you out in seventh grade? So you'd let me off this ship a year and a half later? Is that why I've been making a fool of myself all this time at school, hanging around where I knew I wasn't wanted? Where I knew I didn't have a chance? When I knew I wasn't even in your league? So you'd be useful to me when the time came?"

"Keep your voice down."

"SHUT UP." I grabbed her with a kind of theatricality and kissed her hard. It was a solution learned from the movies and it didn't particularly work. She remained limp. "God, are you dumb," I said in angry frustration as I thrust her from me. "From the moment I first saw you, I've been gaga over you—like everyone else, according to you—but still gaga anyhow. And now you—"

She was crying. For some reason her tears did not fill me with panic, only tenderness, probably because they weren't mine.

"Hey."

"I'm sorry. Oh, George, I'm sorry. I just got scared—I said the first thing that came into my head. The other time was so— It wasn't like this. I—" she broke off for more sniffles. My finger found her face and brushed away the tears as they sprouted.

"It's okay. Come on. It's okay." She stopped crying, subsided into little choking, gurgling noises. I leaned down and kissed her damp cheeks. "Only, you believe me now?"

"Yes." Her arms went around my neck and she gave me a salty kiss. "George."

"What." I didn't want any more of her interpretations.

"Could we—you know"—a very small whisper—"do it again?"

Could we? We could. Did we? We did. By the phosphorescent dials of her little folding traveling clock, it was after three in the morning. Our day had been a long and strenuous one, and we had been hours dancing and necking to reach this point. It made no difference. Our bodies were fueled by excitement, by curiosity, by affection. Together with our exertions we manufactured a scent I had never inhaled before. Parts of us grew bruised and sore. We managed to go through four more prophylactics notwithstanding. The more familiar I became with the process, the longer I was able to postpone my ejaculation. The longer I postponed my ejaculation, the more excited she became. Between bouts we lay wrapped in each other's slickness and talked in whispers, about everything. Our hands fluttered nervously, independent of our conversation, checking swollen damage, stroking, exploring, wandering in and out of various nooks and crannies they had never touched before. I told her the entire history of my obsession with her; I catalogued the events in her life as I had witnessed them—the first pair of high-heeled shoes she'd ever worn, etcetera. The conversation of lovers at such times is of absolutely no interest to a stranger, consisting as it usually does of extensive biographical data regarding people one has never met.

"Did you ever sleep with Dick?"

"No. We lay on the bed in his parents' room in our underwear a couple of times, but that's as far as we got."

My heart leapt. I had had her and Dick Revere had not. I was never too big to be petty.

"Were you really a virgin?" she asked.

"One hundred percent. You seduced me."

"Ha, ha, ha."

"Seriously, I've had only one sexual encounter in my life, and I didn't go to bed with her or anything."

"What was it?"

I told her in detail the story of Olga. She listened with rapt fascination.

"Jesus, George, you were the most precocious eight-year-old I've ever heard of." She wanted to know if my parents were really dead circus acrobats, the Flying Berninis. I told her they were. She shook her head in the dark, her hair sweeping my face like a caress. "I can't believe anyone is really the children of dead circus acrobats."

"Somebody had to do it, so I figured it might as well be me."

She was full of plans. I would join her in Perugia; perhaps I would even join the tour earlier. Go with her to Amsterdam, why not? For a time I joined in these plans. I collaborated, swept along by my love for her, for the sheer miraculous knowledge of life that had given her to me against all logic and all odds. I wanted nothing more than to be hers, completely hers. I wished only to go where she went and make love to her all the time. I listened in an agreeable, trancelike state, lulled by the sound of her voice as she rambled on. I could almost imagine myself, or rather some phantom projection of myself, doing the things she spoke of as she described our summer together, aglow with romantic fervor.

All the time she spoke, however, a dark shadow crawled around at the base of my skull, some niggling detail that in my present exultation I couldn't name. I was asleep and dreaming the pleasantest dream I had ever had. Could I be blamed for not wishing to wake up? My mind waged a blearily impatient battle with encroaching reality (an alarm clock in the distance) and returned, a little more annoyed, a little more desperate each time, to the soothing sound of her soft voice beside me in the dark. I petted her absently as she spoke.

My dream was rudely shattered by footsteps outside the corridor, which stopped briefly by our door. We tensed and grabbed for each other, but almost before we had, the foot-steps had moved softly away. I switched on the light. At the base of the door, slipped across the threshold, lay the reason for the footsteps. A small cluster of yellow and white cards —one for each of the four occupants of the cabin—had been passed in. I walked over to the door and retrieved them.

Where was Fritz? I was no longer dreaming now.

"What are they?" Dottie demanded, sitting up and look-ing in my direction with a little squint at the unaccustomed illumination.

"It's immigration and customs declaration cards to be filled out before we debark at Cherbourg."

"Oh. Turn out the light."

I did as she bid and felt my way back across the room in darkness. Something in her tone as well as her request told me she knew now as well as I that the dream had ended. I slid in next to her and she cringed slightly, a shudder, as though she were suddenly chilled by my touch. This was going to be hard and I didn't know quite how to go about it.

"Why did your parents call you Delilah?"

"Because they're affected," she replied shortly, looking away from me.

"Delilah in French sounds great. Have you heard your name in French?" I didn't know what I was saying or why. "Da-le-*la*."

"I've heard it in French class."

"Is your father really a hotshot lawyer?"

"My father is a vice president at Armour."

"Oh." I had run out of chitchat and decided to try a gambit of hers. "What are you thinking?"

"You're not coming with me, are you?"

"Will you do me a favor?"

"What."

"Will you listen to me? Really listen?"

There was a fractional pause before she spoke; when she did, I heard the fatalism in her voice. "All right."

I took a breath and launched into a long, rambling, sometimes incoherent, sometimes movie-inspired account of my love. I was trying to sound like an adult—she had made clear her disinterest in "boys"—and at the same time to express a set of very real feelings. I suppose much of what I said might be labeled corny by those who had no vested interest in hearing it, but despite its mediocre literary antecedents (Jules Verne wrote the worst romantic dialogue, and Dumas's was improbably high-flown), I nevertheless spoke from the heart. I told her that I loved her, that I had always loved her, that I hoped to go on loving her until the day I died. Perhaps I would and perhaps I wouldn't, I went on, waxing philosophical, and perhaps she wouldn't even want me to, as neither of us could tell what the future held in store. Nevertheless—and here I tried to say exactly what I meant, because it was the most important part—what had happened to us had shown me that life can be kind as well as horrible. Up until now, all I had ever known was the horrible part. You get used to things—a time, a place, a person—and they get taken from you. Or you from them. That, I explained, was all I thought life was. I hadn't understood until now that there was also a flip side—life was a phonograph record—and that sometimes, out of the blue, life gives you something.

"I'm sure most people never get what it has to give, either. For most people you can flip the record over and the song's

just as lousy on the other side. They just starve to death in
China or someplace and never have a chance. Certainly they
never get lucky the way I got lucky tonight. Most people
will not be given you."

"Oh, George." Her hands felt for my face and held it.
She kissed me. "What wonderful things you say."

This was really hard. "They're not all wonderful," I protested gently and, fumbling, took her hands in mine. "I've
got to finish. I started this trip for a reason: to find out
where my uncle is and learn why I haven't heard from him.
I decided months ago that this was very important to me.
I've planned and worked and saved to do this because it was
very important. It hasn't been a long trip and so far it hasn't
even been too tough, except for a few hairy times. I even got
all of this"— I waved my arm around in the dark to indicate
the cabin, us—"and I told you how I feel about that." She
started to say something, but I plowed on. What I was saying
sounded so strange and contrary to my own deepest instincts at the moment that I was treated to the disagreeable
sensation of hearing my own voice, which, if you have ever
experienced it, can be really unnerving. "But what about
Fritz? Was finding him just an excuse to duck out of school
because I wasn't happy there and my grades stank? Am I
supposed to give up on all this stuff the moment I start having a good time? You know I think you're more than a good
time," I explained hastily, "but you know what I mean. This
is a good time, the best *I've* ever had, anyway—"

"Me, too," she interjected.

"But if I say to hell with finding him, doesn't that—I
don't know the word, but it does something to me and to the
whole thing."

"Trivializes," she supplied in a neutral tone.

"So let me ask you something and you've got to promise to answer honestly." She waited in strong silence for the inevitable question. "Would you, in your heart of hearts, like me if I gave up trying to find him because I was having such a great time with you? Would you? Would you respect me?" I almost choked on the improbability of the word. She thought, lying in my arms, but it didn't take her long.

"I guess not—sooner or later." I said nothing for a time.

"What are you thinking?" I repeated finally. It was catching, asking this question. In answer, she reached up and pulled me roughly to her, whispering fiercely into my ear.

"Do it to me. Fuck me good-bye, George." Her words shocked me by their urgency and by her use of a word I had never heard a girl utter. The intensity with which she held me as she spoke and her use of that word elicited yet another erection. I slipped on the last of my rubbers, and slowly, very slowly, as if we were copulating underwater, we made love for the last time. It took me longer than before to climax, but I reveled unhappily in the protraction. I never wanted this to end. As for Dottie, her undulations began to take on a violence and increased tempo of their own. Her moans became louder and they were interspersed with guttural snorts, like the panting of a runaway horse. I was sufficiently startled by what was happening to her to conform to her rhythms, instinctively to follow her lead. All at once her entire body began to quiver from head to toe. She screamed, and then her screams turned to harsh, wracking sobs. She lay curled in my arms, weeping as I held her.

We didn't talk anymore. She drifted into a restless, uneasy

slumber, as if determined to avoid thought. At the moment
I had no wish to find Fritz, whether I respected myself or
not. I just didn't want her to be unhappy. I especially did not
want to be the cause of her unhappiness. This was where it
got tricky. In an attempt to dry the tears with which she had
cried herself to sleep, what might I not be capable of?

When first light came, we dressed in lugubrious silence.
I repacked my rucksack and Dottie methodically removed
her clothes from the closet and folded them into her suitcase.
We sat opposite one another and filled out the customs and
immigration forms. (I had nothing to declare, at least not to
customs and immigration.) I named the cabin next to hers
as mine. We went about these tasks purposefully, and it
struck me at the time that we were now grown-ups, or at any
rate, more grown-up than we had been. I did not attribute
this to the loss of my virginity (though that was certainly a
part of it), but to the choices we had made afterwards.

On deck, all was still. The ship was asleep and the coast
of France not yet in sight. I knew that down below, Dottie's
roommates would be staggering in, hung over and disori-
ented. They could cram their suitcases, stuffing them with
clothes they couldn't be bothered to fold, and sit on them
till they shut, protesting. They would write their names in
the wrong places on the forms. And one of them would have
to find the purser because she hadn't gotten the forms.

The hours passed and gradually everything changed. By
ten the ship was a beehive of activity in preparation for dock-
ing. I took my rucksack with me to the bridge (it was no
longer conspicuous amongst all the other hand-held luggage), and I watched with gloomy fascination as the coast

of France hove into view, then resolved itself into the modern, rebuilt harbor of Cherbourg. To my left and right other passengers chattered animatedly as they jostled for a good view and cameras whirred and clicked like a field of crickets. Most of those on the bridge would not be getting off at Cherbourg. They would stay on one more night until the *Mary* reached Southampton. The sky was grey and unpleasant, but not especially cold. I looked at the sprawling town of Cherbourg—bombed to smithereens during the war and now almost completely reconstructed—and tried to imagine what the future held for me. One thing was certain: There would be no Jake in Cherbourg to give me a place to stay.

After we docked, the huge cargo hatch was lifted open by a crane and they began unloading cars with a hoist that ran on railroad tracks along the quai. I watched for a time, but my attention was arrested by a voice on the public address system. Passengers were advised that the visitors' gangway was now open for those who wished to wander about Cherbourg for the three hours or so that the ship would take to unload her cargo. I had not known about this procedure and it simplified matters for me. I had never intended to board the boat train for Paris. I wasn't certain when Cunard would catch up with me and wished to separate myself from my clandestine association as soon as possible. It now seemed easier to go ashore as a visitor, as though I were returning to go on to England.

I stuffed my obsolete customs form into my pocket, and hoping my rucksack would not occasion comment for a brief visit ashore, I went to the cabin-class lounge and met

Dottie as we had arranged, at eleven o'clock. I explained my decision and the reasons for it.

"When are you going to leave?" She looked around, distracted by the milling passengers searching for each other, their children, lost luggage.

"Now."

She turned to look at me, her face flushed. "I'll walk you."

"What about your group?"

"Let me walk you, George. Don't be difficult."

That was better. I smiled to myself: A touch of her old bossiness was already returning. We walked through mobs to the visitors' gangway and stood next to it.

"Well—" I began, but she cut me off, flinging her arms around me, quite heedless of whatever spectacle we might be making.

"You have my address in Perugia? My dates for American Express in Amsterdam, Florence and—"

"I've got them; don't worry."

"What's going to happen?" she wailed softly in my ear.

"I'll be all right. Really. I promise. Wish me luck."

She squeezed harder.

"I wish you more. And George—"

"What." I was nervous now. She seemed so wound up I was afraid she might do something. I wasn't off the ship yet.

"You taught me something." I started to smirk, but she waved it away. "Not that, dummy. Whatever happens, I will never again confuse intelligence with wisdom."

"Meaning I'm not intelligent."

"Meaning I won't pay quite so much attention to grades next year."

"Lucky for me." But I was smiling again and holding her.

"Shut up, George," she said affectionately. "Don't revert to type. I meant what I said, even if I said it badly. Don't be a creep."

"Sorry." We stood still in the midst of the chaos, clinging to each other. Then we broke apart and I went over the gangway, not looking back. I turned at the bottom, but the thing was too long and the angle too curved. She was gone. Or rather, I was.

My next moves were made like an automaton. I walked through the high, echoing shed, listening to the thunder of a hundred footsteps around me as I signed out for shore leave with a British officer who gave me a chit and impressed upon me the importance of returning within three hours, lest I miss the sailing. He didn't appear to notice or care about the rucksack, and I was too distracted by a wholly new set of emotions to worry about whether he did or not. I proceeded from the sign-out table to the currency exchange, where I cashed in some of my traveler's checks for francs.

As I made my way about the new-arrivals building, concluding my business, a new and long-unheard sound began to assail my ears, only faintly distinguished at first but, as I descended the steps past the waiting boat train towards the outdoors, most definitely audible: *French.* Hearing my own tongue again after all these years (the grotesque efforts in Miss Missel's French class didn't count) crowned my confusion. On the one hand it penetrated my misery with refreshing memories of a happier time and place in my life, and it provided me with a tangible sense of my achievement in getting this far from America; on the other it failed miserably to alleviate my heartache. Not even this vivid a reminder of my accomplishment was sufficient to overshadow or compensate for the sense of loss I now felt.

Outside the pier building, on the cobblestones of France, I turned and looked past the boat train up at the *Queen Mary,* majestic and beautiful as ever. More beautiful now than ever, because of what she contained. Somewhere inside her gleaming black hull and proud white superstructure was a beautiful, wonderful girl I longed for with an ache I could not remember feeling since the day I parted from Madelaine. It was probably no accident—but was it a sadistic twinge of fate?—that they both wore musk. I knew enough at fourteen (it was the lesson my life had taught me) to know that the world was wide and unsafe. I hoped we would live to see and love each other again.

At this point, for a reason I am not quite sure of, I now made an error of judgment. I decided that the most important thing was to get out of Cherbourg as quickly as possible. Now that I had well and truly stowed away and made it in fact as a fugitive from Chicago to Cherbourg, a kind of paranoia descended over me. My irrational thinking was no doubt in part the result of my troubled state of mind and heart. All I wanted to do was walk and keep walking. I would follow the railroad tracks out of town to the next village— my map suggested it would be Valognes—and there entrain for Paris. In my cloudy mental state, my ineptitude at math was my undoing, and looking at the map, I idly supposed Valognes to be no more than four or five miles from Cherbourg. I put away the map and stumbled through the new town of Cherbourg, always keeping the railroad tracks more or less in view on my left. They branched out briefly into a network of yards, but the main line eventually resolved itself. I noticed, with a growing sense of satisfaction as I walked, signs that read Tabac, and other small indications that I was indeed in France. The very air had a peculiar gasoline-laden smell from all the grey Citroens and blue mini-vans. All the vehicles looked tiny after Chicago and New York, like the English Matchbox toy cars. Indeed, something about the entire country suggested to my mind a kind of gigantic miniature, such as one sees in elaborate model-railroad set-ups. Even the cows in the Normandy countryside—when I reached it—looked like props you could lift up and place elsewhere at whim. What was it about America that made it seem huge by comparison?

My steps at first led me through the more populous areas. At one point I stood on one side of a square and watched two orderly rows of blue-uniformed schoolchildren, who couldn't have been much younger than I was, marching in perfect regimentation down the street, supervised by alert teachers, who somehow brought to my mind again the sheepdog of Miss Peterson's parable.

That thought, logically enough, brought me back to the Marcus Leader School. From there it was no great leap to Dottie Kirstein. With a thrill and a pang I recalled the last ecstatic twenty-four hours and my possession of the queen of my dreams. The whole episode seemed more dreamlike and unlikely than ever, now that it was over, and my heart grew heavier in my chest as I tramped past poorer houses and lots of sagging laundry being taken down off clotheslines by fat ladies with black kerchiefs on their heads. The lowering sky matched my hopeless mood.

Outside the town, as it gave way to weeds and an occasional abandoned and dilapidated shack with broken windows, I picked up the railroad tracks at a signal box and started walking between the rails, heading southwest for Paris.

It was as if it had never been. She probably wouldn't even remember. Or if she did, she would deny as much as she could the substance of what happened. If she acknowledged any of it to herself, she would put it down as a shipboard romance, a transatlantic aberration that overcame her good sense and better judgment. Or call it sexual experimentation. After her debacle at the Northwestern party, I had done her a service by showing her that all sex was not a drunken, hostile act.

She had cried to see me go, and I had been full of noble platitudes, stern and correct in my purpose. But now our roles were probably being reversed. I longed to go back and try anything to board the boat train, to be with her again, to feel again the joy of possession, the confirmation of our love in her gold-flecked blue eyes. She, on the other hand, was no doubt already immersed in plans for the tour, meeting the other girls in Amsterdam, and—

Did I say other girls? How did I know it would only be girls? When did she ever specify as much? Had she even implied it? As far as I could recall, she had not even alluded to the other members of the tour. Why not? *Because some of them were boys* was the dark interpretation that instantly sprang with conviction into my mind. With a sinking feeling as I trudged along, I considered this dreary likelihood. Boys to me meant taller, older, more sophisticated rivals, any or all of whom had better grades and would be likely candidates for Dottie's affections as the long summer, with its liberating influence, progressed. She would probably be in bed with one of them before the week was out, panting and groaning in his arms, for she had—as I knew (and she would no doubt discover), a mighty appetite for lovemaking. And the bastard would have an endless supply of rubbers. What had possessed me to give away half my arsenal to Jake? Airy condescension, the theatricality of the moment. Why was I even worried about it? I had no further use for them, anyway. I wouldn't be seeing her again.

Another thought now buried itself in my vitals. Had she ever said she loved me? In a flash I knew the answer. It was only I who had declared myself, while she, the canny bitch, had soaked me dry. She had remained tactfully silent on the subject of her love. As I thought these tormenting thoughts, my stomach throbbed as though my appendix would burst and hot, scalding tears stood in my eyes, making it difficult to see. I remembered my motto—"He Travels Fastest Who Travels Alone"—and cursed myself for having abandoned it. I plodded doggedly on, tripping over the maddening railroad ties and feeling the frame of the rucksack gouge my rib cage like a misplaced crown of thorns. I was not without grandiose tragic imagery at this point.

Soon my body began to ache in earnest. To my left and right as I staggered along were the undulating farmlands of Normandy, with the railroad running down a slight rise between the fields. I grew hotter as the weather grew colder, and my legs began to tighten and protest with each step. My neck and back were being rubbed raw by the bloody rucksack. For a time I walked with my head bent, counting the tar-covered railroad ties as they blurred past beneath me in slow motion. How many railroad ties were there between me and Valognes? Ever and again I would look up in the vain hope of seeing the town in the distance. But I saw nothing except more fields and the railroad tracks stretching to the horizon.

Had I gone in the wrong direction somehow? That thought made no sense whatsoever. To have left Cherbourg in the opposite direction would have been to march into the Atlantic. Besides, the sun's position in the sky behind the clouds at this hour told me that I wasn't following a course up or down the coast. According to my calculations, I couldn't be doing that. Could I? I thought about resting, taking the rucksack (my cross?) from my back and consulting the map again, but the thought of what I might find, of putting the thing back on again, was too much. I slogged grimly on, a bit of plucked straw between my teeth, my body bathed in sweat as it was whipped by the chilly breeze.

It began to rain, lightly at first, and then in a steady, relentless downpour. How prescient had been that image I had had the night before my departure in Chicago. Here I was, I thought with bitter satisfaction, drenched to the skin, fulfilling my prophecy.

Over the sound of the rain all about me, I gradually became aware of another sound—a train was approaching from behind. With awkward, exhausted movements, I turned to see it hurtling towards me in the distance, then clambered cumbersomely off the tracks to get out of its irresistible path. I slid on sharp, wet rocks down the steep embankment of the railroad bed and watched on my hands and knees as the boat train thundered past above me. As the rain pelted down and I watched, panting, sweating and crying, the train carried my love away, snug and warm and laughing inside its sheltering accommodations.

It was a train again, only this time I was not on it, leaving behind my life. My life was leaving me.

I was wet through.

Eighteen
Almost a Dead End

It was a long night. In many ways it was the longest I ever remember. For one thing it began at three-thirty in the afternoon when the boat train passed by on its way to Paris. For the next eight hours I walked, stumbled, staggered and fell by inches towards Valognes. Sometimes I huddled in a sopping mass by the side of the tracks, but it was too cold to rest for very long; I had to keep moving. The rain never let up, either, and the temperature grew colder as twilight came on. I started talking to myself. It began benignly enough, with singing to pass the time, but from songs I soon switched to mumbling, and from mumbling to muttering.

She had never even used the word love that I could recall. I imagined I was talking to Jake, explaining the situation to him, recounting blow by blow the entire episode. What would Jake's comment be? "Sounds like suicide is your best bet," I heard him tell me in my mind's ear. "Only honorable way out." I almost smiled to almost hear his silly response.

Fritz, on the other hand, would pour himself a drink and wax philosophical. "The thing about violinists," I could imagine him saying, "is that you can't count on them for too much. Oh, sure, they like to play duets, but they don't like rehearsing for encores. You know what their main concern is? Keeping the damn fiddle in tune—you guessed it. They can make you crazy with all that tuning. Same thing with reeds. I went with an oboist once, for three days. All she ever did was walk around with a reed in her mouth and lick it and lick it and lick . . ." His voice faded and more general memories of my life with him took over and helped me forget the cold and my feet. I wondered where he was and what he was up to. I comforted myself with warm thoughts concerning our eventual reunion and the laughs we would share. He wouldn't know I had run away, not for some time at least, since it was summer and I planned to tell him David and Suki had let me come for my vacation. He wouldn't inquire too closely—I knew him. He would simply be happy to see me, wherever he was and whatever he was doing. And there was no telling what that might be, I reminded myself. I thought about the night we had slept in the Colosseum—the largest chamber pot in the world—by moonlight. What would it be this time? Would we go to Austria and level Vienna the way we had done for Rome? I had a vivid picture of people sweeping glass shards from in front of the Hotel Excelsior. I remembered other things. Once we had tried to steal a piano. Fritz was unhappy with his own piano, a brown Bechstein that had seen better days, and had his eye on a magnificent Bösendorfer at the Conservatoire that was unpopular because its action was deemed too stiff.

"They're all a bunch of sissies," he'd snorted contemptuously. "They want a piano that does all the work for them and makes them sound like Horowitz. That Bösendorfer's a *man's* piano. You've got to be tough to play it. Tough *here*"—and he drummed a tattoo in the air with fingers like pistons, flexing the muscles in his forearms—"or that piano will eat you up and all your pounding will come out as that, just pounding." We'd gotten as far as sneaking into the Conservatoire one night and casing the place with the idea of renting a truck one day and backing it up to the stage entrance of the recital auditorium and rolling the piano onto it. With uncharacteristic prudence Fritz had finally decided against it. There was too much at stake if things went wrong and too many possibilities for things to go wrong. I wasn't big enough to help him and that meant accomplices, he'd explained to me, wolfing down glass after glass of cognac at Mlle. Isabel's, whither we had repaired in some confusion after our examination. "It's too risky with accomplices," he declared. "I'd always be open to blackmail by one or the other of them and a poor musician is a desperate character—desperate—which is why we're considering this in the first place," he pointed out, stroking his mustache. "They're capable of anything. I might be threatened with exposure by a cellist with two children, or turned in by some damned clarinetist for the reward money to pay his electric bill. Anyone who came to play at the house would see the thing.

"On the other hand—" he pursued still later, with one of Mlle. Isabel's girls cuddled in his lap (I think maybe it was Isabel herself), "on the other hand we could paint the Bechstein black and switch them, arrange a substitution.

How long would it take to notice? They never play the Bösendorfer, that's the point. It's just going to waste there. Or maybe we could hold it for ransom!" This idea pleased him so much he stood up with excitement, knocking the girl onto the floor and waking her up. "Yes, ransom, like the Lindbergh baby. No, no, that's no good. If they didn't pay up I'd have to kill the piano and I'm not sure I could go through with it. I might molest it, all right; I think I'm capable of that. I might play a little avant-garde crap on it, or maybe jazz, but murder? I don't know. With molestation, that piano might be traumatized, but with occupational therapy—lots of Ravel, Mozart, what have you—it might get better. But a dead piano—" He shook his head.

I let him rattle on in my mind. Night fell but the cursed rain did not stop. At eleven or so, I gave up. I slid down the embankment again and propped myself up against the rucksack, unable to move a step. I peeled off my sneakers and socks in the darkness and rubbed my swollen, numbed feet, wincing at the blisters, especially the matching pair of beauties at the base of my Achilles tendons. It was cold but I didn't see the good of opening the rucksack or changing clothes. Whatever was there would shortly be as wet as the rest of me if I put it on.

I got the chills and sat shivering. The minutes passed like centuries. I wondered how I had ever come to be in this desolate and miserable place. A stern voice tried to tell me this was good for me, that it would help build my character, that it had all been too easy—not to say fun—up until now. After all, what was sleeping in a comfortable chair in the tourist bar compared to this? A minor discomfort. Or listening to some inane lecture about fallout shelters in the first-class cinema? To say nothing of— And here my thoughts began yet again to stray in the most upsetting direction of all. I clutched myself for warmth as I conjured up the smooth, warm body that had so lately heated mine, the quivering breasts, the yielding thighs crammed against mine in the narrow berth. The moans and whispered exhortations, the sweetness of her breath, the silkiness of her hair, the divine smell of her sex. Why could I not stop torturing myself with thoughts that repeated themselves like a broken record, endlessly replaying the same bit of tune?

I must have fallen asleep, because I remember waking with a start of terror as the ground began to shake beneath me and a sound like thunder crashed about my head— another train was whipping by. I looked about when it had gone and realized the rain had finally stopped and with it the wind. The sky had begun to lighten and by its faint illumination I made out the time: slightly after four. I tried to stand and was alarmed to find that I could not. My body and limbs were so stiff that it was some time before I could induce them to obey the commands of my brain. At last I made it to my feet and celebrated the fact by peeing onto a patch of already soaking gravel.

There was no going back to sleep. With drowsy, inefficient movements I unpacked the rucksack and put on some clothes that were dirty but dry. I shakily applied some Band-Aids to my feet and warmed them with two pairs of athletic socks before forcing them into my loafers. The wet sneakers and other clothes I wadded into a soggy ball and scrunched in at the top of the rucksack. I put on the green sweater for a time and did some stretches to help my circulation. If I hadn't been in good shape to begin with,

goodness knows how I would have made it through the
night. I had heard of people dying of exposure. I was lucky
to be young and fit.

When I was ready to set off, I removed the sweater and
tied it around my waist. It was colder without it, but I knew
I would get warm walking and I preferred to use it as a pad
at the base of my rib cage where the rucksack had been
digging a path to China. It was hard putting the thing on,
as the water had soaked it and added to its weight. The top
was damp and cold at the base of my neck. I crawled back
up to the tracks and started off again, walking into the
mists and listening to the faint stirrings of life that greeted
the day. I heard the twitterings of various birds I could not
identify, and at one point the croaking of a lone frog. It
was depressing to realize how long it took me to walk out
of earshot of his roaring. As my ears attuned themselves to
these little sounds, they mingled with the crunching of my
feet on the railroad gravel and produced a cacophonous silly
symphony.

I rounded a long stretch of curved track and beheld in the
distance the town of Valognes—at least I hoped it was
Valognes. It was seven o'clock in the morning and the mists
were beginning to burn off before a real sun rising at my
back. It was Valognes, all right, as a sign atop a signal box
assured me. I reached the little train station by eight and
collapsed on a bench in a poorly heated, empty waiting
room.

The place began to show signs of life shortly afterwards.
Porters and station personnel showed up, and then an
elderly woman in dark blue with a number of paper bags
and a tallish grandson of eighteen or so came into the *salle*

d'attente (such as it was) and sat solemnly opposite me. I rearranged some of my clothing and possessions and made use of a poorly maintained WC, splashing some water over my chest and face before realizing that there were no towels to dry myself with. In addition the water was a little slow in coming and rusty when it arrived. I was suddenly reminded that I was back in France, where the plumbing was not to be trusted.

By the time I returned, the ticket office had opened. For the first time in almost four years I had occasion to speak my own language. Either from exhaustion or emotional strain, I was greatly moved by the opportunity that presented itself when I merely inquired what time the next train to Paris might arrive. The ticket seller appeared to find nothing odd in my question or irregular in my accent. In a disinterested voice he told me that a train arriving at ten-fifteen would take me to Caen, where I was obliged to change trains with a ninety-minute layover before boarding the express for Paris, which would stop once, at Evreux. I bought a third-class ticket and almost fainted at the smell of warm croissants and hot chocolate wafting across the sill of the ticket window. I returned to my bench, opened the rucksack with the intention of eating the last of the salami, but under the circumstances the sight of it made me gag and I threw it away.

By ten minutes to six in the evening I was in Paris, inhaling the peculiar, distinctive odor of that city, which greeted me the instant I stepped off the train at the Gare Saint-Lazare. In a breath I was whisked back to my childhood. The sight of the Eiffel Tower and the slate–blue-grey rooftops as seen from the train window in the gold-purple twilight brought a bulge to my throat. It seemed as though I were home.

The first order of business was finding a place to lay my weary head. There seemed no point in going to Marly when it was almost dark and I didn't know what I would find when I got there. If there was no one I knew to greet me, I would simply have to return to Paris and search for lodgings, and I had had quite enough train travel for one day. After my miserable night what I wanted most was a comfortable place to sleep.

I got the métro for Pigalle. It never entered my mind to find a pension for the night. I was only fourteen and didn't want a lot of questions. On the other hand if Le Pussycat or Mlle. Isabel's was still in business, I saw nothing strange in asking them to put me up. They would not ask questions, but they might answer some. If Fritz was missing, someone or other in these establishments might have seen him. If they hadn't, that, too, might be suggestive.

Le Pussycat was no longer there; it had been replaced by a kosher delicatessen, but Isabel's was almost exactly as I left it only bigger, as it had taken over the property next door as well. They were just opening for the evening and Isabel looked exactly the same only a little heavier. When I told her my name, she screamed and threw her arms about me and kissed me affectionately on both cheeks.

"George Bernini!" she cried in her beautiful Parisian accent. "How you have grown! Such a handsome young man, I would never have recognized you. Yes, you are a man, look at you! And where is your Uncle Fritz, that silly boy? No one has ever played our piano as he did. The Chopin always made the girls cry. Where is he?"

I explained briefly that I had come from America to find him. Isabel raised her plucked eyebrows at this, but was of no help. Fritz had not been a guest of hers for almost two years. I listened, trying not to project my anxiety and jump to conclusions. After all, just because he hadn't been to Isabel's didn't mean he wasn't somewhere in Paris—though I had to admit it made it seem less likely.

"Can you put me up for the night? I can pay."

"Don't be absurd, George. We never took money from you and you stayed here all the time. Unless, of course, you want one of the girls. I don't think you'll recognize any of them; they certainly wouldn't know you, so big and hand-some." She looked at me inquiringly, a little smile tugging at the corners of her mouth. I shook my head. "Are you sure? You're about the age to learn the facts of life. There are nice teachers here. No? Well, I will show you an empty bed, but you must share it with César when he comes in. Yes, César is still here. Come." And she took me by the hand. How grateful I was to find a friendly face and a warm heart. I had begun to feel quite alone in the world.

César was the pianist in residence who doubled as bouncer, a kindly old gentleman who couldn't have bounced anybody really troublesome. I had slept with him before. Isabel's generosity did not stop with a bed, either. Seeing that I was fairly done in and traveling in filthy clothes, she had one of the girls unpack my rucksack and take its contents for cleaning to the *blanchisserie* that serviced the house. I was given a hot bath and had my back scrubbed by Diane, the only girl I remembered from my previous visits—and she wasn't quite a girl any longer, though her body, with its tiny breasts and narrow shoulders, was as slim as ever. When

I asked about the other girls, Diane laughed and told me they were married, some with children. They had grown up, gone away, started businesses. One had even died.

"I don't know," Diane said, scrubbing my back in the tub, "I can't seem to settle down. I'm so used to this place, to the routine. But I know I must. I can't do this forever." She spoke dispassionately of these things, like a model objectively discussing how long she would remain photogenic. "After all," she concluded, "I am almost twenty-eight. It is time to make a baby."

Diane looked quite lovely to me. It crossed my mind to do business with her, but something stopped me and it wasn't spending the money. It didn't feel right. I had discovered how wonderful sex was, but I hadn't separated it from being in love and it was Dottie that I loved. I sat instead, letting Diane chatter and soaking off the grime, the sweat and the rain until I almost fell asleep in the tub. I gathered later that it was a lively night at Isabel's but I heard none of it and wasn't even aware of César crawling into bed with me.

I was up, rested and refreshed by nine the following morning, which is to say the middle of the night for the toilers at Mlle. Isabel's. César did not stir as I slipped out of bed and off to the toilet. The only person awake besides myself when I went downstairs was an old scrubwoman mopping the floors and beating a few beaten rugs. She paid no attention to me as she went about her work. I went into the little kitchen and made myself a cup of hot chocolate and helped myself to some freshly delivered croissants, still warm from the bakery. When I returned to the foyer I saw that someone had dropped off my clothes (nicely pressed, even though they didn't require ironing). I took them back upstairs and repacked the rucksack, which was almost dry, leaving only the sneakers, which still wanted a few hours of sunshine to become wearable. I tied them by their laces to one of the outside straps where the air could get at them. They bounced around irritatingly as I walked, but I couldn't think of anything else.

On my way out I stopped in the back room on the first floor, where Isabel still maintained her cluttered office. I sat at her desk and scribbled an affectionate and grateful note. I knew she would be disappointed to wake and find me gone. So would Diane. They would want to know where I had been all this time and what I had been doing, but I could not stay to tell them. The nearer I drew to Fritz, or where he ought to be, the greater urgency the matter assumed in my mind. The more I thought about his failure to patronize Isabel's, the more ominous I found it.

I was about to get up from the desk when another thought occurred to me. Perhaps this was a good time to dash off a note to Dottie, one that would be waiting for her at American Express when she reached Florence. I drew forth another sheet of paper and touched the pen to it. There I hesitated. What did I want to say after all? That I loved her, missed her, was desperate for her. But the words didn't come. Petty and paranoid thoughts stood between me and the page. I found myself remembering that she had not mentioned love and fell into the notion I had held walking down those endless railroad tracks in the rain that she had forgot me, more or less, as she was bombarded by a host of more immediate and spectacular stimuli.

I thought about writing her a chatty letter, as if to let

her know I was alive, but without committing myself to any strong expression of feeling. But if I was wrong in judging her state of mind, she might find my letter unaccountably cool and distant and be hurt or angry.

Had I been older I might have—with application, to use Herman Blue's favorite word—struck a compromise between the two extremes that presented themselves to me. I might have composed something unmistakably warm but not overpowering. As it was, I saw no room in my emotions, nor had I the skills as a writer, for compromise. At fourteen I was still inclined to view things in primary colors, in terms of either/or. The subtle pastel nuances of feeling and reason were yet beyond my ken.

I wrote nothing. In a day or so I would check in at American Express in Paris, just behind the Opera, and see what, if anything, she had written me and take my cue from her. I tore up the sheet on which I had written "Dear Delilah" and crumpled it into the wastebasket.

With the sense of eerie familiarity that pervaded so many of my recent experiences (in which I visited old haunts— even though the *Queen Mary* was technically not the old *Ile de France,* yet it did bring back memories), I boarded the train for Marly. The wood-paneled, hard-seated carriage was the same I remembered though oddly smaller. It was empty leaving the city at this hour of the morning, but the countryside through which it traveled was so altered as to be almost unrecognizable. There were more roads and more houses than there had been only four short years before. Some of the houses had suspicious-looking steel wands growing from their rooftops, feeling blindly at the sky— antennas, indeed, were well named.

The station at Marly-le-Roi was the same, but rue Saint-

Denis had begun to become affected by the onslaught of suburban housing. The field by the railroad tracks, where I had played with Sasha and where I had almost seduced Olga, was now locked from view by a high wood wall on which a posted notice informed the curious that a housing development would shortly be erected by one Giovanni Mischione on this spot, ready for occupancy in early 1958.

The other end of the street—"our" end—was still the same though, again, strangely shrunken. Mme. Berthe's house was painted a different color—yellow—and there were no carefully tended geraniums in the window boxes anymore. There were no window boxes.

I pushed open the gate and walked up the flagstone path, feeling a bit like Pip in *Great Expectations*, though there was not and never had been anything remotely gloomy or threatening about the house. Quite the reverse. My heart leapt to behold it, even transformed, and I could not believe that Mme. Berthe would not greet me dourly at the door and stand aside as I made my way past piles of books to where Fritz would be sitting in the kitchen, slightly hung over (as he usually was about this time), inhaling steam from the spout of the kettle, his head hidden in a large dish towel.

No one answered my knock, however. I repeated it several times, then walked around to the back of the house. There was a new addition, a small annex painted the same color yellow, that abutted the old end of the main hallway. It took me some moments to realize that a toilet had been installed at last. I wondered what had become of my thick white china pot, on which I had scooted about, chasing after Hieronymous.

I inspected the yard. It wasn't precisely overgrown, but

neither had it been particularly cared for. The lawn wanted mowing and weeds had replaced Mme. Berthe's precious tomato beds. The strangest sight that greeted me, however, was the shacklike abode that had once belonged to the Ogareffs. It was much smaller than I remembered it, but this impression was heightened by the fact that it was completely overgrown with untrimmed bushes and trees, so that had I not known what I was looking for, I might have missed it entirely and supposed I was looking at a kind of hill in the midst of the yard. Long abandoned to the encroachments of nature, it had been almost entirely consumed by her. In the midst of all the housing projects tearing apart her domain, this one structure she had reclaimed with a vengeance. I forced aside brambles and branches and, chinning myself on a rotting sill, put my face to a pane of dusty, cobwebby glass and peered inside. It was so dark as to be invisible within. It was as if the Ogareffs—and my shameful encounter—had never been. As if Mme. Berthe had never been.

And Fritz?

I wandered like a lost soul about the grounds, alarmed to find that in addition to all life being absent, my memory was playing tricks on me. Everything was out of proportion and things were not precisely in the places I had remembered them.

For a time I sat, confused, by the front gate, propped up against the rucksack. Down the street I could hear the cries of children at play, but they were not children I knew.

I stood at last, heaved the rucksack onto my back again, and pushed open the gate. I had no very clear idea of where I was going or what I planned to do. In all my schemes and plans and fantasies, it never occurred to me that there would not be some clue to where Fritz had gone. I had come half-way around the world, seemingly to a dead end.

Of course I could—and would—wait by the house to see if any of its occupants presented themselves and ask them, but in the meantime it wasn't so much my mind that was perplexed and stymied as my heart.

Without considering where my steps were taking me, I began to retrace them towards the train station. As I looked ahead of me I saw a bent figure approaching. There was something familiar about him and his queer hobbling gait, but it was some moments before I was able to recognize him. I think it was his use of a cane that confused me; I had not seen him with it before.

Nineteen

In Which I Find My Uncle

It was M. Jacopo, the milkman. He wasn't pulling his milk wagon at this hour; he was simply walking with the aid of a cane and puffing on a stubby little pipe. His grey beard was now almost fleecy white, as was his half-dome of hair, and his face was redder than ever by contrast.

As he drew near, he stopped and looked at me.

"George?"

"Monsieur Jacopo!" I ran to him and embraced him so hard I practically knocked him off his unsteady feet, so pathetically grateful was I to have found one remnant of my life where I had left it. It wasn't until much later, when I reconstructed the moment of our meeting, that I accorded the old man his due for his remarkable feat of observation and memory: After five years and at forty paces (and five years produce enormous changes when they occur in the life of a child), he had known me the moment he saw me.

I held him tightly for some moments, almost not knowing how to let go.

When he released me, he asked the usual questions and I

explained that I had returned to Europe with a group for my summer holidays. I embroidered this fiction with little touches of authenticity, but he did not seem inclined to question any of it. I wanted to ask about Fritz, but felt it was a matter that I should work up to rather than broaching without preamble. I told him I had hoped to get away for the day to see Mme. Berthe and the Ogareffs and had been surprised not to find them.

"Mme. Berthe?" He arched his bushy white eyebrows at my ignorance, and looked at me in surprise. "She has not lived here in more than a year. The house is sold and she and her maiden sister have retired to Aix-en-Provence. She has a daughter there, Mme. Berthe, and they live near the daughter, the two old ladies, and mind the grandchildren. Oh, yes, Mme. Berthe has two grandchildren. Girls, I think, but—" He passed a hand over his mouth as he thought about the sex of Mme. Berthe's grandchildren. I could tell it was a point of honor with him to remember such things. Old men forget, but he did not wish to think of himself as old.

"What about the house?" I interjected, to take his mind off what he could not tell and bring him, in any case, back to my purposes.

"The house?" He turned to look at it and pointed with his cane as if to make sure we were speaking of the same building. "Sold to a businessman. No wife, no children, no milk." He lowered the cane and looked at me in perplexity. "Every day he goes to Paris to work on the train and comes back in the night—like your uncle, only his habits are more regular. Every day at the same times he comes and goes. He has business. The house is always empty in the day." M. Jacopo leaned conspiratorially down to me. "He does not take care of the garden," he informed me. "I think he is too busy with his business." He straightened up and looked back at the house with a melancholy, faraway expression. The neglect of the garden distressed him.

"And the Ogareffs?" I prompted, as much to take his mind from the abandoned garden and its associations as to find out about them. He brightened at once. He liked questions with plain answers attached to them.

"The Ogareffs? In America, with you. You do not see them?"

"America is very large, Monsieur Jacopo. Do you know where they went?"

"I know it is large." He ran a gnarled hand through his grizzled beard, scowling and puffing rapidly on his pipe. "New Jersey!" he exclaimed suddenly with satisfaction. "I get the letter from Sasha at Christmas. It is from New Jersey. The father, he teaches at the university. He is a professor of theology." (*"Il est professeur de la théologie"* —it is almost impossible to render M. Jacopo in English. He sounds wrong.)

I nodded and said that was interesting. Then casually I brought up Fritz, as at the end of a long list. I explained that I had written to say I would be visiting this summer and that my letter had been returned.

"Fritz?" his eyebrows twitched again nervously. "Ah, your uncle was a funny man, so kind to everyone, and *such* a piano player! I would stand out in the street—over there —and listen to him practice. Truly an artist. Music is the joy of the heart for an old man." The thought made him introspective and he broke off.

"Do you know where Fritz is now?"

"Now?" He shook his head, searching his memory. "I haven't seen M. Bernini for—almost two years. I think he and Mme. Berthe—there was something, not a fight exactly. I don't know. I think maybe it was a girl. Ah," he interrupted himself angrily and tore the pipe from his lips, knocking the ashes against one heel. "An old man should not be a gossip. M. Bernini, he went away, but where?" He concluded with an eloquent shrug of his shoulders.

I tried not to look into his face as he told me these conclusive tidings, and I tried not to panic. Before I could dissemble further, he began to speak again.

"You know who could tell? You must ask Olga. She will know." And he smiled triumphantly, revealing rows of irregular yellowed teeth.

"Olga?"

"The little girl you loved to play with when you were small. You loved her better than her brat of a brother. You don't remember? How quickly they all forget, except Jacopo," he congratulated himself. "You don't remember all that red hair and the long braids?"

"I remember. I thought you said she went to America."

He shook his head impatiently and stamped a foot. "No, no. Just the father and the awful little boy. Olga, she married François. You remember François? He was going to be a pilot?" M. Jacopo laughed hugely and clapped me on the back. "Well, he *is* a pilot. For Air France. He married Olga and they live in Ville d'Avray. You want their address? Come with me. I'll get it for you."

I said I hoped it wouldn't be any trouble and he assured

me that it would not. He had retired, it seems, and had too much time on his hands and not enough to fill it. A son had been killed in Algeria; another wouldn't speak to him, or else it was he who wouldn't speak; I didn't quite follow the details. He went to the park and played chess a good deal with another old man, Bertrand, but was otherwise at loose ends. Seeing me provided him with a welcome opportunity to be garrulous and reminisce.

"Do you remember," he said, laughing as we retraced our steps, his arm draped heavily over my shoulder, adding to the weight of the rucksack, "you used to ride on the milk wagon and I would pull you around the yard on the way to Ogareff's? You would always shout for me to go faster, faster, and you would never get off. I had to lift you off, and then if I didn't pay attention, you would climb right back on. One day I was halfway down the rue Saint-Denis when I thought the wagon felt heavy. I turned around and I was still pulling you! And you were grinning like a little monkey—so clever you thought yourself! 'Faster, faster,' you said." M. Jacopo laughed so hard at this recollection that he had a coughing fit and we were obliged to stop while his red face got even redder.

Olga! Seeing Olga after all these years; and married to François! I quaked at the thought of confronting her, and the memory of our "experience" (I never knew what to call it) came over me in an instant like a scalding chill. Would she slam the door in my face when she saw me? Yell for François to come and beat me up? How did I dare face her? I scarcely heard M. Jacopo's prattling as we resumed our maddeningly slow walk to his flat. In my mind I replayed the humid afternoon by the railroad tracks and remembered with a flush the sight of Olga's gleaming white underpants drawing nearer and nearer as I squeezed between her legs. I felt myself blushing, my neck chafing red, as though an angry welt had grown there from when she had slapped me frantic with rage and shame and, dormant all these years, was rising again on my neck.

It took almost an hour at the rate we were traveling to reach M. Jacopo's flat, and another fifteen minutes for him to locate Olga's proper address among his effects. The old man was so clearly starved for company that I curbed my impatience to go through with the confrontation of Olga and allowed him to brew me a cup of tea. His spare lodgings contained very little in the way of decor—an old brown and white photograph behind cracked glass on one wall and a plain wood crucifix on the other. He did have a hobby, though: stamps.

"Would you like to see my collection?" he offered, handing me my cup of tea.

I don't imagine he had ever before shown it to anyone. It wasn't a large collection, nor did I suspect it was especially valuable, but he was very proud of it and sat next to me on the faded purple sofa, flipping through the pages and telling me about the different stamps, where they were minted, when, what was special about them, drawing my attention to their various distinctions. Some were franked and others were not; I didn't know why. I murmured what I hoped were appropriate responses, but I had never been interested in stamps and now was not the likeliest time for me to start. They remained a kaleidoscopic series of colored patches, with an occasional eagle on one or profile on another to catch my eye as they whipped by. I longed to dash back to the train station, but my inadvertent visit was clearly so important to my host that I had not the heart to cut it short.

It was M. Jacopo himself who realized at length that he was detaining me.

"What am I doing?" he asked himself with some annoyance. "You are trying to find your uncle and I am boring you with stamps. Forgive me," he went on, gathering up the books with quivering hands and putting them carefully away, "but I so rarely have the chance to display them."

"It is a very impressive collection."

"Oh. Ah. Um," he responded, but I could tell he was pleased with my grave assessment. He helped me slip on the rucksack, remarking on how heavy it was, how strong I must be to carry it, and pointed me in the direction of the train station.

"Come and see me again," he called from the front door of the building. He waved until I was around the corner.

Finding Olga's house was not difficult, though standing before it, I hesitated. Ville d'Avray was virtually next door to Marly, and trains ran back and forth constantly amongst the outskirt villages of Paris. In addition Olga and François lived almost directly behind the station, in a little red-shingled house of three stories that was probably cheaper than most similar constructions because it had the disadvantage of being so close to the noise of the trains. I walked to it from the station in less than a minute, but stood before the door almost another five, trying to calm myself and assemble my nerve. It was midday, and after the train had left, the street was almost completely still except for the occasional chirp of a bird.

All at once I heard the sound of singing, or rather, of humming. Someone was humming inside the house and it sounded like Olga. I knew my courage would not grow by waiting and that if I wished to locate Fritz I must face her. I knocked. My knock was so feeble that she didn't hear it and went on humming. I knocked again, this time more forcefully than I'd intended. I did not appear to be in complete control.

The humming stopped. After a moment I heard the sound of footsteps. The door was opened and standing in it I beheld an attractive but unremarkable woman of eighteen or so in a red and white checked dress with a polka dot apron over it and a baby in her arms. She regarded me blankly.

"Olga?" At the sound of my voice, her eyes widened slightly with the beginnings of recognition. I didn't know what she was about to do—scream, slam the door, or what. "It's George," I added hopefully.

She hesitated a moment longer, then her expression transformed itself into a broad smile and she came forward and hugged me, including the baby in her embrace. I don't know what I expected but it was not this. I stood awkwardly for the hug, like a tin soldier; by the time it occurred to me to return the embrace, she was already extricating herself. She was still smiling with astonishment and pleasure; there was nothing in her look that hinted at the remotest association of me with our mutual humiliation.

"But this is wonderful," she was saying, pulling me into the hallway. "I can't believe it. You've grown so. What a shame François isn't here to see you. He is flying today. Have you met Paul? Paul, say hello to George Bernini." She took one of his tiny arms like a puppeteer and caused it to wave at me, then laughed at her accomplishment. "I was just putting him down for his nap," she explained, and I kept her company while she did it. As I told my string of practiced lies, she punctuated my tale with coos directed at the infant, who, less interested than his mother in my fanciful narrative, fell asleep during it.

Afterwards she offered me tea, which I declined, but when she asked me if I was hungry, I hesitated, and she elected to make me some lunch. Watching her prepare it, I had disquieting memories of another meal she had once put together. The house was a tiny, narrow one, and the kitchen and dining room were essentially the same. There was colorful blue-and-white-print wallpaper, but the windows were small and the place a bit dark at this postnoon hour. In addition the intermittent roaring of trains across what ought to have been their backyard made startling intrusions on the otherwise restful silence of the place.

As she sliced and seasoned, Olga told me of François' progress at Air France and his prospects for advancement. The couple had their eye on a nice house in L'Étang-la-Ville —to buy, not rent, if François got promoted to some new aircraft for which he was training at the present time. It would be a jet.

When she had done, she set the plate of cold meat and chicken before me with some good mustard and kept me company while I ate. The mustard alone brought back my whole childhood world. One thing you could not get in Chicago when I was growing up there (maybe you could get it, but no one I knew did) was a decent jar of mustard. America's idea of mustard was an affront.

Olga had many questions about Chicago beyond my observations about the quality of American mustard. I answered between mouthfuls. In her questions I heard again the sweet, not terribly imaginative young girl I had known. She had simply evolved into a sweet, not terribly imaginative French housewife. Chicago to her meant gangsters. I saw no reason to cheat her out of this notion, but assured her there were safe parts of the city. Paddy Bauler, who continually urged the point that Chicago was not ready for reform, would have been amused by my descriptions.

"Have you ever been to Princeton?" Olga asked. I shook my head. "Papa and Sasha are living there now. Papa teaches at the university. Next year, when the baby is older, we will fly there and visit. On Air France, of course." She laughed, mightily pleased with the thought. "I can't wait to see them, to see America."

I asked what Sasha was up to.

"In the high school. He says he will be a doctor," she replied, but was unable to suppress a trace of her old impatience. She really didn't like her brother very much. I reflected that I probably didn't either.

By degrees I relaxed in Olga's presence, and if she felt any awkwardness towards me, she never showed it. What's past is long past, she seemed to say, in every word and gesture. We were different people then. She may have been a little dull for some tastes, but she was generous to a fault, a real Christian who forgave her enemies—except Sasha, which made her human.

Eventually I questioned her about Fritz, telling her of my

returned letters and my attempts during my "tour" to find
him. She startled me with a little sideways look, but her
first words fell on my ears like manna from heaven.

"Yes, I believe he is in Paris," she said, avoiding my eyes
and turning on the kettle. "He fell in love with one of the
—musicians, and they wanted to live together. This Mme.
Berthe would not allow. I think in a way she was jealous.
She didn't mind the girls who came and went, but Violette
staying on and on was another matter. Finally she had a
row with Fritz and he left. A big truck came, so big it could
hardly get up rue Saint-Denis, and took away all his books,
the piano. Everything."

I listened to this news with a wildly beating heart, my
hands frozen in place around the utensils. It took such a
load off my mind to know that Fritz was still in Paris after
all. I would see him in no time, even before the day was
out! I looked at my watch, suddenly impatient to get his
address, or Violette's, whoever she might be, and head back
to Paris. But there was something in Olga's tone and sideways glance that gave me pause.

"What's wrong?" I asked. "He *is* in Paris."

"Yes."

I laughed. "He's not in jail or anything?"

"No, no." She busied herself with the kettle again, adjusting the flame more carefully than needed for boiling water.
"I'm not sure really, but François heard from someone—I
can't remember now—that he'd been sick."

"Sick? Sick with what?" To me, sick meant a cold, a
sore throat. My imaginary maladies. I couldn't understand
what she was being so mysterious about.

"He was in the American Hospital in Neuilly."

For the first time I began to feel uneasy.

"The hospital? When was this?"

"Earlier this year. I'm sure he's all better now." But she did not sound sure.

"Do you have his address?" I stood up. She stole another guilty look at me.

"I think so. Just a minute. I thought you knew," she mumbled apologetically as she left the room to get it. She returned less than a minute later with a scrap of paper. Fritz, it appeared, was living at 12 rue Chambord in Neuilly. Not far from the hospital, Olga explained in the same awkward tone.

I can't really remember leaving her, saying good-bye or admiring the sleeping baby. I have the vague recollection of promising to return if I could and see François and Paul when he was more lively. I can't remember much of the train ride to Paris or the brief trip by métro to Neuilly.

Children are funny creatures for figuring things out some-times. The last thing to have occurred to me was that Fritz might be ill. I had never known anyone that was ill. I had known no sickness but my own psychosomatic complaints, and as painful as they sometimes were, it had never really struck me that they might be lasting or debilitating in any way. As David had pointed out to Suki more than once, for someone who was sick, I was alarmingly healthy.

Now, as I returned to Paris and automatically sought the métro for Neuilly, I was gripped by an odd sensation that would not be banished until I set eyes on my uncle and saw for myself that whatever it was had passed. I tried to concentrate on the positive side of Olga's news. I wondered if Fritz and Violette were still together, and if they were, what she was like. It made a kind of reassuring sense now that Fritz no longer patronized Mlle. Isabel's. He appeared to have settled down at last, and I was happy to think this might be the case. Fritz had so much to offer; that was the real reason women were so fond of him. He put out such an abundance of energy and uninhibited goodwill. His appetite for life was catching. Whether he was playing the piano or making love, he brought an irresistible enthusiasm to both projects that swept along all before it. I hoped I would find Violette still with him. Olga had said she was a musician. Perhaps before the day was out I would hear them play duets. It had been a long time since I had heard any live chamber music. I wondered now, as I searched for rue Chambord, how I had managed to endure life for so long without it.

Rue Chambord was not, as it happened, very far from the American Hospital. I walked down some lovely tree-lined streets that were agreeably populated on this golden afternoon with strollers, cavorting children, baby carriages and tradesmen. There were some shops on rue Chambord, a bakery and a small sidewalk café. Number twelve was a building more or less like its neighbors on either side, a five-story grey-cream–colored apartment house with its blue and white tiled street number set in the keystone.

Outside the building and across the street from it, I set down the rucksack and ran a hand through my hair in an effort to make myself presentable. Olga's slip of paper said flat four. Telling myself that he might very likely be out at this hour and that I might have to resign myself to waiting, I crossed over and pressed the buzzer. Almost at once I was buzzed in. I ignored the birdcage wood elevator and rushed up two flights of stairs, jumping them two at a time. Huffing and puffing past apartment doors one, two and three, I eventually located number four on the second floor back. In my excitement and impatience I knocked on the door and rang the bell both.

The door was opened as quickly as the buzzer had been sounded. I found myself face to face with a woman who was slightly shorter than I, with a rotund shape and dark curly hair and almost Arabic olive skin. (So Fritz had finally grown out of his blonde phase!) She had a small, bee-stung mouth and flashing black eyes, which looked me up and down in candid inventory. She frowned at what she saw, her lips compressing.

"Yes?"

"Is Fritz Bernini here?" I panted.

With an automatic motion she looked over her shoulder, then back at me.

"What do you want?"

"I am his nephew, George, from America. I've come to see him."

She frowned still further at this, but before she could answer, another voice interrupted.

"Is that the damn piano tuner? What the hell was keeping him? Send him in here."

I knew that mock-testy voice and was not to be denied. Muttering "Excuse me," I pushed past the short woman and rushed into the strange apartment. In my exulted state I did not observe the details of the place or its furnishings. I simply headed for the room where the voice came from, the room with the piano in it.

Stretched out on the sofa when I walked in was my uncle. He looked at me and I at him. He smiled broadly.

"Well, well, well," he grinned. "Hello, chum, what brings you here?"

And I saw at a glance he wasn't sick.

He was dying.

Twenty

In Which I Learn the Facts

He lay on the sofa, unable to rise. He had lost so much weight his body had almost disappeared. He had always been terribly slender; now he was virtually nonexistent. Even his handsome, thin face was now nothing but discolored yellow skin stretched taut over the bones of his skull, and a pair of glittering eyes. His hair had fallen out in large patches where it had once been thick and dark and lustrous. Atop his eyelids, on either side of the bridge of his pen-knife nose, were two little wartlike dots. I later found out that these were caused by the drugs he took. About the only unchanged aspect of him was his bluff, amused voice.

Almost at once, as if by unspoken agreement, we began lying to one another.

"I can't get up, I'm afraid," he began. "I've had a bit of minor surgery recently, and you know how that sort of thing can affect you. The doctor says it will be a while before I'm up and about again. I'm delighted to see you though, chum; really tickled. What brings you here? Pull up a chair, why don't you?"

I pulled up a chair, my head pounding so with blood that I was afraid I was about to faint. I sat down with a sense of relief, as though I had been swimming over my head for hours and my toes had finally felt bottom.

"I'm on this summer tour—that is, I *was* on it, but it was so boring I asked David and Suki if I could get out of it and come see you."

Fritz looked at the ceiling.

"And they said it was okay?"

"As long as I reported where I was."

He looked at me then, without shifting the position of his head. I chose to face the floor during this sideways scrutiny. "A fourteen-year-old kid bouncing alone around Europe," he mused. "Very progressive," he added, finally relieving me of the burden of his gaze. "Did you have a hard time running me to ground?"

I told him how I had found him. He was amused by the parts about M. Jacopo's stamp collection, Isabel's offer to initiate me into the rites of manhood and especially by Olga and her baby. "Those pilots don't waste any time, do they? Breed like rabbits. If I hadn't needed glasses I would have tried for the air force. You don't walk in the air force."

At this point Violette came into the room and we were formally introduced.

"Violette le Chaiye, this is George Bernini, my only begotten nephew and a scoundrel in the mold of his only bleeding uncle. Be nice to Violette, George, she's very rich. I plan to marry her for her money. Observe the sweater—cashmere in June; that's probably a song title. I should have gone into pop music and made a fortune like Johnny Halliday. But Violette has had a profound effect; for her I have performed miracles. I don't drink anymore. How do you like that? You want to know the secret of happiness?" He leaned feebly in my direction, his face a ghastly mask as he grinned. "Get out of the violin section, particularly the *blonde* violin section. Violette is a brunette and a cellist. I wasted years of my life on a matter of semantic confusion. I stayed with the violins when I should have been with the *violettes*. I am now with the violettes, ergo I am in seventh heaven. Or close to it," he amended under his breath.

Throughout this silly introduction, Violette herself smiled broadly at Fritz and then at me. The smile completely transformed her features; I now perceived her as an impish soubrette type. She came forward as I extended my hand. She took it and gave me a kiss on each cheek at the same time.

"He talks about you all the time," she said, still smiling. "I can't believe half the things he says. You two must have made quite an impression on the Eiffel Tower."

"Just don't eat any meat from Les Halles."

"Oh, the Eiffel Tower," Fritz broke in with a faint whoop that turned into a cough. As he gasped for air, Violette and I instinctively exchanged alarmed looks. "The Eiffel Tower," Fritz repeated, subduing the cough. "Those frogs are lucky it's still standing after we got through with it. What a team of con men we were." He faced me again with his glittering stare. "I can't honestly imagine a little whoremaster like you going normal—like to junior high school in Chicago, of all places. Is that where you are? Junior High?"

"Yes, it hasn't been easy. Chicago is a land without mustard and nobody speaks French." I was trying to fall into our old rhythms and conversational conceits, but I was shaking. Fritz, if he noticed, gave no sign. He made a deprecating sound in response to the absence of mustard in Chicago and rolled his eyes.

"You poor kid. You want some mustard now? Or something to drink? A mustard chaser. How long can you stay?"

"Forever," I blurted. "I mean, can you put me up? I can stay as long as it's convenient."

"Of course we can put you up," Fritz offered enthusiastically, though I noticed Violette had not come forward with this invitation as quickly. "He can stay as long as he likes, can't he?" he asked her, his voice fading on a sharp intake of breath at the end of the sentence.

"He is welcome to stay," Violette said. "You shouldn't tire yourself, you know," she added. He nodded, closing his eyes, as much as to say, "I know, I know," then looked at me again. "I think I'll take a little nap," he whispered. "Talk to you later, chum."

"But—"

Violette made a quick sign to me as Fritz closed his eyes again and I followed her out of the room, carrying the rucksack.

She showed me to a little room with a single bed in it and a chest of empty drawers.

"In earlier times this was the maid's," she explained, pulling open the curtains to admit the twilight. "Will it be all right for you?"

"It will be fine, Violette," I said as she made to leave. "Can I—can we talk?"

"I'm sorry." She returned and sat down next to me on the bed. "And I am sorry I was rude at the door when you arrived. I had no idea who you were and it's been a little—" She hesitated. Clearly she didn't know how to deal with me.

My trouble was, I was a child, or at any rate, not an adult. I knew there were probably grown-up ways to talk about what had happened to Fritz and where I fit into the picture now that I had arrived, but I didn't know the grown-up words to use and was only capable of posing the simplest questions in the plainest language.

"What's wrong with him?"

She jerked a quick look at me and her eyes started to water, but she blinked them furiously dry.

"You're only—"

"I'm only fourteen. In some places that's considered grown-up. If I stay, I'll be bound to find out sooner or later, won't I?"

"Were you really on a tour before you came here?" she demanded.

After a moment's pause to make a decision, I shook my head. "He didn't answer my letters; they just came back to me. So I ran away to see for myself."

"From Chicago?"

I told her about my trip. She listened in silence, staring at the tips of her sensible brown shoes as they swung rhythmically back and forth over the edge of the bed. When I had finished she looked at me, smiling again.

"You're quite a little man, George. I am glad you told me the truth. We've had inquiries about you from your aunt and uncle in Chicago."

My heart stopped, and my blood, as they say, froze.

"From David and Suki?"

"Don't worry, we hadn't heard from you and that's what we had to tell them."

"But now? What will you say now? Please don't tell them.

Please. He wants me. You know that. You saw how glad he was to see me. He asked me to stay."

She made a fist and bit the knuckles before pressing them to her forehead, her eyes closed.

"This is such a responsibility," she said at last, with a sigh. "I didn't bargain for this, you know. I never dreamt any of this would happen. And now you want me to—"

"I'll help you," I declared passionately, and grabbed her fist and held it as though nothing but her consent would gain its release. "I'll help you. You need help. You don't need to lie to them. Just don't tell them I showed up. Please."

"I can't promise I won't. But for the moment I won't. He *was* glad to see you."

"What happened?" I asked again. Even as I insisted on knowing, I hoped she wouldn't tell me. She sighed again.

"He has lung cancer," she said simply, as though crawling out from beneath a crushing weight. "They removed one lung almost six months ago. The question was whether they'd gotten it in time." She paused heavily. "Unfortunately they hadn't. He will die."

It was one thing to intuit Fritz's condition, but quite another to hear it bluntly spelled out in simple French. Apparently when all was said and done, grown-ups used the same words children did. I sat down, or rather fell back on the bed, as though the wind had been knocked out of me.

"Are you all right, George?" She put her arms around me and drew me to her, which had the terrifying effect of bringing me close to tears. I shook my head frantically from side to side like a boxer trying to clear his senses from a blow to the temple. Her response to this was to hold me tighter and press my twisting face into her cashmere sweater. I pulled her against me with all my strength then, hoping that if I pressed my eyes hard enough against her there would be no space for tears to squeak through.

"Isn't there anything they can do?" I wailed into her shoulder. She held me tighter in response and I could feel her torso heaving.

"They tried, George. They tried."

We sat there quietly for some time. Violette cried softly and I concentrated on holding her to take my mind off the possibility that I, too, might create a scene, which was a thought not to be endured. Gradually, as my terror of weeping receded, my mind began to function again, though sluggishly, like an engine misfiring. At first I was simply overcome with the tragedy of it, the sheer hopeless, oppressive sorrow. (Watch it, *mon cher,* better get off this topic.) I went on to feeling sorry for myself in a funny kind of way. I mean, here I had come all the way from Chicago, braved a thousand privations (or so I totaled them at the moment) and even turned my back on the girl of my dreams, and for what? For Fritz; Fritz, who was still a young man, but who couldn't come out to play; for Fritz, who was going to be mowed down before he even had a chance. After he'd finally fallen in love and stopped drinking and everything. After the good things had started to happen to him. (Watch it, *watch it*—you're in danger of a household accident!)

I forced myself to become aware of Violette crying next to me and furrowed my brow, compelling myself to concentrate on her. As I did, it dawned on me that I was not alone in my misery. What had happened was as much a surprise and disappointment to her hopes in life as it was to Fritz or me. And as she had said, she never dreamt it would happen, and now all the responsibility had fallen on her.

"Does he know?" I asked, wiping at a suspicious damp patch on her shoulder.

"He knows, but we don't discuss it. He pretends."

"How long will it be?"

She shrugged, produced a small handkerchief from her sleeve and blew her nose into it like a man.

"A few weeks, according to the doctor."

The timetable almost started me off again. I leapt to my feet and started shaking my head like the punch-drunk fighter and began jerkily unpacking the rucksack, putting various items in drawers. She remained on the bed and watched me. I talked casually over my shoulder. "Does he need medicine? Or money? I have some money—"

She laughed a little bit. "This isn't quite *La Bohème,* thank God. Fritz wasn't lying. I'm rich. At any rate my family is, so he's been getting the best care. We took this place because it's close to the hospital and because it has a room—this one —for a night nurse. But I'm glad you're here." She sprang up and gave me a hug. "It's been hard managing alone. You will stay? It's a lot to ask. I don't know if you know what's involved. You're only—"

"I know. Believe me, this isn't what I expected, either." And it wasn't. I had a funny feeling in my stomach as all the truth began to sink in. "Is it all right if I go for a walk?"

"But of course. I'll get you your own key. You can come and go as you please."

"I'll be back in a little while," I told her at the door of the flat. She nodded and closed it after me.

I stepped out into the cool early evening. It was an indigo such as you see only in retouched postcards or in Paris. I began to walk and kept walking as if by doing so I could leave my problems—or rather, my problem—behind. As I looked about me at the world going on, unconcerned with the tiny drama of a single life being played out behind the unthought-of door marked number four, second floor back, at 12 rue Chambord, it seemed inconceivable that this larger reality should be so dominated by the smaller one, of which only I, as I walked, was aware. Fritz would live—or, as it happened, die—behind that door, and no one but Violette and I would know or be affected by it.

As I walked and let my consciousness begin to absorb the situation and my reactions to it, I began to admit that I didn't much feel like staying. The sight of Fritz terrified me. I had not bargained for anything like the sight of him, half-dead already, that had greeted me when I walked into the living room of the flat and saw him prone on the sofa. I thought longingly of David and Suki and Hieronymous. It seemed preferable to go back and take my chances in Chicago than to witness this. After all, as Violette kept pointing out, I *was* little more than a child and could hardly be expected to shoulder these shocks. It wasn't even as though I were Fritz's child. The whole thing might very likely scar me for life, if it hadn't already. It was bad enough having found Larry Hayes hanging from the gymnastics high-bar. I'd done my bit. Even Fritz, when he thought about the matter, probably wouldn't want me to stick around.

I knew, too, that in a burst of spontaneous generosity, I had offered—no, that's not right—I had *pleaded* to stay. I had held Violette's fist and told her I could help, but the truth was, I couldn't. She could afford all the help she needed, and I was simply acting on reflex at the time, incapable of stopping myself from volunteering. Surely she would see that. They would both see it. As I walked, I told myself that Fritz's illness was not my fault, that it would have happened whether I showed up to see him or not and that it would take its inexorable course whether I stayed or not. They couldn't blame me for returning to America under these circumstances. In fact, if David and Suki knew where I was, I would be forcibly returned.

There was a thought.

All I had to do was figure out how to notify David and Suki and I would be extricated from this mess as if by magic. It would all be taken out of my hands and neither Fritz nor Violette need ever know that I had made any choice in the matter at all. I might protest loudly at my extradition, but as Fritz had once told me in similar circumstances, I wouldn't have anything to say about it.

The question was how to tell David and Suki. The simplest solution was for me to write or, better still, if I could arrange it, to telephone.

I felt better at once for reaching these conclusions, and having reached them, I returned to the flat.

Violette and Fritz were having dinner in the living room on a card table set up next to the sofa. A place for me had been set and Violette had automatically poured me a glass of wine. I had not experimented much with liquor, but the sight of them smiling in welcome as I entered the room made me very thirsty.

"What do you think of the neighborhood?" Fritz asked as I began to eat and drink.

"It's very pretty; there's lots more people and cars here than in Marly. It's more like Chicago."

"We did that on purpose because we knew you were coming, chum. We knew you yearned for the city life, the bright lights of State Street, wherever that is."

Throughout dinner they asked me all sorts of questions about Chicago and my life there. I endeavored to answer them in a lively fashion, but it involved a deal of evasions and outright lying if I was to avoid depressing Fritz with the truth about my friendless existence or my grades or Larry Hayes's suicide. I concentrated on tales of David and Suki, especially Suki, who made for good laughs. I did not tell the stories at her expense, for I found as I thought and spoke of her lately that I longed for her warmth and unthinking support. I longed very much to hear her say again that everything was just fine.

"Whatever happened to Hieronymous?" Fritz wondered. "You used to call him Hairy Mouse, then Harry Mouse, then finally just Mouse. The truth was," he told Violette, much amused, "Hieronymous was a great mouse- and bird-killer. You never saw such technique in a harmless housecat. He'd creep up on innocent sparrows as though he were a miniature tiger."

"A Siamese tiger," I agreed.

"The worst kind," Fritz opined, shifting his position with a grimacing effort. Violette started to help him but he shook his head and stayed put. "The worst thing about a Siamese tiger," he insisted on saying, "is that it's usually connected to another one." I couldn't help laughing. I didn't know if it was the effects of the wine or not. I was beginning not to care.

"Did you hear about the boy who couldn't speak?" Fritz asked us. We shook our heads. "Very sad. He was dumb, couldn't say a word. The parents were reconciled to this tragic deprivation over the years as they passed and the poor thing grew up. Then one night at dinner—he must have been about fifteen—the kid turns around and says, 'This spinach is terrible.' Well! You can imagine. The parents are dumbfounded with shock and disbelief. 'Bernie,' the father says, tears rolling down his face, 'Bernie, my son—you can talk!' 'Yeah, I can talk,' the kid says, 'no big deal.' 'But,' the mother says, 'all these years—all these years and you never said a word!' The kid says, 'Yeah, because up till now everything was fine.'"

It seemed as though I had never heard anything so funny. Violette thought she had never heard anything so funny either. We laughed and laughed, and my hand shook so that I spilled the wine as I poured myself another glass. I grew gayer and blearier. Fritz's joke about the boy who didn't speak was now more than funny. It was tragic that the lousy spinach had ruined his perfect life. I kept this thought to myself, as I knew there was something not quite right with it, but I continued to feel sorry for the little boy with the spinach.

After dinner I witnessed an extraordinary ritual. Violette helped Fritz half-stagger, half-crawl to the piano bench. When she had tenderly seated him on it, gasping for breath and holding on to the top of it as though he were clutching the north face of Everest for dear life, he waited while she took out and tuned her cello. She went about this with utter concentration, pursing her lips in the fashion I had first seen them as she drew the bow across the A string several times, adjusting the peg slightly until she was satisfied, then looking up.

"She's really good," Fritz assured me, looking at me over the top of his skinny arm. Violette said she was ready. "The Schubert?" Fritz asked.

"If you like."

They didn't use music, but played the "Arpeggione" sonata from memory. It was obvious they'd spent a lot of time playing together. Even in my woozy state I was aware of the sympathetic understanding they as a unit brought to the music.

But the most miraculous thing was the change that came over Fritz. Instead of sitting doubled-over and straining for air, he sat erect and completely alert and played with all the style and vigor of his earlier performances. In fact, as I sat there and closed my eyes and listened, it seemed to me he was playing with greater concentration and sensitivity and control than I had ever heard from him. I cannot remember a pianistic performance so free and at the same time so thought-out. I knew something had freed him—he played as though he had nothing to lose. At first I decided it was love that allowed him to play this way. Later I realized it was death. When I was much older I heard music like this once again. Someone played me a recording of the last recital of Dinu Lipatti at Besançon. Lipatti, like my uncle, was dying as he played, and the condition, coupled with his own unique talent, gave to his performance the same feeling of incandescent purity and rapture, almost as though Lipatti were playing under the influence of some powerful narcotic, which, come to think of it, in his condition, he may well have been. For all I know, Fritz's painkiller or killers also contributed to his playing that night, but I do not think so. A drug might sap the reflexes and the judgment if it were to do anything. It might rid you of certain inhibitions, but that wouldn't explain the incredible precision and clarity that went with Fritz's playing.

I sat there and listened to this new Fritz, marveling at his touch and wondering whether perhaps the wine was affecting my hearing, but knowing that it was not. I wasn't drunk —not yet, anyway; I just wanted to be. I was going to leave Fritz to his fate, and Violette to shoulder it for both of them. I was crazy about me.

When the piece had ended, Fritz shrank back into his smallness as though a plug had been pulled somewhere and all the air inflating him to something like his normal proportions had rushed out. He clutched the piano top again, his head resting on his arms.

"Didn't I tell you she was good?"

The night nurse arrived and was introduced as Mme. Klein. She favored me with a starched but not unfriendly smile and helped Fritz get to his bed. I gave him a light kiss good night as he groped his way past me.

Violette came back shortly afterwards and I helped her put away the dinner things. We didn't wash them as a maid would come in the morning, she had explained; just rinsed them and left them in the sink. When we said good night, she did not appear to notice that I had retained the wine bottle, which was slightly more than half-full.

I took the bottle to my room with me and curled up around it like a drunk, swigging from the neck in order to stop my mind and enable me to sleep. This business of being fourteen was neither here nor there. Sometimes I felt grown-up and as capable, if not more so, than most other grown-ups. Hadn't I planned and executed the most intricate escape, gotten from Chicago to Paris on two hundred dollars and a lot of nerve? Hadn't I performed like a grown-up in bed with Dottie Kirstein? Hadn't I trudged thirty miles on a man's legs from Cherbourg to Valognes? Hadn't I coolly cut down Larry Hayes and startled the police with my aplomb?

But I knew, as I posed all these questions to myself between swallows, that such feats as I had managed were those of a strong and clever boy, which, when all was said and done, was all I was.

In trying to get myself drunk, I only succeeded in making myself sick. The feeling began to steal over me as I lay on my back, cradling the bottle like a glass child in my arms. I fought throwing up for as long as I could, but when I realized it was inevitable, I got to the bathroom in time and quietly heaved up a good deal. It had been a long day, starting with waking up at Isabel's. I was suddenly exhausted as well as literally empty.

As I padded back to my room, I passed Fritz's bedroom; the door was slightly open. I stopped and looked. Mme. Klein was giving Fritz in injection in his rear as Violette, on the other side of the bed, held his arms and they looked at each other. When the injection was completed, Mme. Klein helped Fritz back into bed. Violette remained seated next to him. They were obviously in the midst of a discussion of some kind.

"—simply write to them," Fritz said with an effort at sounding businesslike. "He can't stay here, that's all there is to it."

"He wants to," Violette said quietly.

"Don't you believe it," he snapped. "Anyway, I don't care what he wants. Do you think this is what I want? What *I* want?" he repeated sullenly. "But he can't stay. So write the letter like a good girl."

Violette promised she would and I returned thoughtfully to my room.

Twenty-one

King Solomon's Mines

"There were some letters on the hall table," Violette said a day or so later at breakfast.

"Mme. Klein mailed them for you," I told her carelessly.

"Mme. Klein?"

"Wasn't she supposed to? She saw them lying there on her way out and they were stamped. I thought they were to be mailed and told her to go ahead."

"They were." She looked at me curiously, wanting to ask but not daring. I busied myself buttering a croissant and asked how Fritz had passed the night.

"He got a little sleep for a change."

"So you did, too, for a change. Why do you bother with Mme. Klein if you plan to wake up whenever he does, Violette? You're just throwing away your money."

She laughed; it came out slightly brittle.

"Anyway, it's not my money. What are you going to do today?"

"I've got a couple of errands to run," I said importantly. "I'll be back after lunch."

I took the métro to l'Opéra, and sitting on the train, I drew from my pocket the letter addressed to David and Suki. I debated opening it but decided the contents were none of my business. I tore the thing in half, stillborn in its envelope, then in quarters, and threw the fistful of scraps out the window. It was possible that Violette would suspect my interception and sit down and write another letter. For all I knew she was scribbling away that minute and would mail it by the time I returned, while I would never the wiser. Or perhaps she would telephone. There was nothing I could do in the long run to prevent her if she was determined. As it happened, fate had placed the first of her communications into my hands. I had bought a little time; that was all.

I did have some errands to run. I felt there was not enough in the way of distractions or amusement in the flat. I bought a set of Chinese checkers, a game that required absolute concentration, and had the advantage of allowing two, three or four of us to play it at the same time. I bought two new phonograph records, a Rubenstein-Wallenstein recording of the Schumann Piano Concerto Number One and a Rubenstein solo album in which he played music by De Falla and Granados.

I also bought a copy of *King Solomon's Mines* in English. I had mentioned the title to Fritz and he couldn't remember ever having read it. He usually immersed himself in metaphysical tomes (hence all those weighty philosophic discussions on the train in and out from Marly), but I wondered if a story mightn't be more absorbing, or at the very least, represent a change. At any rate it was my favorite story (tied, really, with *The Count of Monte Cristo* and *The Three Musketeers*—I read them when I was supposed to be studying) and the mere possession of it in my hands again gave me a kind of comforting assurance. In times of trouble I had learned to trust art instead of people. Mozart and H. Rider Haggard would never let you down. I knew that if I had well and truly decided to settle in for this horrible event— and it appeared as though I had, somehow—we would all need to busy ourselves and each other, especially when the time came when Fritz could no longer sit at the piano.

As I went about my purchases, I passed the American Express office behind the opera house. This was no accident, though I tried pretending it was, as though shopping in this vicinity was just a coincidence. I knew quite well that I needn't have come all the way in from Neuilly to l'Opéra just to find a bookstore and a record store.

It was hard for me to go in. I felt that I had endured enough of life's disagreeable left hooks and upper cuts lately and wasn't ready to lead with my chin again. I walked back and forth a few times as though thinking it over. Really I was working up my nerve, because I knew finally that I had to make sure.

"Oh, yes," the clerk at the B section said when I showed my passport, "I remember something came in with your name on it." I was sure this was unlikely and disliked her for raising my hopes just to show off her memory. The American Express office in Paris is huge. My mouth dropped open in astonishment, therefore, when she flipped through the pile and extracted a postcard.

"George Bernini," she said triumphantly, and smiled at my stupefaction. "Thought they'd forget all about you, eh?" She handed me the postcard. All I saw was that it was a painting of the *Queen Mary* that the Cunard office gave out

to everyone who sailed on her; they kept stacks of the postcards in all the writing rooms on board.

I walked out of the place on air, hugging the postcard to
my breast as though it were a stock certificate. Before finding
a café in which to sit down and savor it, I postponed the
delicious moment by stopping at a stationery store on the
boulevard des Italiens and getting some paper, envelopes and
a ballpoint pen with which to reply.

On the picture side of the postcard, she had drawn an *X*
in ink along one side of the hull, approximating the location
of the cabin. "*X* marks the spot," she had written as the cap-
tion in the sky part of the picture. I turned over the card, my
breath coming in little jerks. "Dear Sweet One," it ran, post-
marked Cherbourg,

You have not been gone an hour but I miss you already. I hope
you find your uncle and that all is well. I hope there is a card
waiting for me at AMEX in Amsterdam. Running out of space;
help!

Love, Dottie.

PS: [this was crammed into the space above the part for the
address] I am sorry if I am bossy. Don't let me be.
PPS: What's your address?

She said *love*. It wasn't a long letter, but she'd managed to
squeeze in a lot with her exquisite miniature penmanship.
(She drew little circles with which to dot her *i*'s.) I read the
card several times and even managed to decipher a cramped,
incompleted sentence to the effect that she was writing in a
café in Cherbourg before getting on the boat train. She had
been writing while I'd been walking! I read it all again and

again, so greedy that at first I tried to ingest all the words at once and choked on the meaning. Eventually I got myself to slow down and worked my way through it with a forefinger under each precious word. My eyes watered up, but I blinked rapidly: It was the first good news I'd had in what seemed an age of walking, looking and then—God help me —finding. I wiped my eyes with my sleeve, ordered a lemonade to celebrate and set about replying.

Almost at once I became confused. My first impulse was to pour my heart out and tell her everything, but I decided upon reflection that this was probably not a good idea. If Dottie felt I was floundering under the weight of an intolerable burden, it would at the very least dampen her own summer; at the most it might cause her to act rashly. She might take it upon herself to let someone in Chicago know where I was. One thing I must not do was give her my address. The best thing, probably, would be to disguise things a little so as not to alarm her.

I would have to lie yet again. I didn't like the idea of lying to Dottie. On the other hand it was all I seemed to do these days. I wondered, as I took up the pen again and began my fiction, whether lying was not becoming so much a way of life for me, a reflex action, that eventually I would fail to recognize truth when I saw it or to understand its value. When I considered how wrong lying was said to be and then attempted to total up how many untruths I'd told in the last three months, it seemed as though I were completely depraved. If there was a Hell, I appeared likely destined for it. With a faint smile playing about my lips as I wrote, I remembered my exchange with Sasha when he had gleefully pronounced me damned. We had both been proven right.

In which case, what harm either way would a few more lies do?

Dear Dottie:
How wonderful to get your card. Sorry I didn't write you in Amsterdam, but I had a little trouble finding Fritz and didn't have time. This should reach you in Florence, I hope. I miss you, too, though I am having a fine time. It's great to see Fritz again. He's been a little under the weather lately, but is well on the way to being his old self again.

I went on to tell her in glowing detail about the rich cellist with whom Fritz had fallen in love and how happy we all were. I told her what beautiful music they made together:

I know you don't listen much to classical music, but I wish you could hear them play. They are wonderful together. Take care and write again c/o AMEX, Paris. I would really love hearing from you.

Love, George.

I read this distant production unhappily when I was done writing it. My penmanship compared to hers was rather unsightly and hard to read, more like a vicious scrawl. But what really bothered me was the contents of my note, which reflected the overcalculation with which it had been composed. I wanted to rant on about how much I loved her, but if I did, it seemed to follow that I must tell her everything else, which I knew I couldn't do. For the moment I wanted to put my entire life on a back burner and keep it there until everything calmed down, if it ever would.

Feeling like a complete shit, I mailed the letter and returned to Neuilly. There I was reintroduced to Emile Laurent, the famous teacher of composition and theory at the Conservatoire with whom Fritz had studied. Laurent must have been over seventy on this occasion, but he was as trim, erect and dapper as I last remembered him. He wore a little polka dot bow tie, his shoes had spats, his lapel a boutonniere and he carried a walking stick. Nevertheless, he did not strike one as a dandy. Everything was in perfect taste, and his own dignified mien precluded frivolous interpretations of his dress.

He barely remembered me from when I was seven, or whenever it was we had last met, but gravely insisted he would have known me anywhere. The visit I had interrupted appeared rather an awkward one; Laurent did not know how, or perhaps did not care, to dissemble. He and Violette and Fritz sat more or less embarrassed together, making sporadic monosyllabic chitchat on absolutely inane topics (they even discussed the weather) as though they were looking at each other from across the crater left by a giant meteor that, however, social conventions insisted they ignore. With my arrival Laurent had his excuse to leave. At the living room door he turned and remembered something.

"I have a pleasant piece of news for you, Ernesto. Monteux is conducting the Orchestre Radiodiffusion in two weeks. Be sure to listen."

"What's on the program?" Violette asked, giving him his straw summer hat, which perfectly complemented the seersucker suit.

"Oh, nothing much. Thank you. Franck's *Psyche*, Strauss's *Zarathustra* and Bernini's *Equations*."

"What?" we all three exclaimed together. "He must be out of his mind," Fritz insisted in the next breath. "Are you certain?"

"Quite certain. And I'm not at all of your opinion, by the way." Laurent touched his mustache lightly; I suddenly understood that Fritz had grown his as a kind of *hommage* to his teacher. "You'd do well to be a little more tolerant of new music, Ernesto. Sometimes it takes more than one hearing to understand or grasp a new work, especially if it experiments with unfamiliar ideas. Also, Monteux is a great conductor. Try to be a little tolerant."

He tipped his hat, eyes atwinkle, and left.

"I wonder how he pulled that off," Fritz mused when he had gone.

"Fritz!" Violette exclaimed impatiently. "He didn't have anything to do with it. Don't be a silly. You think he tells Monteux what to put on his programs?"

"Anyhow, don't you get a royalty?" I asked.

Fritz laughed and made a familiar sign of approval. "Here's the only practical one among us. He doesn't worry about how, or why; only how much. That's looking at the bright side, chum. They owe me money."

Clearly pleased and excited by the news, Fritz made it to the piano and played two Mozart sonatas (without the repeats) before collapsing with the effort. He had a good nap.

After dinner (and much coaxing by Violette to try and eat more—she talked to him as though urging a child), Mme. Klein arrived and closeted herself with Fritz for his injection. I was becoming familiar with certain words and phrases without knowing precisely what they meant: corti-

sone (still relatively new), morphine, radiation or chemo-
therapy and other grisly adjuncts to the cancer victim's lexi-
con and the vocabulary of his family.

When Fritz was ready for bed, I came in and announced
my intention of reading out loud to him from the book I
had bought.

"*King Solomon's Mines?* No philosophy?"

"You'll really like this," I insisted, looking at Violette for
help. "Just give it a chance."

"I'm going to listen," Violette said. "I will practice my
English."

"Oh, all right."

I started reading to him. I had never read out loud before
and it took me a while to get the hang of the thing. I began
too fast and I had trouble with a lot of Haggard's Boer-
African words, but by and by I improved so that even Violette
could follow the story of Allan Quatermain, Captain Good
and Sir Henry Curtis. Fritz was hooked by the end of the
second chapter and lodged a faint protest when Mme. Klein
insisted I stop for the night. The chapter ended with Quatermain talking about going to sleep and dreaming about José
da Silvestre and the diamonds, and Fritz announced his intention of doing the same thing. Violette, who can't have
grasped all of it, said she was totally absorbed and couldn't
wait for more of the story tomorrow. As she said it, her eyes
shone kindly on me and I felt as if I had done something
clever and good.

"You've certainly provided me with incentive," Fritz allowed as I closed the book. "Scheherazade's incentive," he
whispered more or less to himself.

I forced myself to give Fritz a kiss on his waxen cheek,

went to bed and thought about Dottie, our letters, and masturbated, remembering our time together on the boat.

With the reading of *King Solomon's Mines,* the days became divided into chapters and Fritz grew weaker with each chapter, though his interest in the tale remained unflagging. We listened to the records I had purchased and to others in his extensive collection; we played Chinese checkers; people came to visit, mostly fellow musicians, but occasionally a confrere from one of the odd, crazy jobs. The visits were always strained—everybody talking across the unmentionable meteor crater. Sometimes I felt the very effort it cost Fritz to maintain his jaunty *sangfroid* in the face of continual covert—but always obvious—scrutiny and anxiety on the part of his friends did more to sap his vitality than if we'd all been able honestly to discuss what was happening.

We listened to the Radiodiffusion concert and heard Fritz's composition performed at the end of it. I was astonished, and I think Fritz was as well, by how good it sounded. For Violette, who had never heard it before, it was an unalloyed thrill. Her bias, on the other hand, was obvious and Fritz and I, looking at each other across the room during the piece, took it into account and dismissed her reaction while at the same time marveling at our own. In the middle he raised his eyebrows as much as to say, "Who'd have thought it?" The dissonances and Teutonic heavinesses were still in evidence, but somehow they were not objectionable or jarring or alien, as they had been five years before. In some undefinable way the music had changed. Something had changed. It was no longer best moments from Hindemith crossed with a little of this and a lot of that, adding up to a lot of nothing. Fritz had written better than he knew—

certainly better than I had known, for I had been disappointed when I first heard *Equations,* and I had not been alone.

It was the more remarkable therefore to listen to the sustained applause and audible *Bravo*'s that greeted the work at its conclusion. Fritz cocked his head at the sound, his mouth partially open. He could not quite bring himself to absorb his own relation to the cheering on the radio. The announcer told us what we had just heard and concluded the broadcast. Violette walked up and down, she was so excited, and her eyes shone with delight. I think she was more pleased than Fritz. At any rate she knew how to be pleased more than he did.

"It was wonderful! Darling, it is a great piece!" she trilled. He allowed her to gush for a time and to kiss him, then asked if she would make us some tea.

"They don't know *merde* from Mineola," he groused in the direction of the radio after Violette had left the room. The experience appeared to have upset him in some way.

"That girl was right," I told him.

"Which girl?" He turned his face away from me, towards the wall.

"You know. The one who was with us that night. She said time would tell and she was right. You told her to shut up."

"No, I didn't," Fritz said to the wall.

"Well, you wouldn't listen to her. Anyway, she was right; time *did* tell, and at least you didn't have to be—" I stopped in confusion. He didn't move.

"Yes? You were saying?"

"Nothing," I said in a miserable voice.

"Nothing?" He pursued relentlessly, still not looking at me.

"I can't remember."

"You were saying that at least I didn't have to be dead before my music was discovered to be okay." I was so ashamed that I could not speak now. Fritz, on the other hand, appeared to find the idea morbidly arresting and turned to face the ceiling. "Well, I have to admit you have a point. And she was right. If you live long enough you keep on learning the darndest things." He lavished some irony on the words "if you live long enough." I sat biting my lips and feeling my face burning red as if I had sat in the sun without any protection. He looked over at me with an almost hostile detachment. "No? You don't have anything to say?"

"I'm sorry. I didn't mean it to come out like that." He continued to glare balefully as though I were a sample of some detestable species and he was staring at me through a monocle. "I didn't." Abruptly he switched off his searchlight gaze and returned his attention to the ceiling. "What are you thinking?" I found myself using Dottie's constant phrase.

"I'm scared," he said shortly after a pause. It was the thing I feared most to hear him say. I rose and muttered something about leaving him to his nap, but he wasn't buying any. "Running away, eh? I'm not supposed to embarrass anyone with references to my unfortunate condition, is that it? Don't make life hard for anybody, just wend my way quietly and alone? You little shit. You're just like the rest of them."

"I don't know what you want me to say," I complained in a small voice, looking at the floor.

"I want someone to talk to me," he snarled. "I'm very sick

here; I'm lonely; I'm frightened; I'm in pain and everybody wants to avoid the topic. But me—I can't avoid it." He looked at me pathetically. "I can't talk about it with Violette—it terrifies her—so I find myself telling you and you've got to be tough and take it. You think I don't know what's going on here because we don't talk about it? You think I don't know you know about it? I'm dying." He said it harshly and choked on it. "That's why I'm scared. I'm halfway across the Jordan right now, and yes, I hate you. I hate you because you're all going to live and I'm not." But he didn't sound very hateful.

In an odd way his explosion was a relief for both of us. I went over to him, and not knowing what else to do, I put my arms around him. He let me hug him and hold him for a while. "It's not fair," I whispered. If he heard this, he gave no sign.

"That's better," he said after a time. "I guess that's what I really wanted out of all this—some cuddling. People tend to stay far away from you when you're dying—as I can now testify—but that's when you'd like someone to hold your hand."

I took his hand. Of all his anatomy, only his long, graceful fingers were unmarked by the savage progress of his disease.

"Violette wants to touch you," I said into his ear. "She wants to marry you. Why won't you marry her?"

"Come on." He tried to withdraw his hand but I retained my hold on it.

"I know you have a million reasons, but it would mean everything to her. She's going to be just as upset whether you're married to her or not." He said nothing, but stopped trying to take back his hand. "Will you think about it?" He mumbled something and then asked if I was going to read to him. Violette returned with the tea (which he didn't drink), and I took up the book.

We never alluded to the question of his death again, but something was easier between us after that. We both knew that we knew.

I had insomnia now. When Fritz was awake, I'd be awake. I continued to get letters from Dottie at American Express and to word careful replies. Her letters began to reflect the confusion she was detecting in mine. She was in Perugia now, and I could tell from the way she'd begun to concentrate on the details of her life there instead of on us—including an oblique reference to an attractive Italian teacher in his twenties, clearly designed to goad me—that she was upset, sad or annoyed by my correspondence. Probably all three. There was little I could do but continue to write silly jokes and concoct bizarre or inane anecdotes about life in Paris, always omitting my address. To do otherwise would have been to let her in on the whole heart-rending affair and I could not foresee the consequences of putting myself in her hands. I had been so long not trusting people since I had vowed I would not trust them that now, when common sense told me to confide in her, I could not, but withdrew instead and, stoically benumbed, played Chinese checkers.

Once a week the doctor came and huddled with Fritz and then with Violette and then with Mme. Klein. He regarded me with a mixture of stiffness and unease as he came and went, clearly not knowing what to say to me. It occurred to me that Fritz had taught me something when he had insisted on talking about his own imminent death. We smother each other sometimes in the name of tact. Out of some misplaced sense of decency, coupled with our own terrors, we deprive those in need of talking about their needs. We tell ourselves that they don't want to or need to, but we are lying. Can we really pretend that a man in a wheelchair never thinks about his missing legs? The doctor knew and I knew. We both would have been happier if we could have acknowledged this. He wouldn't have had to avoid my eyes; for my part, the secret aspects of Fritz's journey towards death would not have remained more shrouded in obscure rites and terrifying mystery than they needed to be.

King Solomon's Mines continued to absorb all of us day by day. I got to be a good reader, describing the bloody civil war in Kukuanaland and the machinations of the witch, Gagool. Some of the only truly peaceful moments for all three of us came when H. Rider Haggard transported us out of the steamy Paris of late June and into the beautiful and exotic climes of Kukuanaland and the struggle for power and diamonds going on there. There were frequent deaths and references to death in the novel. At first I was self-conscious reading them, but after our talk about dying I read them simply as part of the story, no longer looking up to see how Fritz was reacting to them.

I escaped from the flat whenever I could for as long as I could. I went to the movies or I just walked. The world was going on without us, and certainly without Fritz. His absence from it would not make such a gaping hole that many would notice it. Again and again I thought of telling Dottie about what was happening, but always I stopped myself. Why bother her with it? Surely then she'd only have to burden someone else. And so Fritz's fatal illness would become meaningful out of all proportion—to people who hadn't even known he was alive. Besides, she might take matters into her own hands and summon help from Chicago.

One day, in the middle of a Chopin prelude, he keeled over at the piano. Violette screamed and I carried him to bed. He was tiny and as I held him in my arms and felt how slight he was, how thin and feeble, I knew it wouldn't be long now.

He finally allowed Violette to marry him. It was a strange ceremony and inevitably grotesque under the circumstances. I was best man and Violette's father, a very wealthy business-man who looked utterly panicked by the whole thing, gave away the bride at Fritz's bedside, while her mother, an over-dressed matronly type, stifled tears throughout the brief service. Violette cried, too. At first I thought her tears were about the hopelessness of the situation, but soon I realized otherwise. She was crying only because she was in love and happy that she had married the man she loved. She was a bride like all other brides. She was the most courageous person I had ever met.

"I hope this lasts," Fritz croaked when the vows had been spoken. Violette laughed through her tears.

I didn't cry. Fritz's instructions to be "tough" merged conveniently with my own inhibitions on the subject. I had come close to incontinence a couple of times, but always I had stopped myself. I rationalized my terror of tears by telling myself that I had to be strong for Violette and for Fritz. Its interesting how strong you can be when you think of other people depending on you. You tap resources you didn't know you had; you bleed yourself white and never feel a thing. I prided myself on remaining housebroken the way some pride themselves on their virginity—the coward's pride in remaining unsoiled.

As a consequence my stomachaches and headaches from Marcus Leader returned to haunt me and keep me awake night after night. I fantasized that I, too, was ill, perhaps desperately ill—as though Fritz's disease were contagious. Certainly I was related to him. Might not the cells in my body betray me as those in his had betrayed him? I lay awake in the dark, horrified by the sound of my own blood coursing through my veins, the very signs that assured me I was alive.

Dottie wrote again about the Italian teacher. The doctor now appeared twice weekly. Quatermain and company were trapped in Solomon's mines by the evil Gagool. There was no way out. Fritz no longer played the piano. I no longer slept. Violette and I were beginning to look like each other, with wan complexions and blue veins throbbing at our temples. I went to more movies. Mme. Klein smiled less and gave more injections. When people visited, very often Fritz was too ill to see them and they wound up attempting to be supportive of Violette and me. We wound up comforting them. I was so far removed from the reality of it by now that I must have appeared to be functioning quite normally. I fetched drinks, took hats and coats, did whatever was needed and needed nothing for myself. When I got desperate for rest, I went to bed with a bottle of wine to quiet the blood in my veins. In the morning a few brown dregs would stain the pillowcase next to where I had lain my head the night before. Those stains made an unhappy contrast to the hairs of Hieronymous I used to find next to me when I woke up. Come to think of it, holding warm and cuddly Hieronymous in my arms while waiting to fall asleep seemed infinitely preferable at the moment to clasping a cold glass bottle.

I wished I hadn't intercepted the letter to David and Suki.

And if I wasn't picking up the phone and calling them now, I was under no illusions as to my motives. It wasn't self-sacrificing nobility; it was simple cowardice. I didn't want to watch Fritz die, but in some way I was even more frightened to leave. He had said I must be tough and I was more terrified of disobeying his orders, of forfeiting his good opinion (for the little time he had left to *have* an opinion), than I was of staying around for the horribleness that was yet to come.

Did I fear being haunted by his ghost if I deserted? In some obscure way I suppose I did. There are certain kinds of people in this world who think nothing of calling up strangers on the phone (having randomly selected their numbers from the book) and shouting or mumbling all sorts of obscenities and insults at them. They have no fear of capture and punishment: They are certain of their anonymity. They know they have only to hang up and no one can determine who or where they are. I could never make such calls. I could never believe but that somehow, sometime, some way, somewhere, I would be correctly identified, flushed out, exposed.

I only stayed because I feared Fritz's reaction—even dead—if I left.

꙰ ꙰ ꙰ ꙰

CHAPTER

Twenty-two

To Be Continued

One day in mid-July I saw the funniest movie I had ever seen in my life. It was a French film called *Fanfan la Tulipe* and starred Gina Lollobrigida and an actor called Gérard Philipe. I don't remember how I came to choose this particular movie, but at the time I was not especially discriminating. I went to anything and everything, hoping to be taken so far out of myself that with any luck I might never find my way back.

I sat in the darkened theatre with a few other afternoon patrons and roared my head off. The film was in black and white, set in the eighteenth century, and dealt with the adventures of a picaresque scoundrel (played by Philipe) who always managed to escape with his life, but that was about all, and in the film's view it was plenty. At one point the mood of the film appeared to turn quite somber. Fanfan was sentenced to be hanged. He went in a cart to a huge spreading oak tree with a rope dangling from it. Drums rolled and tears were shed even by those who had cause to hate him; the atmosphere was charged with pathos and finality. The film had become unexpectedly grim. The noose was placed around the hero's neck. Last rites and last words were spoken. The signal was given, the cart moved out from under him and Fanfan was hanged.

But the branch of the tree broke. Fanfan was miraculously saved by the ingenuity of the scenarists. The other patrons in the cinema applauded deliriously this unexpected rescue, which was not (as I recall) an act of God: Some confederate had sawed through three quarters of the hangman's branch.

I was too shocked with relief to laugh. When I applauded, my hands were stiff and I was late. The film had inexorably unwound to other things. I continued to laugh at the antics of Fanfan and his friends, but the hanging incident and the rescue stayed with me and set my mind working. I realized that somewhere throughout all these weeks I had anticipated a rescue for Fritz. Possibly one of my own devising, as though reading *King Solomon's Mines* would restore him to life. "Can't they do *anything*?" I had implored Violette. I could not believe that we were all powerless, without resources or invention or technology in the fact of this arbitrary thing. If Larry Hayes wanted to take his own life, that was his business. I saw life as a country whose citizens were free to stay in if they chose. Fritz wanted to stay, but he was being forcibly extradited by death. I saw myself as standing idly by and permitting this violation of some moral principle (I wasn't sure exactly which) to happen. How could I, who had either foreseen or else overcome all obstacles in my path, be unable now simply to overcome one more set of customs officials? Wasn't there a paper to filch, a ploy, a bribe or yet another lie that would serve? When I ran out, at this particular juncture, of protests and miracles, I railed against the injustice of it to me personally. Death followed me around, from the fatal accident that deprived me of my parents, to the suicide of Hayes, now to the compulsory death of Fritz. It wasn't fair.

Nor was Fritz's imminent demise the only misery waiting for me outside the moviehouse. The letters from Dottie had stopped arriving at American Express. I couldn't blame her for giving up on me, but I had grown to rely on the letters for my sanity and looked forward to my jaunts into the center of town to get them. Dottie's voice was the only untainted sound in my world, and it was a sound I longed to hear, even if I couldn't really answer back. I was familiar with the same table at the Café de la Paix, where I went to devour them. Now it had been almost a week and I had heard nothing. It was clearly time for me to stop writing, too, and I had. God knows, she wouldn't miss my trivial communications. She was probably deep into her affair with the young Italian teacher, who was handsome, smarter, taller and older. Or he was deep into her by now.

Altogether it was the funniest film I had ever seen. I made up my mind to come back and see it again the next day and to bring Violette. She rarely left the flat now and it would do her good to get out for a couple of hours. I also planned to tell Fritz about the film. I knew it was just the sort of thing he would have loved.

So wrapped in these comforting thoughts and plans was I that, after I rounded the corner and stepped into rue Chambord, it was some moments before I noticed the ambulance parked in front of our building at the other end of the street. The sight of it brought me up short and caused my stomach and heart to change places. I ran as fast as I could and charged through the little knot of spectators before the door.

If I expected a scene of confusion at the flat, I was mistaken. I found Violette in conference with the doctor in the foyer. Only a handkerchief balled up in her right hand betrayed any presence of emotion during their talk. Two stretcher-bearers for the ambulance stood partially to one side, awaiting instructions.

"What is it?" I cried, looking wildly from one to the other of them. "Is he dead?" Mme. Klein appeared and put a gently restraining hand on my shoulder.

"No, no. But he's sunk very low," she explained, taking me to one side. "The doctor wants him to go into the hospital."

But Fritz did not go into the hospitial. Violette knew he didn't want to, and felt there was no reason for him to die in a strange place. As there was nothing they could do for him there that couldn't be done at the flat—and none of it would make the least difference ultimately—Mme. Bernini decided to let her husband die in his own bed.

After the doctor and the litter-bearers had left, she took me in to see Fritz. He was barely conscious and slightly delirious. His eyes kept crossing and uncrossing, rolling around in their sockets like those little steel balls you try to nudge into their holes in those little games from Japan.

"Who's that?" he asked, meaning me, as Violette sat on the edge of the bed and held him.

"That's George," she said.

"George?" He tried to look at her, but his eyes wouldn't focus; it was only by a slight inclination of his head that one sensed he was making the attempt. "Why is he so big?"

Violette looked at me.

"He's big because he is a man now. George is a man now."
She said it very slowly, but the words meant nothing to
Fritz or to me. I didn't feel like a man at all. Fritz simply
repeated his question. We sat together for some time in silence. Finally Fritz spoke again, his words so slurred that
only I, who had lived with him when slurring was not the
exception but the rule, could understand what he said.

"I don't want to fuck this up." They were his last words,
and they were spoken in English.

After speaking, he lapsed into unconsciousness. Night fell
and Violette and I maintained our silent vigil. Fritz made
odd noises in his throat. Later I heard these noises referred
to as the death rattle. They were caused simply enough by
the fact that the dying person cannot swallow his saliva anymore, and it burbles up and down in the throat with every
intake and exhalation of breath. It was a horrible sound.

Violette's parents arrived and so did Emile Laurent a little
later. I don't know how or when they were summoned.

For hours, as we stood aimlessly about the room like
statues, Fritz remained on the edge of a cliff, clutching on to
life with his fingertips, clawing to maintain his hold. But
one by one his fingertips were being pried loose. The only
sound in the room was the noise in his throat. As I listened
to it, one thought kept recurring to me. At the time it struck
me as the saddest thought of all: We hadn't finished *King
Solomon's Mines*. Fritz would never know how it came out.
And we had just been getting to the really good part.

Shortly before ten o'clock the noise stopped. Fritz had
fallen silently off the cliff.

Violette looked over at me and I at her. Bewilderment was

stamped on her face and I knew it mirrored the same expression on my own. Violette's father took her clumsily in his arms and let her cry there. Mme. Klein patted me on the back a little; I knew I was still supposed to be "tough." I was too shocked anyway, I suppose, to worry about crying. Violette's mother called the ambulance and M. Laurent kept his arm lightly around my shoulders as we waited for it to come. When I heard the buzzer, I gently disengaged myself and walked over to where Fritz lay motionless. I don't know why I did it, but I reached out and touched his mustache. It felt just the same as it did when he was alive.

That night, for the first time, I did not need the wine to help me sleep.

Fritz's funeral was attended by a great number of people. I hadn't realized how many friends he had had and how devoted they were. Some boasted only the slightest acquaintance with him, but they showed up anyway. There must have been over five hundred people in attendance at the nondenominational service, and they came from all walks of life. Isabel was there; so were Olga and François, as well as a host of musicians. The coffin was closed by order of the widow, and the eulogy was delivered by Emile Laurent. He was impeccably dressed, as always. He praised Fritz as a courageous artist who battled tremendous self-doubts as he ventured daringly into the unknown reaches of the human heart and spirit to tell the rest of us what he found there. He pointed out that such journeys were not always successful or even profitable in the tangible sense. Very often the explorer returned discouraged or empty-handed. But in the long run, he said, they were the only journeys worth making. Perhaps that is why we remember great artists more than anyone else. They have carried the Good News, frequently at great personal peril.

And in Fritz, Laurent concluded, we had all known an explorer who had accepted his mission in life with unfailing zest and good humor (for all his sense of unworthiness), such that all who came in contact with him were privileged by the association. His appetite for life whetted the appetite of others. It was a tragic loss, Laurent stated with authority, because with the death of the composer of *Equations,* an important new voice in music had been stilled.

"Now Ernesto Bernini is on another journey," Laurent said sadly, "one from which many here suppose he will not return.

"But he *will* return, every time we remember him, and certainly whenever his music is performed, his voice will be among us, whispering in our hearts."

Many people were weeping audibly. I kept my hand over my eyes and looked down, as though I were thinking about what Laurent had said.

The music that followed was spectacular. What I remember the most was a black baritone from America who was carving out a career for himself in Europe (as did many American singers at that time), singing "Come, Sweet Death" with tears rolling down his cheeks. Fritz had accompanied him during several recitals. I had always enjoyed his voice, and he was a regular at rue Saint-Denis when I was there. He came over to sing, and sometimes favored us with lieder, but more often—after a few drinks—launched into the blues and made sounds I had never heard before or since as he got drunk and lamented his life or the life of his parents. He played cards (badly) but adored Fritz. They called themselves "expatriates." I had never heard Bach's song about death before; it struck me as the sweetest and most soothing music I had ever heard. I grew almost calm listening to it, as though whatever had happened might not be bad, even though I could not understand it. While it lasted, the music felt like liquid solace stealing through my veins.

My mood of resignation, however, ended with the song. Afterwards some of us went in black cars to the cemetery in Saint-Cloud where Violette's family had their plot. Fritz was interred beneath a double headstone. When Violette died, she would lie next to her husband. The prospect comforted me in a vague way; it made Fritz lying there seem less lonely. On the way back to Paris we were all silent in the car. Nobody had anything much to say. Someone commented on how nice the music had been and someone else put in that there was lunch waiting for us at the flat. I stared out the window and wondered what I was going to do now. The world was open to me and at the same time closed. I had no plans for the time or for my life. My mind had steadfastly refused to think beyond the possibility of Fritz's death. Now that he had died, it still refused to think.

The car stopped for a red light at Place Marceau.

"I'll be back," I said and jumped out, slamming the door behind me and walking briskly away. I walked without purpose or direction, blind with indifference.

It was a beautiful day. The sky was a cloudless blue and the temperature unseasonably mild. The city was crowded with tourists. It was certainly a wonderful place to be, Paris —crammed with history and knickknacks on every cornice. I walked along avenue New York by the Seine and looked up to find myself directly across from the Eiffel Tower.

"—and for a few francs more, ladies and gentlemen, my young friend here will tell you the history—"

I had to laugh at the recollection. I had to, but I couldn't. I turned away and started off in the other direction. I walked, not really seeing, until I looked up and realized that I had walked all the way to the Café de la Paix. L'Opéra was mobbed with sightseers, flaneurs and foreigners.

I walked to the opera house and looked up at it, begrimed with soot, but beautiful nonetheless. Fritz had taken me there a couple of times, once to see *Carmen* (they had horses on the stage) and once to hear *Meistersinger,* a comedy in slow motion.

Somewhere in my head I heard a distant whistle. The train was ready to move on again and take me with it. But I didn't want to go. I couldn't bear, yet again, to leave all behind. If this was all life consisted of, I really wasn't that crazy to keep traveling. Couldn't you ever find anyone decent to sit next to for the duration?

I walked around the opera house, trying to force myself to think, but reality was overwhelmed by shadows. It seemed that everywhere I looked there were distractions. There was the American Express office where I used to go—it seemed like an eon ago—to get the letters from Dottie that kept me alive.

And there was Dottie.

For a moment I thought it was just another milling American who looked like her. She was leaning up against the wall in dungarees, sneakers and a sailor hat with a tired expression. A second look assured me that it was really she. I couldn't believe my eyes, and when she saw me, neither could she.

I walked towards her as she pushed herself off the wall and brushed herself off with the hat, letting her hair tumble down around her shoulders. I kept expecting her to vanish as I drew nearer, and I could see in her fatigued features that she expected the same thing of me. We stopped a foot or so apart from each other and stared, blinking.

"I've been waiting here for three days, during business hours," she said in a neutral tone, studying me.

"Fritz is dead."

"I knew it was something."

I began to cry on the sidewalk. I knew I must look absurd, but I had no longer the strength to staunch the flow. Or the inclination. Tears cascaded down my cheeks like water from a cracking dam. Soon I was blind with them.

Delilah Kirstein put her arms around me and held me as I wept.

"Come on, George," she said softly into my ear after a time. "Let's go home."